I0633185

YOUNG
BLOOD'S
REVENGE

The Miranda Chronicles: Book V

YOUNG BLOOD'S REVENGE

Susan Old

Zairesue Books Arlington,
Washington 2023

Thank You!

I want to thank you for taking the time to read my book and hope you enjoy it. When you have finished it, I would love it if you took a moment to leave a review of the book on Amazon. Reviews are enormously helpful to independent authors, not only to find out what readers think but also for other readers to find the book and help decide whether to read it. It is the best way for independent authors to get the word out.

You can go to my website for more about Miranda, the nocturnal maniacs and me. If you like you can also sign up for my newsletter.

www.susanold.com
www.amazon.com

Copyright

Young Blood's Revenge
Copyright 2023 by Susan Old. All Rights Reserved
Published by Zairesue Books
This is a work of fiction. The events and people are imagined. Any resemblance to actual events, or to persons, live or dead, is purely coincidental.
ISBN: 978-0-9996242-4-1
Without limiting the rights under copyright reserved above, no part of this publication may be reproduced, stored in or introduced into a retrieval system, or transmitted in any form or by any means (electronic, mechanical, photocopying, recording or otherwise), without the prior written permission of both the copyright owner and the above publisher of this book, except by a reviewer who wishes to quote brief passages in connection with a review written for insertion in a magazine, newspaper, broadcast, website, blog or other outlet.

Cover art by Lily Droeven
www.lilydroeven.com

Cast of Characters
The Mordecai Family

Baron Tristan Mordecai, 2nd most powerful vampire and wealthy publishing mogul. Born in what is currently Lithuania. Ex-husband of Miranda and father of Tomas, Marie and Desmon. Splits his time living in L.A. and Seattle. Once was blindly loyal to the Magus but as his children grew older, he realized that the Magus wanted to use them to solidify and increase his power and hold on the vampire world.

Baroness Miranda Ortega-Mordecai, Head of the House of Sun, the first half-vampire, raised in Rossville, Illinois by Pete and Connie Ortega. Only as an adult did she find out that she is the biological daughter of Sir Omar Sedaghi. She was secretly watched over by various members of vampire society. She moved to L.A. to attend UCLA and to pursue a writing career. Was pursued and seduced by Tristan Mordecai. Mother of Tomas, Desmon, Marie, Jacques, and River.

Miranda's Children
The Triplets – Baron Tristan Mordecai is their biological father.

Tomas, (Oldest triplet) Neat, orderly, and tries to rise above the chaos in his world. A chemistry buff, he developed a sunblock for vampires. Bass player in the Cringe.

Desmond, (Des; Middle Triplet), Trickster, techie, loves to get under his sibling's skin. Lead Singer of the Cringe

Marie, (Youngest Triplet) Headstrong, loyal, bright, and very tough. Hates the Magus but has a baffling attraction to him. Drummer of the Cringe.

Jacques, Thoughtful, kind, and artistic. Father of Alejandro. Keyboard player in the Cringe. Was unaware that his biological father was Alexander the Great until he was a teenager.

River, Miranda's youngest child. Sweet, playful, funny and energetic. Batu is the father.

Lug, The family black Lab, short for Bela Lugosi. Adopted at a gas station on the move to the Pacific Northwest.

Piglet, A pug originally belonging to Alexander, which Jorge kidnapped to get revenge. Now lives at the House of Sun.

Miranda's Grandchildren

Alejandro, Son of Jacques and Loretta

Wendel, Son of Jacques and Loretta

Vampires

Historically Sir and Lady denote the ruling class Haute Caste vampires with HH blood. After brave and exemplary service to the Magus during Alexander's failed coup attempt several Common Caste were elevated to Haute Caste who did not possess HH blood. To the chagrin of many of the Haute Caste, Miranda often refers to them without using their titles.

The Magus aka Desmon Dontinae, First vampire, rules over world vampire society from his mansion in L.A. Born in Mesopotamia with unknown medical disorder and rejected by his father. His mother realized he needed raw, bloody meat to survive. As he began to understand his power he recruited and transformed others to help him build his new society.

Lady Amelia, High school friend of Phoebe from Mirror Point. Became pregnant with Alejandro by Jacques, in a bargain with the Magus in return for being transformed.

Lady Anastasia Romanov aka The Tsarina, Significant other of Sir Omar and the only "surviving" member of Tsar Nicholas' family.

Sir Angel, House of Plows, Lives in L.A. Recruited by the Magus to do his bidding. He began to question his loyalty to the Magus when ordered to spy on the Mordecais and actively act against them.

Antoinella, Aide to Sir Borgia, House of Pentacles

Sir Bartholomew (Bart) The Hierophant Prefers to be called Bart. Lived at Miranda's Rossville, IL. estate to watch over Miranda and her offspring. Now with his significant other, Jeanne aka Joan of Arc, oversees the vampires in Portland.

Sir Batu, Former bodyguard to the Mordecai Clan in Rossville, Illinois. Transformed by ***. Knight to the House of Cups and House of Sun. Father of River Mordecai.

Sir Billy aka Billy the Kid, – motorcycle riding member of the House of Plows and traveling companion to Sir Robert.

Carmen, Manages the Narcissus Club. She is Conon Caste.

Sir Cesare Borgia, Head of The House of Pentacles, London, England

Sir Franco, Knight to Sir Jorge, House of Arrows

Guillaume, Master swordsman, born in France, transformed by the Magus, guardian to Miranda and her offspring at the Granite Falls estate.

Sir Henry, – One of the ancients but not affiliated with any established House. Rejects titles and trappings of Haute Caste. He was Cleopatra's lover and was transformed after her death. Owns the Seattle nightclub Funeral Pyre where his band Carnage performs. Knight and adviser to the House of Sun. (*Gift of Blood*)

Lady Jacquotte, Pirate that spends most of her time in the Mississippi Delta and the Caribbean.

Sir Jorge, Head of The House of Arrows, Caracas, Venezuela

Lady Kabedi, Knight to Lady Kananga, House of Wands

Lady Kananga, Head of The House of Wands, Kinshasa, Democratic Republic of the Congo

Lady (Princess) Khunbish Head of the House of Cups, Mongolia. Replaced Kyoto as Head of House of Cups after being disgraced for participating in Alexander's coup attempt.

Dr. Kyoto, Was once the trusted physician to Miranda and her children. He had grave concerns about the effect of vampire/mortal hybrids on vampire society. He secretly conducted research that resulted in Jacque's conception without Miranda's consent. Was reduced in status to Common Caste and banished to a Mongolian monastery.

Leif, Bass player in Henry's band and was daytime security for Miranda and her family. Significant other to Marie, extremely jealous of her contact with the Magus. In a "botched" transformation (a scheme by the Magus to eliminate him), he became the first day walking vampire.

Lady (Dr.) Lily, Former Knight to longtime love interest Dr Kyoto.

Sir Omar Sedaghi Head of The House of Swords, Doha, Qatar, biological father to Miranda.

Sir Raf – Rogue Haute Caste who loosely leads the Common Caste in Portland. He is not affiliated with any established House. Disdains titles and the reverence given to the Haute Caste. (*Gift of Blood*)

Sir Robert Johnson – B guitarist, singer, and songwriter. Recognized as a master of the Delta blues. Legend says Johnson met a large black man (the Devil) at a crossroad in the south. He took Johnson's guitar, tuned it, then played a few songs and returned the guitar to Johnson. Thereafter Johnson was a master of the instrument. The vampire Robert Johnson claims that it wasn't the Devil he met but the Magus.

Sir Ruben, Brother and Knight to Lady Sarah, House of Plows. Operates online media for the vampire society and purveyor of gossip. Acts as bookie to the undead. Takes bets on the outcome of any crisis in the nocturnal world.

Sir Sam, Knight to Lady Kananga, House of Wands

Sir Sapna, Member House of Cups

Lady Sarah, Head of The House of Plows, Toronto, Canada

Scheherazade/Sybil, Common Caste, The House of Pentacles a very ambitious vampiress. Joined Alexander in his coup attempt against the Magus. Committed other transgressions and was punished by having her powers taken away and being imprisoned.

Sir Steve, Formerly Knight House of Plows, now knight to Princess Khunbish, House of Cups

Lady Teri Park, Martial arts expert bodyguard to the Mordechai family when they lived in Illinois. Was transformed after the family moved to Granite Falls. Significant other to Henry.

Mortals

Benny, Street kid that Jorge and Franco took under their wing.

Clive, Tristan's longtime chauffeur and butler

Dion, Uncle to Sigourney. Owns a diner in L.A. where Sigourney worked.

Gloria, Loretta's auntie who raised her in New Orleans.

Grigoryi, Reformed vampire hunter, former monk, who owes a debt to Miranda for sparing him after having a change of heart during a rogue vampire plot against Mordecais. Now part of the extended family of the House of Sun. Looks after the family in Granite Falls.

Loretta Fontenot, Married to Jacques, mother of Alejandro and Wendel. Goth super fan of the band, Cringe. Raised by her Aunt Gloria in L.A., after being orphaned by the Hurricane Katrina in New Orleans. Biology major at a community college.

Manny Takeda, Salinas Detective, got involved with the Mordecai family when investigating a drug dealer's murder by a vampire. He and his fiancé became good friends of the Mordecais. He keeps tabs on possible vampire-involved killings by checking police reports in the Seattle area.

Molly, Manny's fiancé

Phoebe Gaskins, Gamer girl, who grew up in a small town in the PNW with Amy (Lady Amelia). Significant other to Tomas.

Sigourney Demetriou, BFF of Loretta, got "dragged" by Loretta to a Cringe concert where she first met Des. Computer whiz/hacker. After becoming part of the Mordecai family, she found out that she is a distant relative of Sir Alexander. Is conflicted about her desire to be transformed. Has promised Miranda and Alexander not to make a final decision without discussing it with them.

Tilly, Wife of Clive, longtime housekeeper and cook for Tristan at his Bel Air mansion.

Glossary

Common Caste – Vampires with blood other than HH. Have lesser rights and power in vampire society. In book I, *Rare Blood,* vampiress Lena organized some of the Common Caste to attempt a coup against the Magus

Eye of Horus - The Eye of Horus is an ancient Egyptian symbol of protection, royal power, and good health.

Haute Caste – Elite ruling caste of vampire society. Only those with HH blood can be Haute Caste

HH Blood - Called Bombay Blood, it is the rarest of blood It was first discovered by human science in Bombay in 1952. Only 0.0004% (about 4 per million) of the total human population have this blood type. Haute Caste vampires all have HH blood.

Knight – An aide-de-camp to the Head of a vampire House, highly trusted and performs important and confidential tasks. A Knight may be a personal representative to the Head of a House at important vampire society functions.

Pikes Place Market - 108-year-old farmers' market draws in more than 10 million visitors annually—is justly famous for fishmongers, produce stalls, craft stands and specialty food shops.

Shorts – Term used in the vampire society for mortals or short-lived.

Succubus - A demon that feeds on the sexual energy or as known as "Life Force" of a man through sexual intercourse.

Acknowledgements

To Joel, my hubby who friends refer to as, "My staff". Thanks for everything, 365 days a year.

To our kids... Gabriel, Victoria, Jennifer, and Jessica... I can never express enough love and respect for all your strength and support during the difficult times.

Thanks to Trevor, Dayna and Ryan for inspiring Detective Takeda and your years of public service. Trevor helped get the cop stuff right. Any errors are mine not his.

To my big sis Megan and Dalia, Annette, Dy, Debbie, Peggy, Karen, Ronna, Donna...your encouragement is greatly appreciated.

To Courtney who tames my wild hair and is supportive of my writing.

To Tessa, Kale, and Elijah, who help with our lovable Lab Bela...Thanks for being such great neighbors.

To Susan Brown and Linda Jordan, my writing buddies...I love collaborating with you on 3 Witches Books.

To everyone at the Writers Coop of the Pacific Northwest...helping dreams become books...Thanks for your kindness and support.

To Christine and Susan, beta readers rock. Writers couldn't do it without you.

To David at Paca Pride Ranch for his information about Alpacas.

To the wonderful Readers of vampire books: you make my writing journey worthwhile.

And to the Baristas everywhere, thanks for the great coffee.

Dedication

For Chuck and Jeff

"...rulers come and go, but rock and vampires never die."

Sir Ruben – House of Plows

Chapter 1

Strange Nights

"Do you think vampires are promiscuous by nature?" Phoebe, all wide-eyed asked Miranda. She had popped her head into Miranda's tiny office off the kitchen.

Miranda's youngest child, River, five years old, was taking a nap freeing up some precious time to write. Being Head of the House of Sun didn't leave her much time to wear her author hat. With the chaos in her life, it would take years for her to finish her next book. Phoebe, a gamer girl with guts and a kind heart, was her son, Tomas' girlfriend. The young woman pushed her glasses back up on the bridge of her nose, patiently waiting for a response.

"The short answer is absolutely. Everything, for them, is a competition, like look who they screwed this week. Vampires continue to enjoy sex over the centuries. When you live that long, sports and other hobbies can get boring. At least that's how it seems to me." Miranda hoped to cut the conversation short so she could get back to writing.

"Well, I guess you would know."

Miranda's brows went up. "What?"

The young woman explained. "It must be frustrating for the undead, having centuries of sex and never an outcome. I mean until your mom gave birth to you and then you had babies with the Baron. That changed everything."

"I never thought about them wanting anything from sex but pleasure. I sort of see your point, but the goal of sex for most people is not procreation. Vampires aren't all that different from a mortal bar crowd on a Friday night when it comes to fucking. You give these nocturnal narcissists more credit than they deserve. It's an excuse to preen their feathers." Miranda squared her shoulders and leaned towards Phoebe. "Think about it. I was pregnant for months, went through excruciating labor and delivery several times, while the dads accepted the admiration and awe of their peers."

"They definitely have serious inferiority issues for supernatural beings. It is like they are always trying to prove who has the biggest fangs."

Miranda had to laugh. "True."

"And the Baron has fathered the most children, so…."

Miranda interrupted her. "Phoebe, I promise I'll answer all your questions later tonight when the others get here. I have to get back to my writing."

"Okay. Sure. I'll be in the game room if you need me."

Miranda thought about how she would explain the bats and the bees to the mortals who were now part of her crazy world, then got back to her book.

That evening at the Funeral Pyre, a club catering primarily to the undead, in Seattle, the Cringe were putting their band equipment away after a great set and an encore. Fans loved their dark, sexy, goth look and death metal music of the Mordecai siblings. Little did the audience know that much of their charisma came from their mortal/vampire family genes.

Leif, Marie's lover, helped with her drums. He teased. "Don't you wish we could hear what your mom is saying to the girls tonight?"

Marie gave him an icy stare. "Women! Sig, Loretta and Phoebe are not girls." Long dark hair framed the blue eyes she inherited from the Baron. "And no. If I hear any more about my parents and vampire sex, I'll spew."

He laughed, "But you have to admit, it's been better for us since I became…."

She cut him off by putting a drumstick up to his lips. "It's always been good between us."

Her brother Des, finishing packing up his guitar, grinned. "Wow, you guys haven't tried to kill each other for at least two hours. I think that's a new record." He untied the black ribbon holding back his shoulder length brown curls. "Let's get going." He was eager to talk to his serious girlfriend, Sig.

Tomas, was the oldest of the Mordecai triplets and a neat freak. He straightened the velvet vest Phoebe had given him and turned his attention to Leif. "Get your goth face on, it's time for Carnage." They had warmed up the crowd for the primal seduction of Sir Henry's band.

"Shit! I have to get ready." Leif kissed Marie then the bass player ran to the dressing room.

Jacques stored his keyboard and walked out into the damp night with his siblings. He pulled his leather jacket tight against the chill. Though a year younger than the others he was the only one married with kids. He was glad to be leaving the Funeral Pyre before the Carnage fans lost it. Sir Henry's dark metal music was about to explode, taking the club patrons to rock n' roll oblivion. The North African lead singer was an ancient undead whose vocals could tap into their deepest emotions at will. The vampiric power of his voice beguiled and enthralled the fans.

In the dressing room, Leif was rushing to apply eyeliner and tie his unruly red hair back with a black bandana. He wore a torn shirt exposing his well-defined torso. He hurried out to the stage and strapped on his guitar as Henry was coming on stage. The Haute Caste vampire scanned the excited crowd. He flipped his long braids back over his shoulders, getting ready for his entrance. He was shirtless, wearing a black leather vest and matching leather pants. He touched the Eye of Horus pendant on his muscular chest for luck.

The Cringe had left the crowd wanting more. Leif gave a thumbs up to Sir Henry and roared, "Feel it in your blood!" The crowd howled its approval.

Sir Henry raised a hand and the room fell silent. He called out to the crowded club, "Don't fight the hunger!"

The room thundered with the crowd's chant. "Carnage! Carnage! Carnage!"

An intense guitar riff filled the room. Leif's thumping bass rhythm felt like a punch in the chest, joined by the drummer's pounding beat. Henry introduced the first song yelling, "Never Repent!" A new song that his beloved, Teri, had written. He flashed his fangs, and the crowd went berserk.

It was a typical, if not bizarre night at the Funeral Pyre; the exclusive club for lovers of dark rock. Henry no longer met with fans backstage for 'sips' of their blood. Teri had stopped that when they became monogamous a few years before. That had not deterred his young female fans from idolizing him, nor affected the popularity of the club. The undead who frequented the Funeral Pyre, profited

4

from Henry's abstinence by charming some of the disappointed groupies after the show. The nocturnals were only allowed small 'tastes' from the fans. No one dared cross Sir Henry by taking things to lethal extremes.

Sir Henry was one of the oldest vampires. He was from ancient Egypt and had been Cleopatra's lover. As a result of the manner of her death, Henry had an intense hatred of snakes to this day. After her death he had been transformed and now along with members of the Haute Caste and Common Caste supported and protected the Mordecai clan's House of Sun. None of them could anticipate or prepare for the storm the Magus was planning on bringing to their world. The Magus harbored a long-standing resentment for having been embarrassed by Miranda and her offspring in the past. He had overestimated his power and influence over vampire society. The Magus had been foiled in an attempt to extort the Mordecais in exchange for saving the life of Sigourney's uncle, who had been diagnosed with terminal cancer. The vampire world had been appalled that he had held the life of an innocent mortal hostage, resulting in a blow to his authority. The ruler of the vampire world was becoming increasingly desperate to reassert his dominance over the House of Sun. With the exception of Miranda's House, the rest of the undead society made a show of proper respect and deference to the Magus.

At the Mordecai homestead, an hour north of Seattle, Miranda sat in the living room with the three young women who had stolen her sons' hearts. Or at least been able to put up with their part-vampire behavior for a little over two years. Loretta and Jacques were married in a touching goth ceremony and Loretta was a doting mother to their son, Wendell, and her stepson Alejandro. Sigourney and Des constantly tried to best each other with their hacker computer skills. Phoebe and Tomas used humor when his OCD tendencies and her natural messiness collided.

Miranda invited them to hear the history of her involvement with the seductive undead, straight from the horse's mouth. Though they had heard parts of the story from her kids and others in the undead world, she wanted them to know the full story. "I know you wanted to go to the club tonight with the band, so I appreciate you being here."

Phoebe nervously pushed her brown hair back from her sweet, freckled face and grabbed a chocolate chip cookie. "No problem, we've heard them play a thousand times."

Sig said, "Thanks for being willing to share your story with us. I mean, we've been told stuff, but I was never sure what was true or that we had the whole story." She had spiked her red hair anticipating a weekend at the club, but didn't mention that.

Miranda laughed. "I can imagine some of the stories you must have heard." Her eyes fell to the Dracula tattoo on Sig's arm. She was perfectly suited for their family, and it didn't hurt that she was distantly related to Alexander the Great. The Macedonia King, now a vampire, was very protective of Miranda and her family.

Loretta, initially the hardest of the three to convince that vampires existed, had grown particularly fond of Miranda. "You've been here for all of us, even when we gave you attitude in the beginning. So, whatever you tell us, we got your back." The Cajun beauty had lost her family in New Orleans and had gone to live with her aunt in L.A., where she met Jacques. She always seemed to find the right thing to say. Miranda thought she should change her biology major to psychology.

Phoebe, having been drawn into the Mordecai family drama by a childhood friend, turned vampire, added, "No judgement here. We've all got issues."

Sig elbowed her friend. "What the fuck Phoebe!"

The young woman's pale cheeks reddened. "Sorry."

Miranda chuckled, "It's okay. Really. She's right." She picked up a mug of black coffee; her security blanket. A sip of the bitter brew helped center her. "This is a cautionary tale about dealing with vampires. It is also my life. They're exhausting. You constantly have to be on your guard because you never know what the nocturnal darlings might have in mind."

Sig said, "Like when the Magus blackmailed Marie into 'being with him' in exchange for helping my uncle." Loretta elbowed Sigourney.

Phoebe smirked and side-eyed Sig. "Miranda, we're trying hard not to be offensive."

"It's okay. It will always be painful to think about how the Magus manipulated Marie." She gathered her thoughts. "Let me start with my first contact. Because of my rare HH blood and Knights Templar heritage, vampires were very interested in me. Tristan, the love of my life, royally seduced me. I was a virgin and overwhelmed by everything about him. In time, after a lot of drama, I accepted their reality. It was more shocking when I got pregnant. I assumed the undead couldn't father children. I didn't find out till after the triplets were born

6

that my dad, Pete Ortega wasn't my biological father. That asshole, the Magus dropped that bomb on me."

Phoebe said, "That had to be a big shock."

Unphased, Miranda continued. "Living in the vampire world you never get a break. I found out that a Qatari undead, one of the elites, had had a one-night stand with my mom to get her pregnant. The Magus, through bribery and manipulation, his stock in trade, found out my dad was sterile. He never knew himself. I was in my twenties before it was revealed I was half-vampire. My mom was secretly given HH vampire blood in small amounts in her morning V-8 at their café to help her conceive. The Magus set it all up, and he told me how delighted he was the 'experiment' worked."

"Damn," Sig said, "I knew about your bio dad, but not how it happened. Still, without the Magus, no Des."

"Or Jacques, Marie, Tomas, and the kids." Loretta rubbed her arms. "That's what makes this so hard, it's a mixed bag."

"Sometimes they seem so hot," Phoebe declared, "Raf was the first vampire to come on to me. He was so sexy and demanding. But I found out he only wanted to control me; it wasn't anything good. I don't know what would have happened if you guys hadn't protected me from him." Her expression became a little painful, thinking about the vampire who had tried to make her his mortal pet.

Miranda leaned over and took her hand. "Keep an open mind, but always be wary. I'm not saying let more vampires into your life, or totally trust them. You never know when one of them might look out for you. I hated Alexander when he plotted with Dr. Kyoto to inseminate me without my knowledge. I was young and ignorant. I thought Kyoto was giving me a normal post-partum exam." She took a long sip of coffee to gather her thoughts. The young women exchanged glances.

"It was shortly after the triplets were born; it seemed like he was just checking the plumbing. The Magus punished Alexander and Kyoto. Probably as much as anything, for doing it without his knowledge. Alexander saw the error of his ways, made amends and has protected the family, including Leif, ever since. It wasn't easy, but I eventually was able to forgive him. He is a great ally to have on your side in a crisis. Alliances are ever changing in the vampire world."

Sig smiled. "I'm not going to lie, being very distantly related to him rocks."

Phoebe said, "Those guys don't consider our, you know, mortal feelings, or what we want."

Miranda sat back. "I couldn't stand Angel when he was working for the Magus. He was involved in one of the Magus' plots against us and he had a rare

7

moment of clarity. For the first time he saw the Magus for who he really is, had a change of heart, and put himself at risk for us. That's why I accepted him as part of the House of Sun. Many of the oldest ones have forgotten their humanity and only care for themselves. They see mortals as underlings or playthings. Sir Borgia of the House of Pentacles is a perfect example."

"Or think we are their snacks." Phoebe frowned and pushed her glasses up on her nose.

"My sweet baby won't be anything like them." Loretta crossed her arms. She and Jacques had been spending less time around the nocturnal side of the family since Wendell was born. Miranda did not blame them. Though Loretta had allowed Miranda's distant undead cousin Guillaume, to babysit at their home in Seattle during this get together.

"No," Miranda assured her, "he won't." She put down her mug. "I was kind of a mess after I divorced Tristan. Alexander and Batu were only too eager to comfort me." She could see the young women considering her involvement with the handsome Mongolian and incredibly charming Alexander the Great. "Batu was my bodyguard, back in Illinois, for years before he became undead. There was an attraction between us, but we never acted on it until after the divorce. That's when I got pregnant with River. Tristan had warned me that other vampires would want to have a child by me. He said it would elevate their status in their society. Batu made the vampires in Mongolia happy when our daughter was born. I know he has always had strong feelings for me, but perhaps even sweet Batu had an ulterior motive. On the plus side, now the Mongolian House of Cups is our ally against the Magus."

Phoebe had no filter and blurted out, "Why didn't you use birth control?"

Miranda laughed. "Believe me, I did. I had my tubes tied but I never suspected that my undead DNA would repair the surgery as if it was an injury. So, I've had five children by 3 vampires. I love my kids, but I am so done."

Phoebe bluntly asked what the others were thinking but were afraid to ask. "I know this is kinda personal, but aren't you and Tristan, uh, still active?" They all wondered about the relationship with her ex-husband.

A look of amusement lit up Miranda's face. "I'll just say we're much more careful now. That's as specific as I'm going to be. It may seem strange, but since our divorce, our relationship has been better. It was a kind of wake-up call for him. I'm not saying that he can't be a little narcissistic on occasion, but he's all I want and need now." She took another sip of coffee. "That leads me back to you guys. Be very careful and take your time to trust them. I was fooled by Dr. Kyoto. He delivered the triplets and seemed to sincerely care about me and the kids. Without any of us knowing, he was doing research on the properties of our blood, for the Magus. They are cunning, seductive, powerful and manipulative. They'll promise whatever you desire and will often deliver it, but you may have to pay a terrible price."

Sig asked the matriarch. "Was the last remark aimed at me because the Magus offered to transform me?"

Miranda put down her mug. "Not just you. Every time a vampire flirts with a mortal there's this unspoken possibility that they might be able to become one of them. There is a seductive promise of eternal life." Then she added with a bit of irony and sadness. "It might be worth it if you didn't have to spend it with them."

Phoebe laughed awkwardly, but the others remained serious.

Loretta said defensively, "They aren't all bad: you trust some of them."

"You're right, there are a handful that I do trust. But only those that have always been straight with me and adhere to the code not to harm innocent mortals."

Sig asked, "What about Tristan, Alexander and Batu?"

"I can't say that I trust them completely. Sometimes they do things, with the best intentions, to protect us. The problem is that too often they make decisions without consulting me first. They have been doing it since I married Tristan and I can't tell you how much it pisses me off."

Sig asked, "Is that because they are vampires or still just guys?!"

Miranda laughed. "A good question that I don't have the answer to."

Phoebe said, "You don't trust the fathers of your kids; that's cold."

Miranda explained, "I didn't say I totally don't trust them. I have learned the hard way to be wary. I guess the same could be said for mortals."

Loretta said, "I suppose that's true. She looked troubled about something and bluntly asked, "How do you put up with the killing? They keep saying that they have a code to only take out people that have done terrible things and have escaped mortal justice. I can't get past them thinking it's okay for them to decide who to execute and drink their blood. Jacques promised he'll never transform. I think that's the only way I could stay with him."

Miranda's gaze softened. "The first time I saw Tristan attack a pedophile, I freaked out, threw up and ran away. I understood the guy was a despicable person, but to actually see someone you have feelings for be so violent is traumatic. Over time I learned to accept it, not approve of it. I never want any of you to see that, and especially not the grandkids. Never!"

Phoebe exclaimed, "Kinda like being married to a mafia hitman."

Sig chimed in. "I heard Alexander took out the thugs in Seattle that shot at you. I mean, it's hard to be upset about it when he kept you from getting killed."

Miranda managed a little smile. "Most of my adult life I've lived with and depended on vampires. For a lot of reasons, I owe them, and I don't think I'm better than they are. Even the Magus rescued Marie from a rogue vampire when she was abducted as a baby. It's not something I'll ever forget, but that doesn't mean I will forgive or forget some of the other things he has done."

A heavy silence fell over the room.

Finally, Phoebe said, "You gotta say they're all attractive as fuck."

Miranda smiled and agreed, "Yes, unfortunately they are. Sometimes it's easy to forget what they are."

Sig asked Miranda. "So, I guess you really love your ex? It is kinda weird that you guys are divorced, but still together."

Miranda's expression softened. "He has his moments. I do have to admit that our relationship is getting better with time. After we were divorced and I moved away from him, he bought a condo in Seattle to make it easier to spend time with the kids. Gradually, he became less focused on himself and more sensitive to my needs. That's a hard thing for an immortal and we got back together. He even had his appearance aged, temporarily, so I would feel better about my decision to stay mortal. For someone so vain, adding wrinkles for me had me in tears. Tristan is my true love, and I hate to think of the pain it will cause him when my time comes."

Phoebe stated confidently, "Well that's not happening for a long time." She grabbed another cookie.

Sig said, "You keep this family grounded and balanced. We all need you around."

Lugosi, the family's lab, came bounding in, with muddy paws and jumped on the couch. Grigoryi, part of the extended family and the cook followed behind the black lab yelling, "No Lug. Get down! Come here!" The dog leaped off the couch and managed to snag a cookie on its way back to the kitchen. Grigoryi ran after him, calling over his shoulder, "I'll clean that up later."

Phoebe asked, "What's his story? How did an Italian cook become part of the family?'

Miranda laughed and said, "To make a long story short, he was a monk that hooked up with another monk from his monastery to come to the US to hunt vampires. He has a really good heart and during a confrontation with some rogue vampires, came to our aide. After a while he became part of our crazy extended family. Grigoryi is an amazing cook and baker. He makes sure we eat healthy food and keeps us on a sort of regular schedule. I think Grigoryi might be a better mother than I am."

"I think you are a great mom." Loretta stood. "Thanks for looking out for us. It's getting late and I should get home to check on the kids." She kissed Miranda's cheek. "I totally trust you."

Miranda teared up, "Thanks. I understand why you keep your distance. I would love to see you guys more but I'm sure it's for the best." She turned to the others. "It ain't easy loving a Mordecai."

Later that night at the Funeral Pyre, Leif, a unique day-walking vampire who still loved tacos, climbed the stairs from the basement door to street level. Fog from the Puget Sound drifted through old Seattle. Though most people would think the fog and darkness creepy, it didn't affect him that way. Very little scared him any more except for Marie. He loaded his bass guitar in the passenger side of his truck then stopped suddenly. The scent of rare blood made him turn.

"What freak show let you escape?" he called out.

An attractive female swaggered towards him. Long brown hair tumbled down to the middle of her back, from a tri-corner hat. Scuffed-up black hip boots and a long waistcoat with brass buttons added to her off-beat appearance. A jewel-encrusted dagger peeked out of a black lace bustier drawing his attention.

The vampiress said, "The vampires I know are more polite. But blasted cannons, I get the feeling yer exactly as they say, Day Fanger. Had to see fer myself. Diamond in the rough, and I'm sure a delight in the buff."

He scowled at her and squared his shoulders. "I can smell your HH blood. You're Haute Caste. You want a bite? Is that it? Try me!"

"No. Not yet." Her hazel eyes traveled the length of his body. "Another night I might allow you to warm my bed, but I'm seeking a ride to the Magus' mansion before daybreak. I heard you lived near his estate."

She peered into his eyes. Leif could feel her power roll over him, making him want to move closer. He shook it off and said, "I'm not taking anyone to see that asshole. You're wasting your time. Call an Uber."

"Impressive." She moved closer, pulled out a pistol and pressed the barrel to his chest. "I was afraid you might refuse."

His survival instinct kicked in. With lightning speed, he took a step back and knocked her arm aside. The gun fired and a bullet struck the passenger window of his truck. Henry and Teri, rushed out of the club and grabbed the intruder before she could flee.

The vampiress did not struggle and said, "No harm done here. It was only a little joke that got out of hand. You know me, Sir Henry. Couldn't resist playing with yer fine young recruit."

"Lady Jacquotte," Henry addressed her as they let go of her arms. "May I introduce you to Leif."

There was a mischievous gleam in her eyes. "I prefer captain but cher Henri, you can call me…."

Teri cut her off. "I'm sweet Henry's partner. You can call me Lady Teri."

"Aye, I bet you are." She regarded the vampiress, with short dark hair and a determined look.

A little shaken, Leif said, "You could be Blackbeard, I don't care who you are, but you're paying for my window! I'm out of here." Clearly disgusted he got in his truck, slammed the door, and burned rubber as he sped off.

Undaunted, Jacquotte aimed a charming smile at Henry. "You're looking fine. I like the dreadlocks and you've always worn leather well."

"So, whose idea was it for you to bring trouble to the House of Sun?" Henry asked.

She put away her gun, straightened her coat and said, "Been curious 'bout the newest vampire House and wantin' to meet Baron Mordecai's brood. I also thought I should pay my respects to the Magus. The tales of this new blood got me to leave the Caribbean. How can you stand this cold, dreary place?"

"It has its charms." Henry started down the stairs back into the club. "We should take this inside." Teri, not trusting Jacquotte to be at her back, gestured for her to follow Henry.

Once in the club Jacquotte asked, "Is it true the young Viking stopped the Magus' Komodo Dragon from attacking him?"

Teri said coldly, "Yes. Leif used a tranq gun, so he didn't have to kill it. You are not worthy to even speak to him. You're lucky you didn't harm our friend. Not only would you have to answer to us, but you would have incurred the wrath of the Mordecai family."

"Didn't mean to ruffle yer feathers. Was curious about him." She aimed a charming smile at Henry. "Might I request a room for the day? Then I'll be off to see the Magus tomorrow night."

Teri walked away in a huff. Henry rubbed his chin. "You've always had a gift when it came to getting on the wrong side of people." They heard Teri slam a door behind the stage. "You can't stay with us, but the Empress Hotel is two blocks away. It is owned by the Magus and I'm sure they'll accommodate you."

"Henri, you never turned me away before." Her eyes lit up. "Are you exclusive to that eastern vampiress?"

He felt the pull of her passion, but pushed it away. "I would never deceive her, even for a tryst with you. And never refer to Lady Teri or anyone that way again. You need to evolve Jacquotte!" Making it clear that he was done with her he went to find Teri.

"Damn!" She thought perhaps she had been in the backwaters of the Delta too long. Disappointed, she realized there was no chance of a dalliance with Sir Henry. Tired of sleeping on her schooner she went in search of lodging.

Once she was gone, Henry and Teri came back out to the club. She was fuming. She grabbed a rag and started wiping the bar counter aggressively. "Seriously, a pirate?"

Henry was unsuccessfully hiding his amusement. "She's an old friend. The Mississippi Delta and the Caribbean were safe places for the undead during the height of piracy. The Magus respected their audacious behavior towards the authorities, but disliked the way they treated women. He was quite fond of the few female buccaneers."

"And what about you?" She snorted. She threw the bar rag and it landed on his head. "Why do I even ask? I want to kill someone."

Henry said, "For what it's worth, she revels in causing trouble."

"Great! Keep her away from me!"

The house musician Robert Johnson, quietly playing in the corner, set his guitar down and said, "There's fresh O positive in the back fridge. Just a suggestion." Teri stormed off into the storeroom.

Henry pulled the rag off his head and with a twinkle in his eye said to the legendary blues artist. "I'd ask you to play to assuage her anger, but she might become more incensed."

Robert clicked his tongue. "My, my, Henry. I wish I had been with you back in the day with the pirates. But that was before my time. I can only imagine your crazy exploits."

"Jacquotte has always been difficult, not to mention an amazingly talented criminal. At the end of the pirate era, when the officials were closing in, she was able to disappear thanks to the Magus. One of his more questionable transformations."

Robert smiled. "Who can resist wild women."

Teri emerged with reddened lips. "Apparently not Henry." She took the stairs up to their apartment not willing to wait for the elevator.

Robert laughed. "You think she's more lawless than Billy?" Robert Johnson and Billy, aka, the Kid were unlikely undead traveling buddies. The last several years they had been unofficially part of the House of Sun and stayed in Seattle.

Henry started to follow Teri but stopped to reply. "They are both hellions. Let us hope they are off-setting, not complimentary harbingers of chaos."

On the way to the Empress hotel, Jacquotte noticed a young man pull a reluctant woman into a dimly lit alley. She followed them and hid behind a dumpster. The stench of rotten food interfered with her ability to detect their blood types. She took a step closer, and a large rat screeched as she stepped on its tail.

The young man's hoodie fell back as he turned in the direction of the sound. Not seeing anyone, he was certain they were alone. He forced the struggling female against the brick wall. "C'mon honey. You know you want it."

She tried to push him back, but he was too strong. "Stop it! We only shared a drink, nothing more. Let me go!"

"Hey baby. I've seen how you look at me at work. Be nice." He leaned forward to try and kiss her, but she head butted him.

Blood from his nose dripped down his chin. "Bitch!" He raised his fist to strike, but his arm was stopped by a hand tightly gripping his wrist. He whipped around and confronted the angry face of Jacquotte.

"Yer not worthy to be gator bait!" With blinding speed, she grabbed him by the neck and smashed the side of his head against the wall. As he slid to the ground unconscious, Jacquotte yelled at the frightened woman, "Get gone!"

Without a second thought, the young woman bolted out of the alley, pulling out her phone.

The would-be rapist began to come around and opened his eyes, looking confused. The vampiress smiled, revealing her fangs. Jacquotte cut his scream short by ripping into his throat. She drank deeply and felt a euphoric rush from his fresh, warm blood. The beat of his heart slowed and faded as hers increased. The vampiress wiped her lips on her sleeve and gasped, "Excellent!" She hated wasting so much blood with her messy attack, but there had been no time to plan this meal. Jacquotte knew the undead code required the victim be told why they were being punished, but she figured he would never have understood rape was wrong. The vampiress threw his corpse on the ground like an empty soda can.

Jacquotte felt the wave of the energy of the kill surge inside her. "Yer good for something." She said to the corpse. The vampiress started to walk away, but turned back. She realized she should disguise the wounds caused by her fangs. She pulled out her jeweled dagger and slashed across the bite mark. She

14

effortlessly lifted his body and tossed it into the dumpster. "Tis where scum belong." She hummed a sea shanty, wiping the remaining traces of blood from her face with a lace handkerchief. She heard police sirens in the distance, exited the alley, and hurried to the hotel. She thought to herself. "Seattle's not so bad after all."

Leif parked his truck at the log cabin house he shared with Marie and trekked through the trees to the main house where her mother and some of the family lived. He glanced at Guillaume's house, but it appeared that the resident vampire had already turned in. A light was on in the kitchen as Leif went into the house.

Guillaume had begun life as Gisele but had only felt comfortable in men's clothes. One day, working in a stable as a man, a group of men discovered the secret. They began a brutal attack but were stopped by the Magus and Tristan. The Magus performed the transformation rite and Gisele became a vampire. Centuries later Gisele completed another transformation and had been Guillaume ever since. When Miranda first moved to Granite Falls, Tristan had requested Guillaume to watch over her and the children. He lived in a small house on Miranda's property. In a short time, he had become a close member of the family.

Their old black lab, Lugosi looked up and wagged his tail. Grigoryi, was busy making Italian bread as usual. Leif was glad he could still eat his fabulous cooking. "Morning G, is anyone else up?"

"No. There's leftover eggplant parmigiana in the fridge. You okay?" The graying, pudgy ex-monk worried about Leif's ability to cope with his dual nature. He feared the nocturnal maniac side might take over. "You need something else; there's a fresh delivery in the back."

Leif replied with a half-smile. "Grigoryi, you can say blood. The world won't come to an end and your soul won't be damned. It's just how it is for me now."

Still feeling a bit uncomfortable, he replied, "Sure, whatever you say." He turned his attention to the task at hand, baking.

Miranda walked in. "Hey Leif. How was the club?"

"A shady visitor pulled out a pistol and shot out my side window." He grabbed the leftovers from the fridge and dug in without reheating it. Grigoryi watched with distain.

"Damn! I knew something wasn't right." Miranda had only slept a couple of hours when she woke up with a bad feeling in her gut, then heard Leif in the kitchen. "You're okay? What happened?"

15

"I'm fine." He took another mouthful. "Did you ever in your wildest dreams think that Magus might've transformed a pirate?"

Grigoryi mumbled something in Latin.

Miranda leaned forward with her hands on the table. "No. Though when you think about it, of course he did. Nothing he's done shocks me anymore."

"Well, this Jacquotte turned up outside the club to check me out. She wanted me to give her a ride to 'pay her respects' to the House of Sun. I refused and she almost shot me."

"She wanted a ride here?" Miranda asked.

When he kept eating without answering, she grabbed his plate in exasperation. "Leif!"

"Well, not exactly. She wanted to be taken to the Magus' place. Henry and Teri were dealing with Jacquotte when I left." He took his plate back and finished off the eggplant parmigiana while Miranda tried to make sense of this revelation. "I think she's curious about all of us."

Miranda sighed in exasperation. "We've had two sweet, peaceful years since Wendell was born. Even though the Magus built a mansion nearby he has stayed clear of us. It was only a matter of time before he found a way to screw with the House of Sun and make it seem unintentional."

"She's a piece of work. I came right back here to make sure everyone was okay. I think she came alone." He put his plate in the sink. "Just wanted you to know. I need to get some sleep." He took off out the back door with vampire speed.

Miranda watched his departure. "Do you think Leif realizes how fast he is?"

Grigoryi put the bread in the oven. "Not really. It is difficult to understand why Leif of all people would be granted these powers." He wiped off the counter and turned to Miranda. "Anyway, it's good that Guillaume has taught you how to fight with swords with a pirate around."

Miranda responded, "Aye!" Then she got serious. "The kids, even the older ones, love pirate movies. You know they'll want to meet her, and I bet she's hot. We don't need another unscrupulous vampiress around here. Fuck me!"

Chapter 2

News Spreads

Detective Manny Takeda was at his desk in the Salinas police department, his coffee, sitting forgotten, to one side, was almost cold. He sat staring at a crime report he'd pulled up from the Seattle area. The victim's throat was ripped out, and the body tossed in a dumpster. The body and the dumpster were covered in blood. More blood was left behind than some similar unsolved cases he'd investigated. He checked the location of the attack; it was near Sir Henry's club. Manny grumbled to himself, "Vampires."

He sat back as the other officers were clearing out for the day. He reflected back several years earlier when he had first encountered and reluctantly accepted that vampires exist. Manny was a good cop, but he could never let go of an unsolved case. He was almost fired when he got carried away pursuing a bizarre murder of a local drug dealer. None of the normal explanations had made sense to him and when he continued investigating his boss had suspended him. Determined to get to the bottom of the murder, he continued to check out leads which led to Miranda. That in turn led him to the murder of her dad in Rossville. Poking around into the affairs of vampire society could have dire consequences. The detective was alive today because the Mordecai family took a liking to him, and he actually assisted them in thwarting one of the Magus' plots. Miranda even tried to persuade him and Molly, his fiancé, to stay and help with security. They decided that a little vampire contact went a long way and went back to Salinas.

When he returned to work, he earned a promotion by closing other cases from leads he had turned up investigating the original murder. It wasn't easy, but Manny had come to accept that the undead were a class of serial killers that the law could never touch. He was back in the good graces of the chief and didn't want to screw anything up, but he couldn't forget about the existence of vampires.

He kept tabs on the Mordecai clan by regularly checking the reports from the Seattle area. The woman, from this crime report told the investigating officer that the murder victim had tried to rape her in the alley. An unknown woman dressed as a pirate intervened. There were no other witnesses. He couldn't remember any of the undead ever wearing disguises, much less anything as outrageous as a pirate costume. Manny couldn't ignore the queasy feeling in his gut that had accompanied his previous contact with these killers. He signed off the computer and grabbed his jacket, knowing he should let it go.

His mind raced as he drove to the little house he and Molly were able to buy a few years ago with the money they'd earned helping the Mordecai family. Molly had insisted on accompanying him when he went to Granite Falls to find out more about the Mordecais, to try to keep him out of trouble. A part of him missed the adrenaline rush of their world. Maybe he could talk Molly into a little vacation up north.

An hour later, after Manny told her what he had found and suggested that it might be interesting to visit Seattle, Molly stared at him, mouth agape. She took a breath and ran a hand through her short wavy hair. Finally, she said, "To be honest, a day hasn't gone by that I haven't thought about them. I kept it to myself 'cause I'd been all over your ass to be content staying here after we helped them fight the 'bad' vampires. I have to admit it was tempting to accept Miranda's offer to move up there and work for her. I really like them and can't help wanting to see them again. Sometimes when I think about everything that happened there, I have a hard time believing it was real, even though I know we didn't make it up."

He smiled. "It wasn't your imagination. I get it. It was hard for me, as a cop, to believe it. This latest killing has all their trademarks, except for the amount of blood left at the scene. They usually are neater than that." He raised his eyebrows as a thought came to him. "Maybe it's a wannabe Dracula. Or it could be a new vampire has come to town."

She petted their fat cat, Trouble. "I shouldn't be so excited about someone being killed like that, but do you think they might need us again?"

He grinned at Molly, in her hot pink hoodie. He gestured around their small house, which Molly had worked on to make comfortable and cozy. There was even a *God Bless Our Home* embroidered pillow on the sofa. "Baby, what we've got is great. But you have to admit that once you've met a vampire, normal life and normal homicides don't compare. Let me think about this, and we'll see if the Seattle PD finds any leads on the murderer."

She said teasingly, "So, does this make you want a rare steak?"

He burst out laughing. They had given up meat completely after their bloody visit to Granite Falls. "Veggie burgers and fries, but with lots of ketchup."

The Magus had sent a car for Jacquotte after waking up to an apologetic text from the pirate about the murder. He did not want any unsanctioned attacks in Seattle that might be somehow blamed on him, but she never played by the rules. His plan to appear to make nice with the Mordecai family had been working. His affair with Amelia, the mother of Jacque's older child, allowed him to hear bits of gossip about them. She had been visiting her son twice a month for some time without incident. Though Miranda and Tristan chose to ignore the Magus' move to a mansion with acreage close to them, he had been content to show his maturity and patience until now.

"You must not let her stay!" Lady Amelia's dark eyes flashed. "She'll ruin everything."

"She is my guest. An honored member of the Haute Caste." He buttoned his dress shirt as Amelia rose from his large bed. Straight black hair fell past her shoulders. He gently cupped one of her breasts, then leaned over, kissing her lips. "Don't fret. Jacquotte will be useful in my efforts to learn more about Leif."

Amelia's anger at this vampiress messing with her world shut down any feelings of arousal. She pushed his hand away and went to the bathroom, slamming the door. The Magus shook his head. Jacquotte had not yet entered his home but had already created tension. His fondness for Amelia would not get in the way of taking advantage of this moment. The young vampiress had been a bandage while the wound inflicted by Marie had slowly healed over. He still longed for Marie if the truth be told, but he concealed that. He never let on that Amelia's appearance reminded him of the Mordecai's oldest daughter.

The original vampire had a tall, lean, and muscular frame. He stood and ran a comb through his dark hair, which framed his angular features. His expressive brown eyes could elicit terror or incite passion. The power of the earth ran through his veins, and when the Magus became enraged, he had been known to cause the ground to literally shake. Several years ago, some of the Haute Caste vampires aligned themselves with Miranda against him; that was the last time he had unleashed his unique weapon. The world's first vampire lost face and support when he threatened the Mordecais. His obsession with Marie caused the Haute Caste to question his judgment. The Magus was no longer given the same respect, and he desired to rectify that situation.

He wanted samples of Miranda's and the Mordecai offspring's tainted blood to use as weapons. The vampire world would once more be in awe of his brilliance and afraid to cross him. To his surprise, Miranda's immune system had developed an anti-vampire response that caused any Haute Caste who drank from her or the offspring to become weakened and temporarily lose their special powers. If a Common Caste partook of their blood, they would lose their undead nature and begin aging quickly. He had never imagined that outcome when he orchestrated her birth. He had hoped her blood would have given him the ability to withstand the sun. A faint smile came to his face as he thought about the excitement the Mordecai family had brought to his once-predictable existence. He embraced the challenge to regain supreme, unquestioned dominance over his kind.

Lady Amelia returned from a shower and slowly dressed in tight running clothes and platform sneakers. She knew the Magus was watching her, but she ignored his appreciative stare. The vampiress turned to him, "What will you do?"

"That depends on our guest. Jacquotte has never been easy to influence. She only agreed to be transformed when the authorities were going to hang her."

"She's a criminal. Why did you give her the gift?"

"Should I second guess allowing you to become one of us?" There was a coolness to his response. "She has a special gift and is quite perceptive."

A butler gently tapped on the bedroom door and announced that Lady Jacquotte had arrived.

Lady Amelia ignored the warning in the Magus' tone. "It's my night to visit with Ali. Don't let her get in the way of my time with him."

"You dare make demands of me?" The Magus straightened his shoulders. "I don't care for your tone." The harsh sound of his voice caused her to stop. "It would be best for you to take your things and stay in Seattle."

She swallowed; awareness that she had blown it crept into her psyche. The two years they had been together had emboldened her. "I meant no disrespect, Magus."

He walked to the door and said over his shoulder. "I no longer desire your company." Then he went to greet his visitor.

"Fuck it!" There would be no use in trying to dissuade him. She started packing her suitcases.

Miranda, Tristan, and their grandson Ali waited for Amelia at Tristan's mansion on the shore of Lake Union. Tristan had lived there until his and Miranda's relationship had redeveloped and were once again living together. Loretta loved the house on the lake and rather than sell it, Tristan offered it to her and Jacques as their home for as long as they wanted. It was perfect for Loretta, Jacques, and the kids to be able to keep some distance between themselves and the vampire society, but still be reasonably close to the rest of the family. That evening they had taken Wendell to see a Disney movie. Jacques made a point of staying away from Amelia to keep Loretta from getting jealous. His ex was a ravishing vampiress and, although Jacques only loved Loretta, the two women stayed clear of each other to avoid any tension around Amelia's son Ali.

A red Porsche Cayman pulled up to the front steps. A maid opened the door, and Lady Amelia went to the living room, where five-year-old Ali sat on the couch looking at books with his grandmother. Tristan stood behind them, glanced at the clock on the mantle, and gave Amelia a disapproving look.

"Hi, Ali!" She sat beside him. "Sorry, I'm late."

The curly-haired little boy smiled up at her. "It's okay, Momma Amy. Look, a dragon."

She mussed his brown hair and said, "I love dragons too. Tell me all about it." He was the spitting image of his father, Jacques.

Miranda went into the kitchen to let Ali spend a little time with his mom. Tristan followed and said, "Something is wrong. She is anxious, and her smile forced."

"I noticed. It's got to be the Magus. Who else can get under the skin of a vampire like that."

With a slight smile, he said, "You."

She elbowed him. "Maybe they broke up. Does the Magus have a thing for the pirate?"

Tristan raised a hand to her cheek and kissed Miranda gently. "Do you still think he is capable of feelings for someone other than himself?"

"I wondered if he might've dumped Amy for Jacquotte. Someone new to screw. But you're right, and there would be more to it. His horribleness is up to something."

"You said you heard from Detective Takeda?" Tristan asked, always quite formal.

"I did, Manny said he read about the recent attack here and wondered if we wanted his help. I texted our thanks and said I'd be in touch if we needed him."

"Yes. It's good to have a connection in law enforcement. Though he must regret not being able to arrest nocturnal serial killers, as he calls us."

Miranda said, "If this Jacquotte messes with Leif again, we should just turn her over."

"You might consider that possibility if it amuses you, but there are no prisons that could hold us."

As Miranda was mulling that over, Phoebe and Tomas arrived. Phoebe had grown up in a small town with Lady Amelia, and they were best friends long before Amelia became nocturnal. Phoebe often stopped by during the visits with Ali because she still cared for her. Sometimes Miranda thought Phoebe was too good-hearted to survive in their world.

"Hey, Phoebe." Miranda hugged her and smiled at the unicorn sweater. Her apparel was always interesting.

Tristan said, "Good evening." He tried to extend a warm greeting, but he couldn't pull it off convincingly. "Perhaps you could talk with Lady Amelia before she goes. She seems unsettled."

Phoebe said, "Sure. No problem, Baron." She took in the vampire's appearance. "You pull-off the aging thing well. Not everyone could."

Baron Tristan Mordecai was a tad offended. "Thank you."

As is the case with most vampires, Tristan was very vain and has always been proud of his youthful appearance. After years of a turbulent relationship, Miranda and Tristan finally came to terms—mostly dictated by Miranda—that allowed them to live together again. Not wanting her to be constantly reminded that she would continue to grow older while he would always appear youthful, he sought the help of Anastasia, who had the ability to cause vampires to rapidly age. Tristan had asked her to use her power to temporarily make him appear to be the same age as Miranda. Now they both appeared to be about fifty years old.

Tomas watched, amused by the interaction. Of all the kids, he most resembled Sir Omar, Miranda's biological grandfather. He had Omar's soft brown eyes, high cheekbones, and full lips. He could pull off the dark, brooding look on stage, but his aloof expression would melt into a smile around Phoebe. She once called him "gorgeous," which made him laugh, but he never refuted it.

Miranda, Tomas, and Phoebe shared some cheesecake while discussing the arrival of Jacquotte with Tristan. He had not spent any time in the Caribbean or the Delta during the golden years of piracy. "I only met Lady Jacquotte once at a ball thrown by the Magus in Chicago. She acted ill-mannered and offensive and brough undue attention to herself. I had no desire to become better acquainted with her."

Phoebe said, "If my manners suck, I don't mean anything by it. Just saying."

Tomas grinned. "Oh, we know."

Billy aka the Kid, walked in, leading a large black panther on a leash. Many years before, Tristan had rescued the cat and named her Delilah. She had been his companion ever since. Billy let go of the leash and the black panther ran to the Baron. He petted her sleek head, "Sweet girl. Are you watching over our family?" Her amber eyes seemed to understand his question as she rubbed her nose against his hand.

Billy, along with Robert Johnson, had been recruited to help keep watch over Miranda and the family when they were living in Rossville, Illinois. The two of them had been transformed by the Magus, became fast friends, and traveled the country together. Robert Johnson, the legendary blues guitarist was always amused by the myth that he had gotten his playing ability when he encountered the devil at a crossroads, and they made a pact. The real story, which would be as unbelievable to most people, was that he met the Magus, who transformed him. His enhanced abilities as a vampire vastly improved his musical talent. To add fuel to the myth, Johnson wrote a song called "Me and the Devil".

Even after Miranda and her family left Illinois, Billy and Robert stayed part of the extended family. Henry, so loved Johnson's guitar playing that he persuaded him to become a regular at the club. Johnson's delta blues was an interesting contrast to the hard metal sound of Henry's band Carnage and the siblings Cringe. Since the bands usually played at the Funeral Pyre until dawn, Robert accepted Henry's offer to live in one of the apartments over the club.

Billy had a particular soft spot for Jacques and Loretta, and they persuaded him to stay with them at the mansion. He and Delilah had bonded together, and Tristan decided to let her stay at the at the lake house. It gave him and Miranda some comfort to know Billy was there to watch out for Loretta, Jacques, and the kids at night. Delilah was particularly protective of the children. Billy and the panther were the best security one could ever want.

Billy said to Tristan, "She started pacing in her enclosure, and was a little agitated when she heard a car pull up. I wasn't sure who it was, so I thought we better check it out. Is it Lady Amelia?"

"Yes, it is. There is also some news," Tristan said, "Lady Jacquotte is visiting the Magus."

His eyes lit up. "No shit. I've wanted to meet her for years. Heard she's as good with a gun as a sword."

Miranda frowned. "She shot at Leif but missed."

"No!" He remarked. Then to their surprise, Billy seemed to be amused. He was always cocky about his prowess with a gun and delighted when others fell short of his gunslinger reputation. "That's a pretty big target to miss. Ha!" When he noticed the family's reaction, he sheepishly said, "I'll go and feed Delilah." He disappeared with the panther.

Later, Miranda watched as Ali hugged his bio mom. Lady Amelia kissed the top of his head and said, "Dream of riding a dragon tonight. Love you."

His grandma took him to get ready for bed. Phoebe entered and plopped down beside her friend. "What's up, Amy?"

"Maybe now I can spend more time with Ali." She touched Phoebe's arm. "I fell out of favor with the Magus. I had to move out tonight."

Phoebe swallowed. "Holy blood sucker. Did he hurt you?"

Lady Amelia assured her that she was fine. "Nothing like that. He said I was disrespectful because I criticized him for having that vampiress come to visit. I told her she'd cause problems. I am afraid that somehow she'll get in the way of me being able to spend time with my son."

Phoebe said, "Maybe it's for the best. I'm glad you aren't with him. Where are you going to stay?"

She sarcastically replied, "Maybe I'll go stand on the Seattle pier at sunrise and burst into flames."

"Stop it!" Phoebe hit her shoulder.

"Okay, I'm staying at the Four Seasons. I've booked a suite for a week. That should give me time to find a more permanent place. I like their sheets."

"Amy, you are such a diva. How did you ever put up with growing up in Mirror Point? I used to get excited about going shopping in Marysville like it was a big city. It seems like that was a lifetime ago."

"Well, we weren't exactly living the dream." Lady Amelia asked, "So, how are you and Tomas? I hear he and Cringe are slaying it at the club."

Tomas walked in on the tail end of the conversation. Phoebe jokingly said, "Yeah, they're okay. I mean for a band from Granite Falls."

Tomas trying to look insulted said, "Too bad there aren't any bands from Mirror Point to compare us to."

Lady Amelia snickered. "Phoebe was in the marching band."

Tomas looked surprised. "You're kidding! What did she play?"

Phoebe grumbled, "Tuba."

"Wow." He tried hard not to laugh. "I wish I had seen that. You've got to play for me."

Phoebe threw a pillow at him as Miranda returned. "I don't know what that was for, but I'm sure Tomas deserved it."

Lady Amelia got up, thanked Miranda, and arranged for another visit. On her way out, she told the Baron, "I have moved out of the Magus' house. I'll be at the Four Seasons if you need to get a hold of me for any reason."

He said, "It is the Magus' loss."

The young vampiress was surprised by his kindness. "Thank you."

He watched her go and remarked to Miranda, "There was a time I despised Lady Amelia for getting pregnant by Jacques so the Magus would transform her. Now I pity her for getting caught up in the power struggles of our kind because she honestly cares for Ali."

Miranda agreed. "The Magus has only been using her as a pawn."

Jacquotte took in the luxurious mansion in the woods. She had changed into a cashmere sweater over tight jeans. The vampiress still wore a sheathed dagger on a leather belt because she was accustomed to being armed, although her undead abilities were enough to fend off any mortals.

"Thanks for the accommodations, but doesn't it drive you mad to be away from the world? Not many to seduce or sip from around here."

The Magus smiled, "I go into Seattle or fly back to Los Angeles to whet my appetite." His dark eyes swept over her, remembering past intimate moments. "Besides, sipping from mortals has made a comeback at clubs like the Funeral Pyre, creating easy access."

"Yeah, Seattle is full of possibilities." She flashed her fangs.

"I've checked the police reports, and except for a description by a rather traumatized woman, the police have no clue about what happened. But you've left me with an unauthorized attack in the House of Sun's territory."

Her brow furrowed. "Yer worried about what this upstart Baroness Miranda is gonna think? What the hell has happened to you?" She had known him long enough to be frank.

"The Mordecais! I created a monster, and now I'm challenged trying to rein them in. They are impossible." His outburst was uncharacteristic. The Magus turned his back to her to calm down.

"It's that Marie, isn't it? So, it's true about you and the daughter. You almost had her, but she turned you down. She ain't right. I could never resist you." Actually, Lady Jacquotte could resist anyone, but she was usually in the mood.

His eyes narrowed as he faced her. "Marie was mine for one evening, then it all fell apart. She went back to that mutant you met outside the club." His hands turned to fists. "He's an idiot that the fates have endowed with our powers and the ability to walk in the sun."

She approached him, putting her hands on his shoulders. "How can I help you deal with these ingrates?"

He swept Jacquotte into his arms and carried her to the couch, where he fell upon her. Soon their clothing was being shed as his lips tasted hers. The vampiress' power of attraction was legendary. The Magus' palms rubbed her nipples as they became hard; she began stroking his cock, lightly at first, then in a savage fashion. He let his fangs tease her neck; she gasped, "Yes!"

Jacquotte raised her hips to accept his thrusts as the Magus brought her to the peak of arousal with strokes against her wet folds, finding her nub of pleasure. Her body shook; the first climax sent her into oblivion as the Magus' fangs slid into her flesh. Pain seared her neck before another wave of exquisite sensations overwhelmed her. Their bodies collided again and again. The Magus was bathed in the euphoria he had experienced thousands of times. He swallowed, and with all his willpower, pulled back from her neck before taking too much. His body shuddered with pleasure as he climaxed. She grabbed his arm and bit deep into his wrist. Jacquotte was greedy and swallowed several times.

The Magus pulled his arm away from the vampiress and stood up. "You never know when to stop. Some things never change."

She flashed a charming smile and sat back, letting the energy of his blood invigorate her. "Always ready to accommodate your desires, dear Magus." She stretched and languidly pulled on her clothes. "Now, what shall we do about the House of Sun?"

The next night in Granite Falls, Leif was warming up Phoebe and Sig for their fencing lesson with Guillaume. It was the only exercise Phoebe liked besides the time she spent with Tomas. Sig was in great shape, a natural athlete who loved running, biking, and horseback riding since she met Des.

Leif told them to pick up their rapiers and do warm-up exercises. He corrected Phoebe's grip, and she made a wide sweeping movement.

"Watch it!" Sig cried as Phoebe's rapier scratched the back of her hand.

"Sorry. I'll move farther away." Phoebe was mortified. "Didn't mean to make contact."

Sig started to respond until she noticed Leif staring at the blood on her hand. She grabbed a towel to cover the small cut.

He said, "Later," before abruptly running out the door and almost plowing Guillaume over.

The vampire entered and noticed Sig's injury. He admonished them. "We must be careful around Leif. He is still learning to control his appetite."

Phoebe said, "It's my fault. I probably shouldn't be trusted with sharp objects." She started to remove her padding.

"Nonsense!" Guillaume picked up a rapier. "It was bound to happen. Sig, are you ready to proceed?"

She put a bandage over the cut. "Sure, it's nothing."

"Bon! I know Jacquotte, and I don't think she would duel with someone beneath her capabilities, but there are others, mortal or immortal, who could seek to harm you, so let's begin."

"Great." Phoebe's voice lacked enthusiasm.

Marie was in the large barn making sure the horses were taken care of for the night. Leif found his love and said, "I'm a mess."

She turned and flashed her blue eyes. "And?"

He gave her a wry smile and said, "Sig had a cut, and the scent and sight of blood got to me. My fangs started itching."

Marie walked over and put her arms around him. Her horse, Athena, snorted. Marie kissed him, and they fell over onto bales of straw. They feverishly began to undress each other when a familiar voice said, "Reminiscent of farm animals."

They sat up to see the Magus and Jacquotte with amused expressions.

Marie screamed, "Get out!" Pulling down her shirt.

Jacquotte said, "I came here to pay for the damages to the Day Fanger's truck. I always take care of my debts."

Guillaume and his fencing students ran in, rapiers in their hands. He asked Marie and Leif. "Are you two all right?"

Jacquotte smiled. "Sweet Guillaume. It's been ages since we played with swords. Unfortunately, I'm unarmed."

"It would be my pleasure to challenge you another time, Lady Jacquotte."

The Magus wanting to get back to the business at hand, said, "That would be entertaining, but we're here to make amends for the broken window, then we'll leave you to frolic in the hay."

Marie said, "We don't want anything from either of you."

The Magus made eye contact with Marie and smiled. "Baroness, though always charming, you might want to remove the straw from your hair when trying to sound so commanding."

Leif's hands balled up into fists. Guillaume moved between them, knowing that Leif, even with his assistance, could not take down the Magus.

Miranda burst in and read the tension in the barn. "Stop it! I don't care what happened, but I know who is to blame." She glared at the Magus and Jacquotte. "You are not welcome here."

The Magus took out a money clip and dropped several hundred-dollar bills on the ground. "That should cover what is owed. Come, Lady Jacquotte, as you can see, the House of Sun has yet to learn how to be hospitable."

Miranda stepped away from the door, clearing their path, while staring daggers at Jacquotte. "That unsanctioned kill of a rapist is understandable, but you didn't respect my House by notifying me. You behaved like a careless newbie, not a member of the Haute Caste."

Jacquotte looked Miranda over. "What a scrawny creature. I would make a better Head of your House."

Sig swung her rapier and tore the sleeve of the vampiress' sweater. "Apologize!"

Jacquotte's dagger appeared. Guillaume, with lightning speed, intervened and jumped on the vampiress. They fell, wrestling on the ground. Leif reached out to grab Jacquotte, but Marie threw her arms around his chest, stopping him.

The Magus yawned in feigned boredom. "Enough." Jacquotte got out from under Guillaume and jumped to her feet, staring at Sig. The original vampire placed a hand on Jacquotte's shoulder. "Their ignorance makes them bold." With a lightning move, he took the offending rapier from Sig and dropped it on the ground. "Never draw blood unless you are a match for your opponent."

Sig stepped back wide-eyed and noticed a second small cut on her wrist. She covered it with her hand. "Damn!" The Magus licked a finger leaving a trace of blood on his lips.

Jacquotte was clearly unnerved by the welcome she had received. "I only planned to teach these mortals better manners, nothing lethal. I respect the code."

Marie snapped, "Too bad the Magus doesn't."

The Magus' ignored Marie, letting his gaze rake over Sigourney. "You would make an amazing vampiress. There is still time."

Sig swallowed and lowered her head to avoid looking directly at him.

Miranda crossed her arms. "Your desperate attempt to get in a fight with Leif has failed. And now you've thoroughly pissed us all off. Leave!"

Leif stared coldly at them and folded his arms. "You heard the Baroness."

Phoebe's hand was shaking as she gripped the practice rapier. She glared at the Magus. "I'm a pacifist, but you make me want to stab you."

He pretended to be frightened, and they left without another word.

Chapter 3

More Blood

The Baron had been tending to business in Seattle. When he arrived at the family home, he was livid. "The Magus came here?"

Des, Sig, Tomas, Phoebe, Guillaume, and Miranda were in the living room. Miranda said, "It's okay. He was just reminding us of why we don't invite him over."

Guillaume stood. "Baron, he brought Jacquotte here to undermine our sense of security and again invited Sigourney to transform. The Magus was rude to Marie and then threw money on the ground for Leif's truck repair. It was obvious he was trying to provoke Leif so he would have an excuse to harm him."

Tomas added. "He must be monitoring who is here and who came when you, Des, and I were gone. We know that the Mag-ass wants a sample of Leif's blood. If he had been able to goad Leif into a fight, he could get a blood sample from stains on his clothes. Luckily Guillaume stepped in and stopped him."

Des said. "Probably a lot of the Haute Caste would be on his ass if he attacked Leif." He finished cleaning Sig's wrist. He said angrily, "And he hurt Sig!"

Phoebe said, "When I cut her, it was an accident. What he did was 'sick' and not in a good way."

Sig grimaced as Des pulled a Band-Aid out of the first-aid kit to put on her cut. "Mickey Mouse?"

"It's one of Rivers," he said.

Sig turned to Miranda and the Baron. "What is it about the Magus? I can't get a handle on what his deal is."

Miranda drew in a deep breath and slowly let it out. "Sigourney, he's the most powerful vamp. He gets into your head and fucks with you, gets you questioning everything until you think he must have all the answers. Believe me, he doesn't."

The Baron asked, "Where are Leif and Marie?"

Miranda replied, "Back at his place, cooling off. Leif promised me he won't retaliate, and Marie will make sure he keeps his word."

River came running in, followed by Grigoryi, and exclaimed with all her five-year-old exuberance, "Brownies!"

Grigoryi stood behind her. "It's been a rough evening, so I baked something."

Des picked up his little sister. "No ice cream?"

Her soft brown eyes got big. "Yes! Ice cream."

Miranda stayed back with her ex-husband as the others went to the kitchen. She stood in front of him on her tiptoes for a kiss. He leaned down and responded tenderly. With one finger, she traced the tiny lines near his eyes and then down to the slight sag of his jaw.

She said, "No matter how much Anastasia ages you, you always look better than me, damn it."

He took her hand, smiled, and said, "But you will always love better." And kissed her with more passion.

She stepped out of his embrace. "Later. I'm too pissed at the Magus."

Tristan, looking unhappy, said, "I heard Jacquotte had said you were 'scrawny' and that she should be the Head of your House. I was amazed you didn't retaliate."

"That was the best she could do? There is still time to set her straight. Anyway, Sig was the most upset. She is trying to figure me out."

He smiled, "I wish her luck."

Miranda placed a hand on his arm. "Promise me that you won't go after the Magus and Jacquotte alone. We'll meet with our allies and come up with a plan."

"I wouldn't do anything so foolish. In any case, we must trust the offspring to respond wisely. It is now their time. Besides, shouldn't you use a sexual invitation to distract me? It's much more effective than a prohibition of violence."

"Time and place, babe, time and place. Right now, I need brownies and coffee to help me strategize."

31

Lady Sarah and her brother Ruben were in his suite in their Toronto mansion. Lady Sarah watched him sort through his well-worn tee shirts. She gave a disapproving look at his wardrobe choices and said, "We have to go to Seattle. Lady Jacquotte is of my House. I haven't seen her in ages. She was never happy that the Magus passed that pirate trash by to put me in charge of this House." Sarah ran the House of Plows, which encompassed North America, with the exception of Washington and Oregon. Lady Sarah had agreed to give jurisdiction there to Miranda's House of Sun.

"The House of Plows would have become a den of thieves if Jacquotte had controlled it," Ruben responded, though he thought it would've been more fun with Jacquotte running things.

Sarah continued, "Sir Jorge told me he will arrive in Seattle tomorrow night. The Haute Caste want to know what the Magus is up to." She wore a black leather outfit, and her perfectly curled, long auburn hair framed her face. She regarded his typical unkempt appearance. "You should dress better when you represent our House."

Having heard it many times before, Ruben ignored her comment and shoved some of his favorite rock icon T-shirts in a backpack. "Sister, do you ever wonder why the Magus doesn't go medieval on the Mordecais? You know—take them prisoner or simply destroy them?"

She sipped from a crystal shot glass, then said. "He'd never kill the goose that lays golden eggs. Don't you see how important their blood is to all of us?"

"Their blood is toxic to us. It's what keeps me from making a move on Marie." He straightened his Judas Priest shirt and ran a hand through his unruly red hair.

She scoffed. "Like you'd ever have a chance with her. She walked away from the Magus."

"Yeah, but she likes rock gods."

Sarah shook her head. "You don't play anything but a fool."

"Harsh." He checked his phone for gambling updates. "I'm good with our existence the way it is, and I've made quite a bit taking bets on the royals. Wendell's birth netted me a small fortune."

"You better hope Jacques never finds out."

"Hey, even Des bet with me. He made fifty grand. He was sure the baby would have HH blood. I think the siblings will keep their bets private."

"Who else bet?"

"Tomas, he lost ten grand."

Sarah said, "Let's hope he gets over that."

Ruben rubbed his chin. "Since he fell for that Seattle babe, he's harder to rattle. He even suggested I donate his losses to a homeless shelter."

Sarah gave him a questioning glance. "Well? Will you?"

He turned his attention back to his phone and distractedly said, "I'll get right on it."

"We don't have time for that. Do it on the plane. We must get going. Our House will not be left out of the action."

Ruben grinned. "You're afraid of Lady Jacquotte's influence on the Magus."

"I don't know what you're talking about. Now grab your stuff!"

He started humming a sea shanty as he finished packing.

She gave him a dirty look. "Stop it, or I'll burn all your Ramones T-shirts."

Ruben scoffed. "You wouldn't dare!" But he stopped humming.

Phoebe and Tomas were hosting a game night in the Seattle condo they were given by the Baron. Sig and Des were the reigning champs of "Throne of Death," a post-apocalyptic battle between werewolves, vampires, witches, and zombies. Marie played without a partner as Leif wanted some time alone. She hoped taking care of his goats would improve his mood. "So, Leif is with his four-legged kids, and Jacques is helping with his boys."

Des smiled. "Jacques doesn't want to lose again." He looked at Tomas. "Good thing losing doesn't bother you."

Phoebe taking up the challenge, "Oh yeah? Well, we aren't going to be just werewolves tonight. We're bringing on the witches!"

Sig exclaimed, "You can't do that!"

Tomas countered. "Sure we can. Jacques said he'd be glad if we took over for him. Des never plays by the rules, and we decided to follow his example."

Des said, with a sly grin, "No problem." He glanced at his partner. "Sig and I got this."

Marie pushed a button on her controller and all hell broke loose on the big screen. "Die Vampires!" A mega zombie sent a blast into the head of one of Des' undead warriors.

Sig cried out, "She's playing the atomic zombies against us! Crap!"

Two hours later, the room was quiet as all the players ate pizza and marveled at the amazing destruction they had rained down on each other.

Des said, "That was epic. Too bad Jacques and Leif weren't here."

Phoebe snorted. "Yeah, to see you crash and burn."

Marie said, "Leif doesn't need video vamp attacks to light up his brain. I hope he figures something out soon. He's been so edgy. Dark thoughts take over, and he pushes me away."

Tomas hugged her. "Sorry, the dude is struggling. Leif got hit by a cluster fuck truck. It's gonna take time for him to get used to his new life. But he will."

"It's the Magus' fault," Sig said. "He wanted Leif to die when he tried to transform. That fuck-up resulted in a bloodsucker who walks in sunlight and still loves pizza. He is having a hard time trying to figure out how to live in both worlds."

"My hero." Marie finished her pizza. "That freak visiting the Magus isn't helping. She's trying to get under his skin."

Des said, "Could you believe how Mom let that vampiress insult her? She's in much better control than she used to be."

Sig put down her slice. "I should've skewered her. She's bad news."

Tomas said to no one in particular, "Fuckin' pirate."

Marie said, "Mom never forgets shit like that. I learned from her that you gotta play the long game with vamps. Jacquotte will regret being on the Magus' team."

Des said, "I wish we had some atomic zombies for real."

Leif crept up through the closest line of tall evergreens to the Magus' mansion. It was a three-level masterpiece of stone, wood, and tinted picture windows that faced west, away from the rising sun. The metal roof panels extended out to provide a wide overhang protecting the rooms from direct sunlight even if the drapes were opened. The daylight vampire was impressed at the ingenuity of the design.

Lights were on in the large, great room at ground level, which opened onto a deck. He raised his binoculars but did not see anyone moving about. Fear began to dampen his bravado. His breathing became shallow. Leif questioned his impulsive decision to check out the enemy and turned around to go back home before he was missed by Marie. The wet ground helped muffle his footfalls. He inhaled the cool air scented with pine and felt calmer.

"What the..." Leif was thrown to the ground and looked up to see Jacquotte straddling him with a dagger pointed at his heart.

"Steady. It's silver." Her eyes showed no mercy.

With every ounce of control, he lay still, not knowing how his hybrid body might respond to her silver blade. Though it might not kill him, silver could cause a bad reaction in vampires and cause wounds to heal slowly. He knew of the many rumors that this vampiress had taken many lives. "I thought silver weapons were outlawed."

She smiled. "I'm a pirate vampire. Different rules, lad." She leaned over him and let her free hand gently trace the outline of his jaw, then touched his lips with her fingertips. He started to bite her, and she cackled. "Easy, not yet." Her hazel eyes held him. "No need to tell anyone else about our chance meeting. Can I withdraw my blade?"

Leif nodded, and she slowly straightened up. He started to get to his feet, but she grabbed his wrist. Her touch was cool but pleasurable. He asked, "Why are you here?" The scent of her HH blood mixed with her unnatural scent was causing a reaction.

The light of the full moon reflected in Jacquotte's eyes. "I had to find out for myself. Never been much for believing tall tales." Her voice took on a soft, compelling nature. "You're much more than I expected."

She leaned forward, aware that his mind was burning to taste her passion. Slowly, cautiously they kissed, unsure of the storm that might follow. The coolness of her lips and the pressure of her breasts against his chest fueled the fever inside him. A feast of sensual taboos filled his mind. Leif took her down to the ground and all restraint was gone. The rage, the urgency, and the desire were all overwhelming. Clothing went flying as the primal nature of their sexual needs blocked out the world.

She kissed him as though plundering a treasure chest. Jacquotte stroked his hardness from the tip to the base with enthusiasm. Leif moved down to pleasure her. He delighted in her wetness, licking her clitoris until she moaned and cried, "Now!" Her body ached for more. "Enter me!" Her nails dug into his back as Leif moved up and entered her again and again. He had never felt so out of control. Their hips collided with rhythmic force. On the edge of climax, Jacquotte pulled her hair away from her neck and commanded, "Bite me!"

Consumed with blood hunger, Leif bit into her throat. The hit of fresh blood was a euphoric rush that overwhelmed his senses. The age-old forbidden pleasure of vampires burned in his brain. He could not stop himself from drinking more until Jacquotte pushed him away but kept hold of his wrist. "Enough! Don't bleed me dry, love."

Her fangs tore into his wrist. He laid back, succumbing to the pain, which was quickly replaced by rapture. "That was wild," he uttered. His mood quickly changed as thoughts of Marie filled his heart with shame. Part of Leif hoped Jacquotte would finish him. She released him, withdrawing with a sigh of satisfaction.

They lay side by side as the dreaded reality of his betrayal sobered Leif. "No! No!" He grabbed his clothing and moved away.

Jacquotte sat up, grinning, "But darlin', you probably saved me from beheading you. I was going to claim self-defense. Now, if I can get a little specimen of your blood." She pulled a syringe out of her jacket.

"Fuck off!" He panicked and ran back toward his home a few miles through the woods. Leif tried to push the thoughts of Jacquotte's body out of his mind, but the taste of her lingered. Guilt and vampire pleasure were at war in his brain. Leif got to the edge of the freezing cold river, stripped, and dove in. He tried to wash away any trace of her, even taking a mouthful of water and spitting it out. The current carried him a little way downstream. Shivering from the icy water, he climbed out on the rocky shore and made it back to where he had dumped his clothing on the bank.

"What the hell is going on?" Miranda yelled from the tree line.

He tried to cover himself, swallowed, and said under his breath, "Fuck!" It was no good lying to her. She was the closest thing he had to a mother. He hoped she would not abandon him now. Leif pulled on his clothes and slowly walked over to her, panting, filled with self-loathing. "I screwed up."

The matriarch stared icily at him. "You are such a dumb ass. That vampiress got to you, didn't she? Crap! Marie will want to kill you both. Guillaume woke me up after he noticed you had taken off."

He hadn't noticed Guillaume, or anyone else in the woods when he was with Jacquotte. "Did he see me with Jacquotte?"

"No. I saw the scratches on your back before you put on your shirt. She marked you for a reason. Guillaume is so angry that he is afraid to be near you right now."

"What am I gonna do?"

Miranda cautioned him. "You underestimated them. I get it. It's why I've got five kids by three vampires. The good news is she didn't destroy you. I meant it when I said I'd have your back, but I didn't think it would become so literal. Many vampires are jealous of you, and only a House aligned with me can offer protection while you grow stronger." She noticed that he had started to shake from the cold. "Let's get you back to the house before you freeze to death—if that's possible. You're going away for a while."

Chapter 4

It's Complicated

The next evening, Phoebe and Tomas were in the family garage, which he had turned into a lab. He was developing a sunscreen that would allow vampires to tolerate sunlight. She asked, "So that's it? Leif goes off somewhere, Marie is mad as hell, and nobody wants to talk about what happened?"

Tomas picked up a test tube and twirled the contents around. "Pretty much. My mom or Leif will let us know what's going on eventually. You just have to trust them."

"Whatever." She was looking out a window towards the driveway. She poked Tomas and pointed. "She's getting pretty handsy with that stranger."

Tomas walked over to the window. His mom was embracing a tall man with dark brown hair wearing a stylish suit. "That's not a stranger. It's Jorge. I guess I should say, Sir Jorge. He's the Head of the House of Arrows. They have been pretty close for years."

It was a long hug. "Close like she was with Batu and Alexander?"

He chuckled. "See that other guy? That's Franco, Jorge's knight and lover."

The other man was slightly slimmer and his hair was a shade lighter. His suit was dark copper and matched his shoes. "Woah, serious fashionista."

"Tell him that. He'd love it."

She considered her Pokémon sweatshirt, jeans, and purple sneakers. "I think I'll stay in here."

Tomas hugged her and said, "I like your style. Flaunt it, gamer girl!"

Her anxiety went up as Miranda, Jorge, and Franco entered the garage. Tomas shook hands with Sir Jorge and Sir Franco. "This is my girlfriend, Phoebe. You can be open with her."

She thought about her high school Spanish class. "Buenos noches."

Franco looked at her attire. His eyebrows went up, and he asked, "Retiring so soon?"

Phoebe looked down in embarrassment. Tomas said, "She's the one who escaped from Sir Raf."

Jorge took her hands, and she felt a sense of comfort. "We are not all like him. Thank the gods. I hope the House of Sun is treating you well."

"It's a lot to take in, but I like living with the lead guitarist for the Cringe." She smiled at Tomas.

Franco remarked, "Gads. I hope your taste in music improves."

Phoebe said mockingly, "Gads? Who says that?"

Sir Jorge saved the moment by teasing Franco. "The hipsters of the 1930s. Tomas, how is your ultra-sunblock coming?"

Tomas proudly picked up a jar from a table. "Guillaume has been able to tolerate the sun for two hours in the early morning and late afternoon with almost no side effects. I'm trying to develop a non-toxic fire retardant before I make it stronger. Dad complained of getting a rash."

"Outstanding!" Sir Jorge patted him on the back.

Miranda said, "Let's go in the house, and I'll get you up to date on our situation with the Magus."

After they left, Phoebe asked. "Where will they be staying?"

"They've got a new place in Seattle." He put the jar down and walked over to her. "Alexander and Jorge got into it over Franco once. Jorge kidnapped Alex's pug to get revenge. They worked things out, and all now swear to be loyal to the House of Sun, but they don't hang out together unless it's unavoidable."

"Alexander and Franco?"

Tomas said, "Yep. Alexander once told me that he's attracted to intelligence and character."

Phoebe snorted. "And nice bods." Then she remembered what had happened with Miranda and Alexander. "Sorry, I didn't mean anything bad by that."

"Don't worry about it. I'm not offended. Our family is complicated. I'm just glad you haven't run for the hills." He smiled and added, "yet."

"I guess things can get screwed up around here. Like Leif. I get why he split for a while."

In the house, Miranda served her guests small glasses of O positive while she drank black coffee from a mug that said, 'What the Fuck!'

Franco fluffed the pillow on the couch before sitting. Jorge gazed fondly at his close friend. He had first met Miranda while posing as a student at UCLA. The Baron had asked him to keep an eye on her. He remembered how innocent she once was, a young woman beginning her writing career with the normal concerns of a graduating student, totally unaware of the vampire world.

Franco said, "Nice mug."

"The kids gave it to me. It's the House of Sun motto."

"Of course it is."

Sir Jorge finished his beverage and carefully placed the glass on the table. "My dear, aging suits you. Now tell me about the Magus' latest obsession with your family."

They discussed the Magus' residence and his inviting Jacquotte there. Then her voice became a whisper. "She seduced Leif in the woods. He was so ashamed of himself, I was afraid he might do something...."

Franco interjected, "...foolish and dangerous."

Jorge asked, "Does Marie know?"

"I'm trying to give her a little time to calm down before she finds out exactly what happened."

Franco asked, "Where is this poor excuse for a vampire?"

"Someplace I don't think Jacquotte has ever been. I have to keep her from influencing him any more."

Jorge nodded. "He drank from her. Now they will have a connection, though when Leif becomes stronger, he'll be able to fight it."

Franco said, "If he wants to. I remember Jacquotte having her pick of suitors."

Miranda looked clearly unhappy. "Others can have her, but she can't have Leif."

"Is he going to Mongolia?" Franco was quite pleased with himself for figuring it out. "I'm certain that's the only House Jacquotte has not visited. Her chaotic adventures always make news."

Miranda's lips tightened. "It's the safest place for now. Leif needs time to get his act together."

Jorge agreed. "That makes sense. What about Dr. Kyoto? Isn't he running the Magus' research under the watchful eye of Princess Khunbish?"

"He was, but Batu explained our problem to her highness. Last night she expelled Kyoto from Mongolia for some reason or other to allow a safe place for Leif. Kyoto is on his way back to L.A."

"Your handling of this crisis is admirable." Jorge smiled.

With a bored expression, Franco said, "Impressive." He yawned. "Now, when do we get to see all your offspring? And tell me, are you and Tristan planning any more surprises?"

Miranda smiled at Franco. She knew the deadly assassin that hid behind his snarky comments and fashion sense would do anything to protect her family. "I'm done adding to the population. Guillaume took River for dinner and a play date with Ali and Wendell at Tristan's home. Jacques and Loretta are living there now. They should be back soon. Tomas and Phoebe are living at Tristan's old condo in Seattle, Des and Loretta have an apartment near them."

"Well, I hope you let the children stay up late and sleep in. Where are the fathers?"

Jorge was peeved. "I think he means Alexander." He stood and walked over to the picture window. "Nice view of the river at night."

Miranda said, "Tristan and Alex are at the club conferring with Sir Henry about Jacquotte. I thought I should stick close to home. Batu went to Mongolia with Leif. I was afraid to send him alone since he isn't in control of his fangs yet. Or other parts, for that matter."

Jorge said, "I'm relieved to hear that." He gently patted Miranda's hand. "I would gladly speak with Marie if you'd like."

"Thanks. I was thinking of sending her to Las Vegas to stay with her grandfather and Anastasia, to keep her away from the Magus. As good an idea as that might be, I can't make her do anything. Des and his girlfriend Sig are staying with Marie at Leif's house."

Franco asked, "Are Des and his red-head still going after the Magus on the web?"

"Absolutely! They are partners in cyber-crime. Sig and Des have moved a small fortune out of his offshore accounts and donated it to charity. They also messed with his skincare firm, so he can't research sunscreen without it all being given away to his competitors. They have been careful to do enough to be a bane of his existence but not enough to cause him to retaliate. He doesn't want another confrontation with the House of Sun and our allies. I know they have something planned, but they told me I'll find out soon enough."

"Brilliant! No one has ever challenged him like the Mordecais." Franco smiled.

Marie came in with Des and Sig in tow. "Hola!" She gave the visitors hugs. "I guess you heard about that bitch, Jacquotte. She did something to Leif, and now he's in hiding. She's a malicious disaster in a bustier. And what's her deal walking around with that stupid knife in her belt?"

Franco joked. "I told her to stop accessorizing lingerie with daggers years ago."

Des said, "The Magus is always looking for a new way to fuck with us. That's the only reason she showed up."

Miranda got down to business. "So, we've got another serial killer in town. One that we don't like. Any ideas of how to get rid of her?"

Jorge said, "It's worse than that. She's not simply a vampiress; she fed off a succubus she killed two centuries ago. Ever since then, her power to seduce has grown enormously. Even I would have to be vigilant around her."

"Not me," Franco asserted.

Grigoryi entered and took in the visiting vamps with trepidation. He was always leery of the motives of vampires outside of the 'the family'. "I hope you're here to help." He placed a plate with freshly baked banana bread on the table.

Franco quipped, "We didn't come for your cooking."

Grigoryi collected the empty glasses and left the room without another word.

Des scoffed, "I'd think after all this time, Greg would have gotten used to our crazy world."

After a brief pause in the conversation, Marie let out a long audible sigh. "Poor Leif." Marie found her anger and disappointment towards him begin to diminish. No one openly admitted Leif had sex with the vampiress, but she knew it had to be the reason he took off so suddenly. "Leif's not the most woke man when it comes to women, but he wouldn't have a chance against a vampire/succubus."

Des agreed. "None." He grabbed a slice of Grigoryi's fresh banana bread.

Sig said, "If men can't deal with her, it's got to be the women who take her on."

Tomas said. "I have to admit she sounds pretty hot."

Phoebe elbowed him. "Is that why you wanted to watch a pirate movie last night."

Des cracked up. "Seriously, bro?"

Sig gave Des a dirty look. "And you mentioned I'd look good in a bustier."

Jorge said, "See how powerful she is? She sows jealousy, dissension, and heartbreak wherever she goes. We came as soon as we heard she was here."

Miranda said, "Rumor has it that Sarah and Ruben will be here soon."

Franco warned, "There's bad blood between Lady Sarah and Lady Jacquotte." He paused, noticing Phoebe's puzzled expression. "I didn't mean that literally."

Sig said, "I'm having a hard time wrapping my head around the fact that succubuses—succubi—whatever—exist."

Grigoryi returned with coffee for the offspring. He placed a tray of mugs on the table and said, "A succubus! Dio ci protegga. God protect us!" Then he crossed himself.

Franco said, "That won't help."

Grigoryi huffed. "You may not think so, but it makes me feel better." He went back to the kitchen.

Miranda laughed. "Franco, knowing you has made even me pray more."

Jorge said, "Amen!"

Phoebe shook her head. "You people aren't right."

Miranda stood and crossed her arms. "As the head of this dumpster fire, I'm asking that we not invite any more of our nocturnal allies here. I think we need to take care of this problem ourselves. With the help of the present company, of course." She regarded the kids. "Des, let Jacques and Loretta know we need to meet. I'm trusting the next generation to find some new creative ways to deal with threats from the Magus."

Jorge responded, "We shall be glad to add our guidance and skills."

Marie gave Jorge a sad smile. "I wish I could be transformed, on a temporary basis. If for no other reason than to kick Jacquotte's succubus ass. I know most of the Haute Caste respect the Magus, but he's a sociopath who doesn't care about who gets hurt if anyone gets in his way."

"Never forget what a very cunning and powerful being he is. He hasn't lived this long and amassed so much power and influence by chance," Jorge warned.

Franco said, "He did invent the guillotine."

Sig blurted out, "No fuck, seriously?"

Franco explained, "He wanted a way to permanently 'end' anyone who opposed him and posed a serious threat. Not wanting to attract attention, he allowed the Frenchman, Dr. Guillotine, to take credit. Even the undead can be disposed of if they lose their heads, so let us all keep ours."

Chapter 5

The Land of the Mongols

Batu and Leif were bundled up against the cold as they left Mongolia's Chinggis Khan International Airport in a van provided by Princess Khunbish. They would stop at a safe house to rest during the day before proceeding to the House of Cups headquarters in Choibalsan. Chang, a vampire serving the Princess, drove them, looking smug. "I hear that the House of Sun is weak."

Batu shook his head. "On the contrary, I now wield more power with greater wisdom because of my connection to both Houses."

Leif's breath came out as steam. "Meet me at high noon and we'll see who is weak." If the others were like Chang, Leif wondered if being sent to the House of Cups would be helpful with his anger management issues.

Batu touched Leif's shoulder. "I didn't want to leave River, but you needed to get away from Jacquotte. So, we shall make the best of this. Don't mind, Chang. He has Haute Caste envy."

Chang countered, "We're of the same blood type."

Batu replied with a self-satisfied smile. "But you haven't been favored by the Magus and elevated to the Haute Caste rank."

Leif said, "My blood wasn't special. It mutated when Angel screwed up my transformation."

Chang glanced in the rear-view mirror. "Are the Day Fanger rumors true? You weren't joking about meeting in daylight?"

"That's right, I'm amazing." Leif pulled his blanket tighter. "Can you turn up the heat? And I need some food. I mean real food. There's gotta be a burger place or even noodles."

Batu noticed Chang's look of disbelief. "We've got to get him dinner so he doesn't kill us in our sleep."

Chang wasn't sure if Batu was joking. "Sure, no problem. There's a café near the safe house where we'll stop before sunrise. It's at the halfway point to the Princess' palace. We'll get something there." He shook his head. "Seriously, you're the only one who…."

"… is so royally screwed up." Leif turned around, grabbed a bag of blood from a cooler, slurped the contents loudly, and then burped.

Chang muttered, "Unbelievable."

Batu with a disapproving look said, "Mongolia will never be the same. How was it with Jacquotte?"

Leif considered the question for a moment. "Terrible and fantastic. I lost control. She had to push me off her so I wouldn't drain her. But I'll tell you both something, just in case you're ever with her. She said that fucking me made her decide to spare my life." Leif got with an arrogant look added, "Yeah, I'm that good."

"So that's why Marie hasn't killed you yet." Batu held back a laugh.

Chang gripped the steering wheel tighter and tried to focus on the road.

Leif said, "But it wasn't worth it. I'd give anything to be back home with Marie. I'm afraid she'll leave me when she figures out what happened."

Batu's expression became serious. "I'm sure she has already figured it out. We all know that Marie had an ill-advised rendezvous with the Magus. What you did certainly wasn't worse than that."

Chang's nodded in agreement and said, "I heard all about that, even here."

Leif's concerned gaze fell on Batu. "Do you think Marie will decide it was only fair that I had sex with Jacquotte?"

"Probably not." Batu considered how well he knew her mother. "Mordecai women are complex and mysterious. With all that I think she might forgive you. Even if you don't deserve it."

Chang said, "I'd like to find out how complex the Baroness is." He recalled how fierce Miranda was during the rogue vampire rebellion that he had ill-advisedly participated in.

Batu replied, "I'll make your funeral arrangements."

Leif cautioned Chang. "She's exclusively with the Baron. He's not the most forgiving guy. Forget a coffin. He'd probably put you out in the sun to fry."

Batu grinned. "But Chang, it might be worth it."

"Fuck you!" Chang spat out.

Chang stayed quiet during the drive the next night until they arrived at the mansion on the outskirts of Choibalsan. They passed several mortal guards as the van drove over a gravel drive to the main entrance. It was a sturdy yet attractive structure with white walls, columns, and red-tiled roofs on several connected buildings. A large yurt was set off to the side next to a fountain.

"Can the security guys be trusted?" Leif asked.

Batu said, "Absolutely. For them it's an honor to serve the Princess, a descendant of the Great Khan."

Chang parked the van and the trio walked up to the entrance. Tall, heavy looking, carved doors were opened for them as they approached. The guards' clothing was a combination of East and West. Wool military coats with fur hats pulled down to the top of their eyes. Leif noticed each carried pistols, long knives, and compound bows on their backs. The guards scrutinized them carefully, but said nothing as the small group entered the building. They walked down a long hall that led to a large audience chamber.

"Wow!" Leif couldn't stop himself from staring at a very small woman, in traditional Mongolian garb, wearing an ornate headdress. She was sitting on a carved wooden throne atop a raised platform. Standing beside her was another little person with blond hair and a sword fully half his height. A fire pit in the middle of the room provided heat as its smoke rose to a small opening in the ceiling. The floor was covered in Persian rugs, and antique brass lanterns hung from the ceiling shedding a warm glow. Incense permeated the room with the scent of cedar.

"Bow," Batu whispered to Leif. The three of them bent from the hip almost in unison.

The Princess rose. "Sir Batu and Leif, come forward."

Chang moved to the side of the room. As the others stopped a few feet from the throne, the blond man came forward, and Batu leaned down as they embraced.

He regarded Leif. "So, you're the latest surprise from the House of Sun. Welcome. I'm Sir Steve. A knight of the House of Cups." He shook Leif's hand, and his grip strength was surprising.

Princess Khunbish said to Leif, "We are closely allied with your house. We offer you protection and training to enhance your gifts."

45

Batu elbowed Leif, who was momentarily tongue-tie at the sight of the exotic-looking ruler. The mortal vampire said, "Thanks. I'm kind of blown away by everything that's happened."

She smiled and said to Batu. "Leif shall spend a night among the wolves. With you by his side, of course. Whenever you think he is ready."

"What?" Leif's voice an octave higher than normal.

"Princess Khunbish, my young friend, does not understand the honor you bestow upon him. I will explain it to him later. I thank you on behalf of Baroness Mordecai."

"Sir Batu." She smiled. "How is River?"

He answered, "She has an affinity to horses; like her ancestors."

The Princess was obviously pleased. "Excellent!"

Leif said, "She's a sweet little girl, but she doesn't let her nephew Ali push her around."

She stared at Leif. "One must be careful exposing a gentle nature and affection for others. It can be used against you."

Sir Steve informed Leif, "Sir Sapna will give you a tour of the palace. He will see that all your needs are met. Rest well, your training will begin tomorrow."

A tall man of Indian descent appeared out of an alcove. He was dressed in a high-collar shirt and silk pants. His short and neatly trimmed hair emphasized his regal cheekbones and piercing stare.

"Hi. I'm Leif." He held out his hand, but the vampire ignored it.

"Good, you know your name. Follow me."

Leif glanced at Batu, who gestured for him to go ahead. Leif followed his guide down a hallway that ended in a kitchen with an odd mixture of modern appliances and a stone fireplace with a cooking pot.

Sapna said, "Your meals will be served here. The Princess does not like the smell of mortal food."

Leif saw a loaf of bread on a counter and broke off a large piece. While chewing, he mumbled, "Thanks."

Sapna was a little put off by Leif's table manners. "Follow me; your room is around the corner. It's next to the servants' and guards' housing."

Leif trailing behind Sapna said, "I guess you don't like having to show a commoner around."

Sapna, ignored the comment and opened the door to a large room with a plush bed, desk, and adjoining bathroom. It may have been part of the "help's" quarters, but it was first class to Leif. His backpack had been brought in and was on top of the fur throw on the bed. The vampire stepped aside. "Tomorrow you may explore the grounds, but you are not to visit the city." He started to walk away but stopped to add, "Perhaps you'll earn my respect, but that is doubtful. You might start by zipping your fly."

Leif looked down. "Crap!" He worried that the Princess had noticed.

Leif slept until noon the next day, and it took a minute to orient himself when he woke. From his window, he could see over the stone walls surrounding the property to a glimpse of the open plains. He had been told in no uncertain terms to stay on the grounds of the palace. Leif put on the sturdy clothes and suede coat with a fur-lined hood placed in the room for him. He tried not to think that someone had entered his room and left the clothing while he was sleeping. His empty stomach rumbled.

He went out into the hallway. A male guard said something gruff in Mongolian, then pointed down the hall. Leif followed his nose back to the kitchen.

A woman with gray hair done up in braids, wearing a long dress, gestured to a chair at a small table. There was a sweetness to her round face, pink cheeks, and warm smile. Sitting in the kitchen made him miss home.

She set a bowl of steaming mutton dumplings in front of him. Then she brought a plate of grilled beef, and buttered bread. Leif's eyes lit up as he started chowing down. The cook was pleased and gave him a large mug of milk tea. She watched him finish the meal, then pulled a small cup of blood from a refrigerator and handed it to him with a serious expression.

Leif felt a little awkward about his dietary needs as he took it. Despite the filling meal, he was craving what she offered. "Thank you."

He made a little bow hoping it was the cultural thing to do and left the kitchen quickly. He needed to get outside and feel the sun, proof he had not completely turned. The Day Fanger made his way through the hallways to the front door, and a guard appeared and unlocked it.

Leif blinked as his eyes became accustomed to the bright sunlight. It was cold but clear, and he could see for miles to where the city of Choibalsan began. An avalanche of emotions overwhelmed him, and he started to run straight out of the gates onto the stark flatlands. Though he might get in trouble for leaving the palace grounds, it felt worth it. Leif kept going for a couple of miles and stopped on top of a small hill. At a discrete distance, a guard on horseback watched him.

He should have been out of breath, but he wasn't. His vampire nature was constantly renewing his strength and increasing his stamina. He yelled, "Fuck you!" to no one in particular, and roared with laughter.

A woman's voice startled him. "Who are you?" Her thick accent sounded like the Princess'.

He turned to see a petite Mongol, with long dark hair and fierce eyes. Though bundled up against the cold, he could tell she could not have weighed more than 120 pounds. The scent of her blood type was mixed with a light perfume. "You're AB, like Batu."

"What? How could you know that." She took a step back spooked by his comment.

"I can smell your blood type," he said as though it was like noticing her eye color. "I'm Leif, from Seattle. I mean America. I'm staying there." Leif pointed to the mansion, and noticed the guard on horseback was still tracking him. The guard silently watched them, motionless. "What's your name?" Leif asked the woman.

"Ask Chang or Batu. Tell your friends I remember their crime."

"What do you mean?"

"They owe me." She looked him over carefully. "You are not like them. You don't belong here."

"You're telling me."

"You should leave." With that, she stormed off toward town.

Leif dropped down and sat cross-legged, watching her disappear. He wondered if she could pose a threat to anyone. After being around Marie and her mom, he learned never to underestimate a pissed-off female. He would talk to the House of Cups about their need for daylight security. Though safe from Jacquotte, this refuge was as chaotic as home. "Crazy ass vampires," he said to barren landscape.

Marie found her mom reading to River in the living room with their black Lab Lug at their feet. They had adopted him as a puppy at a gas station on their move to Washington. They named him after Bela Lugosi, the actor responsible for making Dracula a horror movie icon. Marie sat for a moment, sipping a mug of coffee, remembering story time when she was small. She and her brothers had loved it most when their dad read to them with a lot of dramatic inflection. Those were happy times in Illinois on a small farm outside the town where her mom had grown up. Then the kids began to understand how weird their family was. They realized that Bart, the guy who took care of the horses, only came out at night, and he had a small fridge with bags of blood for his 'special diet.' Their dad never approved of vampire costumes on Halloween and hated vampire movies.

There were amazing birthday parties at the Magus' mansion in Chicago when he still protected them before things got ugly.

She smiled at her younger sister, hoping she would be sheltered from the mayhem and tragedy of vampire society. Marie's ability to trust the undead, even her father and biological grandfather, Sir Omar, would never be whole because of the murder of her grandpa Pete Ortega. The all-powerful vampires weren't able to protect him. Two deranged monks who wanted vampire blood to give them powers killed Pete while trying to take him hostage. Marie knew that they had been given help by some Haute Caste who disapproved of them as part mortal and part vampire. Only Lady Antoinella of the House of Pentacles admitted any involvement and declared the murder of Pete a terrible mistake. She now pledged loyalty to Miranda, but it would never be enough to satisfy Marie.

"What's up, hon?" Miranda interrupted her musings.

"Can we talk?" Marie pointed at River.

Miranda said, "Sure."

Marie hugged her little sister. "Why don't you help Grigoryi make dinner?"

River giggled. "I good cook!" and went off to the kitchen with the dog following her.

Marie moved closer to her mom on the couch. Her eyes searched the tired matriarch's face.

Miranda said, "I'll tell you what you want to know, though you may have already guessed it. Leif went to Mongolia. Batu is with him. Princess Khunbish and Sir Steve are offering protection and training."

"And?"

She hesitated, then went on. "Jacquotte got to him. He's not ready to take on the Haute Caste."

"Nice way to say he screwed her." Her eyes flashed with anger.

"You know he was helpless against that vampire succubus. I found him in the freezing cold river trying to wash her off of him. All he could think about was how you'd react."

"In the freezing river?" Marie shook her head. "I could've picked a brighter guy."

Miranda swallowed a laugh. "But not with a bigger heart."

"Do you think he'll be able to handle this daylight vampire bullshit?"

Miranda reassured her. "Yes. But he needs time. We need to be patient with him while he figures out how to live in both worlds." She tried to sound confident, but her eyes held worry. "He's a mystery unfolding before us."

Her daughter asked, "Can we order a guillotine from Amazon for the Magus and Jacquotte?"

49

"Your grandpa Omar is quite good at beheading people with his sword. That would be much more discrete."

Marie's eyes lit up.

"I was only kidding." She hugged her. "You're such a Mordecai."

"Says my mother, Miranda Ortega, who cut off the nose of a vampire."

"Okay. You're definitely an Ortega-Mordecai."

Marie laughed, then got serious. "All of us have been working on a blow to the Magus' empire. That keeps me going. I'm glad Sir Jorge and Sir Franco are staying in Seattle if we need them." She looked down at her mug. "I miss Leif so much. I know I should be furious at him but for a grown man he can be so naïve sometimes. He gets lost driving in Seattle. I can't imagine him in a foreign country."

"Send Leif a text message. Tell him you forgive him. I have faith that Batu will protect him."

"I'm not sure that Batu, or anyone can protect him from himself." She studied her mother for a few seconds then stated firmly, "You are the only one I trust."

Miranda teared up and changed the topic. "What's this blow to the evil empire involve?"

She managed a grin. "Stay tuned."

Twilight in Mongolia found Leif sitting in the kitchen, finishing off a platter of kebabs. Chang entered and stretched. "You seem to like it here." He sat across from the new arrival as the old woman brought him a small cup of blood and said something to her in Mongolian.

"Did you say thank you?"

"Yes."

He saw Leif's confused look and said, "It's Bayrl-laa."

Leif tried a few times with limited success. The old woman, not wanting to be rude, tried to stifle her laugh.

Leif said, "English is tough enough for me."

Chang said, "You should stick with that. I want to warn you. If someone offers something to you make sure you don't say 'No'. They'll regard it as rude, and you don't want to offend anyone, especially the Princess."

Leif finished off his fifth kebab. "I met a woman I'd be afraid to say 'No' to today. She seemed pissed off at you and everyone else here."

"That had to be Odgerel. Where did she approach you?"

"I guess that could have been her. She wouldn't tell me her name. She was petite with long hair and an attitude that would scare a bear. She said something about your crime spree. I was out walking, and the guard followed me at a distance but didn't pay any attention to her."

"The guards underestimate that woman. But I saw her stab Batu once. Never turn your back on Odgerel."

"Seriously, and she is still walking around?"

Chang looked around the room to see if anyone was listening, lowered his voice, and continued, "Her boss was a local politician who would go into drunken rages and abuse his wife and children. One night he was in a particularly foul mood, and after he severely beat his wife, he went to the barn and beat one of his horses to death. That poor excuse for a man was Batu's first sanctioned kill, with my help. In fear of her job, Odgerel had been forced to submit to him and was in the house that night. When Batu attacked Hulagu, she snuck up behind him and stabbed him in the back. I pleaded with Princess Khunbish to spare her. Odgerel has been harassing us ever since. I don't know how much longer the Princess will tolerate it."

Leif poked Chang and laughed. "You've got a thing for her!"

"Shut up!"

"Just saying. Don't worry, I won't tell anyone, but it's kind of obvious. If I can help, let me know."

Batu entered and announced, "Time to train."

Chang muttered, "Later," and left.

Batu asked, "What's up with him?"

"I met a hostile local today," Leif replied.

Batu grinned. "I heard. She's not one of my fans. Chang is protective of her, but he's playing with fire."

"I was wondering, does the whole town know the truth about the House of Cups?"

Batu said, "No. Like the rest of our society, we try to keep as low a profile as we can. They think Princess Khunbish is a wealthy eccentric descended from the Great Khan. She's the richest person in this area, so everyone looks the other way if there's anything unusual happening or even a suspicious death. A lot of the local economy is supported by the Princess. It never comes back on her, and her name is rarely spoken aloud. It means 'not human.'"

"Not everyone looks the other way. Odgerel is carrying some kind of grudge. I heard that she stabbed you. Is that true?"

"Yes, it's true. You learn a lot your first kill, like always watch your back. Let's get going. I must prepare you."

"Prepare me to kill? No, not me. I'll fight to protect myself or others, but that's as far as I will go."

Batu sighed. "You've got so much to learn, Day Fanger."

Chapter 6

Unimaginable

Sir Raf was in the library with Lady Jacquotte and the most ancient vampire. His blond hair, broad shoulders, and perfect features stirred Jacquotte. His phone beeped, grabbing his attention and a look of annoyance from the Magus.

Raf held up his phone and said, "Phoebe texted that I should be a better vampire and that being undead stunted my emotional growth. What does that even mean?"

Jacquotte said, "You surely don't expect me to know the answer."

The Magus remarked, "I'm surprised she would communicate with you."

Raf smiled. "She wants to think I'm not evil because she was attracted to me. Is it because she can't admit to her darker inclinations, or does she have a savior complex?"

Jacquotte declared, "You both need therapy."

The Magus frowned. "I've always considered most mortals beneath contempt, especially when they have the nerve to condemn us, considering their history of wide-scale atrocities. Phoebe and the Mordecais are not condemning anyone. They are admonishing us. Extraordinary. Until this moment, I never saw it so clearly."

Jacquotte scoffed. "What do they want? Shall we take an oath to live on cattle's blood? I'd rather sunbathe."

An alarm chirped as a few vehicles drove onto the property. On a monitor above an ornate desk, strangers in business attire and a local news reporter with a cameraman approached the front door. Raf and Jacquotte looked surprised at the visitors.

Jacquotte asked, "Do you know any of them, or why they are here?"

The Magus, without showing any break in his composure said, "I'm not sure what they want, but I have no doubt who is behind this."

The butler entered and announced, "The leader of the county Girls Scouts, the Granite Falls Mayor, and some news people want to interview you about your donation of this property."

Raf suppressed a laugh. "Horribly brilliant! It has to be the Mordecai siblings."

The Magus glared at him, then shook his head. "Never have I been up against such worthy opponents. Perhaps I should be glad they have not transformed."

"But they are multiplying like rabbits." Jacquotte stifled a grin. "What will you do?"

Raf suggested, "Tell them it was a prank, but you'll make a contribution."

"No. I will not be made a fool of in public." The Magus responded to the butler. "The Mayor, the reporter, and the Girl Scout leader may meet with me, but no cameraman."

"Of course."

A few minutes later, the wide-eyed mortals entered the opulent library. There was no home in the town of Granite Falls that came close to the size and décor of the mansion. The Magus stood in front of a marble fireplace wearing a black silk shirt and black dress slacks, silently staring at the intruders. Raf eyed the brunette reporter in a short skirt and began introductions.

"Welcome. This is Mr. Desmon Dontinae. I'm his assistant, Rafael, and my coworker Jackie." The vampiress gave him a cold look. "Please be seated." He gestured to the velvet couch and matching chairs.

As they settled on the large couch, the Girl Scout representative started to talk but was cut off by the Mayor. "I'm Fred Quinn," the tall, balding man began. "As Mayor, I have to say your offer to turn over this magnificent property to the Girl Scouts is the kind of generous spirit the people of Granite Falls are known for."

The reporter leaned forward, almost coming off the couch. "Mr. Dontinae, I'm Carol Kasai from King 5 News. Why did you decide to do this? An unverified news source said you wanted to make up for many years of, and I quote, 'Cutthroat business dealings.'"

Jacquotte, unable to contain herself, cackled. She drew the attention of the visitors. The Mayor's stare stopped where her long brown hair fell over her tight V-neck blouse. He caught himself and looked back up at her face and swallowed. She ran her tongue over her lips, and he tore his eyes away, adjusting his sitting position.

The Magus said, "Thank you for coming. I kept my decision a secret until all the details were worked out, but my security was apparently compromised." He aimed a charming smile at the reporter. "Please don't take that attack on my character seriously. I'm very private, and few are allowed into my intimate circle. Of course, those who are jealous of my success will try to discredit my charitable acts."

The middle-aged woman finally spoke, "I'm Mattie Green. I represent the Board of Directors of the Girls Scouts of Western Washington. The generous financial donation this week from your Public Affairs agent, Ms. Mordecai, will help improve our educational programs and outdoor facilities. But the addition of this property will help Girl Scouts for many years to come." She held out a tote bag. "We are grateful. It's not much, but we wanted you to have a sampler of all our cookies."

The butler rushed over and took it.

The Magus said, "I appreciate your thoughtfulness. I know you must have many questions, and I'll have one of my lawyers contact you. I shall remain on the property for a few months, which will provide plenty of time to arrange the transfer of ownership. Now, I hope you will respect my desire for privacy."

Jacquotte said, "Your audience with Mr. Dontinae is over. He's very busy."

The Mayor stood, "Of course." He reached out to shake the hand of the young-looking millionaire, but the Magus stood and turned away.

Raf took up the role of genial host and guided them out with light banter. His hand lightly grazed the reporter's arm at the door. She smiled and remarked, "You're cool. Maybe we could have a drink by a warm fire when you get off work."

Her flirty expression made clear that she was interested in more than an interview. A dalliance with a reporter could have dire consequences if not handled with extreme care. He flatly said, "Perhaps," and left it at that. He took her card and smiled.

The mortals left with a sense of having been permitted a peek into the secret world of the very wealthy and could not wait to tell others about it. Raf mused that it was a shame the reporter would never be aware of the shocking truth about the Girls Scouts benefactor. That would be a career-launching story.

When he returned to the library, the Magus was fuming. "The audacity! The hubris!"

Raf added, "The brats!"

Jacquotte shook her head. "I can't believe they pulled this off. They should be pirates. Bless their conniving, ungrateful hearts."

Raf asked, "You'll give it up? All this?"

The Magus's shoulders slumped, and he sat down with an air of defeat. "It's the Girl Scouts. What kind of bastard could disappoint them?"

Raf said, "I think this is what Phoebe meant when she said I should be a better vampire. This trickery is giving you the appearance of one."

"Of course." Jacquotte walked over and rubbed the Magus' shoulders. "Use it to repair your reputation. Do not let them see that you've been bested. Who could publicize your generosity?"

Raf said, "Ruben. He is the ruler of vampire social media."

The Magus sounded more irritated. "Ruler?"

"Uh, poor choice of words. The purveyor of gossip and gambling."

"Demand that he announce my good deed right away. Emphasize my desire to help these children. I don't want the offspring to spin their version before I do." He stood and seemed to regain his sense of dignity. "I shall make Ruben my public affairs agent and have him tell the Girl Scouts that Ms. Mordecai was fired."

In Choibalsan, Leif was laughing so hard that a guard barged into his room. He held up the phone and said, "It's okay. Good news." Then waved him out of the room. Alone again, he asked Marie, "It was on TV?"

"It was great! They showed the house and the butler telling the cameraman to stop filming. Then the Mayor made a statement about how Mr. Dontinae did blah, blah, blah and that he had wanted to keep his generous gift to the Girl Scouts a secret. I can imagine him trying to keep his cool while the officials told him what he had done."

"Damn! The Girl Scouts. That's frickin' hilarious."

Marie sighed. "I miss you bae."

Her boyfriend didn't respond, afraid he might break down, and after an uncomfortable silence, he asked, "Is the band playing this weekend?"

Leif couldn't see her smile. She knew he would rather talk about anything but feelings. "Sig has stepped up to keep us focused on playing at the club."

"Sig won't let Des screw around." Leif stopped wishing he had used a different expression.

Marie said, "Look, I told you we're okay, and I meant it. That vampsuc doesn't matter. I'm not saying I'm happy about what you did. After what happened between the Magus and me, I understand their power to control and manipulate. She has been around a long time and has had a lot of practice. We won't let the Magus or his minions come between us. You got that?"

"I got you." Someone knocked on his door. He heard Batu call him. "I have to go. The Princess wants to see me. I'll call soon. Tell everyone I'm fine. Stay away from the bastard." Then he whispered, "I love you." And put down his phone.

By now, he could find his way to the audience room by himself. When he entered, it was empty. He looked about until a guard gestured for him to follow. They went out a back entrance to a building too luxurious to be called a barn. It was a heated hotel for horses with fancy brass lighting fixtures and tiled walls. The stalls had raked dirt and clean hay for the pampered small horses draped in tailored velvet blankets. They lifted their heads, eyeing the stranger, and neighed. As he walked to the other end of the building, Leif noticed the horses there were standard size with brushed manes and glistening coats.

Princess Khunbish stood on a platform that put her at eye level with Leif and Batu. Sir Steve, as always, was at her side.

"Hi. Nice barn. I've never seen that breed of small horse before. Is it for...."

Batu coughed suddenly, afraid Leif would refer to the size of the Princess and Sir Steve. "They're a famed Mongolian breed. Their short, strong legs carried the Mongol armies. They are spirited, loyal horses able to survive long journeys."

The Princess continued the explanation. "Leif, my ancestors would at times combine horse blood with alcohol to help them survive the dangers of conquest. In many ways, the lives of these fine horses and the survival of my people are intertwined. As you ride out tonight, you will see a dozen horses in a pasture that are never ridden and under my protection. They are some of the last of their species of wild horses in existence, the Takhi or Przewalski as the west calls them."

Steve added, "There are more horses than people in Mongolia. Nowhere in the world are horses more central to daily life than here. Mongolia is called the Land of the Horse, and Mongols are the best horsemen anywhere. Most of the children around Choibalsan can ride better than you, Leif."

Khunbish nodded. "Much better."

Batu heaved a heavy saddle into Leif's stomach. He grabbed it and let out a breath. "We're riding now?"

Sir Steve answered, "The full moon will guide you to the place of wolves." He winked. "Have fun!"

Batu tugged on his arm. "You heard him. I've got a heavy coat and a bed roll for you. Let's go."

Leif shrugged, then grimly smiled goodbye to the Head of the House of Cups as he followed Batu to a stall. They saddled up two of the larger horses, identical black stallions except for a diamond-shaped patch of white fur on the head of Leif's horse. He wished Marie were here to coach him. He'd been thrown once and never completely regained his confidence as a rider.

"Don't embarrass the House of Sun or me. I thought you were supposed to be a tough Viking."

"Fuck you." He made sure the saddle was strapped on correctly, then hoisted himself up, only to land on his ass as the horse moved at the last second.

"He doesn't like you. Here give him this." Batu handed Leif a carrot.

Leif stood up, rubbing his butt. He grabbed the carrot and held it out to the stallion who eyed him suspiciously. Luckily a couple of chomps later, the horse allowed Leif to rub his head. Then with all his courage, Leif hauled himself up into the saddle. "I am so glad that none of the Mordecais saw that."

Behind him, he heard someone laugh. He turned to see Sir Steve put his phone into a pocket of his tunic.

Batu said something loudly in Mongolian, and both horses moved through the open doors of the building. Leif asked, "What's with Steve? I mean, he's American, right?"

Batu said, "They met when the Princess made a rare visit to the States, and I was part of her entourage. She left me behind to be Miranda's bodyguard and brought Steve back here. Love, lust, and devotion at first sight. They are inseparable."

Leif said, "Then you and Miranda, you…."

"…had an affair. It's over, but we remain close." He glanced at Leif. "I've moved on."

Leif shook his head. "I don't think I could ever get over Marie."

The vampire looked off into the distance. "Perhaps. None of us know what fate will decree."

Leif flicked his reins and moved ahead of Batu. "Fuck fate. I make my own."

Batu said, "If only it were that simple my young friend."

Chapter 7

Capitol Crime

Sir Franco and Sir Jorge had bought a condo in the Capitol Hill neighborhood, an old but up-and-coming area of Seattle that attracted artisans and musicians. It also had become a magnet for LGBTQ people. It was a surprise when their evening stroll was interrupted by a man yelling, "There you are, acting like a little bitch. I got you now!"

A middle-aged white man was yanking the arm of a teenage boy with one hand and slapping him with the other. Then he dropped him on the sidewalk and kicked him in the ribs.

Sir Franco got to the man first. He threw the abuser against a brick wall, then held him up by his neck as he struggled to breathe. "I hate to soil my hands with you."

Sir Jorge kneeled by the youth. "Are you okay?"

The blond boy shook his head and, through tears, said, "It's nothing. Don't hurt him. He's my father."

Sir Jorge shot a threatening look at the man struggling hopelessly against Sir Franco. "You don't deserve this child." He gave a barely perceptible nod to Franco. The vampire hit the man's head against the wall knocking him out.

The boy cried out, "No!"

Sir Franco walked over, rubbing his hands with a scented handkerchief. "Sweaty bastard. Don't worry, I didn't hit him that hard. He's unconscious, but he'll be fine."

Sir Jorge used his vampire charm to comfort the trembling teen. "We mean you no harm. You need a safe place to recover from your injuries. Your ribs are bruised, if not broken. Do you want that disgusting excuse of a father to beat you again?"

The 14-year-old had been on the street long enough to know help wasn't free. The mission wanted your soul, and the pimps wanted your body. "I don't do tricks."

Sir Franco said, "Me either, except with cards. Our friend, Henry has a club near Pioneer Square, The Funeral Pyre. I'm sure he'd give you shelter if you'd sweep and mop the place."

Sir Jorge added, "But no drugs, and he won't let anyone underage drink either. He is an ethical person. Years ago, he helped someone get off the street. He's now the bass player in his band. You have no reason to trust us, but your alternative is bleak, so I think you should take a chance."

The teen, still sitting on the ground, looked at his father, who groaned as he regained consciousness. "I appreciate you helping, but maybe I should go to the shelter."

"Wouldn't he find you there?" Jorge asked.

The young man took a deep breath, then put his hand to his side and grimaced. "I guess you're right. It's not like I have a lot of options." He slowly and painfully got to his feet, looked around, then said, "Okay, I'll go with you. For now, anyway. I'm Benny."

"You want to stop at urgent care first? We'll cover it for you."

"I think I'll be fine in a couple of days. I've had it worse than this before."

"Thank goodness you're not a drama queen," Franco responded and led him to the car.

Benny wrapped his arms around his chest as they made the short drive to the club. Franco showed him backstage to a dressing room and told him he should wait there. The youth groaned as he painfully settled into a stuffed chair in the corner.

Franco handed him a glass of water and said, "Jorge and I are going to talk to Henry. We'll be back in a few. You're safe here."

Benny sat back and closed his eyes. "Dad," he mumbled. His eyes became watery. The members of the Cringe entered in all their goth finery and noticed Benny blinking back tears and looking miserable. His anxiety was palpable as he started to get up, holding his rib cage. Startled, Benny said, "I don't want to intrude. Maybe I should leave."

Des said, "Hey, sit back down. It's okay; Franco said you needed some help. We're dressed like this for the show. I'm Des. Those are my brothers Jacques and Tomas."

"Yeah, don't introduce me." Marie came forward with a first aid kit. "I'm Marie. Jorge said you got beat up. I know this is a weird situation, but we want to help. Let me see your injuries." She kneeled beside him.

He winced as he started to speak. "I'm Benny." There was something about the young woman that made Benny trust her. "It hurts if I take a deep breath, and my arm got twisted."

Marie had discovered she had healing skills while helping with Leif's goats and the horses. A gift she hadn't revealed to others. She dug around in the kit and pulled out an instant cold pack. She said, "Hold this over your ribs." Then while trying to hide it from her brothers, who had moved closer, she put her hands on the arm that had been twisted by his father. Her energy seeped into the swollen tissue soothing the deep bruising and sore muscles. Marie couldn't mend bones, but she could help with damaged tissue.

Tomas elbowed Des. They could feel the energy emanating from Marie. Jacques leaned over, watching how her hands gently moved over the injured limb.

Benny asked, "Are you a doctor? That feels a lot better."

"No, with three brothers beating on each other all the time I've picked up a few tricks."

Des joked, "Who knew you were Florence Nightingale?"

Jacques said, "I've seen you massage the horses, but I had no idea you had that ability with people."

Marie faced her brothers with a fierce stare enhanced by her Cringe makeup. "Do not tell anyone!"

"Whatever," Tomas put his hands up and backed away.

Benny said, "Thanks, it already feels better." Which seemed to ease the tension in the room.

Des said, "I won't even take the chance of telling Sig. We don't want the Magus to know anything more about us."

Reacting to the tension in the room Benny, in a small voice asked, "Thanks, but I can go if…."

Jacques cut him off. "No. Stay here. Henry will be around after his set. The fans get loud and crazy when he plays. You don't want to be out there by yourself. We'll hang out with you. What kind of pizza do you like?"

Benny hesitated before saying, "Chicken and pineapple."

Tomas was amused. "I can tell you're from Seattle." He called in an order. A minute later he got a text. His eyes blazed as he threw down his phone. "Damn it, Phoebe!"

Benny flinched and looked at the exit. Des noticed and said, "Hey, calm down, you're scaring the kid."

Tomas slid into a chair. "Sorry, it's my girlfriend."

Benny said, "That's okay. I get it."

Marie and Des turned towards him and tried to hold back their laughter. Jacques said, "I already like this kid."

Tomas was brooding. He picked up his phone and reread Phoebe's message again. "She's going back to Starbucks. She said she needs a life, a way to support herself with or without me."

"Imagine that." Marie pulled up a chair. "You're not the center of her universe."

Lady Antoinella, a knight to Sir Borgia of the House of Pentacles, left her bed at noon and silently crept to a damp room at the bottom of their Venetian villa. She knew Cesare was deep in the slumber of the undead. She no longer slept with him, though his ardor for her had not diminished. She had slowly lost respect for the Haute Caste vampire who was content to serve as a vassal to the Magus. Once, Lady Antoinella had worshipped the Haute Caste but had become disillusioned since rising to their ranks.

She opened her computer and logged into a Zoom chat of a few trusted nocturnal women.

"Ladies, what we speak of must stay between us to protect the existence of our group. I swear I will not confide in Cesare about our deliberations." Since cameras could not capture the images of vampires, they used avatars when meeting online. An avatar of a Renaissance woman with long dark curls represented Antonella. "As I was once of the Common Caste, I am privy to their increasing unrest and desire for more representation in the Parliament and better treatment overall. I feel the Magus is ignoring this threat to our society as he obsesses on his campaign to control the House of Sun."

Lady Kananga's avatar of an African woman in gold robes lit up next. "Sadly, I concur. I hoped he would have learned from his loss of stature when his attempts to harass the Mordecais into submission failed. Our leadership is failing at a crucial time and we need it to evolve to protect our survival. We must not ignore the Common Caste unrest."

Lady Cassandra, the legendary Seer, represented by a woman in flowing white robes, added, "We must protect the Magus from his own nature. For thousands of years, none could pose a threat to us as he created and protected our society.

Until now, that is. We all owe him a debt that cannot be repaid. Even so, we must soon be ready to remove him from his role while putting another in his place until he has recovered his judgment and insight."

Lady Lily's avatar was a Japanese woman wearing a blue silk kimono. "I concur he must be protected from himself and taken to a secret location away from his blindly submissive supporters." They all knew she meant Dr. Kyoto, Lady Sarah, Lady Jacquotte, and Sir Borgia.

"As you know," Lady Anastasia began, "Removing a ruler brings up painful memories for me, but in this case, I too, agree."

Princess Khunbish had been waiting to hear what the others had to say. "We previously decided how we shall achieve this. Now we must stay vigilant as we wait for the right moment. Our current task is to agree upon a new interim ruler. They must be feared and respected by the other Haute Caste yet able to deal with our society's issues." She paused. "I do not wish to be considered as I have no camaraderie with those of the Common Caste."

Lady Anastasia said, "Let us meet again in a week to discuss who will assume leadership. I submit that we should continue to keep the Baroness unaware of our deliberations and plans to protect her family for now. The Magus must be made to understand that the Haute Caste have carried this out, not the Mordecais."

Lady Antoinella added, "We will take responsibility for this rebellious act."

The others signaled their agreement, and the screen went dark.

Chang was making his rounds when he heard a sound behind the horse building. He silently made his way around the barn and came up behind a figure kneeling beside a water pump. He jumped on the trespasser, forcing her to the hard ground. She cried out a curse against his mother.

He put a knife to Odgerel's throat and whispered, "Lower your voice so that we can talk without alerting the guards." She grudgingly agreed. "I'll let you sit up, but you must not run or attack me. In return, I won't slit your lovely throat."

She sat up slowly, keeping her gaze on Chang. He remained inches away, holding his knife at his side. Odgerel spit out, "Why do you work for her?"

Chang scanned the area and listened to the night to be sure no one was approaching them. He whispered, "Because I hope to stay in her good graces until I find a way to go to Los Angeles to pledge my allegiance to the most powerful of our kind."

"Have none of you any shame? You are executioners with no regard for the consequences of your actions. When you killed my boss, you took away any chance I had of ever leaving Choibalsan. I'm back to working in a noodle shop!"

"So, it wasn't true love?" Chang chuckled.

"You live in her palace and have the nerve to belittle my struggles?"

His eyes became cold. "I have not always lived in a palace: I have survived by my wits after following the losing side in a grab for power. Do not tell me of your struggles. If you could get beyond your self-pity, you might use your brains to find a way to leave Choibalsan."

She felt his pain, though she didn't want to. Odgerel slowly raised a hand to his cheek. "Let us help each other."

Chang heard footsteps of approaching guards. Knowing he couldn't risk being caught "consorting" with the enemy, he raised his knife and yelled. "I'm taking you to the Princess!"

"Pizda!" She cried out the Mongolian version of 'Fuck!' and swung at his head, but he quickly subdued her.

Two guards came around the corner, and Chang puffed out his chest and ordered them to lock her up until he could speak with the Princess. Chang strode away quickly, trying to compose himself. "Pizda is right," he said to himself.

Chapter 8

The Talk

Miranda, keeping a neutral façade, regarded the succubus-vampiress the next night at the Funeral Pyre. No disgust, anger, or pity showed as she said, "Sit down." Her black hoodie and jeans showed she felt no need to try superficial means to impress the pirate.

Jacquotte warily sat across from her at a table in a small upstairs apartment. Their eyes locked as Miranda rested her hands on the table and scrutinized her new adversary.

The vampiress said, "Nice of Sir Henry to give us a private place to parley."

Miranda looked over Jacquotte's outfit. She wore a knee-length, red brocade pirate coat with black velvet lapels, cuffs, and brass buttons. Underneath the coat, she had on the modern-style clothes the Magus preferred. Miranda suppressed an eye roll and said, "Nice coat."

Jacquotte, missing the sarcasm, stroked one of the lapels, smiled, and said, "Thanks! Now tell me what's on yer mind, Baroness? Just so you know, I don't resent you sending my newest conquest away. I figure Leif will find me again some night."

Miranda frowned. "From my experience, there are two kinds of lovers. One will cherish your body and soul; the other will overwhelm your senses but not your heart. You are the latter—a dazzling display with no substance. Most vampires fall into that category eventually unless they find real love. I guess you're unlucky."

The vampiress leaned back a little. "You know nothing 'bout me. I can have any...."

"Stop, you're making a fool of yourself. Leif was no great conquest. You went after an immature vampire, not yet in control of his abilities or emotions."

Jacquotte jumped to her feet, and hissed. "You should thank me. I was given permission to enslave him with my passion or take his head as a trophy. He is lucky I'm not partial to trophies."

"Permission?" Miranda studied her latest opponent through narrowed eyes.

The coldness on Miranda's face made Jacquotte take a step back. "I'm the Magus' partner in crime."

"More like a sacrificial lamb. Didn't you wonder why the Magus didn't personally punish Leif? Don't you think he wanted to sink his fangs into the mortal who broke into his house, set off fireworks, and embarrassed him to the whole vampire world? The mortal lover, my daughter, has chosen over the Magus?"

"I figured he thought it was beneath him." Jacquotte struggled to sound confident. "So, he let me have a little fun."

"It's all about our blood and what it can do to your kind. Marie's blood put the Magus into a coma. Our blood can strip Common Caste of their vampire natures."

"That's not possible! Those are rumors you started to make us fear your family."

"It's all true; all you have to do is ask him. Or you could track down Sybil. She escaped the Magus' experiments. He was using my blood on her, she almost died; but I've heard she's recovering her power. Have you not heard the stories of the Great Alexander having his powers temporarily taken away with my blood for his attempted coup against the Magus?"

"I did hear of those things, but I thought it was exaggerated rumors."

"The Magus wanted to see if it was safe to take Leif's blood before he attacked the Day Fanger. He used you like a lab rat in one of his and Kyoto's experiments. You seem fine, so I'm guessing Leif's Common Caste blood type doesn't have the same effect as our HH blood."

"Over the centuries, detecting lies has helped me survive." Unease swept over her as she realized Miranda spoke the cold, ugly truth. "You tell no lies. That dishonorable bastard set me up." She sat back down.

Miranda tilted her head and asked, "Why did you spare Leif?"

Jacquotte leaned forward with her elbows on the table, wondering how quickly she could grab Miranda by the throat for making her feel so stupid. "He was fun. The Haute Caste are experienced in pleasure, but it becomes a bit routine." She flashed a malicious grin, trying to cover her anger. "He was wild. You should borrow him from your daughter sometime."

Even though she knew better, Miranda took the bait. The tension between them rose. Jacquotte's hand slipped to her dagger. The Head of the House of Sun closed her eyes and held up her hands. The air suddenly felt damp, and the temperature dropped. Miranda began rubbing her hands together, then cupped them, forming something.

Jacquotte stood. "It can't be!"

Miranda aimed and fired. A hard-packed small snowball hit Jacquotte's nose with enough impact to cause her to stagger. A small trickle of blood ran from Jacquotte's nose. With an amused expression, Miranda said, "Though still mortal, I am half vampire and have the power of water. I've got what some of your kind call freakish abilities. It would be best if you remember that I regard Leif as a son. If you do not want your schooner to mysteriously end up on the bottom of the harbor, I would advise you to stay away from him. You should turn your anger towards the Magus. He's always at the center of shit storms."

Jacquotte regarded Miranda in a new light, as though she was seeing her for the first time. "Only a few of the ancient Haute Caste I know of have elemental powers: the Magus, Sir Henry, and the Baron. There are rumors about others but clearly not you! You're just a half-blood."

Miranda held one hand up and turned her palm down with her fingers waving. Moisture concentrated over the vampiress' head, and droplets began to fall on her. She flew across the room to the door, stopped, then turned back to Miranda, trying to compose herself.

Jacquotte said, "I've always had a fear of lightning. I wonder what else yer capable of, but I am sure I don't want to find out."

Miranda looked at her with narrowed eyes. "Then leave us alone, and leave Seattle. I won't be the aggressor, but the House of Sun will harshly respond to any action against us. I don't make idle threats."

Jacquotte asked, "I've always wondered, is it true you cut off the nose of a member of the House of Pentacles?"

"Yes. Why does everyone ask me that? He attacked me when I was pregnant."

With new gained respect for Miranda, Jacquotte thoughtfully, said, "Your appearance, especially the signs of aging, make it easy to underestimate you. Baroness, I believe you employ that to your advantage."

Miranda allowed a small grin. "Being underestimated and the element of surprise has helped me defeat more than one unwelcome vampire."

"I'm sure. Your offspring giving away the Magus' property to the Girl Scouts was a nasty but impressive move. His need to appear as a modern enlightened creature, supportive of women made it impossible for him to back out of that arrangement."

"Appear to respect women? Really? He is a self-absorbed fool." The matriarch crossed her arms. "He wanted half-bloods but doesn't have a clue about how to deal with us or anyone with a backbone."

Jacquotte's stare softened. "You would've made a fine pirate with your gifts. If your sons approach me, all bets are off, but I won't go out of my way to seduce them. I will respect your power. It's part of my personal code if bested. I'll give you this; you can tell Marie that from this moment on, her man is safe from me. My word is always good, especially if given to a woman."

Miranda looked unmoved. "Trust has to be earned."

"Aye, Baroness." She opened the door and quickly left the club.

Jacquotte walked down the street, needing to clear her head before returning to the Magus' powerful presence. "Shit," Jacquotte growled. She didn't want to risk a sudden squall sinking her boat. Now she understood why Sir Henry was aligned with the House of Sun. With the Baron, they had three elementals who could unite against the head of their world. The thought of being used by the Magus as an ignorant subject of an experiment pissed her off. She knew better than to confront him about it.

Sensing someone coming up behind her, Jacquotte stopped at a corner in front of a bar. She noticed movement nearby. Turning, she saw a couple getting out of their car, heading to a Mexican café. Relieved, she drew in a breath. A tap on her shoulder made her jump. Jacquotte whirled around, slipped a hand inside her coat, reaching for a dagger.

"Easy pirate. I'm Sir Angel."

She closely watched the stranger, still ready to pull her weapon.

"I worked for the Magus until I came to understand who or what he really is. That changed my perspective on him. I had a change of heart, and now the House of Sun has my loyalty."

She appraised the tall American with Latin vibes from head to toe. He had straight hair pulled back in a ponytail and wore tight-fitting sports clothes, which accentuated his build. She stopped at his Air Jordans. Being a thief by nature, she had a good idea of what those chic clothes and shoes cost, but his cologne could not hide his Common Caste blood.

"Sir? I think not."

"The Magus granted my title, and when I joined the House of Sun, the Baroness said I could keep it. Shall we discuss why anyone would consider you a lady?"

"You're a bold one. I've never heard of you, but I'll believe your tale for now, Sir Diablo."

For fun, Lady Jacquotte allowed her succubus side to reach out to him. Angel swallowed and moved a step back as her scent radiated seductiveness, like a hit from an opium pipe. He shook his head to clear it. "I've been around a pure-bred succubus in L.A. Memories of enjoying almost being sucked dry messes with your allure. Sorry."

"You're a surprise. You pulled away from a succubus, but I destroyed the one that came after me and took their power."

"Impressive. Sir Steve helped trap one that came after me, then burned the carcass to make sure I'd be safe. He's a knight of the House of Cups in Mongolia now. He detests all of them. I suggest you never visit the House of Cups and forget ever hooking up with Leif again."

"I'm amazed by the devotion you all have for that young blood." She relaxed, and her scent changed. "No worry. One taste of him was enough." Her eyes cascaded over Angel. "It's too bad you're so jaded."

"Perhaps if you came on to me using only your vampiress charms, that might change."

"Not tonight; I've got to head back to Granite Falls before the Magus misses me."

His gaze hardened. "You should leave before he grows tired of you."

She tried to come back with a snarky remark, but the chill in his voice unnerved her further. "I appreciate the warning. You should look me up if you're ever in Key West." She disappeared into the night.

Downstairs at the club, Miranda reinvigorated herself with a mug of coffee. Lady Teri asked if everything was alright. Miranda nodded. "Everything is fine. I am sure she got my point."

The vampiress called out to Benny and waved him over. "This is Benny. He is the kid Sir Jorge and Sir Franco took in."

Miranda checked out the nervous teenager. Benny looked back shyly, then smiled. "Teri told me you figured out about the nocturnal natures of some of my friends. That was pretty smart. I'm mortal and feel quite safe here. You don't have anything to worry about." She wasn't ready to explain her relationship to the undead. "My kids play here in the band, Cringe."

"I met them." Benny's eyes held a glint of sadness. "You must be a cool mom."

Miranda wanted to grab the abused kid and take him back to Granite Falls, but at the moment, she had too much on her plate dealing with the Magus. "Thanks. You don't have any family?"

He glanced at Lady Teri, "After my mom died from cancer, I left home so my father would stop trying to beat the gay out of me. She used to protect me from him. The street was better, but not much. I panhandled, ate from dumpsters, and slept under the stars. One of the worst things is, it's hard to keep a sleeping bag dry in Seattle." Benny shivered when he thought about it. "After being here for a little while, I realized some of you disappeared during the day and saw the blood bags in the back fridge. It didn't take long for me to figure it out. Not saying you're not terrifying, but you treat me better than my father or the assholes who chased me night after night." His big blue eyes were shining as he looked at Miranda. "Teri gave me an apartment, my own place."

Lady Teri gently touched his arm. "Jorge and Franco were going to pay for you to go to a boarding school on the East Coast to get you out of here before you found out about us."

"It's okay. Look, I won't tell anyone. I'm no snitch, and I like this place." He gave her a tight smile. "I figured you weren't going to, you know, turn me if you hadn't yet."

Miranda thought about the hell Benny's life on the street must have been for him to be grateful to live with nocturnal freaks. She gently patted his hand. "It's called 'transforming.' It is never forced on anyone; you must have the desire to be nocturnal."

"Seriously? You mean not everyone who gets bitten...."

"...Becomes like us?" Teri finished for him. "No. It's rare for someone to be allowed that honor. It's not often we bite. I'm a relatively new one, so I've only had bagged blood." She didn't think the fang play when she and Henry were alone counted.

"You're nothing like—you know—in the movies."

She smiled. "Maybe a little. We police ourselves and have a code. We're never to go after an innocent, but we sometimes intervene with people that society would be better without. People that harm kids, drug dealers that evade the law, that kind of thing."

His eyes got big. "Predators going after predators."

Miranda changing the subject, asked, "Can we be sure you won't tell anyone?"

"I'll swear on a Bible." He swallowed nervously. "Would that be wrong?"

Miranda and Lady Teri giggled. Miranda said, "No. But it's not necessary. I think we can trust you."

Benny's eyes fell to his fidgeting hands. "One thing. I gotta know that you won't go after my dad. He hurt me 'cause he's messed up, drinks too much. I don't want to see him again, but I don't want him killed."

Lady Teri's gaze softened. "I'll talk to the others. None of us will take his life." She imagined that, in any case, his father's lifespan would be shortened by his lifestyle. "So, do you want to stay here for now? You are free to go anytime you want. If you stay, we'll figure out how to get you enrolled in school."

His face brightened. "Yes!"

Sig parked off the road a little way from the entrance to the Magus' mansion. She crept onto his property, trying to convince herself she wasn't making a huge mistake. She could see a Humvee and a limo through the trees, suggesting he was in the residence.

A hand reached around Sig's head and covered her mouth as strong arms pulled her back into the dark forest. She bit down hard and tried to kick her assailant. Fear that no one would ever find her body gripped her. A muffled scream escaped her mouth.

"Ssh! Sigourney, it's me, Alexander." His grip let up, he pulled a handkerchief from his pocket and wrapped his hand.

She turned to her regal, distant, relative. "You scared the crap out of me." She felt a tingling sensation on her lips.

He whispered, "I didn't want to speak so close to the house. Have you lost your mind?"

She was close enough to feel his cold, angry stare despite the darkness. "I wanted to ask the Magus why he thinks I should become a vampire." She shivered and brought her arms up around her chest. "I tasted your blood. Oh my God!"

"Quiet! It wasn't enough to do anything to you. Calm down."

Alexander wanted to put his arm around her to comfort the confused young woman but worried she might take his affection the wrong way. Instead, he merely said, "Meet me at my place. We need to talk." He disappeared into the deep shadows.

The great warrior was giving her a choice. Take a chance on what the godfather of the undead might tell her or trust the vampire who had a one-nighter with her very great grandma. She ran to her car, realizing the mistake of sneaking up on the Magus' home. She was grateful for Alexander's intervention. The door was wide open when she drove up to the front of his home.

She walked in, a little tentative. Inside the comfy living room, he sat at a chess board in front of a fireplace as though nothing unusual had happened. Alexander looked up and gestured to the seat opposite him.

She managed a smile and said, "Thanks. I'm sorry about your hand."

He waived his hand, dismissing the apology. "It's nothing. We heal quickly." Alexander sat silently, contemplating the position of the chess pieces. After a moment, he picked one up, made a move, leaned back and asked, "Did you lie to Des about where you would be?"

"I didn't lie, but I didn't tell him I was skipping class."

He scrutinized her. "Was it easy to be deceitful to your lover?"

She bit her lip. "Easy to do but not easy to live with."

Alexander moved a pawn and said, "Your turn."

Sig shook her head. "No thanks. I'd never win."

"Which is why you shouldn't play with the Magus either." He paused, watching defiance come to life in her eyes. "You are more than worthy enough to become a vampiress. The question is whether you're willing to pay the price for the rest of your unnatural existence."

"You mean to watch people I love die of old age?"

"And to witness the world die, over and over again. I was foolish enough to try and build a small palace in the Nevada desert, reminiscent of one of my homes when I was king of Macedonia. After defeating the Magus, I planned to become the new nocturnal king with Miranda at my side." For a moment, his face lit up, then his countenance saddened. "Even I am subject to foolishness and arrogance. Everything and everyone will change except us. Life is but grains of sand continually falling through our fingers."

His loneliness touched her deeply. "I had no idea you were so unhappy."

"The Mordecai family now, is my only true source of joy. Jacques, Ali and little Wendell are all that matter." His lips grew taut. "I'll not allow anyone to harm them."

She drew back a little. "I would never!"

A steady cold stare pinned her to the spot. "You would transform with the best intentions, heal the sick like your uncle with your blood. Unfortunately, the miraculous recovery you made possible would spark the curiosity of some medical researcher. If they even suspected some component in your blood was the cause, it potentially could expose our society. Some greedy CEO would see dollar signs and have corporate mercenaries hunt us down."

"I was extremely careful with my uncle."

He shook his head. "We couldn't take that risk, broke into the lab his doctor worked with, destroyed the blood samples, and put a virus in their computers. We made sure there was no evidence of how your uncle recovered."

"I had no idea."

"You are not the first to underestimate the dangers to our world. As I said, your intentions may be good, but you are young and naïve." He huffed, then continued. "The Magus transformed Jeanne d'Arc, Hannibal, and me knowing we would quickly grasp how easy it would be to raise an army of vampires. He chose us because he believed we also had the clarity of judgment to understand how disastrous that would be to our kind and the world." In a dramatic gesture, he swept all the chess pieces onto the floor. "So, for the most part, we have used our strategic abilities to conceal and protect the undead. Though I did lead a group of rogue vampires against the Magus, I never used them against mortals."

Sig leaned towards him and touched his folded hands. "You've given me a lot to think about."

He stood abruptly, crossed over to the fireplace, and turned to face her. "Do you understand Leif's importance to our world?"

"He's a new breed. Mortal but more vampire than the Mordecais."

"Exactly! Daylight has always held the vampire world in check. Leif's existence changes everything. I was relieved when he was sent away. I hope that in Mongolia, he will gain the wisdom and maturity needed for someone with his gifts to make responsible decisions, not childish antics like setting off fireworks in the Magus' house." A small smile came to his face. "Though it was amusing."

"With all his power, the Magus still envies Leif."

"We all do. It's one of the reasons the Magus pressured Marie for a taste of her blood. Fortunately, it temporarily diminished his powers instead of giving him any new abilities."

"But he won't give up."

Alexander scrutinized her. "The Magus never relents. He'll find a way to profit from Leif's creation or destroy him out of jealousy."

"Shit!"

"Sigourney, you must give me your word that you won't seek an audience with the Magus alone without speaking with Miranda or me first. If he persuaded you to allow him the honor to transform you, you would become beholden to him. Who knows what he might demand of you? He might try to use you against Leif. Not to mention the pain it would cause Des."

"I promise," she agreed without hesitation. "I was being so stupid. I need to know if that is what I'm meant to become."

"Our destiny is very much of our own design. Sigourney, descendent of my blood, you don't need to transform to manifest your talents." His expression became dark. "The Magus tends to bring out the worst in us, except for the Baroness. Somehow, she has always managed to best him in remarkable ways. You could learn much from her."

There was something about the way he said, 'Baroness' that drew Sig's attention. "You love her."

"You are quite observant. My feelings are no secret. It's why the Baron will always resent me."

"But she chose him."

"So it seems. Goodnight, Sigourney."

She did something quite unexpected. She hugged Alexander the Great quickly and said, "Thanks grand uncle. I owe you." Then left.

As he turned back to the fire, a rare tear fell down the King's cheek.

Chapter 9

Mortals Unite

The Cringe entered the dressing room where Benny was playing a car racing video game. He tried to concentrate on his game and not eavesdrop as Des loudly launched into concerns about his girlfriend.

"How can I trust her? She was supposed to be at UW." He pulled out his phone. "The app shows she is in Granite Falls. What is she up to? I don't know what is going on. I have to get back to Granite."

Marie poked Des, pointed, and said, "Hey, it's the kid. Hi Benny. How are you feeling?"

"Better, thanks. A doctor Henry knows came by. He said my ribs aren't broken or anything, only bruised."

Tomas saw Benny's score on the video game. "Little dude, 20,430 points, that's insane!"

"Thanks. I guess I've played it a lot." He was a little embarrassed by the attention and quickly changed the subject. "I watched you guys rock the club. You're fucking dope. Your mom came by before. She was really nice to me."

Jacques nodded in agreement and said, "Momzilla has her moments."

Tomas' phone beeped; he read the text. "Damn It!"

Marie shook her head. "More trouble in paradise. Is it Phoebe?"

"She took the evening shift at Starbucks. I told her to wait for a day shift opening, but she's so stubborn. Phoebe thinks I'll dump her eventually, kick her to the curb. She wants a safety net."

Benny said, "You gotta respect women."

Tomas turned back to Benny and snapped, "What?"

Benny lowered his head, tucked in his chin, and said, "Nothing." He was sure they were about to throw him out.

Jacques said, "He's right. Have faith in them."

Des mockingly said, "Like how you trusted Amy. How did that work out for you, bro?"

Marie shook her head. "Stop acting like controlling assholes. Oh wait, you weren't acting. You need to talk to your girlfriends and work it out. Poor Benny's heard enough about your relationships."

Tomas patted Benny's shoulder. "Sorry about snapping at you. Welcome to our screwed-up lives." He noticed Benny tense up. "It's not too late to ask for a ride somewhere if you want to leave."

Benny looked unhappy. "But I like it here. I got nowhere else to go where I won't get hurt or freeze my nuts off."

Des grabbed one of his leather jackets and tossed it to Benny. "Then dress like you're a member of our crew."

"Seriously?" With watery eyes, Benny put the jacket on over his hoodie. "Thanks! Tell me if you want me to do anything."

Tomas said, "Four large to-go black coffees from the bar. It's gonna be a long ass night."

Marie said, "C'mon, I'll get you on the good side of the bartender."

After they walked out, Des shook his head. "Marie Antoinette Mordecai called *us* controlling. I wish Leif had heard that. He had to go all the way to Mongolia till she chills out."

"Seriously!" Jacques looked at his phone. "Loretta left some chicken in the oven for me. Damn I love that woman. If not for Loretta, I'd have nothing going for me except banging fans."

"Yeah," Des said, "I miss those less complicated relationships."

Tomas glanced at Des. "Everything is a little more complicated for us. Without being transformed, we have enough vampire DNA to give us abilities. Even though she denies it, Maire can heal. I can always tell if someone's lying; Jacques has super semen, and Mom can make it rain. What's your special talent? You never said."

Des cocked his head. "My swagger, my voice, my stage persona."

Jacques burst out laughing. "Being a vain douchebag. That's your power."

Des flipped him off. "Asshole!"

76

Princess Khunbish directed Leif to accompany Batu on a trip. The location and purpose were not explained to Leif. Batu was sound asleep in the small yurt-like tent he and Leif had erected near a craggy rock formation next to a stream. Leif, having trouble sleeping, had been awake for several hours. He had quietly left the yurt and went out to sit on the bank. He was sensing trouble in his gut but was unable to identify the source. Even though the last text from Marie said everything was okay, he knew the Magus would never stop messing with them.

He burst out angrily, "I should be there!" as he kicked some pebbles into the stream. The sun wouldn't set for a couple of hours which gave him too much time alone, hounded by guilt. The surrounding area was stark, with only a few small trees, and many of them were dead. Unable to sit any longer, he walked along the stream until he came to a boulder and sat down to take in the barren steppes. The air was crisp, and he detected the faint scent of smoke.

The wind made an eerie sound; sensing a presence, he scanned in all directions, finding no sign of anyone. Suddenly, a rock struck him in the shoulder from behind. Leif snapped his head around, but no one was there. He rubbed the spot. "What the fuck?"

He noticed a wolf's head, partially obscured by the brush, staring at him with one golden eye. He was about 6 feet away from it, and Leif was surprised the animal could have gotten so close without him detecting it sooner. His heart raced as he picked up the scent of the beast. Suddenly a dozen others silently appeared and surrounded him.

He realized that it would do no good calling for Batu. The sun would fry him. He doubted even he, a day vampire, could survive being torn apart by wolves. Resigned to his fate, he said aloud, "So, this is how my screwed-up life ends." His paranoid side imagined the Princess might be doing the Magus a favor by getting rid of him.

The large gray wolf with the golden eye slowly approached; Leif tensed as he waited for the snarling and gnashing of teeth to begin. A woman's voice called out a command, and the wolf laid down but continued watching Leif.

A diminutive woman appeared, seemingly out of nowhere. She had a white-painted face with heavy black shadow around her brown eyes. Her steady gaze seemed to penetrate to his very core. A red and black cloth was tied around her head. The small woman stood several feet away and extended her hands from the sleeves of a green silk tunic. She held smoky quartz wands and aimed them at him. Speaking in English, she said, "If you raise a hand to me, the wolves will attack."

In a shaky voice, Leif said, "Princess Khunbish sent me out here. I don't know why, and I don't know who you are or exactly where I am. But if you keep your wolves away from me, I'll leave."

She rotated her head side to side, cracking her neck, making Leif jump. Another wolf let out a long slow growl. She whispered something, and the beast quieted down.

"In your culture, I would be called a witch or a shaman. My people call me Idugan. I've been waiting for your arrival."

She turned and walked to a green spot downstream with bushes and a few trees. The wolves followed her, and Leif started to turn back to his camp with Batu. "No thanks," he called, "I am meeting a friend."

She made a shrill sound that stopped him in his tracks. He felt compelled to follow her, drawn to the witch as he had been drawn to Jacquotte. Leif trailed after her to a tiny oasis. She sat on a fallen tree trunk next to a small fire. Without a word he sat beside the strange woman and stared into the flames. He reacted to the sweet musk-laden scent of her pheromones. "Are you a succubus?" Staring at her face, Leif expected to be seduced.

She laughed quietly and replied, "I am more powerful than that. I am a Mongol witch. Rulers tried to destroy us, but I never abandoned our people."

Without knowing why, he felt compelled to explain. "A ruler wants to kill me."

She turned, staring into his eyes. "Yes, I know. Look into the fire." She held out the two dark gem wands and tapped them together. An odd sound reverberated from the flames as warmth filled his chest. The witch chanted in an ancient tongue, and the smoke took on the witch's scent. The wolves faded away, and Leif focused on the flames as they became more intense.

She stood and moved in front of Leif. She raised her wands and touched his cheeks with them. He felt an unusual tingling sensation but nothing like the sexual reaction he had with Jacquotte. It was a sense of joining of powers, kindred spirits enhancing each other. She whispered, "I know your pain."

Tears filled his eyes. "No one understands. For once, I have power, but I'm still weak."

Idugan dropped the wands into the fire which flared up. The flames formed an orange and yellow glowing orb. Leif reached out to shield her.

She stepped aside and said, "No! Look into the flames!"

He looked into the ball of light and suddenly saw a warrior wearing a Mongolian sheepskin vest, a traditional felt hat with fur earflaps, a bow, and a quiver of arrows slung on his back. The warrior took off his hat, and wavy red hair fell to his shoulders. "That's me!" he shouted.

Suddenly a dust storm in the orb clouded the image, and when it cleared, a giant blue dragon with glistening scales landed in front of the warrior. "Shoot it!" Leif urged his image.

The Idugan put a hand on Leif's arm. "Keep watching."

The warrior in the vision stood spellbound as the dragon touched its great head to his chest. Leif gasped as a burning sensation assaulted him. He brought his hands up, covered his heart, and sucked in a deep breath. The orb dissipated, and the fire went out. Leif, without warning, fell to the ground unconscious. Sometime later, he woke, shocked to find he was alone and wondering what the fuck had happened. He questioned whether it had been real. The sun was setting, and the cool evening air made him shiver.

The image of the witch haunted him. "Idugan!" He called out and began searching the area. Halfway back to their camp, he sank to his knees, crying out, "I think I'm losing my mind."

A familiar voice asked, "Did you bring 'shrooms with you?"

"No!" he slowly got to his feet. "You know I don't do drugs anymore. My life is freaky enough. I could swear I met this witch named Idugan." Leif stopped when he saw how Batu was staring at him.

The vampire sniffed the air, slowly scanned the area, and seeing nothing unusual turned his attention back to Leif. "Take off your jacket and shirt."

"Why?"

Batu pointed. "Because someone, or something burned a hole in them."

Leif looked down and saw the blackened spot about the size of his hand. He ripped off his jacket and shirt. On the left side of his chest, over his heart, was a brand of a fierce dragon with fire escaping its mighty jaws. He mumbled, "It wasn't a nightmare."

Batu had a wide-eyed look of surprise on his face. "Leif! Why you?" He examined the brand closely. "Unbelievable! Come, we must return to the palace. I'll explain what happened as much as I can. However, I can't understand why it happened to you. The Princess will know more about what this means."

Chapter 10

Who did What?

Miranda sat on her back deck, wrapped in a thick robe, cradling a mug of coffee, when Tomas, Des, and Marie returned from the Funeral Pyre. At three a.m. the yelling started. She kept them out on the deck, hoping they wouldn't wake River.

"You haven't seen her, so where is she?" Des had wild eyes. "If Sig is with the Magus, I'll destroy him!"

Tomas yelled, "Why do you and Phoebe have to be so stubborn? You're both making me crazy. I'm gonna split wood till I calm down."

Miranda mumbled under her breath, "Right! You're not stubborn at all." She looked up at the shining stars and wished she could be somewhere else.

Marie headed off to Leif's house. "Later, Mom, and good luck with the bro drama." She only got a few feet away before she stopped dead in her tracks and cried out, "What the hell?" She came back and showed Miranda her phone. It was a picture of Leif with his dragon brand on his chest.

"Maybe it's some kind of custom there," Miranda said, though she knew Batu didn't have a mark like that. "That must've hurt."

"He says a shaman did it. He's in over his stupid head. I'm telling Leif to get his ass home, or I'll go drag him back myself!" Marie ran off before her mom could try to convince her to wait until they knew what was going on.

Miranda rolled her eyes and took a big sip of coffee.

Des demanded loudly again, "Where's Sig?"

"I'm right here!" Sig answered as she emerged from the trees.

"Where the hell have you been?" Des rushed over and examined her neck.

"I haven't transformed, and no one bit me. I promised your mom I'd wait awhile to decide what I am going to do."

Miranda was amazed that Sig had taken her advice.

Des looked sullen, and asked, "You didn't answer my question."

Her eyes flashed. "None of your business. I don't have to report everything I do to you!"

"You went to see the Magus!"

A voice came from where Sig had emerged from the trees. "She was with me."

Des lost it and yelled at Sig. "Are you that desperate to screw a vampire?"

"Wow! I can't believe you said that." She shoved him aside. "That's it! We're done!"

In a flash, Alexander was on the deck next to Des. He grabbed Des by his shoulders, and it became apparent he was using one of his powers and inflicting systemic pain on Des. "What is wrong with you? Apologize to Sigourney!"

Des withstood the throbbing ache in his muscles and stared daggers at Alexander. "What were you two doing?"

Alexander lost control, picked him up and tossed him across the yard. Des bounced against the barn wall and slid to the ground. Miranda ran to her son, but before she could reach him, he got to his feet and pushed her away. "I'm fine."

Relieved that he wasn't hurt, Miranda said, "Lucky you've got vampire DNA."

Alexander turned to Sigourney. "I'll talk with him after he cools down. I'm sorry you had to experience this."

With trembling lips, Sig snapped at Des, "Fuck you!" Tears welled up in her eyes.

Alexander said coldly. "In the barn, Desmon. Now!"

Miranda walked back to the deck as Des followed Alexander into the barn. She motioned Sig to sit and said, "Stay here. I'll be right back," and went into the house.

Miranda returned, handed the trembling Sig a mug of coffee and settled in her chair across from her. She could hear Tomas splitting wood behind the house to work off his anger at Phoebe. Since he was a teenager, Tomas would work off his anger and add half a cord of firewood to her winter supply whenever he got upset. She always had plenty of wood. The matriarch looked at the barn wall contemplating what had just occurred. She was sure the Magus was somehow behind all this chaos.

Sig said, "Alexander saved me from making a big mistake."

Miranda patted Sig's arm. "That's what I figured."

Alexander, having regained his composure, stood calmly in the fencing barn, his arms crossed, watching Des pace. The young man finally stopped and faced him. "Are you going to tell me what happened?"

Alexander spoke loudly, like an attorney during an interrogation. "Do you love her?"

Not to be thrown off topic, Des demanded, "Answer me first!"

Alexander, once the king of the largest empire of the ancient world, said, "Sigourney and I spoke in confidence, and I must keep my word. You will have to ask her that question. So, tell me, do you love her?"

Des blurted out, "I think so."

A spark shone in Alexander's eyes. "Think harder. Your relationship with your true love is a sacred trust that must be protected and nourished. You do not subject them to humiliation."

Des felt a sliver of shame prick his consciousness for a second, but then he considered who was lecturing him. His eyes narrowed, and he stepped closer to Alexander. "Seriously? Are you saying I'm a slimeball? You're the one who knocked up Sig's ancestor, not to mention secretly, artificially inseminating my mom! Alexander the Great Douchebag!"

Miranda heard a loud crash, and Guillaume ran from his house to the barn as Des went flying through a window onto the grass, followed by Alexander diving after him. Miranda started to yell at them, but Tomas jumped into the melee, and she knew it would be useless. Instead, she held her arms to the night sky.

Sig felt the air become damper, and a chill ran through her. She watched Miranda raise her arms, higher, as though gesturing to the stars to intervene. Icy rain began to fall, but a deluge became centered on the brawling men.

Tomas pulled away first, looking up at the sky, then over at his mother. Alexander eyed the battered Des and declared, "We're done here!" Soaked to the bone and muddy, Alexander mustered his dignity and marched away toward his house. The rain dissipated.

Des scrambled to his feet, almost slipping in the mud. "Damn it, Mom, I almost had him."

"I almost had him," Tomas mocked. "In your dreams, dude."

Des swung at his brother, who grabbed his arm and wrestled him to the ground. Guillaume came out of the barn with towels and a medical kit and separated them. "Words, not fists, young Mordecais."

Tomas turned away and walked past his mother and Sig. "I'm staying here tonight so I don't go all asshole like Des." He looked down at his shirt and glared at his brother. Always the neat freak, Tomas warned his sibling, "These stains better come out of this shirt."

Miranda gave a mildly irritated look. "Stick it in the washer; you can wear one of your dad's shirts."

Des walked over to Sig, covered in mud and blood, with a towel over his shoulders. "I know I should be sorry, but I still don't know what happened."

"You're sorry all right. I'm going to the condo." She stormed off.

He looked to his mom for a shred of sympathy and support. She shook her head. "You fight first and ask questions later. Sometimes you act just like your father. Go get cleaned up." She went into the house.

Every part of his body ached as his adrenaline level crashed. Lug came up to him, "At least you're on my side." The dog lifted his leg and relieved himself. Des didn't even move out of the way. "I probably deserve that. Fuck me."

Jacquotte rushed into the Magus' living room, where he was meeting with Lady Sarah and Sir Ruben. A fit of jealousy flashed in her eyes. "You won't believe the exquisite chaos I witnessed at the Mordecais." She ignored the visitors, only wanting the Magus' attention.

"Go on," he commanded coldly.

"From what I could see, Alexander and Des were fighting about that girl with the red spiked hair. The Baroness put a stop to it with a contained rainstorm. After Alexander marched off, Tomas started to go at Des, and Guillaume broke that up. At that point, I removed myself before being detected."

A show of delight momentarily played across his face. "Sigourney must still be considering my offer." He picked up a potted plant with a bow and card attached. "For you from the Baroness."

She grabbed it and read the card.

Keep your word.

Miranda

Sarah let out a laugh. "She sent you a succulent."

The Magus's cold stare rattled Jacquotte. "Care to explain, my dear?"

Jacquotte looked directly into the Magus' eyes, not wanting to show weakness. "The Baroness asked me to meet her at Henry's club. Couldn't ignore a summons from the head of a House, could I? She's concerned I might have another dalliance with the Day Fanger." She looked at Lady Sarah and could see the surprise in her eyes. Jacquotte's confidence returned. "Apparently, she didn't like how he succumbed to my charms and demanded I back off. I agreed to leave the young one alone. But only him."

Ruben was salivating at the news. "You and Leif! Marie must have lost it. How did you manage to get him alone?" Ruben did not notice the Magus frown at the mention of Marie.

Jacquotte with a smug look said, "He came to me."

Ruben said, "Right. I can imagine." He felt the succubus pull, and it took all his restraint not to approach her. The legends about the vampiress were true. He noticed the stare his sister was giving him. Ruben now understood why Lady Sarah had always bad-mouthed Jacquotte and had, until now, kept him away from her.

The Magus cleared his throat. All eyes fell on him. "You should have consulted me before meeting with the Baroness."

Jacquotte felt like someone was gripping her throat as his eyes held her. Her hand went to her neck. "I'm sorry," she croaked out. "I don't know all the rules for dealing with the half-blood." The choking sensation went away. "I'm hoping you've got someone else in mind for me to become—familiar with."

Ruben closely watched her, hoping, against all odds, it would be him. She smiled and shook her head, able to read his desires. The Magus watched the subtle interaction and appeared amused. "I would like the three of you to assist me as I take down one of the offspring."

Lady Sarah sat up. "As long as you do not intend physical harm, I will assist you." She had qualms about his demands despite her fear of the Magus.

The tension in the room increased as the Magus fixed his displeasure on Lady Sarah. "You would choose them over me?"

"No," she declared, "It's our code, the Book of Blood. They are innocent, though inexorably linked to our world. They do not warrant physical punishment."

The Magus displayed a grim smile. "True. I would not have you go against the code. I only wish to teach them a lesson about sabotaging my plans. Did you know they secretly gave my home and land away to a charity?"

Ruben couldn't stop himself from laughing. "Audacious!"

"You're amused?" The Magus raised his hand; Ruben fell to his knees, coughing. After a moment, the Magus lowered his hand and released his hold. "Let's hope you will also find my prank entertaining."

"Sure," Ruben gasped for a breath. "Whatever you need, dear Magus."

Chapter 11

The Dragon

Princess Khunbish studied Leif, kneeling before her in the great hall. He had removed his shirt, exposing the brand on his chest. She came down from her throne and approached him slowly, stopping within arm's reach. She raised her hand and reached out toward the dragon over his heart. Before her fingertips touched the brand, she pulled her hand back as though afraid it might burn her. "How is this possible? I sent you to feel the strength of the wolves, to attempt to bond with their spirits, even though I knew it was unlikely with your heritage." She shook her head. "I never expected you to return with the blessing of the dragon bestowed by Idugan."

Leif asked. "Is that a good thing?"

Sir Steve and Sir Sapna stood by her side, all their attention on the mortal with the most extraordinary luck. In exasperation, Khunbish threw her hands in the air, and said something in Mongolian, then returned to her throne.

Sir Steve looked down at Leif from the platform holding the throne, and said, "It's more than good. It's unbelievable. You've been given another layer of protection. No one is sure how this will manifest in you, but some measure of wisdom and powers of the dragon has been gifted to you."

"Cool." He glanced at Batu, who was smiling. "Ah, maybe I could go home now. This will help me stay out of trouble, right?"

The Princess merely said, "No."

Batu touched Leif's shoulder. "I'll tell Miranda what has happened so she can explain it to the family. We have to figure out how this will affect you. We also need to continue training you to master your vampire nature. Once you have made some progress, I'll gladly accompany you home." He turned and looked up at Princess Khunbish. "I would like to return to care for my daughter River."

Khunbish nodded, then returned her attention to Leif. "Go over to the fire pit and put your hand in the flames."

Leif stammered, "I don't think that's a good idea."

"Do it!" she commanded.

With some apprehension, he slowly walked over to the fire. The embers glowed brightly, and the flames rose, ready to burn his flesh. Batu stood nearby as Leif put his hand out, barely letting his fingertips near the fire. He closed his eyes, unable to watch himself do such a stupid thing. He whispered to Batu, "I can't do it myself. You have to do it for me."

Leif felt Batu guide his arm by the elbow, slowly pushing it into the flames. Leif held his eyes shut tightly, waiting for the inevitable pain. Rather than the expected agony of the fire, he felt a weird tingling sensation. Without thinking, his eyes popped open, and he croaked out, "Holy crap!" His hand was engulfed in flames, and he barely felt the heat. His skin was intact and perfect.

Batu let go of his arm and said, "Not only can you walk in the sun, but you're impervious to fire. Every vampire's wet dream."

Leif examined his hand, slowly pulling it back from the fire. He brought his hand up to his face, scrutinizing it closely. After a moment, he lowered his arm and turned toward the Princess. "I'll stay here another week; then I have to go home." He paused, then added. "I appreciate your hospitality."

Everyone's eyes were on the powerful vampiress. Khunbish's intense stare caused Leif to swallow nervously and step back. Batu prepared to step in front of Leif to protect him from any punishment she might aim at Leif.

Instead, Khunbish' s eyes sparkled, and she let out an unexpected burst of laughter. "By the gods, I have never been so surprised by a mortal. If anyone else showed such disrespect, I would've had their heads. Perhaps Tengri and Thor have united to humble us all. I must admit that I am baffled by the abilities granted to you. Make good use of the time you have left here."

Batu bowed, and Leif followed his example. As they left the audience chamber, Batu said, "Let's go for a ride."

Leif complained, "My ass is still sore from our last adventure. Besides, I'm starving."

Batu replied, "It drives me crazy that you are always hangry."

They detoured to the kitchen, where the old woman who seemed to live there quickly filled a large bowl with dumplings and mutton. Leif struggling with Mongolian, managed, "Bayarlalaa." The old woman was delighted at his effort to say thanks and his obvious enjoyment of the food as he devoured the stew like he was starving.

Batu stared at him. "In all the time I've spent here, I have never once seen her smile."

Between mouthfuls, he said, "Maybe she likes redheads."

Batu said something to the old woman. She burst out laughing and replied to Batu in Mongolian. Leif stopped eating and asked, "What did she say?"

"She thinks your hair looks like the wool of a sick sheep."

Leif went back to wolfing down dumplings without a response. There was no way he'd insult the cook. When he was finished, he turned to Batu and said, "Wish I could see the Magus' face when he finds out I can't burn."

Batu advised. "Let's keep that a secret for now and only share it with the Mordecais when we return home. We don't want your advantage to get leaked to the Magus before you figure out how to use it."

"I hate keeping secrets. Sometimes it sucks to be so great."

Batu, exercising all his self-control, let the comment pass without responding.

"I know who Thor is, but the Princess also mentioned Tengri. Who is that?" Leif asked.

"The god of the eternal blue sky. The creator of other gods, kind of like Zeus. You're proof that Tengri has a wicked sense of humor."

On a side street bordering Green Lake Park in Seattle, Kirk Franz sat in his van studying the homeless camp made up of a patchwork of RVs and tents. He noticed a few sad souls in the freezing rain, moving quickly to their temporary abodes as it neared midnight. One, in particular, attracted his attention. A woman with an unsteady gait was walking to a small tent away from the others. He hadn't seen her here before. She disappeared then a lantern flickered on inside.

"Perfect," he thought. "I'll put her out of her misery before she has a chance to become known to the other miscreants. She'll be just another Jane Doe." The forty-five-year-old Franz, in all black garb was all but invisible in the darkness. He pulled a length of nylon cord out of his backpack, placed his hand on the hilt of the hunting knife on his belt, and sucked in his paunch.

Kirk was sure the police would catch him sooner or later, but he hoped to reach his goal of taking out at least a dozen of the filthy street people first. He justified his homicidal rage by assuring himself these bastards were using his hard-earned tax dollars to get high and avoid working. Kirk could at least stop some of them from ruining his country. This 'slut' would be his third victim. He imagined becoming a folk hero to the "law abiding taxpayers" of this country.

The unusually heavy rain had everyone in the encampment hunkered down and masked any sound the killer made as he got out of his van and approached the tent. Kirk wore a long dark coat and a black balaclava, making him a shadow in the darkness. He approached the tent from the rear, listened for a moment, carefully cut a slit in the canvas, then poked his head through the slit. A lantern on the ground was turned down low. In the dim light, Kirk saw a sleeping figure lying on top of a sleeping bag. The smell of alcohol was strong, but he didn't detect the usual scent of someone who didn't have regular access to a shower. A knit cap was pulled down to her eyes, and he could not help but feel attracted to the defenseless woman. Kirk had not raped any of the unwashed homeless yet, but he felt his body respond to her, which surprised him.

He leaped on the woman putting his knife to her throat while putting the other hand over her mouth. "Don't scream, don't fight me!" Her body emanated a strange calm as she opened her eyes and nodded. An uneasy feeling spread over Kirk. He had never had this reaction from a victim. He wanted to terrify her. "Do exactly what I say!"

Again, she merely nodded without a trace of fear in her eyes. Kirk removed his hand, and she said, "You should know, submitting is not my thing." Jacquotte reached up, wrested the knife from his hand, and threw it across the tent. She quickly flipped him onto the ground, rolled on top of him, and smashed her forehead into his face.

His futile struggle against her superior strength was short. "Don't! I've got money!" he whimpered, losing all vestige of his serial killer bravado.

"I only want a little taste!"

Kirk was terrified, as her fangs flashed in the light of the lantern. He struggled in vain as Jacquotte bit deep into his neck. Pain and then silent screams overtook him as he succumbed to her appetite. When his heart stopped beating, the vampiress withdrew, wiping the blood off her mouth on his shoulder.

The Magus and Sir Ruben silently slipped into the tent. The powerful head of the undead was displeased. "I told you no fang marks."

She shrugged. "Vampires gonna do what vampires gonna do."

The Magus bristled. "Use his knife, slash his throat, and break his arms and legs. Then you know what to do with the body. No more mistakes!"

Jacquotte said, "Delighted. I can't wait to see how this plays out. C'mon Ruben, give me a hand."

The Magus gave a final look around the tent and said, "It has been some time since I personally attended the removal of a 'Worthy Target.' I forgot how exhilarating it can be." Without another word, he quickly disappeared into the night.

After Jacquotte disguised the fang marks by slashing Franz's throat, Ruben stuffed the body in the sleeping bag. Neither gave a thought to the newly deceased. Another wretched excuse for a human being. A Worthy Target that the vampire code deemed society better without. He carried the wrapped-up body to Kirk's van while Jacquotte folded the tent. An old woman lugging a plastic bag to a trash can noticed them but looked away as if she had seen nothing.

Jacquotte stepped toward the woman, but Ruben pulled her away and said, "Let her go. As far as she knows, we're packing up our stuff." They loaded everything into Franz's van and were on their way to finishing the dirty deed and improving their standing with the Magus.

Chapter 12

It Can't Be

The security system at Jacques' and Loretta's went off at three in the morning. Jacques jumped out of bed, grabbed his tablet and checked the camera feeds. In the front of the house, red and blue flashing lights lit up the area. The camera at the door showed police walking up to the entrance.

Jacques said to Loretta, "Go to the kids. I'll see what is going on." Loretta looked scared, so wanting to reassure her he said, "It's probably nothing. I'll take care of it."

Loretta was surprised at how calmly he took command in a crisis. She ran to the childrens' bedrooms. On the way she grabbed her phone, and speed-dialed Miranda. A sleepy Miranda answered, and Loretta quickly said, "The cops are here. I don't know what is going on. We might need you. I'll call you right back as soon as I know more."

Miranda got out of bed and replied, "I'm on my way."

There was pounding on the front door, accompanied by someone yelling, "POLICE!" Jacques pulled on a robe and hurried to the front door before it was kicked down.

He opened the door to find a detective in a suit standing in front of four uniformed officers. He asked, "What's going on?"

The detective gruffly asked, "Are you Jacques Mordecai?"

"Yeah, what's this about?"

The gray-haired grizzled man held up a badge and said, "I'm Detective Johnson, Seattle PD." "There's been an incident. Do you own a blue Volvo?"

"I didn't know owning a Volvo is a crime." The cop's vague answers and line of questioning increased his apprehension.

The detective ignored Jacques' comment. "We believe your vehicle was involved in an incident. We are looking into it as possible manslaughter. We need you to come with us and answer some questions downtown."

"What? No fucking way. My car is right there in the driveway!" Jacques started to point past the officers and realized his car was missing. "Fuck! Where's my car?"

Loretta came to the door with Wendell in her arms and Ali at her side, clutching her hand. Jacques turned to her and said, "Call Mom and tell her to call our lawyer. I'm not sure exactly what is going on. Someone must've stolen the car and, I guess, used it in some kind of crime."

A growl from behind the family caught everyone's attention. Billy stepped forward, trying to hold Delilah back.

"What the fuck!" the detective's calm demeanor vanished. He drew his gun and pointed at the panther. The other officers took a step back and also drew their weapons.

Jacques stepped in front of Johnson and held up his hand. "Wait! Don't do anything crazy. It's okay. She's our family pet. The kids play with her. She's not going to attack anyone. Everybody, calm down." He stared directly into the detective's eyes. Johnson took a step back, unaware that Jacques was using his vampire ability to influence him. He explained, "They can only growl to express themselves. She's not threatening anyone."

Another officer said, "Yeah, that's true. I saw that in a National Geographic show. Big cats can't purr or anything."

"Shut up, Phillips!" The detective snapped.

Loretta said, "Billy, please take Delilah back to her room."

Billy shot a dirty look at the police, then said to Delilah. "They're making much ado 'bout nothing. Let's go kitty."

The detective lowered his weapon, inexplicably feeling off his game. He'd taken people in for questioning a thousand times without any problem, but this was nuts. As Billy disappeared with Delilah, Johnson gave a small nod to the other officers, and they re-holstered their weapons.

Loretta told the detective, "He's been home all night. My husband hasn't done anything wrong!"

Johnson regarded the kids. "Ma'am, someone will contact you for a statement later. I think you should take the kids back in the house." He turned to Jacques, "Let's go."

One of the uniformed officers pulled out his handcuffs and approached Jacques. Wendell and Ali started crying as they saw their dad about to be handcuffed by the police.

Jacques turned to the detective and asked, "Am I under arrest?"

Johnson turned to the officer preparing to handcuff Jacques and shook his head. "Uh, not at this time, but we would prefer if you would voluntarily come with us to the station and answer some questions."

Jacques said, "Fine, let's get this cleared up. I also want to know what happened to my car. Give me a second." He went and hugged the kids and told them, "Be good for your mom. I'll be home soon."

One of the cops escorted him to the patrol car. As Jacques got into the back seat, the officer said, "Get in, Panther King." He shot one more look at the house and muttered, "That's gotta be illegal."

Jacques, trying to control his anger, replied, "We have a permit and an approved enclosure in the back. Don't fuck with our cat." Jacques was so upset by the events that he didn't even realize that he was still wearing the dressing robe he put on to answer the door.

The officer slammed the door harder than necessary and looked back at the luxurious house on the lake. "Must be nice." He turned to the detective. "My kid's got a hamster."

Miranda was yelling into the phone at Tristan who was in L.A. on business. "They took Jacques to the police station for questioning on some trumped-up charge. Get your slick lawyer to have him released. I am at the lake house, and Loretta filled me in. We'll wait to hear back from you. The stench of the Magus is all over this."

"Calm down. I'll call the lawyer now. He'll make sure Jacques will be okay. I will fly up tonight. Alexander can be helpful trying to understand the machinations of the Magus and who has aided him."

"Calm down? I understand what's going on. It's a god damned power play. This is another one of his schemes against the House of Sun in his attempt to control us. Meanwhile, I've got two grandsons crying for their dad."

Tristan had been holding his phone a few inches from his ear. Miranda was beginning to wind down, and he moved it back to his ear. "You've got to think clearly to help Jacques. It might be helpful to contact Manny. He might know someone on the Seattle PD and can find out what evidence they have on Jacques."

Miranda took a breath. "You're right. I'll call Manny now." Without another word, she abruptly hung up. She stared at the phone and said, "Damn! I must be getting old. I miss being able to slam the receiver down."

If not for her fear for Jacques, Loretta might have been amused hearing Miranda say her ex-husband was right. "Who is Manny?"

"He's a detective in Salinas that started looking into the unsolved death of a drug dealer that had been killed by Lady Pauline in Salinas. She had recently been transformed and hadn't quite gotten her act together. She didn't cover her tracks well and it raised questions. Manny couldn't let it go, and his investigation eventually led him to my dad's death in Rossville. He can be unbelievably tenacious and ended up coming to Granite Falls with his fiancé. It's a long story, but we told them the truth about us, and now they are good friends. They even helped us fight off an attack by Raf and some rogue undead. We tried to get them to move here, but I guess we are a little too weird for them. In any case, we can trust them both."

Loretta wiped her reddened eyes and asked, "Your contacts and money will make a difference, right? You'll have the best lawyer?"

Miranda touched Loretta's hand, and a wave of reassurance flowed over Loretta. "Yes, we will and you know that I'd walk through hell to save my boy."

Amy pushed aside the butler, who was trying to block her way, and ran into the Magus' living room. She interrupted an intimate moment between the Magus and Jacquotte. Eyes blazing, Amy screamed at him, "You bastard!"

Unruffled, the mighty ruler stood and faced Amy; completely naked. Irritated by the interruption, Jacquotte fell back on the sofa. "Actually, it was my father that was a bastard. My parents were married. The butler came over to assist him in getting redressed. Jacquotte, glowering, started pulling on her clothes.

Amy lunged forward with her hands up to grab his neck. He raised his arm, unleashing a wave of energy that sent the unwanted visitor reeling back into a chair.

Jacquotte, unabashedly still naked, scowled at the intruder. "I was about to reach an epic orgasm. You have impeccably bad timing."

Amy lashed out at the Magus. "How could you? The code says never harm innocents, never harm children! Ali and Wendell are traumatized!"

During the exchange, the Magus had been getting dressed. He waved the butler away and straightened his cuff. "None of the adult Mordecais are innocent. Did you know I always protected them and their mother when they were children? None of them know the meaning of the words gratitude or respect. As for the little ones, they'll get over this temporary loss of access to their worthless father."

Jacquotte added, "Probably do those brats good to suffer a little, prepare 'em for life."

Amy launched herself again, this time on Jacquotte, knocking her to the floor. The Magus watched with amusement. Amy grabbed a fistful of Jacquotte's hair, and the pirate effortlessly flipped her over. They landed with Jacquotte straddling her, holding a dagger to her throat. Jacquotte looked to the Magus. "Just give me the word!" She snarled.

A very long minute passed, punctuated by the vampiress' heavy breathing through bared fangs and nasty stares.

The Magus chuckled. "The Mordecais have inspired so many memorable moments since their creation. Enough! Get up and compose yourselves before I decide that you both may no longer be members of the Haute Caste."

In Salinas, Manny called Molly as he was leaving work. "You're not going to believe this. You know how we were talking about visiting Miranda? She called me a few minutes ago. Jacques got arrested, and she said the Magus had him set up with some bullshit charges. She asked if I knew anyone I could call on the Seattle PD that might be able to help. I told her it would be better if we could come there to help clear him. She said she would ask Tristan to arrange transportation. I got leave from work for a family emergency. You good with that?"

"Are you kidding? I'll start packing right now. Jacques? Seriously? He's the nicest kid. You'd think if any of them would have gotten arrested it would've been Des," Molly said. "I'll call in sick and get the neighbor's kid to take care of Trouble."

Manny grinned. "You would've made a great cop. Nothing rattles you. Not even jumping back into a situation with a bunch of vampires."

At police headquarters, Jacques was in a small interrogation room. A phone had been brought in and he was talking to Miranda. An officer was watching him through the one-way window but couldn't hear what Jacques was saying.

Miranda, at the lake house, had the phone on speaker with the family and had conferenced in Alexander, who was still in Granite Falls.

Jacques told them that he was being charged with manslaughter. "They found my car a mile from the house, and a body was under it. They are saying that I ran the guy over, abandoned the car, walked home, and pretended the car was stolen."

"Your dad already called the lawyer, and he should be there soon. Don't say anything until he gets there." Miranda's voice cracked.

"I know. I told them I'm not talking until the lawyer gets here. They did the whole booking thing, taking my picture and fingerprints. They wanted to draw blood, too, but I told them to fuck off unless they have a warrant. I'm not that stupid. Are Loretta and the kids okay?"

Loretta said, "I'm here, baby. They're all fine. Grigoryi is here with your mom to help with the kids."

"I love you." He tried to keep his voice steady. "Have you found out anything about the guy that died? I swear I don't know him."

Des said, "Sig and I were able to get into the PD database. His name is Kirk Franz. None of us have ever heard of him, and we can't find any connection to us. We're still running a background check. Mom called Manny, and he is coming up here to help."

Jacques sounded dejected. "Detective Manny? This is bad. I hope he can find out something."

Alexander said, "Jacques, we'll bring you home as soon as possible. Whatever it takes. We're sure that the Magus is behind this. I promise you he will regret ever causing any harm to our family."

Tomas said, "This dead guy can't be simply some rando dude. He must be a Worthy Target they used to frame you. I don't think even the Magus would have some bystander killed just to set you up. Henry is talking to his street contacts to get more info on the guy. I know he can't be an innocent victim.

Marie said, "Batu and Leif are returning from Mongolia early to help. It'll be okay, little bro. We all have your back."

Jacques said, "Hang on a sec, one of the cops wants something." They heard someone in the background talking to Jacques. He came back and said, "Guys, I have to go. They're taking me to a holding cell. You gotta get me out of here. I love you, Loretta, hug the kids for me."

Early that evening, Phoebe sat at a back table at Starbucks, munching on lemon cake and holding her phone, looking unhappy. She was startled when someone sat across from her at the small table.

"You seem distressed. Life is a million papercuts until you finally bleed to death." Raf gave her a sly smile.

She tried not to show how unnerved his sudden appearance made her. "No surprise that you'd be an expert on bleeding."

He looked genuinely concerned. "Why so unhappy?" His power to charm prodded her.

"You must know about Jacques." She took a long drink of coffee before replying. "I know that the Magus framed him. The family is trying to help, but I can't be there."

"Can't or won't?"

"You sound like Tomas. Why is it so hard to understand? I need this job. I've got to have a way to take care of myself. I can't depend on anyone else." Her voice got a little loud, causing the other customers to look their way. A couple of the baristas were also staring, but at her handsome visitor.

"Clearly, you're making a choice. I applaud your desire to be independent." He reached out to touch her hand, but she brushed him off. "If you ever need anything. You know I'll be available to you for anything you need: money, a place to stay, or even lust without the complications of love."

She got up abruptly. "Fuck off!"

At that moment, Tomas walked into the coffee shop. He rushed over to Raf and knocked him to the ground. "Stay away from her!"

Raf was on his feet in a split second, his face inches from Tomas'. In a low, threatening voice, he said, "I've killed for less. Don't tempt me."

Customers and staff watched: a couple of customers pulled out their phones to video the confrontation.

Phoebe grabbed Tomas' arm and pulled him away. "Don't; he's not worth it."

The manager walked over, frowning. "Phoebe, get your friends out of here now if you want to keep your job."

Phoebe whispered to Tomas, "Please wait for me. I'll be done in half an hour."

They turned their attention to Raf, who said, "Another time, Phoebe." And quickly disappeared.

Tomas apologized to Phoebe's supervisor. "I'm really sorry about that. It won't happen again. Please don't fire her."

The older woman disapprovingly shook her head at Tomas. "Clearly, it wasn't her fault. I'll give her a chance, but you have to leave now and I don't want to see you or that other guy here again."

Tomas walked out with his head hanging down. Phoebe swallowed and went behind the counter to prepare for closing. One of her coworkers said, "Not bad, Phoebe. I'd shag them both. Might be worth it, losing a job over them."

Phoebe said, "Not the blond. Trust me."

In the parking garage, Tomas was waiting next to Phoebe's old Mustang. He kicked the tire, then leaned against it. He had vowed to his mother he wouldn't let vampires get between him and Phoebe. His arms were still sore from splitting that cord of wood. Tomas considered making some wooden stakes next time.

His love appeared with a sad expression. "Tomas, I didn't know he was coming. I didn't want Raf there. You gotta know…."

"I do." He grabbed Phoebe, kissing her deeply as though trying to leave a mark on her.

She came up for air. "So, I guess we're okay." She stayed in his arms, resting her head against his chest. "I've still got my job. They're having a hard time finding help. But you and Raf are booted from the place."

Tomas said, "Sorry if we got you in trouble. I lost it when I saw him. He's scum. He has no right to…."

"Shh, it's okay now." She looked up at Tomas. "How are Jacques and Loretta?"

"He's still in jail. We've got a court hearing tomorrow. Dad was able to get the date moved up because he and Henry had spent years buying political friends. Mom is ready to kill the Magus, so there's that."

"She won't try anything stupid, right?"

"Don't worry. The Head of the House of Sun is gathering our allies. Her payback will be carefully thought out. The Magus' ego will never allow him to believe he made a stupid mistake in going after us again, but he did."

Phoebe said, "I'm sorry I couldn't be with everyone. Jacques and Loretta don't deserve this shit. Let's go home." She paused before getting into her car. "You had a chance to get me fired, but instead, you stood up for me. Thanks."

Tomas shook his head. "Thank Marie. She said it was good you had a job and that I was being a self-centered dick."

Phoebe chuckled. "I always liked Marie."

Chapter 13

Twists and Turns

Jacques was led through a world of gray walls and steel bars. He was stuck in a holding cell with several guys covered in tattoos and a drunk who smelled of piss sleeping it off on the floor. They eyed Jacques in his silk robe and laughed contemptuously.

"Hey, princess, it looks like you got lost on the way to the palace." A short guy with a mohawk sneered at Jacques.

The biggest guy with the most tattoos, said, "Leave him alone. I've seen him play at the Funeral Pyre."

"I don't give a shit. I need a little entertainment. You gonna sing for me?" He moved in front of Jacques, his eyes blazing with hate.

Something welled up inside Jacques from the dark side of his nature. "Big mistake, asshole." With surprising strength, he hit the bully in the gut so hard he staggered backward, then Jacques delivered an uppercut to the chin. He teetered for a second until his knees buckled. Then he crumpled to the floor unconscious, blood trickling from his mouth, where he had almost bit off his tongue.

The other guys in the cell pulled the unconscious man over beside the drunk. An officer came down the hall to their cell, yelling, "Is there a problem here?" Jacques had moved so quickly that the surveillance cam had only picked up a blur and the sorry aggressor falling.

The guy who had recognized Jacques said, "Nah, the whiskey finally kicked his ass."

Before Manny and Molly arrived in Washington, all had agreed it was essential to keep the Magus from knowing that they had come to help Jacques. They decided to stay away from Granite Falls where one of the Magus' minions might see them. Miranda had made a reservation for them at a small boutique hotel in Tacoma.

The evening they arrived, Manny and Molly treated themselves to a nice dinner at a restaurant overlooking the Sound. After dinner, they strolled along the waterfront, stopping to admire the view of the lights on the islands across the water. In the peaceful quiet, they heard what sounded like a kitten crying from behind a trash can a few feet away. Molly went over and squatted down as a little scrawny brown tabby kitten walked over to her and rubbed against her ankles.

"Aw, Manny, he looks like he's starving." She picked up the kitten, cuddled it against her chest, and it immediately started loudly purring. "We have to help him."

"What are we going to do? We can't take him back to the hotel."

"Why not? I saw other people staying there with pets. Let's take him to our room, and tomorrow we can go to a vet to find out if he is chipped. We can't abandon him out here."

"I can't believe I am saying this, but okay, we can keep him until we find who he belongs to."

"See, that's why I love you. You pretend to be a tough cop, but you can be a big softy."

Holding the cat in one arm, she hugged Manny with the other, as they walked back to the hotel. Shortly after they settled in, there was a knock at the suite door. Molly looked through the peephole and then stepped back. Sounding scared, she whispered, "Manny, it's one of them."

Manny grabbed his gun, went to the door, and checked who it was. He relaxed, turned to Molly, and said, "Nothing to worry about. It's just Angel." He opened the door, ushered Angel in, checked the hallway, closed and locked the door.

The vampire looked up at the TV tuned to a football game. He picked up the remote and shut the TV off. He turned around and said, "I preferred her reaction to yours."

Manny approached Angel and said, "It is good to see you." Molly was surprised to see them fist bump. Manny explained, "When I got those big breaks in the human trafficking case and that drug ring bust, it was because of his help."

Angel bowed. "I asked him not to tell anyone. I would hate to be mistaken for a good guy."

She smirked, "Then you should change your name."

Angel ignored the comment and picked up a box of cat food. "Do you always bring a cat when you investigate crimes?"

Manny and Molly sat in nearby chairs. "Molly is always prepared in case we find a stray."

"Maybe she should have my name." Angel changed the subject, getting to the serious business at hand. "I understand you've been told about the Magus setting up Jacques. We need to get the police to investigate the victim."

There was another knock on the door. Manny checked who it was and started to open the door. Before he could swing the door back, it flew open, and Manny was pushed aside by Sir Henry. "Good evening."

Molly smiled. She remembered how the sexy undead hunk had helped them battle rogue vampires. "Hi! You do like to make an entrance. Still throwing fireballs at snakes?"

He displayed a charming smile. "Not since your last visit to Granite Falls."

Manny said, "Glad we're all on the same team now." However, he did not sound terribly enthusiastic to see Henry.

Sir Henry took Manny's chair and pulled a file out of a leather backpack. "Here," he handed it to the detective. "The man who was killed was on the top ten of Seattle's Worthy Target List, but his entry was mysteriously erased with no one taking credit. Highly unusual and suspect." With more than a hint of sarcasm, he added, "It's almost as if someone wanted to cover something up."

Manny took the file, and Molly's asked, "Worthy target?"

Angel said, "We have a list of criminals who have escaped justice. It is a collection of lowlifes that society would be better without. People that sell drugs to kids, abuse their families, human traffickers, and the like. If the Justice system doesn't deal with them, we mete out their well-deserved punishment. As a side benefit, we get a fresh meal. It's a win, win."

"Not for them." Molly, still not used to the ways of the vampire world, was a little uncomfortable.

Manny flipped through the file, looking at surveillance photos and newspaper stories. "Damn! You think he was a serial killer?"

"We know he was," Angel asserted. "One of Sir Henry's friends looks after the homeless and noticed that he 'happened" to be around almost every time a homeless person was killed. He's the one that took the pictures. So, do you still feel bad for him?" She didn't reply.

Sir Henry explained to the mortals, "We found out the body under the car also had a slashed throat. An odd injury for a hit-and-run. It is commonly done to hide any bite marks. It is clear that the Magus set up Jacques for the murder. Despicable behavior, even for him. The ancient one has lost all sense of ethics and direction. His desire to exact revenge on the Mordecais for his injured ego has taken him over the edge."

Manny was engrossed in the evidence before him. "He stalked and killed the homeless. What a bastard." His attention went to Sir Henry. "I knew Jacques wouldn't hurt anyone. What do you need from me?"

"I can't draw any attention to the club by reporting this, and I'm afraid it will take too long before the police respond to an anonymous tip. They might pay attention if it comes from one of their own. Do you know anyone on the force in Seattle?"

"I did meet a sergeant at a DEA conference. I can get a hold of him and say I got a tip from a C.I. You know, confidential informant. It's worth a try."

Henry stared intensely at him, and Manny's gut tightened. The vampire said, "It has to happen soon. We don't want the Baroness to be forced to make a deal with the Magus."

Angel chimed in, "Or maybe worse, taking some kind of direct action against him. We don't need another war."

"Okay, I'll call him tomorrow morning. I can text Angel and let him know how it goes." He was hoping to avoid more contact with Sir Henry.

The little tabby poked its head out from under Henry's chair and jumped into his lap. To everyone's surprise Henry began petting the kitten who happily settled into his lap and started purring loudly. Henry, pulling his attention away from his new furry friend said, "It was unfortunate that I broke your windshield when we first met. I wasn't sure if you were a friend or foe of the Mordecais."

Manny replied, "Yeah, we weren't sure about you either."

Molly said, "No problem. We owe Miranda a lot. She helped us buy our house. Anyway, that Magus is a prick. Manny and I will gladly do whatever we can to help."

Henry said, "Great! I'll inform the Baroness."

Manny said, "Just one thing. What was the deal with that rapist murdered in the alley by someone dressed as a pirate?"

Henry replied, "An enterprising out-of-town guest of the Magus was hungry. She's been warned. It was an unsanctioned killing. We try not to draw attention to ourselves."

Angel added, "If you meet a vampiress who reminds you of a Pirates of the Caribbean character, run the other way."

"Seriously?" Molly's eyes lit up. "She wasn't in any of Miranda's books."

Angel grinned, "There's a lot she left out, like me."

Henry said, "That vampiress doesn't usually bother women, but Manny, she could put you in a world of hurt, and you'd ask for more. Stay away from Lady Jacquotte."

Now Manny was intrigued. "I've been around several female vampires and kept my head."

Sir Henry regarded him coldly. "She has been tainted by the blood of a succubus."

"A succubus? No way!" Manny responded.

"Way," Angel smirked.

Molly looking a little stunned, said, "First vampires, now a succubus. Next, you will tell me there are werewolves."

Angel and Henry exchanged glances but remained silent.

Henry cleared his throat and said, "I must return to the club. Angel will keep an eye on you at night. We don't think you will need any protection during the day. Unlike the Mordecais, the Magus doesn't have trusted mortals to assist him. Let Angel know if you need anything or find out anything useful." He gently lifted the now sleepy kitten, stood, placed it in Molly's lap and left.

Manny closed the door behind Henry and decided not to wait until morning to contact his friend on the Seattle PD. He made a few phone calls but was unable to get hold of him. He was able to leave a message, and received a promise he would get a call back in the morning.

The suite had a small kitchenette, and Molly decided to make some tea. She asked, "Angel, you want something?"

He replied, "The Magus' head on a plate."

Manny returned a grin. "I don't think I can deliver that, but I can at least work on pissing him off."

In the morning, at an expedited arraignment, Jacques was charged with manslaughter. The Baron used his influence to get bail for Jacques. Posting the exceedingly high bail was no problem for Tristan, and the family was able to bring him home.

Loretta ran to Jacques and tightly hugged him as soon as they uncuffed him.

Miranda, Tristan, Alexander, Marie, Des, Sig, and their lawyer looked on with relief.

Detective Johnson watched, obviously annoyed. He leaned over to an officer beside him and whispered, "Some half-assed rich guys with connections downtown. Nobody gets a hearing this fast, much less bail for murder. His pampered ass should have stayed locked up."

Alexander's enhanced hearing missed nothing. He turned to the detective and spoke in a loud, aggressive tone. "You would keep an innocent man behind bars? Isn't everyone innocent until proven guilty? Perhaps you should change careers."

The force of his stare caused both officers to step back. Some primitive sense of self-preservation kicked in, and they didn't respond. After the group had left the building, the detective asked, "How the hell did he even hear me?"

"I don't know. But do you really think the goth kid killed that guy? The street cams showed him coming home from the club like he said before the murder. His security system showed him pulling into their driveway."

Detective Jonson shook his head. "Right, but after that, there was some kind of 'glitch' in the security system, and it showed nothing for over an hour. Pretty Boy thought it would be enough to cover his moves. It makes me sick that people with that kind of money think they can get away with anything."

The officer rubbed his chin. "What about this Kirk Franz? I spent hours trying to find a connection between him and the kid. Nada."

"Keep digging. There has to be something. I'm going to check out the vic's house again."

Chapter 14

Uproar

Jacquotte, in all her naked splendor, left the Magus' bed, where he lay spent. Even for him, the trysts with the succubus were becoming taxing. She had absorbed his lust and enough blood to feel satiated and invigorated for a week.

The vampiress pulled on his black robe and sat in a chair. "I know what your problem is, old friend."

He lay on his side, watching her with fascination. "Do tell."

"There's a reason you summoned me instead of another to seduce the Day Fanger. I know why you obsess over the mortals." She watched his reaction.

A wave of emotions briefly washed over him; then, he turned his back to her. He did not want her to bring up details from the past. "Spend the rest of the night on your boat."

"I expected you might say that." She got up and dressed quickly. "But I've got something for you. One night you might thank me." She fished an envelope out of a pocket, left it on the bed, and quickly disappeared.

He lay without moving for an hour, torturing himself with what she might have left. The Magus turned over and picked up the envelope. Old regrets and longing rose up in his chest. He tore the envelope open and found a card with an address. His eyes welled with tears despite every effort to stop them. "No!" he cried out and went to the fireplace. He dropped the offending paper into the flames with trembling hands, but it was no good. The information was seared into his brain. "Damn, Jacquotte!"

At the marina, Jacquotte stepped onto her 102-foot three-masted schooner, *Fortune*. She gathered her crew of devoted blood donors who had sailed to the West Coast with her. "We'll head south, maties, to Los Angeles in a few nights."

One of the men looked over her shoulder and said, "You've got a visitor."

A light on the dock outlined a shadowy figure with a rapier in hand. "Lady Jacquotte! You wanted to challenge me. Are you still game?"

A slow grin came to her lips as she saw Guillaume approach. "It will be my pleasure!"

She ducked down into the cabin and emerged with her weapon. Jacquotte leaped onto the dock and waved off assistance from her crew.

"Just so we be clear. I helped frame the young one, but it wasn't my idea. Refusing the Magus never ends well."

Guillaume dropped his coat on the dock and got in position, raising his rapier. "Shameful, even for you. Crossing the Baroness never ends well either."

She lunged first, but Guillaume jumped back into darkness and then suddenly sprang up behind her. Jacquotte whipped around and found the tip of his sword at her neck. She came up under his arm, but he sliced her cheek. She stammered, "You drew first blood! I yield. Damn!"

He saw her reach for a dagger, but with a flick of his rapier, her dagger flew through the air and clattered on the dock. "Cheat! You have no honor!" Guillaume felt her try to use her succubus power to confuse him. "Don't waste your energy. Your tricks won't work on me."

"It was worth a shot." She grimaced as he held the tip of his weapon over her heart.

"Do not ever harm any of the Mordecais or members of the House of Sun again. I won't behead you, but I can ensure you'll need a long recovery. This is your last warning."

He withdrew his rapier and quickly disappeared into the night. She hung her head, unaccustomed to defeat, climbed back aboard, and went below grumbling, "Curse that House of Sun."

The next day Leif watched the kid cleaning tables in the closed club. "Hey, what's up?"

Not having heard Leif come up behind him, Benny jumped at the sight of the intruder and ran away, shouting, "Lady Teri!"

"I'm Leif. It's okay. I play in Henry's band." Leif smiled. "And you don't want to wake her for nothing. Trust me. She gets cranky when her sleep is disturbed."

After the long flight from Mongolia arrived in daylight, Leif had left Batu asleep on the jet. He wore a loose Mongolian shirt, jeans, and sneakers. Not the goth look Benny was getting used to at the club. Benny scrutinized the big man with wild red hair and asked, "You're not one of them, are you?"

Leif scratched his head, held up a finger, and headed for the back room. He returned carrying a large glass of O positive and set it on the bar. "I am, but it's complicated."

Benny stared at him in disbelief. "But you were outside in the sunlight."

"I told you it was complicated. I'm sort of a mutant. For now, that's all you need to know." He picked up the glass, took a long drink, and wiped his mouth with the back of his hand.

The elevator behind them opened, and Sir Henry stepped out. "You're loud enough to wake the undead."

Benny was prepared to see a fight, but to his surprise, the two men hugged each other.

Sir Henry said, "Thank the gods you're back. We can use your help with Jacques. I heard some rumors about what happened to you in Mongolia."

Leif pulled the loose neck of his shirt down, exposing the brand on his chest. "A shaman there did this to me." He then whispered to his friend and mentor. "I'm flameproof now."

Sir Henry had seen much in his centuries, but even he was taken aback at the sight of the dragon. Needing to speak privately with Leif, he told Benny to sweep the entrance. When the boy was gone, he reached out, tentatively touched the dragon brand, and sensed a flash of heat. "I've seen this mark only once before. It was on a trader long ago it is very rare. Let's see what you can do. Put out your hands, palms up."

Leif obliged. "I wanted to talk to you before I went home. There's more to this, right? I mean, can I—you know, do fireballs?"

Henry placed a small napkin in Leif's hands. "Concentrate on the napkin. Picture it starting to burn."

Leif looked at Henry a little skeptically. He shrugged and focused on the napkin. He was startled as sparks tickled his palms. And soon the napkin caught fire. He rubbed his hands together and put out the flames.

"Yes, you've been given the elemental power of fire. Very few of our kind have any kind of elemental ability." Sir Henry took a deep breath and looked at the young man with concern. "You must guard your temper and learn to control this gift. You don't want to unintentionally burn someone who triggers your anger."

"Unintentionally? Why shouldn't I turn the Magus into a kebab?"

Henry's voice was firm. "He deserves to exist despite his unfortunate lapse of judgment. Like you, he is one of a kind. He is the original. Without him, none of us would exist. He is more powerful than you think. Even with a surprise attack, you could not defeat him alone. No other vampire comes close to his power, with the possible exception of the Baron. Perhaps you could get to that level in time with training and practice."

"Fuck it! What good is any of this if I can't help the family?"

"I suggest, that for the time being you stay here. It is best for you to stay away from the Magus. Call Marie. She'll tell you the same thing. You must learn patience, strategy, and timing. Not to mention some anger control."

Leif looked unhappy. "I feel like Superman just got told to stay Clark Kent. I want to take on anyone who messes with us."

Henry shook his head. "Time and place, Leif. With vampires, it's a war of well-thought-out moves. Keeping your abilities secret can make all the difference. If played well, it can be a big advantage. If not, it can be used against you. You must develop cunning and strategy to combat the Magus. Trust that Miranda, the Baron, and especially Alexander can help you with that."

"I'm not stupid!" he blurted out, immediately regretting it.

"No, but you're impulsive. The Magus knows that. He can easily use a mention of Marie to trigger jealousy and take advantage of your rash response." He paused and put a hand on Leif's shoulder. "When I first met you, alcohol and drugs were your way to suppress feelings. You got your act together and don't use anymore. It's time to grow more comfortable with your emotional response. You got clean by learning to gain control, by using your self-talk, and concern for others. Now you will need to control your emotions more than ever."

"But I have this overwhelming urge to kick the Magus' ass."

"I'm not saying you can't strike back, but you must not do it alone." He walked back to the elevator. "You can stay in your old apartment. Leif, you have a way of draining my energy. You have exhausted me; I'm going back to bed."

Leif pulled out his phone and called Marie. "Hey baby, I'm back. Can you meet me at Henry's?"

Chapter 15

Manny and the Darkside

"So, it's Detective Sergeant, now, nice." Rick Montoya smiled at his friend. "I'm not surprised after you put that drug kingpin away. It even made the news up here. I should be pissed at you. Because of your great police work my captain put more pressure on us."

Manny shrugged. "Sorry about that. But you gotta do what you gotta do. Maybe I can make up for it. I got a C.I. who has been hearing things about a killer targeting people in homeless camps. He was once homeless himself, and he still has some contacts. He asked around, and a van was seen at some of the sites of the killings. He checked into it and was able to get a couple of pictures of the vehicle."

Manny passed the file to Frank, but the Seattle cop held up his hand. "Wait a minute. Why are you involved in murders here? And why are you just handing this over to me? What's your angle?"

Manny took a breath and tried his best to tell convincing half-truths. "I know this is out of my jurisdiction, and I don't want to start a turf war. I met the C.I. a couple of years ago on another matter. He wasn't sure what to do about this, so he contacted me, and I said I'd see what I could do. I'd appreciate it if my name doesn't come up. I'd rather not get pulled into it."

Rick seemed a little skeptical but flipped open the file and examined the pictures. His eyebrows raised. "This guy in the van, your C.I. thinks he's the perp?"

"He does. Look at the last photo, my C.I. got a good shot of the vehicle, and you can read the license plates. I didn't want to have to start answering questions about why I was involved, so I figured I'd talk to you and let you look into it."

Rick took a sip of his black coffee. Manny drank his soy latte and hoped his friend would take the bait. "I've never trusted latte-drinking cops, but I'll make an exception because it's you. If this pans out, I'll buy you an espresso machine. The mayor has been on our asses to find this homicidal freak."

Marie entered Leif's old apartment and smelled smoke. She opened a window. "You okay? What's going on?"

Leif came out of the bedroom smiling. "Light My Fire!" He held up his palms, and tiny flames started to rise up.

"No!" She rushed over to him wide-eyed. "Like Henry, you're like Henry."

"And it's all because the Magus sent Jacquotte after me. Silver lining."

She took a deep breath. "Okay, you can put it out now."

He closed his hands into fists, and the flames disappeared. "You okay?"

"Blown away by you and worried about Jacques, he's home with an ankle monitor. Do me a favor. Wait to use your new gift until we clear my brother. We can only deal with one crisis at a time."

He moved away from her. "You all act like I'm a dangerous moron. Like I'm going to burn up shit for fun. I've learned a lot."

Marie looked at him and bit her lip. "Didn't mean to harsh your buzz, but...." She pointed to some burnt trash in the waste can.

"Henry is helping me figure things out. But it's cool, right? I mean, you have to admit that."

She rolled her eyes and then hugged him. Leif gently held her face and teased her lips with a light kiss. She said, "Light My Fire, goat herder."

Manny sent a text to Angel, telling him that Sergeant Montoya would look into the killings. Molly was driving them over to Franz's house. Des had provided Manny with the address. Over the years, as a result of his experience with the vampire world, Manny had become obsessed with serial killers, and he was sure the Seattle PD hadn't found any evidence that would incriminate Kirk Franz.

Although he knew the Seattle PD had already searched Franz's house, he wanted to check it out himself. Franz had lived in a small two-story home in a working-class neighborhood. He and Molly cruised down the street past the house to get a feel of the area. It was late, so only a couple of the other houses on the block had any lights on. Fortunately, there were no pedestrians. The last thing he needed was someone to report him as a prowler. He had Molly turn into the alley and kill the lights as they pulled up to the house. Manny said, "Stay put and keep an eye out. I'll be in and out in no time."

"Be careful!" Molly pouted because she wanted to help search the serial killer's house.

Manny had turned the car's dome light off, so it didn't come on when he opened the door. As he got out of the car, the kitten jumped out and tried to follow him.

Molly said, "Don't worry, I'll get him, go ahead and do your thing."

Manny scanned the area and, not seeing anyone, quickly headed to the back door. Fortunately for Manny, the door had an old knob lock and no deadbolt. He put on a pair of latex gloves, then pulled a stiff square of plastic from his pocket, and quickly slipped the lock. The house was relatively neat, but it was obvious the police had already been through.

He quickly checked the kitchen, which was clean, with no dishes in the sink. He opened all the drawers, found nothing interesting, and headed to the living room. It was simply furnished but appeared comfortable. There were pictures on the walls of white men posing in camo, all holding guns. Manny found it somewhat disconcerting.

He moved into the bedroom, and his eyes immediately fell on a framed picture of Hitler on the nightstand beside the bed. "Crazy racist fucker," he mumbled. The closet had a small assortment of gray clothing, camo, and hunting gear. He checked the shoe boxes and found ammo but no guns or mementos of past kills. Manny picked up the nazi picture and carefully opened the back. A couple of driver's licenses and a state ID card fell out. He recognized the names. "Got you!"

Since the Seattle police considered Franz a victim, they hadn't done a very thorough search. He left the frame face down with one of the IDs peeking out and decided that would be enough to leave for Montoya. Manny didn't want it to be too obvious. As he took one more look around the room, Manny heard a car in the driveway at the front of the house. He rushed back through the kitchen, locking the door on his way out. He tucked his gloves in a pocket and headed toward the alley.

"Stop! Police!" Manny turned and was surprised to see Sgt. Montoya coming around the side of the house, flashing a badge. He seemed equally surprised to see Manny. "What the hell are you doing here?"

Thinking fast, Molly rushed up to them, holding the skinny tabby and a bag of treats. "Honey, I found Sam." She did her best to look shocked by the presence of Montoya. "What's going on?"

Manny said, "It's a little embarrassing, but I had the plates of the van run and wanted to cruise by and take a look. I got out of the car, and the cat jumped out." He made a point of petting the loudly purring feline. "I didn't mean to step on your toes."

Detective Johnson came out of the back door and joined them. "Montoya, who are these people, and what are they doing here??"

"Just a couple of folks chasing their cat. I'll find out if they know the guy or ever saw anything." He tilted his head toward the house and said, "Why don't you start checking the house and I'll be right in."

Detective Johnson grunted and walked back inside. He didn't like interference in his investigation, but the sergeant had been given jurisdiction by the mayor's office because it was rumored the vic wasn't so innocent. His slam dunk case was getting messy.

Montoya held his hand up toward Manny and said, "I don't even want to know." He turned and followed Johnson into the house.

Molly and Manny headed back to the car. Manny reached over and scratched the cat's head. "Well, little buddy, you saved my butt tonight. I guess we will have to adopt you now." He drove off before there were any more embarrassing questions.

Montoya and Johnson methodically went through all the rooms and found some violent porn hidden under the bathroom sink. Montoya said, "Sick fucker."

Johnson picked up the framed picture by the bed. His face became grim as he opened the back and pulled out the stack of id cards. He flipped through them, then handed them to Montoya. "Do these people look familiar?"

Sargent Montoya was relieved they had found something solid and hoped to hell it hadn't been planted. Montoya scanned the photo IDs. "Holy shit! My C.I. was right. I recognize a couple of them as the homeless vics that were killed around Green Lake. I'll get this to forensics and see whose prints come up. We need crime scene to tear this whole place apart."

Johnson said, "Have them put a rush on it. The Mayor is on my ass and we need to wrap this whole thing up. I thought we had that kid dead to rights and now this crap turns up."

Montoya had noticed the finger of a latex glove hanging out of Manny's jeans pocket and knew he was going to have a sleepless night until he got the report from forensics.

"You think this pervert was a serial killer wannabe?"

"It sure looks like it. Makes you wonder who would take him out."

Detective Johnson had a sinking feeling it wasn't going to be Jacques Mordecai.

The family gathered at Jacques and Loretta's house. Miranda had insisted no other vampires, except the family in Seattle be present. Though Sir Omar and Lady Anastasia had wanted to join them, Miranda was worried the police might be watching the house, and it was never a good idea to call attention to the undead. Sir Henry and Lady Teri remained at the club with Billy and Robert.

They were waiting on two things. The results of the final autopsy on Kirk Franz and a meeting Sir Jorge and Sir Franco were having with the Magus.

At the nocturnal ruler's residence, the tone was polite. "Sir Jorge, I appreciate your desire to be an arbiter between the House of Sun and me, but it's simply a petty squabble, a tit for tat, as they say. They have robbed me, damaged my image, and in return, I have caused damage to their sense of security." The ancient vampire smiled confidently as he sipped blood from a crystal goblet.

Sir Jorge's voice was even. "You have raised the concern of those Haute Caste who are close to them. Others wonder if your pride is not causing you to become short-sighted and act erratically."

The Magus looked at Franco, wearing an elegant suit, leaning against the fireplace. "What do you think? Has my behavior become erratic?"

Franco straightened his jacket, to give him a moment to formulate an answer. "Dear Magus, you're capable of terrible harm, but that does not seem to deter these mortals. I don't think this approach is worthy of your great intellect. It feels more like someone lashing out, a sophisticated tantrum."

Sir Jorge managed to hide his amusement. "Tell us, what do you want from them?"

The Magus rose. "Obedience, respect, and cooperation."

"And blood, of course," Sir Franco said.

The Magus' eyes tore into Franco, causing him to put a hand to his throat and cough. Sir Jorge said, "Please do not injure my knight."

The Magus then turned back to the Head of the House of Arrows, and Franco took a deep breath. "Yes, he is right. I do wish to continue my research into their blood and how it has mutated. I would grant them almost anything they desire

112

for samples of the offspring's blood. It would allow me to unravel the secrets which have given them some of the powers of our kind and the ability to endure the light."

"If they do not agree? Then what?" Sir Jorge pressed him.

The Magus simply said, "But they must, or one by one, I shall inflict human misery upon them until they do."

Sir Jorge stood. "Dear Magus, the course you are on is costing you the respect of many besides the Mordecais. I hope you will reconsider."

His brow furrowed. "You mean to say the House of Arrows is also under the sway of these rebellious children?"

Sir Franco responded. "We are but following the code you wrote that has provided the framework for our society."

The Magus' clenched his fists, attempting to keep his temper under control. Sir Jorge said, "We shall say good night and wish you well. Come, Sir Franco."

They left the ruler of the night staring into the dying embers in the fireplace.

Once back in their Capitol Hill home, they called Miranda, and she put them on speaker phone to include the rest of the family. They relayed the chilling conversation they had with the Magus. Sir Jorge told Miranda, "In the centuries I've known him, never did he seem so blinded by an obsession. I have never seen him so prone to anger and lashing out in his quest for revenge. He has always been the epitome of patience and control."

Tomas responded first. "He is constantly probing to find our weaknesses. He's been pressuring Sig to transform, bringing Jacquotte here, and setting up Jacques. And that's this week alone. He thinks he can get what he wants by attacking the people we love."

Marie said, "Not to mention the botched attempt to kill Leif with a fake transformation."

"Yeah," Leif agreed, "That didn't turn out like he planned."

Loretta's sad countenance touched them all. "I'm worried for the kids. I mean, even if he got your blood, it would never be enough. I know he'd come after Ali, River, and Wendell."

Phoebe pushed up her glasses and uttered, "We should kill him."

Des cheered, "Go Phoebe."

Sir Alexander said, "No. He's dangerous, but he keeps our society from imploding. He is essential to maintaining a balance of power."

The Baron added, "The Parliament rules by his design. It can rule in his place if he needs time to reevaluate the way he has reacted to our family, but if he ceased to exist, the vampire world would become chaotic, and battles for control would be terrible. The Magus knows this, which is why all attempts to diminish or take away his power have failed except for Miranda creating the House of Sun."

Miranda touched the Baron's arm. "We represent his worst mistake or greatest achievement. He doesn't know what to do with us. He thinks of us as unruly children."

Leif shook his head. "That asshole doesn't think of Marie that way."

Marie said, "Leif's got a point. I mean, the bottom line is he's lonely. The Magus can always find someone to rock his world but not touch his heart. I think that's why he went after me."

"The spurned lover wants to put me away. Can we focus on that right now?" Jacques asked, exasperated by the turn in the discussion. "Just saying."

Normally Marie would have flipped him off, but everyone knew he was right.

Des was looking at his tablet. "Hey, it's the autopsy report. Manny got a copy and sent it to Angel. He forwarded it to us. It says the dude was dead before he was run over by the Volvo. The actual cause of death was blood loss resulting from a slit throat."

Miranda grabbed the tablet. "Finally, proof!"

Sir Jorge said, "Outstanding!"

Jacques asked, "That's all great, but I don't know if it's enough to clear me?"

The Baron showed an uncharacteristic gesture of affection, putting his arm around Jacques' shoulder. "We'll have to ask our lawyer, but I'm sure it will help prove your innocence."

Alexander who had been quiet during the discussion spoke up, "Jacques is right. All of that is helpful but we need more concrete evidence to prove who actually killed Franz."

Sig said, "It's not likely you'd slash his throat, and then run over him with your own car."

Des grinned. "You know, being accused of killing a serial killer might help with the band's social media presence."

"Fuck you!" was said by several people present.

Miranda's eyes went from Alexander to the Baron. "We've got to do something special for Manny when this is all over."

Loretta said, "First we have to do something special to the Magus."

Chapter 16

More Evidence

The next day at the club, Loretta and Miranda were relieved as Manny told her that evidence was coming to light about Franz. Also, the time of his death was determined in the autopsy and could help their case. The mortal friends of the vampire world made her feel less alone. Under Jacques' bail conditions, he was on home confinement, with an ankle monitor, and was home with the kids. It was ten a.m., so a little light came in through the tiny windows near the ceiling on the back wall. Even that small amount of sunlight showed all the scars on the wooden tables and other flaws around the room. She thought of how stark it seemed without the magic of the music, controlled lighting, and club patrons. Benny wanted to be helpful, got coffee for everyone. Miranda hugged the teenager, telling him he could stay and hear what was happening.

The matriarch looked at his innocent face. "Benny, you've been on the street. You know more about the homeless than any of us."

He replied with a sad smile, "Whatever you need, Ms. Mordecai."

Loretta cleared her throat. "We've got to find someone in Green Lake Park who saw this Franz guy around the homeless encampment. We need something that might support the photos of the van and prove that Jacques wasn't involved. Somehow, we need to connect the dead guy to the murders, maybe get something on his killer."

Manny added, "Sgt. Montoya said he's going to Green Lake at noon to ask around, and you can join him if you want."

Benny cringed. Miranda asked, "What is it?"

He wasn't sure if he should say anything, but he wanted to help. "Bad idea having a cop with you. If they see him, you'll get nothing."

Loretta said, "He's right. I was going to ask the sergeant to stand by in case of trouble, but maybe we should meet him around the corner from the park to be sure he isn't seen."

Manny frowned. "Montoya looks even more like a cop than I do." He unconsciously touched his short hair. "Benny should go with Loretta. A teenager and a woman pleading for info to save her husband have a better chance than any of us."

Benny sat up a little taller. "That's what I'm sayin'."

Molly sounding disappointed said, "I wish we could be there, but the sergeant thinks we're on our way back to Salinas. He doesn't want anyone thinking we tampered with evidence, though we kind of did. You all stay safe."

Manny asserted, "We discovered evidence and didn't tamper with anything."

"And we rescued a stray," Molly added.

Miranda hugged her. "You've both been great, but now it's up to us."

Sgt. Montoya sipped his dark brew as Loretta, Benny, and Miranda met him up the street from Green Lake Park near the homeless camp.

"I was told you could help with the investigation. I trust the source, so I'm not sure what you'll find. My officers have already been all over this area and talked to everyone. As usual, no one heard or saw a thing."

Miranda started to speak, but Loretta held up her hand. "No offense, but do you think people living on the street want to be seen talking to the police? I'm the wife of a man who was falsely arrested and I am not sure I want to be seen talking to you. I've got some cred here."

He fidgeted with his coffee cup and then threw it in the trash. "I guess you have a point." He gestured toward the camp. "After you."

"I think you should stay back until we say it's okay," Loretta said. She clearly was in charge, and Miranda was enjoying the show. Sgt. Montoya, not so much, but he wanted to solve this case. "Benny and I will go in. Hang tight."

Montoya leaned against his unmarked car and watched as they went between the RVs and tents in this makeshift community. His career could take a sudden setback if it looked like he was helping a murderer get off rather than catching one. "I hope to hell this leads somewhere."

Miranda was quiet and watched Benny and Loretta move around the camp. After several minutes she said, "You know my son is innocent."

Montoya retorted, almost automatically, "Of course he is. Everybody accused of a crime says that. But the circumstantial evidence...."

Miranda cut him off. "The evidence is bullshit. He was framed by someone you can't touch." She shut up, wishing she could take it back.

"Oh really? I arrested a state senator once, so don't tell me who I can and can't touch."

Miranda held up a hand and said, "Never mind. Forget I said it."

"Look, whatever your family is involved in, you should come clean if you want me to help you."

He was so sure of himself, but Miranda was not about to shake up his world by asking if he'd arrest a vampire.

Her phone beeped. "They found a witness, c'mon. They'll meet us at the corner."

"Bethany, please tell this officer what you told us. It can help save my husband from going to prison," Loretta pleaded.

The old-looking woman with long gray hair scanned the street as though afraid others might be listening. Loretta gently touched one of her calloused hands. "It's okay. I promise we'll put you up in a hotel after this. I'll owe you big time."

Bethany looked the sergeant over, then Miranda before starting. "Well, the other night, that guy who was murdered, I saw him sneaking over to a tent by that tree there." She pointed to an evergreen on the outskirts of the encampment. "I saw him a few times. He'd park his van, watch us, and sometimes walk around, but he wasn't walking a dog. Always gave me the shivers. So, I kept an eye out for him. I'm sure it's that guy who was run over."

Sgt. Montoya spoke softly, surprising the others with his change in demeanor. "Bethany, I'm Sgt. Montoya. Please tell me what happened the night when he went to that tent?"

"You promise this is confidential?" The sergeant agreed and she continued.

"A woman that was walking like she was drunk went into the tent. The guy followed her and went around the back. After a few minutes two other people showed up and went into the tent. They didn't look like they belonged here. I had to be careful so I kept my distance and didn't hear what they were saying. You gotta watch yourself around here. They were all wearing dark hoodies, so I couldn't see much. I need new glasses, but...."

"Go on..."

117

"The funny thing was, that only three people left the tent. One man was there for a minute, then disappeared. Then the woman and the other man started packing up the tent and carried everything over to the creep's van. I didn't see him leave, and I never saw him again. The woman didn't seem drunk when she left, like when he had followed her when she first showed up. Weird huh? Then it was like they disappeared into thin air. That was some Agatha Christie bullshit." She looked around again. "And I won't be testifying in court."

Loretta handed Sgt. Montoya a piece of paper. "Her vision's not too bad. She wrote down the license plate number."

He turned to Bethany and said, "Thank you, ma'am." He handed her his card. "If I can ever help you."

Miranda touched the sergeant's arm. "Make sure my son gets cleared. We're going to keep our promise to Bethany."

"If you help her, I can't use her as a witness."

Miranda said, "I figured that, but she doesn't want to testify anyway, so I'm hoping you can use street cams to show the van showing up when people were killed."

Sgt. Montoya nodded. "I'll make it a priority."

True to their word. Miranda paid for four weeks at a hotel near Pike's Market after taking Bethany for some new clothes. She also gave her enough cash to tide her over. She and Loretta promised to get her an apartment anywhere she wanted in the city. Benny helped her with the bags of new clothes.

Loretta smiled at Bethany. "We'll call you soon. Thanks for helping my family."

The woman was in tears. "I want you to know that I'm not a druggie and didn't always live on the streets. After my husband Freddy died, the medical bills ate up everything we had, and I lost our home." She wiped her eyes. "I hope your son will be okay! God Bless you!"

Loretta walked into their house and found Jacques overseeing Ali reading books to Wendell which involved unusual animal noises. Delilah would raise her head when Ali roared, then lower it as though not impressed.

"I'm home! And you're not going back to jail!" She rushed over and knocked him down on the couch.

"How can you be so sure?"

Loretta told him everything that had happened. "Now they have to find that van."

Jacques said, "I'm so lucky to have you in my life." He kissed Loretta, then gently pushed her aside and touched his ankle where the monitor rubbed. "Can't wait to get this off."

The kids climbed up on the couch, with Wendell needing a little help. Ali said, "Momma, I'm hungry." Wendell chimed in about his lack of nourishment.

Loretta smiled. "Tell your dad he's cooking." Living amidst the vampire society, caring for the children's everyday needs centered them.

Jacques picked up the phone. "Who wants tacos like my grandpa used to make?" The kids responded enthusiastically, and for the first time since the nightmare started, Jacques felt a sense of relief.

"Hot damn!" Montoya exclaimed. The van, with the license plate number the woman from the homeless encampment gave him, matched the one in the photos he got from Manny. He had put out a BOLO on the van, and it had been spotted by a patrol car, abandoned in an industrial zone in front of a junkyard. Earlier, Montoya found that the van had been leased by Franz. He called Detective Johnson and brought him up to date on the new info. Johnson said he would meet him at the location and to tell the patrol officer to guard the van but to touch nothing.

Montoya and Johnson arrived at the location almost at the same time. The crime scene unit was already there and waiting for them. Johnson wasn't too happy with the possibility of having his whole case blown up, but being an honest ethical cop, he wanted the case closed properly. He pointed to the van and said to the crime scene techs, "Let's do this." The team opened the van, and meticulously began their search. Johnson, Montoya and the techs were surprised by the amount of evidence left behind.

There was a bloodstain on the floor, an unusual knife with a jeweled handle, a gun, and ammo that matched the box they found in Franz's closet. Montoya commented, "How stupid could these assholes be?"

Johnson replied, "I've stopped asking that question years ago." He looked at his watch and said to Montoya, "Once these guys finish going through the van, they'll tow it in and they will be at it for hours. Our shift is just about over, let's go grab a beer."

They headed to a nearby bar and grabbed a booth in the back. Johnson said, "Rick, I have to hand it to you. I was sure that kid had done it and was ready to close the case. He may be a rich, privileged punk, but even if I don't like him, he didn't deserve to go down for this. A lot of guys wouldn't have kept pushing like you did. Maybe I've been at this too long and have become too cynical. I have enough years in, maybe it's time to retire." Montoya didn't know how to respond, so he didn't say anything.

Later, the forensic crew found a long strand of brown hair and more blood stains that matched the homeless people that were murdered. Nothing that linked Jacques to any crime was found in the van. The only fingerprints identified belonged to Franz. To further clear Jacques, a strand of the same brown hair was found in the Volvo that didn't match Jacques or any of the family.

That night at the Seattle P.D. headquarters, the Mayor called a press conference to announce that they had caught the serial killer. The old detective insisted that Montoya be up on the podium with him, standing behind the Mayor. He congratulated the work done by the police department in front of the local media for solving the homicides that had haunted the struggling citizens in the homeless camps. The Mayor went on to promise to do more to protect the homeless and ease their suffering. By the time the Mayor was finished it sounded like he had personally closed the case and was about to bring homelessness to an end. Johnson had heard it all before, and nothing had changed as far as he could tell. No one seemed to care about who killed Franz anymore.

As they walked away Detective Johnson said to Montoya, "I think I am getting too old for this shit."

The next morning Sargent Montoya sent a text to Manny:

Thank your C.I. for me, and please stay in fuckin' Salinas. You're getting an Espresso machine from Amazon

A few days later, Bethany left the hotel salon feeling like a new woman. Her gray hair was soft and curly, falling to her shoulders. She wore designer jeans, a sweater, and boots. It felt so good not to be broke. She went for a walk around the hotel and stopped in her tracks. A homemade poster stuck on a light pole made her wince. She started to question her good fortune but decided to trust her gut.

Bethany pulled out a phone Miranda had given her and caught Loretta in the middle of making pancakes. "It's Bethany. Loretta, I hate to bother you, but I need to know about that kid Benny. Is he safe?"

Loretta pulled the skillet off the stove and asked, "Why? What are you talkin' about?"

"There are missing kid posters with his picture by the hotel."

"Benny's fine. Poor kid was on the street, and friends took him in. He left home because his father beat him. That poor excuse for a parent probably misses his punching bag. Our friends are trying to get custody and get him back in school."

The old woman sighed in relief. "That's all I needed to hear. Glad I called you instead of the police. He's a good boy. You take good care of him."

Loretta said, "We will. Thanks for the heads up." She put the skillet of half-cooked pancakes back on the stove. "Fuck, it's always something with this family."

Chapter 17

Not Amused

In an unusual temper tantrum, the Magus pounded his fists on the fireplace mantle as he listened to the news broadcaster describe how the strange manslaughter case had turned up a serial killer and exonerated Jacques. "Blasted Mordecais!" He turned and faced Ruben. "How could you have been so careless and left all that evidence behind for the police?"

Ruben nervously swallowed. "It was Jacquotte's idea to ditch the van at the junkyard. She said they'd crush it, and no one would ever know."

Lady Sarah tried to look serious, but a tiny smile revealed she was actually pleased that the Magus was unhappy with Jacquotte. She asked, "Ruben, how could you have trusted her judgment?"

The Magus yelled at his butler. "Pack up all my belongings! Call the movers to empty the house next week. I never want to step foot in this backwoods cesspool again. Arrange for my jet to take me to Los Angeles!"

Lady Sarah rose and inquired, "Have you need of us?"

The Magus glared at Ruben, then turned to his sister with a tight smile. "Yes. I desire you take a message to the Baroness." The Magus stood in front of the fireplace; flames were reflected in his dark brown eyes. "I shall offer the House of Sun a treaty of sorts. If they wish me to leave them alone, I must be paid in blood."

Lady Sarah took a deep breath, then said, "I will convey your message."

Ruben avoided looking at the Magus and said nothing but thought that the Magus had lost it when it came to the Mordecais. After all his failed attempts to control them, he was going to try again. "Shall I return to Toronto?"

The Magus shook his head. "I'd like you to help me with an event at the Narcissus Club. You might even like the music this time." His expression darkened. "I haven't forgotten how you both found excuses to avoid attending my last ball."

Ruben's hand went to his throat, afraid the Magus might slash it out of spite. He managed to respond, "I would've embarrassed myself if I tried to waltz. I'm sorry you were offended."

Lady Sarah felt compelled to speak up as head of her house. "We regret not attending that party. Let us make it up to you this time."

"Oh, you shall."

Miranda met Lady Sarah at Pike's Market the next night. They agreed to keep the meeting between the two of them as the offspring were not ready to be civil with anyone representing the Magus.

Miranda noticed Lady Sarah studying her closely as they sat in a restaurant overlooking the sound. It was a favorite place for her to take the kids and rendezvous with others when she was newly divorced. Unfortunately, tonight would not be an enjoyable meal of salmon tacos.

"You've really aged," Sarah said. "More than I expected. Is it true the Baron has allowed a temporary change in his appearance for you?"

"Yes, he did and now appears to be about fifty."

"Extraordinary, especially considering how vain…."

"I'm not discussing the Baron or our personal appearance with you." Her stare was cold. "Cut the chit-chat and get to what the Magus wants—this time."

They stopped their conversation when a waiter came over. Miranda ordered coffee and cheesecake. Lady Sarah asked for a cabernet.

Sarah checked to make sure no one was close enough to overhear, then said, "He wants a blood sample from each of the offspring and Leif."

The waiter returned with their orders, giving Miranda a little more time to respond. Once he walked away, she asked, "I expected that. What is he offering?"

She took a sip of wine. "As a show of good faith, he will see that all charges against Jacques are dropped, and someone in the press will laud him as a hero."

Miranda chuckled and took a bite of cheesecake. "The police are about ready to drop charges anyway. As for the other, we don't seek or want publicity. The Magus isn't offering anything of value to us."

"He is also offering to leave the offspring alone and let it be known that they are under his protection for the next thirteen years." Sarah shifted uncomfortably.

Miranda face darkened with anger. "Ali and River. He's planning to go after them. Damn his eternal lifespan!" She looked out at the Sound for a few seconds. "Is it for their blood, or is he shifting his interest to River? By then, she'd be nineteen or twenty, and he would consider her old enough for his schemes."

"I have no idea. The Magus confides as little as possible in others. You and I haven't always been on opposite sides; I supported the creation of your house. Please consider giving him the blood to make peace for now. Perhaps, later on, he will not even be interested in your other children."

Miranda motioned to the waiter. "Can I get a to-go-box, please?" Her stomach was too upset to eat her dessert, but she'd never waste cheesecake because of the Magus. The matriarch said nothing more until they were out on the sidewalk. She breathed in the cool, damp night air. "He knows Wendell has HH blood. I have no doubt he'll be after him to transform when he's an adult. I think his obsession has crossed the line to madness trying to force us to comply with his demands. Giving in to him will only encourage him to make more demands."

Sarah studied the face of the woman she'd followed closely from birth. "Take a night to consider his terms. He left for Los Angeles with no desire to return here. The property will go to that charity. No one in our world has bested him like you. Take that victory and consider giving the Magus something, so he can save face and keep him from retaliating." She touched Miranda's sleeve. "I told him I won't harm your children."

"Well, Sarah, that's hard to believe when you're his messenger." She purposely snubbed her by not using the vampiress' Haute Caste title. "I'll speak with the family. We will decide on the best course of action together. The Magus can expect a response after he speeds up clearing Jacques."

Jorge watched Franco shamelessly dancing to disco at their martini bar in the Capital Hill neighborhood while flirting with a tattooed bodybuilder. Jorge hid his smile by focusing on removing an olive from his martini. His attention was drawn to the door as two beautiful creatures entered and made a beeline for their table.

Raf caught most of the attention, but a female bartender stared openly at Jacquotte.

Franco disappointed the young man he was dancing with by slipping away as he tried to kiss him. He knew that Jorge was amused by flirtation, but anything more could result in the loss of life, so he spared the mortal that grisly romantic end.

Franco slid into a chair. "Welcome friends."

Raf asked, "Shall we cut straight to why you invited us here?"

Franco laughed. "Straight?"

Jacquotte smiled. "Apparently, anything goes here but that."

A waiter came over and only had eyes for Raf. The vampire curtly ordered a Negroni, and Jacquotte cleared her throat to get the server's attention. "Sorry to disappoint, but you're wasting your time with him. His kink is women who reject his advances. In any case, I'll have a Mojito."

The waiter said, "Pity," and went off to get their drinks.

Jorge appeared amused. "I invited you here to benefit from my advice concerning the Mordecai family. Leave the House of Sun alone."

Jacquotte kept her eyes on Jorge. "I only agreed to spare the Day Fanger. Why do you care if I entertain myself with Tristan's spawn?"

Raf sipped his wine and leaned back. "Jacquotte, you would be wise to watch what you say."

Jorge's expression remained calm, but Franco gave her a clear warning. "We consider them family. We take any attack on any Mordecai as a personal offense."

She replied, sounding surprised by their tone, "It was vampire sex, and Leif was more than willing."

Franco rolled his eyes. "Says the siren. You must be an inadequate lover if you have to lure them with your Delta Voodoo."

She shouted at him angrily, "Take that back!"

Jorge put his hands out, "Enough. Too bad you can't reach for your dagger Jacquotte, but it is with the evidence collected from the van."

She gasped. "The police have it?"

Raf answered, "Yes they do and I am so glad I had nothing to do with that clusterfuck."

"Speaking of clusterfucks," Franco said, "you're obsessed with the fair Phoebe, Tomas' lover. You caused a scene at her place of employment. Sad."

Jorge finished his martini. "How do you think that will end for you?"

Now Jacquotte smiled. "The Baron, or Sir Omar, will have his head." She took a big swig of her drink.

"Or we will," Jorge said without a trace of emotion.

Raf said, "You do know that I'm under the protection of the Magus."

Franco patted his shoulder. "Sorry, but you're an easily replaced lackey, even if you are Haute Caste. Besides, we own this bar, and our security guards are armed with silver knives."

Raf's eyes widened, he pushed up in his chair, and he nervously looked around the club, checking the exits. "That's prohibited."

Franco merely smiled in response.

Jorge said, "Not for mortals."

Jacquotte shook her head. "I never expected to find so many powerful, respected brethren ready to defend these mortal pests. The Baron, I understand, because of his strange attraction to Miranda, but for the House of Arrows to risk the Magus' ire, that is surprising. Very well. If I agree to let the offspring be, will you pay for my drink and allow my safe departure?"

Jorge said, "Yes. It would be my pleasure to see you leave." He signaled to the well-dressed guards at the entrance and pointed to Jacquotte.

"Sorry, Raf. No hard feelings, love." She left the club with amazing speed.

"Shit!" Raf grimaced. "I had nothing to do with Jacque's arrest and the Magus had me contact a reporter to put out a story about it all being a big mistake. It'll be on the channel five news."

Jorge asked, "Will you leave the offspring and their significant others alone?"

With a slight smile, he countered, "You wouldn't impose your will on a mortal. If Phoebe contacts me or seeks me out, that would be her choice. But I will not initiate any more interactions, and I have no desire to feel the sting of a silver blade while carrying out the Magus' plots against the Mordecais."

Franco said, "We respect free will, even if it involves stupid choices. You may go." He gestured to his staff to let Raf pass.

Raf sauntered out with all his unnatural charm as though full of confidence, but his eyes never left the bouncers until he was safely out the door. Silver would not kill him, but it would make him weak and unable to protect himself from other undead. He mumbled, "Fuckin' House of Arrows."

Chapter 18

The House of Sun

The next night the family assembled at the Seattle house at 10 p.m. so all the undead allies could attend. Guillaume stayed in Granite Falls to keep an eye on their place. Grigoryi insisted on sending cookies and muffins with Miranda.

They began by replaying a news broadcast.

"Carol Kasai here reporting from the steps of the downtown courthouse. A judge wasted no time dropping all charges against local musician Jacques Mordecai, who had been accused of manslaughter. In a surprising twist, there is evidence that the victim, Kirk Franz, has allegedly murdered three homeless people in Seattle parks. Mr. Mordecai's cooperation with the police helped them uncover Franz's alleged crimes. Authorities still don't know who tried to frame Mr. Mordecai."

Cheers erupted, and Jacques pulled up a pant leg showing his sore but unshackled ankle. "I'm not going to sue for false arrest," he said smugly. "But I don't think I'll get any speeding tickets for a while."

Miranda sat between Tristan and Sir Henry. "I've called our war council together to have a unified response to the Magus."

Lady Teri was on another couch with Des and Sir Robert. Sig was barely on speaking terms with Des, so she sat on the floor with Phoebe and Tomas. Sir Billy brought some chairs from the dining room for Sir Jorge, Sir Franco, Alexander, and Sir Batu.

Loretta was hugging Jacques as Angel arrived and asked. "What's up?"

Jacques ignored his question, but Loretta smiled warmly, "He's free! They got nothing on him."

Angel returned the smile, then turned to Miranda. "So, how do we take down the Maggot?"

She responded, "Carefully, in a way he would not expect. Any ideas are welcome. The bastard kept his word to help get the charges dropped and got the media to report that Jacques helped close the case. But he's got a huge demand."

Tomas angrily said, "Our blood."

Billy scratched his head. "So, an arsonist helps extinguish the fire he started and wants a reward?"

Phoebe replied coolly, "Fight fire with fire. We can burn down his mansion."

Tomas blinked. "Pheebs!"

Leif rubbed his hands together. "I could do that."

"No!" Several people yelled out together.

Tristan scanned the room. "You cannot go after the Magus impulsively with individual strikes. Besides, he has returned to L.A. The house now belongs to the Girl Scouts."

Des displayed a mischievous grin. "I got a plan, but it will be messy. It was inspired by watching River and Ali. It will seem like we're playing nice, and then, *Wham!*"

Franco said, "I can't wait to hear this."

After an hour of discussion and lots of raised eyebrows, Miranda looked around at those gathered. "Do you all feel strongly that we should do this?"

The offspring and their partners signaled their enthusiasm. Jorge shook his head, "The House of Arrows will support the House of Sun even if we object to this insane plan."

Miranda said, "I'll contact Sarah, tell her Cringe will perform at the Narcissus Club, then give the Magus what he asked for."

Angel gave a thumbs up. "You'll need a good exit strategy."

Tristan said, "I would have never imagined this form of retaliation, but I'll support you. I'm sure you'll be aided by those who are discontented with the Magus." His attention fell on Sir Jorge and Sir Franco. "I don't know that I can say that this is the wisest plan, but I shall be wherever the Baroness needs me."

Sir Jorge leaned forward. "We shall protect the offspring."

Franco quipped, "You mean babysit."

Miranda bit her lip and looked around at her children and their partners. "I hate to say this, but I'll stay with Ali, River, and Wendell. It's time for Tristan and I to step back and let you show your strengths to the vampire world. If it's okay with Loretta and Jacques, we'll keep the little ones safe in Granite with help from Guillaume and Grigoryi."

Jacques said, "Great!"

Loretta elbowed him. Jacques clarified, "I mean, it would be great if you watched the kids."

Loretta added, "It's good timing 'cause my Auntie Gloria and Sig's uncle are going to be in Vegas that weekend. I won't have to explain being in L.A. and not visiting them with Wendell and Ali."

Loretta was looking forward to being in the city without munchkins, even if it involved going after the Magus. She needed a little non-mom time.

Tomas glanced at his mother. "Mom, we love you, but you'd probably get pissed, start a blizzard, and ruin everything."

With a straight face, Des said, "You know you can trust us."

Franco started laughing as the others tried to rein in their amusement.

Alexander had been unusually quiet during the entire discussion. At the end, he said, "This is how Rome fell. But that wasn't a bad thing."

Before everyone left, Loretta pulled Jorge and Franco aside and explained about the missing person posters.

Jorge said, "We'll have to visit his father. I had hoped to avoid seeing the wretched excuse for a man again."

"Thanks." Loretta asked, "Can you get the posters collected up too? It wouldn't be good if that sergeant saw them."

Franco said, "We can have a couple of employees from our bar take care of it."

Loretta smiled. "I'm glad you're spending more time in Seattle. Jacques and I will have to visit your place on a date night when things settle down."

"Date night? How quaint. We miss the debauchery of Caracas, but Seattle has its share of intrigue, thanks to your family. It's growing on us." Franco then whispered something to Loretta.

She blushed and said, "Don't tell anyone. I'm waiting for the right moment when things calm down."

Jorge said, "It's your scent."

Franco added, "Disguise it with perfume."

She looked relieved. "Thanks. You're the best vampires."

Jorge and Franco felt an odd affection for the mortals, a tingle in their hearts but did not speak of it, and they quickly left.

At about one a.m., Miranda, Jacques, and Angel met with Molly and Manny in their hotel room. The matriarch was apologetic. "Sorry, you couldn't hang with the family this visit. We want to let everything cool down, and we don't want anyone getting suspicious about Jacques having connections to the police. Next time you must stay at our place in Granite Falls. You could go hiking, and there's even an alpaca farm up the Mountain Loop from us with guest yurts, Alpaca Pride."

Molly's eyes lit up, "Alpacas?"

"Yes, and llamas. Let me know when you can visit us again—on an actual vacation next time." Miranda petted the scrawny tabby. "This is the cat you found?"

Molly picked up the little guy. "He's a sweetheart, and we went to a vet. No collar and no ID chip. No one seems to be looking for him, so we're adopting him."

Manny said, "If not for me, she'd bring every stray home, but I think we do owe this little guy. Anyway, we'll take you up on the hiking and the yurt next time we're here." He good-naturedly shoved Angel, "Keep your maniac friends out of the news feed. Seriously, I don't want to have to wonder if I know who murdered a rapist in Seattle. You have no idea what it does to a cop to let a perp get away with it."

Jacques was a little teary-eyed. "I owe you big time! Whatever you need, seriously, just ask." He reached into his pocket and held out an envelope. "I heard you might be getting married soon, so in case we aren't able to be there, here's a present from Loretta and me."

Manny put up his hands to refuse, but Molly grabbed the envelope. "Thanks!" She didn't even look inside; she quickly shoved it in her purse so Manny couldn't return it.

Manny said, "That wasn't necessary, but thank you. We couldn't stand seeing you falsely accused. Of everyone, you're the last person I'd suspect of...." He stopped and looked at Miranda. "Sorry."

"No problem, he seems like the nicest of the bunch, but they all have their moments. Anyway, I don't blame you for wanting justice when it comes to our nocturnal maniacs. If not for Ali, River, and Wendell, I'd go Blade on some of these undead assholes."

Angel chuckled. "We're lucky you're a grandma."

"There is no way I can ever thank you for what you have done. It seems every time we see you it involves some kind of family drama. If you ever need anything, we're here for you. And my offer to come work for us still stands if you ever change your minds."

Everyone exchanged hugs, said their final good-byes and headed home. After they left, Molly couldn't help but think about how good Angel smelled. She tactfully asked Manny, "What is it about vampires? Why aren't I repulsed by them? I mean, I'm a freakin' vegetarian."

"Because we can sense that they're fucked up people like anyone else, despite the immortal bloodsucker disguise."

"Wow! I think you're right. I never thought about them like that." Molly didn't add how attractive she found some of them. She started packing. "Let's go home; I miss Trouble." She petted the thin Tabby. "Sam, you're going to love your new brother."

"And I think that I'm ready to get back to some normal mortal mayhem. A little vampire drama goes a long way. Sam? I don't know. I think he needs a name that inspires attitude if this cat will be living with Trouble." Manny thought for a moment. "Samurai!"

Chapter 19

For Benny

"We should end his miserable existence," Franco grumbled, carrying a briefcase.

Jorge took a breath. "No. Benny would find out and be plagued with guilt. Let me reason with him."

They arrived at a small apartment in a rundown building. The walls of the stairwell were covered in graffiti. After pounding on the door several times, it was opened by an unshaven, pale man holding a beer can in one hand. He was wearing a stained tee shirt and worn jeans that looked like they hadn't been laundered in some time. From conversations with Benny, they figured he was only in his forties, but he looked much older. He looked at them with a suspicious expression and gruffly asked, "What do you want?"

Jorge masked his disdain for Benny's father and calmly said, "We're here on behalf of your son, Benjamin, Mr. McMurty."

He squinted, cocked his head to one side, and asked, "What about him?"

Franco asked, "May we come in and discuss his future?" He pulled a hundred-dollar bill from his wallet and held it out.

McMurty grabbed the cash. "Sure. But I'm keeping the money no matter what."

"Of course, I never doubted it," Jorge said.

They quickly scanned the small apartment. Days of dirty dishes were stacked in the sink, the trash can was overflowing, and a pile of dirty clothing covered one side of the stained couch. McMurty mumbled, "I wasn't expetin' company.

That damn kid hasn't been here to do his chores. So, what's your interest in Benny? Where is he?"

Jorge responded in an even tone, "He is safe and recovering from your last beating."

McMurty stepped back, clutching his beer. "I remember you! You're the guy that threw me against the wall. I should sue you."

Franco pulled a document from his inside pocket. "No need for that. We're about to make you a very generous offer. We are prepared to pay you $50,000 to give up your," he coughed, "parental rights to Benny."

Jorge added, "Benny may contact you at any time if he chooses, but you will agree to no longer pursue him."

His mouth hung open, and he farted. Franco said, "Let's get this over with."

The father's eyes lit up with greed. "I want more!"

In a flash, Franco was holding him by the throat with one hand and brandishing a knife with the other. "Nothing would give me more pleasure than for you to reject our offer."

Jorge placed the document on the coffee table, placed an expensive gold pen on top, and said calmly, "Sign it. And we'll give you this." He popped open the briefcase to show the cash.

McMurty croaked out, "Okay! Let go of me!"

"Gladly." Franco released him, stepped away, and straightened his suit. He sniffed the air and said, "Now you can afford soap."

McMurty signed the papers and said, "You know, even though I signed this, he'll always be my kid." He reached into the briefcase and grabbed some of the money. "Can't change that. Suckers." He held the pen out to Franco.

Franco looked at McMurty's unwashed hands and said, "That's alright, you can keep it." With a look of disgust, Jorge said, "Luckily, Benny also has his mother's genes. You are a poor excuse for a human being and don't deserve to be called a father."

They quickly left the apartment and walked back to their car without another word. Jorge remarked as they got into their Tesla, "When I saw you hold that blade to his throat, that was so...."

"Hot." Franco lowered his eyes from Jorge's face to the bulge below his waist and leaned into him.

"Mi amor," Jorge whispered as they kissed. "I'm in no condition to drive."

Franco unzipped his lover's pants and slipped his hand over the hard cock he had enjoyed for centuries. He watched Jorge close his eyes in anticipation. Franco lowered himself to be able to pleasure his lover. Jorge's natural scent unleashed memories of ecstasy. His mouth greedily accepted the throbbing shaft again and again until Jorge pressed against the back of the seat, gasping, "Franco."

He sat up, pulling a handkerchief from his pocket as Jorge adjusted his clothing. The knight of the House of Arrows said, "Back to our place now! I won't relieve my passion in this vehicle, though that was delightfully trashy."

The head of the House of Arrows rolled his eyes. As they drove, Jorge glanced at his partner. "When I saw you dancing the other night, it reminded me of when I first saw you delighting men at that forbidden salon in Caracas."

Franco smiled. "I recall a member of the elite trying to appear bored while undressing me with his eyes. Then we danced, and though you ignored my clever banter, your gaze and hands possessed me."

"Centuries pass, and my passion for you, my desire to have you, doesn't fade." Jorge kept his eyes on the road. "You still drive me mad."

"You're welcome." A barely perceptible smile appeared on Franco's face. "The bitter truth is we owe all this to the Magus. If not for meeting him, you might have succumbed to the pressure from your family to marry one of those well-bred women."

Jorge made a rude noise. "They wanted me to sow my seed, breed, with no concern for my happiness. I wasn't surprised that when we disappeared, they claimed I had been lost on an expedition in the Amazon."

Franco rubbed his thigh. "Here we are. Now I expect you to explore my body like the Amazon."

Jorge kissed him passionately. "Mi amor, it is always an adventure with you."

Lady Pompadour was intrigued by the message from the Magus. She sat on a divan looking out on her garden in the moonlight near Versailles. The ruler of the vampire world requested her presence in Los Angeles to assist him in dealing with the House of Sun. Pomp's on-and-off relationship with the Mordecai family ended sourly when she tried to arrange for Phoebe to go with Sir Raf. Luckily the Magus appreciated her loyalty. For the once mistress and advisor to a king, attention from the most powerful vampire was all that mattered.

"Sacre bleu," she said to herself, then called for her maid to pack for the trip. She would have appreciated more notice. Lady Pomp strolled into one of her three walk-in closets. "I have nothing to wear!"

Miranda paced in her bedroom. Tristan, watching her, appeared amused by her antics. He finally spoke, "It must be done. As head of the House, you must respond to the Magus. Hearing from Lady Sarah is not enough to seal this agreement. He kept his word and assistance in getting Jacques released."

She stopped inches from him, with her face slightly turned up. "Despite the surprise, the kids are planning, I hate the feeling I'm doing exactly what he wants."

Tristan's intense blue eyes drew her in. His voice was soft and compelling. "You will appear reasonable, but we both know the Magus has no idea how his abuse of power will play out."

"Being reasonable is not one of my strong points."

He gently placed a finger on her lips. "I know."

"Okay, I'll try." She sighed, then picked up her phone and sent a text to the Magus.

> **The family has agreed to your request. It will happen at the Narcissus Club, at the end of the Cringe performance in two weeks**

She showed the message to Tristan. He nodded, and Miranda sent it before succumbing to temptation and adding some insult. Within a minute, she got a reply.

> **Splendid!**

Miranda lay on the bed and started wiggling out of her clothes. "Your turn. Make me forget this whole shit show for an hour."

His shirt and slacks fell to the floor. "Only an hour?"

Her eyes took in his lean, muscular body, clearly responding to her demand. "We'll see."

Lady Cassandra slowly sipped lavender and Chamomile tea as she steadied her nerves. She had secured a safe online meeting for those brave or foolhardy enough to act on their concerns about the Magus. His dangerous and vengeful attack on the House of Sun had gone too far, even for some of his staunchest supporters.

Cassandra opened the meeting. "I'm sorry this call is happening when some of you would be resting, but the time has come to hone our plans. The Magus' plot to send Jacques to prison failed, and now he is demanding samples of their blood."

Lady Antoinella shared the news of the invitation Sir Cesare had received to attend a spectacle at the Narcissus Club. "It seems like the House of Mordecai is about to give him samples of their blood, and it is to be witnessed by some of our kind."

Antoinella asked, "Will the Baron or Sir Alexander join us? I would value their input."

Cassandra was not surprised Antoinella wished for their help. "I have not included those close to the Mordecai family who wish to tear out the Magus' throat because they tend to be overly protective. Nor Sir Omar, despite his usually calm, controlled temperament."

Anastasia chuckled. "Their beloved grandfather wishes to decapitate the Magus at the moment, which Miranda and I have forbidden."

Lady Kananga said, "I, too, was invited. This event may aid our plans. Who else was invited?"

"Not I, nor Sir Omar." Lady Anastasia replied. "I believe the Magus worries that our family ties might lead to confrontation with him. We are both quite upset but have been reassured by the Baroness that all will be well." She paused. "But as I thought, Sir Omar is willing to help us. We will be ready when the time comes."

Antoinella said, "Borgia applauds the Magus' unscrupulous actions. I've not openly disagreed as I do not wish to arouse his suspicions. He must stay in the dark about our plans."

Lily added, "Batu returned from Mongolia as soon as he heard of the egregious attack on his family. I dare not divulge to him what we discuss as he would surely tell Miranda of any plans."

Kananga added, "They would battle it out with the Magus, oblivious to the possible blowback to the rest of us and many of the mortals connected to the House of Sun. They would probably end up destroying each other."

The Seer spoke again, "The age of the rule of brute power has passed. We must show the Magus a novel approach that will heal his wounded pride and leave our society stronger and more resilient. Whatever we decide, it must be clear in the end we were responsible, not the Mordecais. That would only give the Magus justification for future actions against them."

Antoinella's voice became somber. "The risk falls on us."

Cassandra said, "Yes, and he has not been the most forgiving leader in the past." She paused. "If any desire to decline involvement, please leave now but say nothing. None present will judge you."

Whether it was due to concern for the Magus or fear of appearing weak before the others, all the avatars remained.

Kananga got to the point. "Are we in agreement that our ancient leader needs to be removed from power for his own protection?"

Cassandra added, "Temporarily, of course. Please raise your hands." All the avatars made the same gesture. She took a sip of tea as she felt a sense of relief.

Lily said, "I grieve to see our once brilliant leader so tormented by his obsessions with lust and control."

Cassandra's voice was soothing. "Our wise, powerful benefactor is still there. We just need to give him what modern parents call a time-out. We must allow him a safe space to come to terms with the changes in our society that he cannot control. He must learn to honorably exist with the changes for our kind to survive."

Kananga said, "You are proposing an abduction?"

Anastasia responded, "Yes. Taking great care to cause as little injury to him or ourselves as possible. Cassandra and I can see no other way to stop the harm he has brought upon himself and our society."

Antoinella said, "Marie and her siblings are his main target. His focus on them could be a distraction that will help conceal our actions. Like you, I wish to act soon, but we must wait for the right moment."

Lily said, "The Mordecais can have no part in this. Not even the Baron. It must be clear that the Haute Caste of several Houses are responsible when the time comes. Though I have not been invited, I volunteer to be one of those who put hands on him when he is taken. That is if we can figure out a way for me to get close to him."

"I think I have a solution that will enable you to do that," Anastasia said.

After an uncomfortable pause, Lady Kananga added, "As will I. The others will make it possible for us to sedate and move him."

"Yes," Anastasia replied. "Now, let us find an opportunity soon. I can offer a secure place for his respite when we secret him away."

Cassandra ended the meeting with, "Dear sisters of the night, your courage will ensure our success. I have seen changes that I dare not speak of yet. I propose that Lady Kananga, Lady Lily, Lady Antoinella, and I carry out the first phase of our plan with Lady Anastasia and Sir Omar taking charge of the second phase."

All were in accord, and the call was over.

The next night, Marie was practicing her drums at the club while waiting for her brothers to show up. Leif had gone to the grocery store with Benny. Marie had insisted they eat more than takeout and sent them off with a list of basics for healthy meals. It was heartwarming to see Leif take Benny under his wing.

Marie was startled to see a figure silently approach from the shadows. "Oh, it's you! What are you doing here?"

Lady Cassandra smiled and came behind the drum set to hug Marie. "My child, how are you?"

"I'm fine. Leif is changed, but we're still together. Life goes on, I guess." Marie stared at the vampiress, wearing a Seahawks hoodie and matching sweatpants. "That's a little casual for you. Going incognito?"

Cassandra smiled. "I thought I would try a different look to fit in with the locals." They sat down at a small table, and the Seer gently touched Marie's hand. "I had seen glimmers of Leif's rise, but I had no idea he would be so powerful. He is lucky to have you to guide his path."

Marie's eyes glistened. "He is a good man and has a good heart."

"I know, and hopefully, that will save him from some of his darker inclinations." She withdrew her hand. "But I'm not here because of Leif. I have a great favor to ask of you, and it must remain a secret for now—from everyone."

"What do you want?" Her eyes flashed. "I've always trusted you, but you're giving me the creeps with this secrecy. What are you up to?"

Lady Cassandra glanced around the club, making sure no one was nearby. She whispered, "An effort is being made to protect our kind and the Magus from himself during his current instability and lapse of judgment. That is all I can say. It will all become clear after your concert at the Narcissus."

"Will this help Leif?"

"It will benefit all of us if we succeed. Though the Magus will not see it that way at first, if ever."

Marie thought about the fact that she was being given a request by the Seer, who had protected her family when they needed sanctuary.

Cassandra continued. "I have a small request of you that will aid us in our efforts."

"Tell me what you need, and I will gladly do what I can to help."

"It's too early to torture me with your cuteness," Des uttered, glaring at Wendell.

The little one was delighted to find his uncle and auntie crashed at his house on Sunday morning.

Sig struggled to sit up. "Little dude, go see your Mom and Dad. They love it when you wake them up."

"OK," he grinned and left a dinosaur on the bed. "Play later."

Des groaned. "I hope someone makes him undead." He pulled a pillow over his head.

"Des!"

"Just so he'll sleep during the day."

She sat up and yawned. "I feel for these kids. What a weird childhood."

Des reached a hand out, slipping it under her teddy. "Don't you feel for me?"

She batted his hand away. "C'mon, it's only been a couple of hours."

He heaved a dramatic sigh and threw a pillow against a wall. "My childhood sucked. Don't you want to assuage my fragile ego?"

"You mean massage your ego, you idiot." She climbed out of bed. "Anyway, I'm focused on fine-tuning our plans to assault the undead patriarchy."

He followed her into the bathroom. "It's hot when you talk about attacking the Magus."

She shoved him away, closed the door, and yelled, "You think it's hot when I order pizza."

He tried to ignore his disappointed dick. Des sat on the bed and muttered, "Because you are all that matters."

None heard his confession. He had never felt so vulnerable. Years of being the king of shallow relationships had left him unable to defend his heart when it came to Sigourney. Sex with her was more than lust. It was the only time he wasn't besieged by loneliness or putting on a show of callousness. There was so much Des wished to say, but he would wait until after the concert at the Narcissus. He did not want any distractions when he bared his soul to her.

Jacques called from the hallway. "Pancakes! C'mon, get decent. We're taking the kids to the alpaca ranch."

Sig emerged from the bathroom, and Des asked, "Do alpacas eat children?"

After breakfast, the ride to Miranda's was uneventful, except for Wendell losing his pancakes on Des.

"You had to make them with blueberries," Des moaned.

Sig laughed until her sides hurt. Luckily, Wendell quickly recovered after they made a pit stop at the house in Granite Falls to clean up, get some Dramamine and pick up River. Miranda waved goodbye, glad to have a little time to herself but asked them to come back for dinner.

Des moved to the front with Loretta driving while Jacques and Sig managed the kids in the back seats of the Escalade. Finally, they arrived at the Paca Pride guest ranch in the foothills of the Cascades with alpacas, chickens, turkeys, and a llama named Zeus. Grigoryi often bought fresh eggs from the ranch. Visitors from all over the world came there to hike and kayak. Many camped or stayed in very comfy yurts, often called "glamping."

David, one of the owners, greeted them with a warm smile. After introductions, he said, "Grigoryi sent me a text you were coming. If the kids want to feed the alpacas, I've got some apples set aside. Just move slowly, and it will be fine."

Sig looked around at the large alpine house and gift shop surrounded by meadows and forest leading up to the mountains. "You're not far from the town, but it's so peaceful we could be a million miles away."

The host made a sweeping gesture. "It's a lot of work but worth it. I'm from New York, and we lived in Seattle before moving here. We wanted to create a place in the country that was welcoming to everyone."

"You succeeded," Loretta replied.

Ali shouted, "That's my apple!"

River countered, "Mine!"

Des remarked, "It was peaceful."

Jacques took charge and made sure each kid had a treat for the alpacas. Wendell immediately started eating his apple. David laughed and gave him another one. The curious creatures lined up along the fence by their barn. River stood back, not sure about these odd-looking horses.

"Where are the unicorn horns?" She looked puzzled.

"They're alpacas," Sig replied. "They're special too, but no horns."

Des said, "Look, it's fine." He walked up and tried to pat one on the head, but they all moved back a step.

Ali held out an apple, and they returned. He chuckled. "They don't like Uncle Des."

Jacques said, "Maybe 'cause he smells like puke."

When the apples were given out, David let the children visit with the chickens and turkeys. Loretta got a little tearful when she saw how much fun the kids were having. She nudged her husband. "We gotta do this kind of thing more often. You know, give them a more normal childhood."

Des heard her. "A goth queen getting up early to feed the flock in Doc Martens?"

"I don't mean the whole farm scene, just you know, regular kid stuff, away from…."

"…my side of the family." Jacques nodded. "You're right. It's just that I never had that. No baseball games with a father, no camping trips, like most people."

"But Dad taught us how to remove blood stains," Des remarked. "Not to mention a pet panther."

Loretta hugged Jacques and flipped off his brother. "I know what you mean, baby. We'll find a way."

Sig watched Des lean against a fence post as the llama, Zeus, reached over the top of the fence and licked his head.

"What the hell?" He jumped forward, stumbled, and fell to the ground.

Sig laughed. "Serves you right."

He sat up, ran his fingers through his damp hair, and said. "I live to amuse you."

Chapter 20

There Are Rules

Alexander paced as Tristan quietly regarded a display of swords on the wall. Leif, Batu, and the adult offspring gathered in the fencing barn. Guillaume pulled up chairs around a small table with a thin leather-bound book in the center.

"What's up?" Jacques asked.

Des looked around. "Are we waiting for Mom?"

Tristan and Alexander moved to the table. Tristan placed a hand on the book. "She won't be coming as she has refused to acknowledge the legitimacy of the *Book of Blood.*"

Marie said, "She thinks it's maniacal ramblings of the Magus."

Alexander shook his head. "I would normally agree with the Head of the House of Sun, but the book of laws is essential to keep our kind from devolving into a self-destructive society."

Tomas asked, "We know that no one is supposed to be transformed against their will and that vamps are supposed to get permission from their House or the Magus to take out a Worthy Target. What else?"

Tristan shook his head. "Clearly, the Magus' behavior has caused your lack of understanding and respect for the laws of our kind, but they have prevented wars between our Houses for centuries."

Des countered, "But the Parliament created by that book hasn't done shit to keep rogue vamps or the Magus from going after us."

Leif said, "It's all Haute Caste lies." Worried that he might have insulted Alexander and Tristan, he added, "I didn't mean any offense."

Tristan picked up the book and turned to the last few pages. "Sir Batu tried to read this to your mother when River was born, but she never let him finish."

Batu rubbed his forehead. "She grabbed the *Book of Blood* and threw it against the wall."

Marie said, "Go Mom."

"She missed the section that pertains to the use of our blood. Pay attention." Tristan began to read, "Our vital fluid, the source of our renewal and powers, shall not be bartered for financial gain or privileges." He gave them a moment to let that sink in. "It shall only be given for transformation or shared between lovers. It may be given sparingly to a mortal of excellent character to extend their life, or if they are ailing or grievously injured."

"So that's how the Magus justified giving some of his blood to Sig's uncle to treat his cancer," Des said.

Marie added, "Exactly! But he used it as leverage for some of my blood."

Alexander nodded. "That is why we will support your plan. He clearly bartered for 'privileges.' That has weighed on my mind since he did it. There should have been a consequence to his violation of the code."

Tomas, "Please tell me he wrote a punishment."

Guillaume shook his head. "The Magus believed that no one would dare break the laws concerning blood. Apparently, he felt he is exempt from the law."

Tristan stated, "So let us consider the role each of us will play in bringing down the Magus in front of an audience of his most loyal followers."

Tomas stood. "I think you'll want to see what I ordered from Amazon. It's in the garage."

They all followed him out. Marie was trailing the others. She wanted to tell them about Lady Cassandra's visit but had been sworn to secrecy. She had always respected and trusted the Seer, and her gut told her to do so now.

Leif called back to her, "You coming?"

She hurried to his side. "This scheme is crazy enough to work."

Lady Jacquotte entered a bar on a back street near Pioneer Square and regarded the patrons. Several men checked her out, but she put them in a 'Maybe later' file. She continued to survey the bar and stopped at an odd pair. One of them was wearing a bowler hat with brown hair that peeked out from under the hat. The other had braids and wore a ruffled dress shirt.

Robert gave her a sweet grin, and Billy took off his hat as she approached. They stood until she was seated. "Gentlemen, I hope yer not about to threaten me as Guillaume did."

Robert pressed his hand over his heart and feigned being offended. "Never would I want to ruin the possibility of knowing such a lovely and clever vampiress."

Billy added, "I got no qualms 'bout being rude if it will protect the Mordecai family."

Jacquotte smiled. "Good cop, bad cop?"

Billy replied, "I don't think either of us has been referred to as good, except for my aim and Robert's guitar picking."

Robert laughed and said, "And I know that no one has ever confused us with officers of the law."

Jacquotte studied them with half-closed eyes. "Damn, if that Baroness hasn't put a spell on all of you. I gotta know why you two would dare stand with her against the Magus. I understand that Guillaume is related to the Mordecais, but you two, I don't get. Are you suicidal? Have you lost your minds? You're not even Haute Caste."

"You may not be aware, but we have been elevated to that status. But we haven't let it go to our heads, have we, Sir Billy?' Robert emphasized "Sir" to poke a little fun at the pirate.

"Not in the least, Sir Robert." Billy smiled. "The Baroness, well, that's just plain instinct. We see the writing on the wall, and it isn't in the Magus' handwriting."

She narrowed her eyes again. "What?"

A waitress came over and took their orders for spiced wine, the establishment's specialty. Billy gave her a charming smile and a big tip when she returned quickly with their order.

He looked at Robert. "I think I might have plans for later."

"You didn't notice the angry stare from the bartender. I keep telling you to pay attention. Jealousy almost got me killed." Robert still felt a shiver when he remembered a lover poisoning him before his transformation.

Lady Jacquotte snickered. "Honestly, I think she's more into me. Trust me, a succubus always knows." She took a sip. "Now answer my freakin' question. And I don't want some long-winded bullshit explanation."

Robert put down his drink. "Which one was that? I lost track."

With exasperation, Jacquotte repeated, "Why would you two stand against the Magus? I wouldn't think that would be the smart choice."

"Well, darlin', the Magus hasn't changed with the times. He experimented with life and now has no idea how to deal with the results. The Mordecai family is kind of like his personal Jurassic Park."

"Jurassic Park?" She knitted her eyebrows, confused.

"It's a movie. Never mind. You should get out more," Robert advised.

Billy added, "Kind of like Frankenstein, except the villagers like the new monsters."

"I can't say that I'm that thrilled with your 'villagers.' Even if I don't care for his self-indulgent pastimes, we owe the Magus," Jacquotte retorted.

Robert played with his glass. "Gratitude is due, so we're trying to help him see the error of his ways."

"How is that going to happen?"

Robert picked up his glass and turned to Billy.

"By showing him that he must accept this new vampire society of half-bloods. He will have to learn to roll with it," Billy answered.

Robert grinned. "More to be revealed in Los Angeles. I don't think you want to miss the gala at the Narcissus Club."

Billy pulled something out of his inner jacket pocket and placed it on the table as they stood.

Jacquotte grabbed it. "My dagger!"

Billy said, "The Baroness wanted you to have it back as a show of good faith."

"That was kind of her." She looked around the bar. "Hate to say au revoir, but my dual nature needs a lot of nutritional support. Can't go as long without sustenance as you two."

Robert smiled. "Of course."

Billy added, "If I were you, I wouldn't overindulge. You wouldn't want to piss off the House of Sun."

She watched them walk out and muttered, "Damn." She hated to admit it, but the Baroness was growing on her. Jacquotte considered how the Mordecai clan had been able to retrieve her dagger from the police evidence room.

The pirate moved to the bar and sat beside a man wearing a knock-off designer suit and a fake Rolex watch. He stood out as a pretentious jerk. She surreptitiously inhaled and noted O positive. "Perfect," she said to herself.

"Excuse me?" The nicely groomed, bearded man turned towards her.

"Your cologne, I appreciate the scent of Cartier." She almost purred. She sensed his pulse rate increase with anticipation.

With a confident gleam in his eyes, he asked, "May I order a drink for you?"

"Perhaps we could go somewhere more private to get acquainted," she suggested.

Her succubus charm was overriding his hesitancy about hooking up with a stranger so quickly. "I'm Vincent. Are you new to the area? I don't believe I have seen you before, and believe me, I would have remembered. If you'd like to go somewhere else, my car is parked around the corner."

Jacquotte smiled and let her eyes travel down his body. "Yes, I'd love to see more. I've heard the Four Seasons is fun." She watched him cringe as he considered the expense. His veneer of wealth was starting to crack.

"Okay, sure, for a drink."

She faked a look of concern. "If that's too—much for you, I'll just...." She started to turn away.

"No, of course not." He put a twenty on the bar and followed her out.

When they arrived at his car, he made a show of opening the door to his leased Mercedes. She slid in, allowing him a good look at her cleavage. He went around to the driver's side, and once he was inside, she moved her hand over his crotch and teased a reaction.

A groan escaped his lips. "I don't even know your name."

She let her charms overwhelm his senses. He pushed a button that lowered the seat backs and grabbed her.

"I can be whoever you would like if you're willing to pay the price." They kissed deeply then Jacquotte moved her lips to his neck as he fondled her breasts and felt her nipples harden.

"You're certainly better than any of the others I ever met at this bar." He said, eyes half-closed.

Jacquotte wasn't running on bloodlust. This was just a distraction. She felt his hardness through clothing against her thigh. "I don't want money."

"Anything. I'll give you anything!" He was struggling with his zipper.

"This is all I want, love." She licked a spot on the side of his neck, then sank her fangs in.

"Stop!" The searing pain took his ability to speak as he slipped into unconsciousness.

Familiar euphoric energy gave the vampiress a contact high. She noted Vincent's mortal blood was bland compared to the taste of Leif or the Magus, but it would do.

"Get a room!" An old man walking his dog slapped the hood of the car and then hurried away.

"Fuck!" Jacquotte stopped herself before she drank too much and pushed the limp body off her. "Time to part ways." She didn't want any more attention after the news coverage about the rapist attack. She returned the seats to the upright positions and positioned her blood donor as though taking a nap. "Sweet dreams." She knew his ego would prevent him from ever saying a word about their encounter to anyone.

When the vampiress got to the marina, she ordered her crew to set sail for Los Angeles and headed below deck. The crew noticed her reddened lips and felt relieved she was satiated. The pirate paid well, but a few of the crew had become borderline anemic. She reappeared wearing her antique tricornered hat and stood at the helm. "The Seattle Sound is way too calm for me. We must go to the open sea. Cast off!"

It was anticlimactic as they motored out of the harbor into the Sound. It would take hours to get to the Pacific. She stayed in command until the dawn began to break, then went below to her dark cabin. She had time to consider how to play the Mordecais and the Magus to her advantage before arriving in L.A. and keeping her word to a very old friend.

Chapter 21

Preparations

Tomas prepared bowls of ravioli as Phoebe settled in after her evening shift at Starbucks. "Thanks for cooking, hon." They sat at the small kitchen table.

"Thank my grandpa Pete." He smiled and put the Italian comfort food in front of her. "He taught me how to cook." He watched as she heaped a half pound of Parmesan Reggiano on top.

"Damn, girl. No one eats that much cheese."

"Don't be a hater." She took a mouthful. "Mmm."

"I have a proposition for you."

She eyed him suspiciously. "So that's what we're calling it now."

"No, not that. This is business. I want to invest in a café and have you manage it. I was thinking pastries, maybe some bagels with coffee, tea, and smoothies."

She dropped her fork. "Fucker! Why can't you let me do my own thing? You are such a controlling asshole."

"You sound like my mom." He immediately regretted that slip.

"Tomas!" She shot to her feet and glared at him.

Realizing he had said the wrong thing—again, he clumsily tried to change the subject and asked, "More cheese?"

Phoebe took a deep breath and sat back down. After quietly eating half the bowl, she said, "I want ownership."

His eyes got big. "Sure! I won't have anything to do with it. You know, except eat there sometimes."

She smiled. "And you'll give it to me to run as I see fit?"

"I have only one request. Pick a location somewhere in Snohomish County. Everett, Marysville, or any place you want, but with a little distance from my family."

She laughed. "Seriously? So, I guess you don't want me to establish a café in Granite Falls."

"Well, no." He flashed her a mischievous grin. "A little too close to House of Sun Central. Is it a deal? Will you quit before our gig in L.A.? I really want you to be there."

"Is all this about Raf? You think I'll hook up with him if I'm left alone for the weekend?"

He walked over and pulled her into his arms. "You know that I would do anything to protect you from him or any other bloodsucker. But that's not what this is about. I want you to see us hold our own against the Magus and his cronies. Share that moment with me. I'm sure Raf will be there, but I totally trust you, Pheebs."

Phoebe's heart was about to burst. "Tomas, I love you. Whatever happens, know that. I'll quit my job and be there for you, but you've got to keep your word when we get back. I want to make sure that we are on the same page. This will be my place to run the way I want. I will be working for myself, and one day I'll pay back every cent you put into my café."

Tomas kissed her gently, but Phoebe's lips demanded more. Soon the remains of the bowl of ravioli hit the floor as they began making love on the table. "All that cheese," he mumbled as they tore each other's clothes off.

"Shut up." She ran her hand over his hard cock. He was on top of her in seconds, reaching down to her soft folds.

"You're so wet," Tomas uttered. He went down on her, kissing her nub as his fingers moved inside.

She moaned, "That feels so good." Her hips rose to increase the pressure.

"I can't wait!" Tomas moved up his mouth, licking her nipples before kissing her again.

Phoebe uttered, "Now."

He plunged into her sweet wetness again and again. She moaned, "Fuck me harder." The creaking table suddenly gave way and crashed to the floor.

"Don't stop!" she cried out, gripping his fine ass with her hands. Her lips traveled up the side of his neck, and she sucked his earlobe. She knew that drove Tomas crazy.

He entered again harder; spasms of pleasure took over as their climax halted the rhythmic movements. "Wild thing," he collapsed beside her on the remnants of the table.

"Cheese does that to me."

Tomas said, "We should stock up."

Sig and Loretta were in Seattle buying clothes for the trip to L.A. "Oooh, that's it!" Loretta exclaimed. "I'm ready to be creepy as hell." She held up a black mesh V-neck top adorned with silver, red-fanged skull beads.

"Here." Sig handed over a necklace with a silver dagger charm.

"Yes!" She laid it over the mesh top. "What about you?"

"I've got a Morticia costume, wig and all."

Loretta asked, "Does Des has a thing for her?"

"Yeah, it was his idea. I agreed because the chic vamp snobs will be all Gucci'd and Prada'd up, and I'll be the classic vampiress with a Dracula tattoo."

"The Narcissus Club is about to be rocked by the dark side of the Mordecais." She looked down at her inch-long black and red nails. "Jacques will have red streaks in his hair."

"We'll be legends." Loretta asserted. "I don't care about the club rules. I'm taking a video with a hidden camera."

"Perfect!"

"I gotta do this for Wendell and Ali."

Sig scoffed. "You're doing this for yourself."

"Well, that too. I need a break from this motherhood thing. You know I love the kids, but damn, I want to find a balance and get revenge on that freak Magus."

"No shame in that. We've all got reasons to go after that douchebag."

Loretta picked up a pair of dangling silver fleur de Lys earrings. "Nola style."

Sig's eyes lit up. "That's it. Of course. We should throw Mardi Gras beads from the stage to get everyone to come close!"

"You're evil, but I love it."

Jacques was in the garage helping Des take an inventory of the supplies for the concert. "It's all here." His phone pinged. He checked the screen and turned to Des, "Sig says we need to order a ton of Mardi Gras beads. I don't know what for, but she said she'll explain later. Good thing we can get anything overnight from Amazon." He slapped his brother on the back. "Remember that trip to New Orleans our senior year? I think it would be cool to live in the French Quarter."

"I don't think you want to tell your girlfriend about how we had to bribe the cops when that goth chick turned out to be undercover." Jacques shook his head.

"I thought she was into me." Des grinned.

"You think every woman is into you. Sometimes I can't believe we shared the same uterus. I do have to admit that Nola was our best vacation ever. The blues, the food, the…."

"…ladies!"

Miranda walked in. "What ladies?"

Des quickly tried to cover. "Sig, Phoebe, and Loretta. They'll have our backs at the club."

"All I have to say is you better not screw up with Sig again. She just started talking to you after that stupid jealous shitstorm. If you break up, I'm keeping her." They all stared at Miranda, who never failed to surprise them. "Oh, dinner's ready," she added.

After she left, Des mumbled. "She gets the Mom of the Year award."

Jacques said. "I'm glad she's keeping Sig. I think I like her better."

Des punched him in the arm.

Chapter 22

The Homestead

The next evening at the Funeral Pyre, Benny packed his new clothes that Jorge and Franco had bought him. He was sure the Gucci suitcase wasn't a knock-off. He carefully packed his Air Jordans and Doc Martens. He had never owned three pairs of shoes before, much less designer brands. He decided to wear his old Converse high tops today. They told him it could be muddy in Granite Falls.

He gave a last look around his apartment, wondering what he was getting himself into. A knock at the door broke his melancholy musing. Marie poked her head in. "Hey, Benny, we gotta go. Teri's waiting in the car."

Benny carried his suitcase down to the car. After Teri helped load his stuff in the back of her Prius, he climbed into the back seat. They were driving him to Miranda's place to stay until everyone attending the Narcissus Club event got back from L.A. He wasn't sure what was happening, except the band was planning to get revenge on the vampire who had framed Jacques.

As they got on the highway, Marie asked, "You okay?"

"I'm good. Are you sure your mom won't mind me staying there? I'd be fine being alone at the club until everyone returns."

"You're afraid we're dumping you? Benny, it's not like that. My mom wants to be sure you're safe while we're in L.A., and so do we. We'll get you back to the club when the gig is over. You know that Jorge and Franco are arranging legal custody." She gently socked him on the shoulder.

"Yeah." He gave her a tight smile. "I've never been looked after like this. I mean, not since my mom died."

"Kid, you are stuck with this crazy, dysfunctional family until you want to leave. River is my little sister, Ali and Wendell are Jacque's kids. Wendell is a teddy bear, but beware, Ali and River can be a tad scary."

"Everyone there is mortal?"

Marie explained. "Not everyone. The cook, Grigoryi, is. Then there is Guillaume, our great-cousin. He is not, but he is one of the most honorable vampires I know. He lives on the grounds and teaches fencing."

"Sword fighting? Cool."

Teri continued, "Marie's dad will be there too. He's usually pretty good at calming Mom down. Except when she's really pissed at him. They've got a long history, but nothing for you to worry about."

"Right," he said but made a mental note to be out of sight if sparks started flying.

"And if you see a cougar, call for my dad. He's good with big cats," Marie told him.

He wasn't sure if Marie was joking. "Is it too late to go back?"

Marie reassured him. "You have nothing to worry about. Everything will be fine. Leif and I are flying to L.A. to join the others after we drop you off. We'll be back in a few days."

After driving for almost an hour, they were on the road that led to Granite Falls when Benny pointed to the road ahead. The headlights of the car illuminated a deer. Benny excitedly said, "Wow! Watch out. There's a deer up there?"

"I guess you don't get out of Seattle much." Teri said.

"We camped when I was little, but then, well, not after that."

Teri hated that sad puppy look he got whenever he thought about his life. "You'll see them running around all over almost daily here." As they drove over the bridge, she said, "That's the south fork of the Stillaguamish River. We're almost there. The house is up this road."

"Wow! This is like in the middle of nowhere."

"Kinda. Mom likes it that way."

They turned into a gravel driveway and stopped in front of the house. As they got out of the car, an old black Lab ran towards them, wagging its tail and ignoring the fat pug nipping at its heels. Benny dropped to his knees as both dogs tried to get his attention. Marie got a little teary-eyed. "It's the first time I've seen you look so happy."

He scratched Lug's head with one hand and petted the excited pug with the other. "I always wanted a dog. But my dad said they were too much trouble."

Marie made a mental note to tell Jorge and Franco.

Miranda came out on the deck, followed by the munchkins. "Welcome, Benny, mi casa es su casa. It's what my dad used to say. My house is your house, and I mean it sincerely". She made introductions. "By birth order, this is River, Ali, and Wendell."

River came over and picked up the pug. "Piglet is Alex's, but she's staying here too."

"Hi, River and Piglet. Nice to meet you both," Benny said.

Ali came over and high-fived Benny. Wendell tried to copy Ali's smooth move but stumbled and fell on his butt. Benny reached out and steadied him. "Hey, little man. Let's try that again." To Wendell's delight, the second time was successful.

Grigoryi came out on the deck and announced, "Dinner is ready!"

Miranda completed the introductions. "And this is Grigoryi, a long-time family friend."

Marie put her arm around Benny's waist and whispered, "Just so you know, sometimes my dad acts like he's got a stick up his ass, but he's really a good guy. Try and ignore it, and you should probably call him Baron."

Teri patted him on the shoulder and said, "You'll be fine. They are all good people. They will take good care of you. We have to get back to Seattle now."

Marie hugged all the kids and her mom. Before Miranda let go, she said, "You be careful and watch out for your brothers and Leif."

Marie smiled and said, "I always do, Mom. We'll see you soon."

Teri and Marie got in the car and took off.

Benny stood in the driveway and watched as they drove away. He nervously wondered if he might be able to hitchhike back to Seattle if things didn't work out.

Miranda put an arm around his waist and said, "Come inside. I'll show you your room. It has a view of the river."

Benny gawked as they walked through the house. "Wow, this place is incredible. Thanks for taking me in. I'll do the dishes or anything you need."

Miranda laughed. "I can always use help with the kids. Grigoryi is very particular about his kitchen. Don't even try to load the dishwasher."

After Benny was settled in his room, everyone gathered at the kitchen table for dinner. Grigoryi closely scrutinized Benny. "You should eat more."

Miranda rolled her eyes. "He tells everyone that." Though she did think the kid was on the skinny side.

The little ones were delighted with the grilled cheese sandwiches and started to make a mess slurping the tomato soup. Miranda helped Wendell. Grigoryi gently admonished the children. "Use your napkins."

Benny said, "It all seems so—I don't know—normal here." He stopped, realizing that must have sounded rude.

Miranda smiled. "Looks can be deceiving, but we try. It does get a little weird in the evening, but we're used to it."

Ali said, "Our family is weird."

River said, "You're weird!"

Ali aimed a spoonful of soup at River. Miranda quickly grabbed his hand in time to prevent a food fight. Miranda laughed and said to Benny, "This is as normal as it gets. They get it from Batu and Alexander."

Benny didn't ask about what she meant. Teri had told him about the family tree, so he knew a little about their history. He smiled, "Weird doesn't seem so bad."

Chapter 23

Treachery

Lady Kananga, Lady Antoinella, and Lady Lily arrived separately at the elephant refuge near Twentynine Palms around midnight. The Magus did not know of his party guests' early arrival to L.A., except for Antoinella. She had told the Magus and Sir Cesare that Lady Cassandra had promised to read her fortune, so she excused herself and took off shortly after landing in Los Angeles.

The Magus was so caught up in his visions of a display of power over the House of Sun that he did not detect her dishonesty. She had left Cesare with him discussing how to collect the offspring's blood in a tasteful yet humiliating ceremony. They didn't realize that their attitudes had cemented Cassandra's desire to go through with the "betrayal."

It was her first visit to the sanctuary where Lady Cassandra and Sir Hannibal took care of a dozen elephants that had been rescued from poachers in Africa. The ageless warrior had established the sanctuary as a way to atone for having taken the giant creatures into battle long ago.

As Antoinella drove up to the electric gate of the sanctuary, it rolled open onto the acreage that contained several huge barns and a large ranch house. She parked her Jaguar next to the Spanish fountain in front of the house. A figure in a long purple dress greeted her warmly. Lady Cassandra said, "Vampiress power."

A grin lit up Antoinella's often somber countenance. "It does feel liberating, even meeting like this."

Someone in overalls pushing a wheelbarrow came around the corner. He stopped and hailed them. "Welcome, Lady Antoinella."

She was surprised to see Sir Hann in such casual attire, engaged in manual labor. "Thank you. I hope you will be so kind as to give me a tour later."

"It would be my pleasure." Then he continued with his chores.

Cassandra shook her head. "If he gets you in that garage that he calls a museum, he won't stop talking about his exploits. Try to stay with our large guests instead."

Inside she joined Lady Kananga and Lady Lily in the spacious living room. Lady Lily said, "No time to waste; we must get right to it."

Lady Kananga, without preamble, said, "I've made a list of the Magus' most loyal supporters." She handed a piece of paper to each of them.

Cassandra said, "Manners, ladies. First tea. Then we can plan on the take down of the nocturnal patriarchy."

After Cassandra served them all tea, Antoinella raised her dainty cup. "To the revolution!"

For three hours, they considered the many ways their plan could fail and countered each disaster with a solution. They were relying on Lady Lily's medical expertise, Lady Kananga's ability to charm the Magus, Lady Antoinella's closeness to Sir Cesare, and Lady Cassandra's visions. Their scheme would piggyback off whatever chaos the offspring created and garner help from allies who would come forth if they succeeded. Vampires were, by and large, a fickle bunch.

"Marie," Cassandra said, "was willing to help us as I assured her that we ultimately had the same goal. She remains in the dark concerning who is involved and what will transpire. She only asked that we wait until the end of their performance to act. She promised to wait to tell the others until it is necessary."

They all knew the Magus could literally bring the Narcissus club crashing down on them if he felt threatened. Secrecy was crucial. They also wanted to keep their heads as the Magus had invented the guillotine for treacherous vampires. It was essential to act with haste to protect everyone involved.

Lady Kananga yawned and asked, "Will you excuse me? I have some logistic calls to make before I retire."

"Of course." Cassandra answered, "I believe we have covered all the main issues. There are only a few details left to firm up."

Rising from the couch, Lady Antoinella asked, "Is it too close to dawn for a little visit with the elephants?"

"Not at all. You can find Sir Hann out in the largest barn with the male elephants. Please feel free to join him." Lady Cassandra smiled. "You will forever have my gratitude for engaging in this endeavor."

Lady Lily watched Kananga and Antoinella leave, then turned to Cassandra. "She seems eager to get a tour."

"Yes, and I'm sure Sir Hann will be delighted by her company even though she's a Roman." Cassandra asked, "Speaking of grudges, have you forgiven Kyoto for his behavior towards the Mordecais?"

"Yes." Her gaze looked distant. "But after a brief reunion, my feelings for him began to wane. I've been keeping company with Sir Batu."

"Excellent choice. He has been a good father to River. When he transformed, I worried he might be too kindhearted and become hateful towards what he had become, but he has found balance."

Lady Lily smiled. "Yes. He would be formidable if anyone tried to harm those he cared about. The Magus does not realize the passionate opposition he has created by going after the Mordecais. I had once helped Kyoto research their blood's properties. I would not engage in that type of research again."

Cassandra put a hand on her arm. "Your skills might be needed to help the Mordecais and Leif understand their unique nature, but I am glad to hear that you will never again engage in the Magus' search for a weapon to harm our kind."

Lady Lily was about to ask if that certainty had come from a vision, but Lady Cassandra quickly got up and went to her chamber without another word.

Sir Hannibal was treating the giant creatures in the barn to carrots and apples when Antoinella entered. He waved her over. "Don't be wary. They are more gentle and polite than most people. Marie named this one Leif."

She reached up and gently ran her hand down the large ear. The rugged-looking skin was softer than she imagined. The beast moved his head towards her, almost causing her to lose her balance. "Okay. Easy." She grabbed a carrot and let Leif take it. "I hope Leif appreciates having this namesake."

"That wasn't the point." Sir Hann's eyes lit up. "The Magus rescued this elephant for Marie, so...."

"She found a way to offend him." She asked, "Why are you willing to help us go against him?"

He hung his head deep in thought for a moment, straightened up, and stared directly into her eyes. "Perhaps for the same reason you risk so much. Something is wrong with the Magus. The society he built and protected for centuries is falling apart due to abandoning his code. He lost my respect when he started targeting Miranda and the children."

158

Her eyes glistened. "I feel the same about Cesare. He supports the Magus in his cruel and ruthless attempts to make the Mordecais submit to him."

The ancient warrior raised her hand to his lips, turned it, and gently kissed her palm. "You are a delightful surprise from what I expected. The House of Pentacles has a long history of corrupt and unprincipled behavior. You are welcome here anytime."

A small smile betrayed her attraction to him. "Perhaps after the concert. Goodnight, Sir Hannibal."

After she left, Leif playfully nudged Hann with his trunk. "Here's an apple. I'm glad you like her. I have a feeling you'll see a lot more of Lady Antoinella."

Tristan and Miranda were sitting on the back deck the next night, bundled up against the evening chill. Grigoryi came out to check in with them.

"The kids are settled in watching a movie with Benny. Do you need anything before I retire?"

"Thanks, G, we're good. Dinner was delicious."

Tristan said, "Goodnight, Grigoryi."

They sat looking across the yard toward the river. The surface of the water sparkled, lit up by the full moon. They sat in comfortable silence, listening to the water rippling over the rocks and the muted cries of owls in the woods. Miranda turned to him and kissed his cheek. "Thanks for agreeing to stay with me and let the kids take on the Magus alone. The vampire world must begin respecting them. We must have faith in the kids and let them find their place in the world." Although she could sit forever looking at his handsome features, thoughts of the upcoming event intruded. "It's driving me crazy not knowing what the kids are planning. I doubt I will get a decent night's sleep until this is over."

"Decency is vastly overrated. In any case, I am pretty sure that I can provide you with a distraction to help you relax."

"I'm counting on it. But tonight, I just want to be held. Damn, Magus! The great libido killer."

He put his arm around her shoulders, and she nestled in closer. "I will share a secret with you, but you cannot tell anyone. I'm only telling you to allay your fears."

Her eyes widened as she turned towards him. "What haven't you told me?"

"The offspring are not the only ones to plot against our ruler. That is all I am at liberty to say."

Miranda's voice got higher. "Do the kids know about this?"

159

"Marie has some vague idea about what is planned but not the specifics. She has been sworn to secrecy as well."

"What if I threaten no sex until you tell me?"

With confidence, he said, "You won't." and kissed her.

She eventually pulled back a little. "You fucker."

"Now you're in the mood?" He gently pushed some unruly curls away from her face.

Benny poked his head out the door, cleared his throat, and said, "Excuse me, I don't mean to interrupt. The kids are ready for bed. Wendell fell asleep during the movie."

"Thanks, Benny. We'll be right in."

Benny disappeared, and Miranda told Tristan, "You know I hate secrets. We'll 'talk' later. I'll find a way of getting it out of you."

Chapter 24

Finding Safe Harbor

Jacquotte's schooner pulled into Marina Del Rey and set up for a few days' stay. The crew of mortals was given shore leave when Lady Jacquotte rose from the depths of her unnatural rest. They needed to build up their "stamina" for the next leg of their journey.

She rented a car and drove to the Narcissus club in search of liquid sustenance. She had never been to the renowned night spot of the undead society. The industrial look of the exterior of the building gave way to a luxurious dance club inside.

Jacquotte wandered to the back of the club. She stopped to look at the mural of Narcissus gazing at his reflection in a pool. Approaching him from behind was a Komodo dragon. The Magus had the dragon added to honor his pet Komodo, Dorcus. In the center of each table in the club was a small bowl of water. Although vampires' reflections do not appear in mirrors, for some unexplained reason, they could see themselves in still water and indulge their vanity. There was even a large, ornate pool at the edge of the stage.

Not especially vain, unusual for a vampire, she was amused at the mural and the reflecting pool. Jacquotte found Raf giving directions to a group of Common Caste staff.

"The Magus expects everything to be perfect. It is imperative to give all in attendance the right impression. Keep their glasses filled and treat any Haute Caste with respect due to royalty. Am I clear?"

Carmen barked back, "The staff knows what to do!"

Others grumbled and gave Raf annoyed glances as they walked away. Jacquotte said, "They don't seem very enthusiastic."

Raf sounded annoyed as he greeted her. "Lady Jacquotte! So, you decided to come even though you're on the outs with our dear ruler. You're such a loyal criminal." He gestured toward the low-ranked Common Caste, setting up tables and chairs. "They'll do whatever the Magus wants out of fear and with the hope he might notice one of them and bestow his favor on them. I find that sad."

Jacquotte scrutinized him. "And what about you?"

"I'm homeless at the moment. The vampires in Portland have scattered, though I suspect they'll stay loyal to the House of Sun. They used to look to me for guidance and wisdom, but now they regard me with suspicion, so I've moved on." He gave her a flirtatious grin. "Of course, I might be persuaded to voyage to a new harbor."

"Not with me. I've had my fill of narcissistic assholes like you. Good looks can only hide so much ugly." She turned away dismissively and headed to the large kitchen. "I'm in need of supplies."

He followed her and appeared amused as she took several bags of blood out of a fridge and put them in an insulated container from the blood bank. He looked into the cooler and said, "I should charge you for that."

In a flash, she threw him against the cooler's stainless-steel door and held her dagger to his throat. She heard gasps from some of the Common Caste watching the exchange. Carmen called out, "You should cut him!"

Raf ducked and rammed his head into Jacquotte's chest, knocking the pirate to the floor. She was back up in a second, and they began circling. Raf grabbed a butcher's knife from the counter. His eyes glowed angrily towards the vampiress who had embarrassed him in front of the other undead.

Carmen, as head of the kitchen, moved between them. She winked at Lady Jacquotte and frowned at Sir Raf. "We'll never be ready if you two Haute Caste don't take your royal selves out of here and go play somewhere else." She handed a box of provisions to the pirate and glared at Raf.

He gave Carmen and Lady Jacquotte an angry look. "I won't forget this." He left without giving them another glance.

Jacquotte looked surprised. "You're not afraid of him?"

Carmen ran a hand through her short dark hair and straightened her back for emphasis. "Fuck no, he's all talk. Besides, the Magus needs us to do the work for his party. You don't expect any of the Haute Caste to get their hands dirty."

Jacquotte nodded toward the box and said, "I thank you kindly for the provisions." With a throaty laugh, she added, "And intervening so I didn't have to kill Raf."

Carmen gestured to the staff, who had stopped working to watch the drama, to get back on task. Once they returned to work, She leaned closer to Jacquotte and whispered, "Thank Angel, he gave me the heads up that you went up against the Magus and might need help." She reached into the fridge and handed her another bag of blood.

Jacquotte's brows creased. "Why is he being nice to me?"

"Hell, if I know," Carmen answered. "Angel and I go way back, so I didn't ask him. A word to the wise, from the rumors I'm hearing, you probably won't want to stick around when the music starts." Then she went into the ballroom and yelled at someone to go on a blood bank run.

On her way out, Jacquotte noticed that the figure in the mural on the wall of Narcissus resembled the ruler of the night. He regarded his reflection in the water as the Komodo Dragon drew near. She thought, "Something is seriously wrong with the Magus."

The band and their significant others had settled in at the Baron's mansion in Bel Air. Miranda had insisted Delilah fly down with them as their guard panther. But the large feline hated flying and was a little grumpy. Des took her out to the swimming pool and threw beach balls to her. She destroyed three before he said, "Enough, girl. Come on, and I'll get you a treat."

Des led her to the kitchen and pulled a meaty cow bone out of the fridge. Delilah sat up and swiped at it. Des let it go quickly. "Hey, watch it. You know better than that."

Sig watched her take the bone out through the oversized cat door. "I can't help but think she should be free on the Savannah stalking antelope."

Des explained, "She was a kitten when Dad saved her from a poacher. The mom had been killed, and she was left an orphan. He knew she wouldn't be able to survive in the wild alone. So, he decided to raise her. That was 40 years ago. Mom jokes she's the only female that Dad has stayed with longer than her."

Sig looked perplexed. "I didn't know that big cats lived that long."

Des sat on a stool beside her. "They normally don't. Dad periodically gives her a little of his blood. It keeps her healthy, and she ages more slowly. He does that for Tillie, Clive, and Jasper. They have been with him for a long time. The Magus does the same thing with some of his staff. I don't know for sure, but some of the other Haute Caste probably also do that. It's hard to find people to work for them that can deal with the whole vampire world thing."

Des grabbed a piece of Sig's cinnamon roll, and she snapped, "Hey! Get your own."

With his quick reflexes, he snatched his hand away before she could smack him, popped it in his mouth, and smirked.

"Jerk! Why doesn't he do that for your mom?"

"Because of her vampire DNA, she is already healthier and ages more slowly than normal mortals, but that only goes so far. Several times over the years, Dad gave her blood to help her recover from injuries and slow her aging. Now she refuses to take it anymore. She can be incredibly stubborn. I get that she doesn't want to transform, but, for some reason, she is determined to die of old age like any mortal." Talking about his mother's decision upset him, and he went silent. He got up and grabbed a mug of coffee.

"That has to be hard for you guys. And for your poor dad. I mean, he's so powerful, and he'll have to let her go."

Des turned away from Sig and blinked back tears. "We have more vamp DNA than she does, but we still don't know how slowly we will age. I don't get it. Who would want to get old and die except her? None of us have a burning desire to transform, either. It's fucked up that we have to choose."

"You're telling me." She came up behind Des, wrapping her arms around his waist. She said, "I'm beginning to understand how my vampire wannabe crusade must be hard for you. I'm sorry." He turned and kissed her gently. It didn't take long for the kiss to grow in intensity. Caught up in the moment, he picked Sig up and laid her on the kitchen table. Des leaned over her, trying to unfasten his jeans as she started taking off her T-shirt. Before they could accomplish that, Loretta and Jacques walked into the kitchen.

The younger brother said, "Dude, we eat on that table."

Loretta chimed in, "There are a dozen bedrooms in this place. Control yourselves." Behind Jacques' back, she gave Sig a thumbs up.

Tillie walked in, ready to fix breakfast, and noticed them straightening their clothes. She was used to their antics, ignored it, and asked, "Anyone want some eggs, bacon, and bangers?"

"Sig scrunched up her face in confusion and asked, "What are bangers?"

Des laughed and said, "Sausages."

"Thanks, Tillie. Maybe later."

Tillie shook her head. "You're like the offspring. Now let me get to cooking." She pointed to the doorway. "All of you, out of my kitchen."

That afternoon the Cringe and their partners gathered in the living room where the furniture had been pushed aside for the band equipment.

Tomas started going over the plan. "We're only playing two songs. No requests. Nothing they expect. I want to play 'Rage!' at the end."

Loretta spoke up. "We've been working on something. Let's do one cover song for the finale."

Tomas started to object, then Leif raised his hands. "You have to listen to something. We've been practicing."

"We?" Des looked around.

Sig, Phoebe, Loretta, and Leif stood. They followed Loretta's lead and sang a Capella to the entire band's astonishment. It was the perfect song for that night, and they harmonized beautifully.

Marie picked up her drumsticks and added a beat, Jacques started playing the melody on his keyboard, and Des came in with a bass line. Tomas picked up his guitar, layering riffs to increase the intensity of the music. They all joined in on the chorus filling the room with the song. At the end of the song, they were quiet for a second then Jacques began applauding. "Killed it!"

Tomas smiled. "Oh yeah, we're definitely doing that." He high-fived Loretta. "And then we'll give the Magus what he asked for."

Chapter 25

Night's a Beach

At the Rooftop Lounge in Laguna Beach, Lady Amelia approached a man sitting at the end of the bar. The smell of mortal blood on an empty stomach was annoying. It wouldn't take much to entice one of the males that watched her move through the lounge in a short black dress and high-heeled sandals.

She came up behind the man who had invited her and whispered, "I want to bite someone."

"Manners." Sir Angel turned to face her. "I have a table outside on the deck."

They sat by the edge of the rooftop bar, looking out on the dark sea. It wasn't cold, but the outdoor heaters were turned on as Southern Californians tended to complain when it fell to 60 degrees. A server brought them two glasses of Cabernet then Sir Angel surreptitiously topped them off with O positive from a flask.

Between sips, Lady Amelia asked, "So why did you want to meet like this?"

His eyes swept her pleasing features. Long, black hair framed Amy's lovely dark eyes and fell about her graceful neck. "You're back in the Magus' good graces. What happened?"

"He wants me to witness his victory over the offspring. The Magus thinks my presence will annoy Loretta and Jacques. He doesn't realize I'm grateful to them for letting me have a relationship with Alejandro. I wouldn't do anything to harm them."

"You're not afraid of the Magus' temper?"

166

"My son is my priority. If I arouse the Magus' anger, I'll deal with it." She finished her drink. "You brought me all the way out here because you didn't want anyone to see us together? Why?"

"Since you mentioned arousal." He finished his drink before continuing. "Do you remember the first time we met at the club in Seattle, before you had been transformed?"

"Of course, you were the first vampire to pay attention to me." She watched him closely. "You let the others know I had HH blood and got me introduced to the Magus."

"And I killed that perv in Mirror Point who was stalking you."

"That was the first time I saw anyone draw blood. I never thanked you for protecting me."

A sad smile played on Sir Angel's lips. "Because I was Common Caste, and you were all about becoming a member of the Haute Caste." He paused, then said, "I have fancied you since the first night I saw you. Amy, you were completely blown away by our kind, and I feared taking advantage of you."

He reached across the table and gently stroked her hand. Her eyes narrowed as she said, "I thought you were pining away for Loretta. Everyone's heard that rumor."

"Like the ones about you having feelings for Jacques? Some desires must be left behind so we don't miss the delights that are truly possible for us."

Lady Amelia's voice became softer. "I don't know what to say. Now is not the time."

Sir Angel withdrew his hand. "You're still obsessed with the power of the Magus."

"I have to do everything I can to protect Ali."

"Keep telling yourself that. I'll see you at the Narcissus Club." He walked away quickly.

Lady Amelia stared out into the darkness. The server approached with the check. Lady Amelia handed over the money with a grin and thought, "Total Angel move to stiff me."

An hour later, the Magus stood on the patio of his mansion overlooking Paradise Cove, looking up and contemplating the stars that were seemingly unchanged in his centuries of existence. The energy of the night flowed in his veins; the crisp ocean air invigorated him. He turned to his loyal visitors with a satisfied smile.

"Sir Borgia, Sir Raf, and Dr. Kyoto, what news do you bring?"

Sir Borgia's jeweled hands emphasized his response. "Our world eagerly awaits the subjugation of the Mordecai siblings."

Dr. Kyoto had a more restrained response. "I'm certain it will be a memorable evening."

Sir Raf stood and walked to the edge of the patio. He bore an anxious expression. "The Common Caste are skeptical you'll be successful. They believe the House of Sun is changing our society. The Mordecais give them the false hope that all vampires will gain the same privileged status."

Sir Borgia spat out, "Regardless of merit!"

Lady Amelia emerged from the house. "Good evening. Have I missed anything?"

The Magus glanced at Sir Raf. "Nothing worth repeating."

She saw Raf's discomfort and snickered. "Is there anything I can do to help with the preparations for the party?"

"Adorn yourself in the loveliest of gowns." The ruler of the night turned on the charm, and Lady Amelia feigned being receptive.

"Of course." She couldn't resist needling Sir Borgia. "Where is Lady Antoinella?" she asked with feigned innocence.

Sir Borgia bristled. "She is a guest of Lady Cassandra's tonight. Antoinella has a fondness for the great beasts."

"And Sir Hannibal? He'll be there as well, I presume." There was a mischievous gleam in her eyes.

"Yes, she is honored to be staying with both of the ancient ones, but the invitation was from the Seer." His tone was cold.

"Lady Amelia," the Magus warned, "do not antagonize my most loyal friend."

She moved back towards the house, "Of course not. If you'll excuse me, I have to make some wardrobe preparations for the event."

After the door closed, Sir Borgia said, "She does not merit the title of Haute Caste."

Dr. Kyoto replied, "Ah, but she meets the only requirement. The good fortune of being born with HH blood."

The Magus reluctantly conceded the point. "She struggles to balance her wild nature, ambition, and tenderness of heart. I find her intriguing and quite baffling."

Sir Borgia added, "And a troublemaker."

Dr. Kyoto smiled. "Yet we all find her appealing."

The Magus turned somber. "One can never truly trust a vampiress." Then he excused himself.

Lady Amelia was surprised when the Magus entered her guestroom without knocking. Trying to tease him, she asked, "Care to help me pick out shoes?"

The heat in his gaze began undressing her. "I want you now!"

She had once melted into his arms but not tonight. "As long as you promise to protect Alejandro from whatever you might do to the Mordecais. Then I will be yours every night."

"You would barter your passion?" He appeared amused by her nerve.

"I would do anything for my child. Having sex with you is more like a reward."

He drew her into his arms. Lady Amelia felt her body tingle in all the right places. Despite his narcissism, he was an unselfish lover. Vampires regard sex as recreation and try not to complicate it with emotional attachment. She knew many vampiresses would love to be in her place at that moment, but her thoughts drifted.

The Magus let his lips graze her neck. "Your mind gives you away, my dear." His ardor suddenly cooled. "You stand no chance with Jacques if that is who you are thinking of."

Lady Amelia took a breath and moved back. She saw the disapproval in his eyes. "Not Jacques. I know he is devoted to Loretta. I can't help but wonder if it is possible for me to find love like the Baron and Miranda have." She almost mentioned his failed attempts to woo Marie, but self-preservation prevailed.

"We are beyond those fairy tales. I remember how enthusiastic you were about your first kill. In time you will see how much alike we are." The Magus looked at her accusingly. "How could you ever imagine that I would hurt a child? Perhaps after the celebration at the club, you will be truly deserving of my passion again." He turned away and said, "Wear the Jimmy Choo heels. Good night."

Chapter 26

Family Matters

"They got married!" Loretta yelled excitedly. She read and reread the text message on her phone as the siblings played hockey in the mini-rink behind Tristan's Bel Air mansion. Delilah was startled by her loud outburst, and Des smacked Jacques in the head with a puck while he was distracted.

"I'll kill you!" Jacques said, blood running down his face as he skated towards his brother.

Tomas got between them. "Stop it! Let Sig look at your cut!"

Sig got out the first aid kit and started cleaning the wound.

Jacques barked at Des. "That was a dick move!"

"You'll be fine by the time we perform."

Jacques winced as Sig cleaned the cut. A normal mortal would have had a concussion, but the young Mordecais were 75% vampire, making them incredibly strong and resilient. Sig used a large bandage to cover up the gash on his temple. Fortunately, he'd heal quickly.

Jacques reached up and started to touch the dressing. Sig lightly slapped his arm and told him to leave it alone. He asked Loretta, "Who got married?"

Loretta was all smiles. "Dion and my auntie. They eloped in Las Vegas."

Sig cried out, "Oh my god! You're serious." Her uncle had never even been engaged before. He was a confirmed stubborn bachelor who devoted his life to running his burger joint and taking care of Sig.

Des looked confused. "Wow. I can't believe they got so serious. I mean, what's the point when you're that old."

Loretta gave him an icy stare. "They're in love."

"Yeah, but old people…."

Sig slapped the back of his head. "Be glad I don't have a hockey stick."

"Okay, okay." Des held his hands up in mock surrender.

Phoebe grinned. "There's this film, *Ripples in Time*, I saw in a psych class about seniors getting it on."

Tomas started laughing. "We'll get a copy for Des. If he could read."

Sig said, "He might be that old before he has sex again."

Jacques sat beside Loretta. "Tell Gloria and Dion we're all very happy for them—even Des."

"They said they are going to stop in Seattle the day after the show on their way home to see us. That means we have to leave right after the concert."

Jacques straightened his shoulders. "Sure, we can do that."

Marie took off her goalie mask and gloves. "Leif, can we manage that time frame?"

He thought for a moment. "We can do it, but remember, we can't fuck around during the performance. Rock the club, do the deed, then get out. That should get us back to Seattle by morning. You know we're all going to be anxious as hell to get to the grand finale anyway."

That night Des and Sig drove along the Pacific Coast in his dad's yellow Lamborghini. "This makes me think about when I first told you about my family."

The cool coastal air flowed around them as they sped along. "Right! That night we were driving this same highway." She stared at his brown wavy hair blowing in the wind. She leaned over and kissed his cheek.

He swerved a little. "Hey, watch it." After a quiet moment, he said, "I knew that night I wanted you to be with me, I mean—really with me."

"No matter what?"

"No matter what!"

"It's funny that Loretta was your devoted fan at the beginning. That night she convinced me to see the Cringe play, then she noticed Jacques."

"And you fell for the lead singer." He wiggled his eyebrows.

"Not at first. I thought you were an egotistical jerk." She crossed her arms.

"But to know me…."

"…is to be sure you are." She punched his shoulder.

"I'll give you my autograph anytime, baby."

171

She pointed. "Hey, pull into that parking lot along the beach." They parked in a dark corner of the lot where some seagulls were hanging out by a dumpster. "There's no one around. C'mon, in the water!" She ran from the car, ripped off her T-shirt and jeans, and didn't stop until she was knee-deep in the waves.

He ran in behind her, shedding clothes, and grabbed her waist. "I love your crazy ass!"

"Marry me!" she yelled. A wave almost knocked them over.

"You finally asked."

They embraced, and he gave her a long, intense kiss as an even bigger wave sent them sprawling on the beach. They came up gasping for air with his hands still on her breasts. She pushed his hands away and said, "Dude, I like you groping me, but someone's stealing the car."

"What the fuck!" he sputtered and turned to see their car pulling out onto the highway. He was about to run when another wave crashed over them.

They got to their feet and waded out of the water. Sig put her arms around him. "Let's not waste the moment. You can't outrun a Lamborghini. I'm sure you'll get the car back, but this night will only happen once."

Des pushed her wet hair away from her intense eyes. "You're perfect."

Practical, even at the most intimate times, Sig grabbed their dry clothes and made a no-sand zone for their lovemaking. They lay down, pulling at their undergarments to free their bodies. His lips teased her nipples, and she felt his stiff cock press against her thigh. Des touched the soft wet folds that held her clitoris until he found the pearl of pleasure.

"Yes," she gasped. Her hands began massaging the length of his shaft.

They kissed hard, their mouths seeking to own the other. The scent of their bodies mingled with the ocean air blocking out the world as they entered the depths of passion. For a short, sweet time, nothing else existed.

She gasped, "Now!" and guided his cock, and he thrust inside her. Again and again, she lifted her hips to meet him. He pleasured her clitoris with each thrust. The waves crashed, the gulls cried out, and they collapsed in a state of sensual bliss.

After a few minutes, Des sat up, straddling her. His expression was full of sleepy delight. He bent down, kissed her breasts, then stood. His phone rang as he handed Sig her T-shirt.

He pulled the phone out of his jeans. "What's up, Clive?"

"The Highway Patrol called. It seems someone was joy riding in your father's car. I believe they were going 120 miles per hour."

"That's a relief they caught 'em. We went for a walk on the beach, and when we got back, someone had stolen it." Sig started laughing, and Des frantically

172

waved with his free hand to get her to stop. "Can you get Leif or someone to pick us up? I'll text our location."

The old butler discretely asked, "Will you need dry clothes?"

"What? No. We're fine. We just need a ride."

"As you wish, Desmon." He ended the call, but Des was sure he heard a chuckle before he hung up.

They finished getting dressed and sat on a cement bench under a light, away from the dumpster. "Damn it, Tomas and Marie will never let me forget this." He saw an old van parked at the far end of the lot. "I bet whoever took the car was in that."

"Well, they had a good time for a little while. Will your dad be pissed?"

He put his arm around her shoulders. "You're cold." Des kissed her forehead. "With us around, Dad is kind of used to things happening to his stuff." He laughed. "Remember when we got in a brawl and tore up the ice rink?"

Sig touched his cheek. "You are all such brats. I've got a serious question; don't get mad."

"Is this about marrying you? I meant that."

"No, but for some insane reason, I meant that too. I wondered, while we were having sex, did you feel the urge to bite me?"

He took a breath and stared out at the ocean. "I promised to be honest with you. "Yes."

Des returned his gaze to her and saw love in Sig's eyes. "It's okay, baby. I felt your fangs when we kissed. I wouldn't mind a little bite."

His mood suddenly darkened. "This is not a game! I won't be like them."

With perfect timing, the Baron's Bentley glided into the parking lot with Leif at the wheel. Marie jumped out and picked up on Desmon's anger. "Beach Party gone wrong?"

"Let's get out of here." He climbed into the back without waiting for Sig. Marie hugged Sig. "You okay?"

"Fine! We had a good time for a little while." Looking at Des, glowering in the backseat, she asked, "Can I sit in the front?"

"Sure." Marie got in the back with her brother and stared daggers at him.

He avoided her look and said, "Forget it. It's nothing."

Oblivious to the drama, Leif headed to the police station and said, "I got dibs on driving the Lamborghini home."

Next to the Mordecai mansion in Bel Air, Sir Jorge, Sir Franco, Alexander, and Angel met at the Baron's guest house. It had a sleek Scandinavian hardwood feel. The lack of antiques and priceless paintings that filled the main mansion made it seem like an odd place for the Haute Caste. The Baron made a ridiculously large offer to the owners several years ago to enable him to expand his home base.

They gathered in the living room. Sir Franco sat back on the blue leather couch and tried to avoid eye contact with Sir Alexander. Sir Jorge sat in a chair between his lover and the one-time ruler of the ancient world.

Angel sat on the other end of the couch and marveled at the jealousy and resentment that permeated the room. "You have to get over yourselves if we want to work together to help the offspring."

Alexander scoffed. "I have no axe to grind. My only concern is for the Mordecais." His polychromatic eyes fell on Franco.

Jorge would never admit to his issues. "We settled our differences years ago. Now we must consider how to protect them when the program ends. What they have planned for the Magus will undoubtedly spark the Magus and his minions to anger, and they will want retribution."

"On a Biblical scale," Jorge said. "Let us each be responsible for the safety of one of them and their partner. I will take Marie and Leif."

Alexander was quick to say, "Jacques and Loretta."

Franco chose Tomas and Phoebe. That left Angel with Des and Sig.

A slight look of amusement came to Angel's face. "Wherever Des goes, there is chaos."

Alexander smiled, "Ah, but my descendent Sigourney is grounded and resourceful. She will be helpful if there is a snag."

Jorge shook his head. "Doesn't she spend every waking moment fighting the urge to become like us? Hardly stable."

The tension in the room went up a notch. "I have discussed her appreciation for our kind with Sig. I assure you she will not act impulsively."

Angel intervened. "Enough. Take it outside or focus. Come on, with the offspring, you know something will go sideways. How will we help them get safely out of the club when that happens?

Franco said, "Angel, that is where your close association with the servers will be useful. Isn't Carmen still in charge of the staff?"

Franco's tone was condescending, but all Angel said was, "Yes."

Franco continued, "Perhaps you can use your influence with them to side with us."

"I've already worked that angle. We won't know for sure if they'll side with us until shit starts going down." Angel asked, "Where the hell is Sir Batu?"

Alexander replied, "There is an issue with the House of Cups. A Mongolian prisoner escaped from Princess Khunbish, perhaps with help, and may be headed this way. He's trying to track them down so they don't complicate our efforts."

"Very well," Jorge crossed his arms. "We'll fill him in later and assign him to back us up. I'm concerned Leif may go berserker with his newfound abilities. Sir Henry said he'll take care of any flames Leif might let loose."

They continued discussing escape routes and alliances that might be beneficial to the offspring.

Once plans had been finalized, Angel said, "It's good so many vampires resent the Magus. The brilliant godfather of the undead has no sense of how to stay in power besides using fear."

Alexander said sadly, "Yes, I had a little experience with that. Despite our differences, I can only hope it is not too late for him."

Chapter 27

The City of Angel

"What are you doing here?" A voice whispered, making Lady Jacquotte jump.

Angel silently slipped from the shadows of a shipping container at the harbor. The pirate cocked her head toward a group of men standing beside an expensive Mercedes parked alongside an open shipping container. In the dim light, they could make out several women cowering inside. "My vampire duty. I found Anatoly on the Worthy Target list. He is the well-dressed one and is trafficking those young immigrant women. He forces them to cooperate by threatening to report them to immigration. He has taken away all their IDs and has them with stacks of cash from his operation in the trunk of his car. He is the slime of the earth." They watched the man in an expensive suit gesturing and apparently giving instructions to the dock workers.

"Ah, but you haven't asked permission." He put a hand on her shoulder.

She didn't refute his accusation. Angel's scent and presence were alluring; she allowed his touch. Jacquotte whispered, "Would you deny a visitor a bit of nourishing amusement? I'd ask the Magus, but he's obsessing about his grand event."

"Is he even speaking to you? Actually, this is House of Sun territory. You should get Miranda's permission first."

"I don't believe she would have a problem if this lowlife was dealt with."

Angel bent close to her ear. "Probably not. Why don't we share."

Her eyes narrowed. "Fine, but I get the first taste."

"Of course. You take the Russian, and I'll take care of his help."

Alright, follow my lead." Lady Jacquotte moved silently, with vampiric speed. She appeared, seemingly out of nowhere, behind Anatoly. "Excuse me," she said and pulled a cigarette case from her vest pocket. "Do any of you gentlemen have a light?"

Anatoly was short, broad-shouldered, and probably weighed 300 pounds. He wore a custom designer suit and had large gaudy rings on both hands. His men started to move toward the intruder. He looked her over carefully and signaled for them to stay back. "Are you lost? Not a good place for a woman alone. It's a lucky thing you found me."

As he approached, she began to let her succubus powers of attraction loose. Not only did Anatoly's eyes light up with increased interest, but the dock workers began to follow him.

The criminal assumed she was a prostitute. He pulled out a lighter, and his fat lips formed into a smile. "Come work for me. I make you rich."

She leaned in close, lit her cigarette, then blew smoke in his face. He leered at her and reached out a hand to grab her. Before he could touch her, Jacquotte clamped her hand around his wrist. He screamed as she easily twisted his arm. There was a loud snap as his arm broke, and she threw him to the ground. She kicked him in the head, rendering him unconscious.

The swift assault threw the workers into a panic. Angel approached them, threw up his arms, and yelled, "Boo!" They quickly ran away and disappeared into the stacks of containers. Angel stood and watched their retreat, amused by their lack of loyalty. He went over to the open cargo container and told the women inside that everything would be alright, and they were free to go. He walked to the Russian's car and opened the trunk. He pulled out a duffle bag containing the women's IDs and a good deal of cash. He handed the bag to one of the shocked women. "You all can leave now, but you should all hire a lawyer."

The women stood for a moment in shock. The one holding the duffle bag said to Angel, "I don't know how to thank you."

Angel replied, "There is no need to thank me. I'm sorry this happened to you." He took a business card from his wallet and said, "Call this lawyer and tell him Angel said to take care of you."

The women murmured thanks and then, with the money and IDs, ran off into the night.

While Angel dealt with the women, Lady Jacquotte had dropped to one knee, pulled Anatoly's head up by the hair, and sank her fangs into his neck. She drank greedily, then stood and wiped her mouth with a lace handkerchief and called to Angel, "I saved you a little."

Angel effortlessly lifted the bulky, heavy body and bit the other side of the dead man's throat. He loved the sensation of his fangs tearing into flesh. He swallowed a few times, then dropped the body and turned to the vampiress, casually leaning against a container. "You didn't leave much."

She burped. "Sorry. But he was A, my fav type, besides HH."

Angel pulled a folding knife out of his pocket, slashed Anatoly's throat to cover the fang marks, then took his wallet and jewelry to make it look like a robbery gone wrong. "Let's get out of here. I'll show you my city." He was tired of pining for unavailable women.

She was drifting on a blood high. "Sure, Sir Angel. Thanks for not getting in the way of my dinner."

They drove up to the top of Mulholland Drive and parked at an overlook. Thousands of lights spread out below. The moon played peek-a-boo with some clouds. He wanted to touch her but refrained, unsure if she would use her abilities on him.

Jacquotte smiled. "Nice touch handing over Anatoly's cash to the women. What was the business card you gave them?"

"A lawyer friend of mine. He works pro bono for anyone I refer to him. I paid for his law school. You never know when a lawyer might come in handy."

"You're hard to figure out. Never expected you to be so benevolent."

"I have my moments. But I'm feeling less than saintly now." His eyes showed appreciation for her beauty. "But I'm not sure what price I'll have to pay."

She moved closer. "I used my succubus ability to suppress Anatoly's suspicion and allowed me to get so close. It takes several hours to build my power back up." With a lecherous grin, she added, "You're safe—for now."

He started to place a hand on her cheek, then pulled back. "I find it hard to trust you. No offense intended."

"None taken, but I'm telling the truth." She looked into his soft brown eyes, then lowered her eyes to his red-stained lips. Jacquotte slowly leaned closer until their mouths collided, Angel responding to her passion. The pressure from his body bent her back against the window. His hands worked to pull down her bustier. She rubbed his cock through his pants while trying to undo his zipper. His hardness excited her as his tongue teased her neck.

A loud knocking on the window made them jerk to sitting positions.

Angel mumbled, "Crap." He quickly straightened his clothes and looked at the scowling policewoman staring through the window. She made a "roll the window down" motion. He opened his window, smiled, and politely said, "Good evening, officer."

A second police officer slowly approached the passenger side of the car. Jacquotte rolled down her window, smiled at him, and used her vampiress charm to calm him.

The policewoman bent down, shined her flashlight into the car to get a good look at both of them and check the back seat. "Keep one hand on the dash, slowly take out your wallet, and show me your license and registration."

"Sure, no problem." He did what was requested.

She took his documents, said, "Stay in your vehicle," and walked back to the patrol car.

The other officer stayed near the car, keeping a close eye on the couple. Jacquotte smiled at him and asked, "What is the matter? I'm here visiting, and my friend was showing me the view. Surely that does not pose a danger to the public."

Feeling a strange attraction to Jacquotte, the officer cautiously took a step back and said, "Sorry, ma'am, but we often find some underage drinking going on up here."

Her eyes got big, and she fluttered her eyelids. "I'll take that as a compliment, but I haven't touched alcohol in years."

Angel sank down in his seat and tried not to laugh.

The policewomen returned. "Here's your license Mr. Camarillo. I would suggest not parking here. There's been an uptick of criminal activity and carjackings at night."

"No problem, officer, we'll be going."

The police officers returned to their vehicle, waiting for Angel and Jacquotte to leave. As they drove away, Jacquotte asked, "Mr. Camarillo?"

"It's the name of a city famous for a now-defunct State Hospital. They locked up a vampire years ago. It didn't go well for the hospital staff." He smiled. "One of my favorite aliases."

She reached over and touched his cheek. "I'm sorry we were interrupted."

"Me too. I better get you back to the Marina Del Rey before sunrise." He turned on the ignition.

"How do you know where I'm staying?"

"Jacquotte, this is my city. I've got friends and informants everywhere." He turned the car around and headed back to the road.

"Like Carmen at the club. Thanks for looking out for me, but I hate owing a debt to anyone."

He smiled. "Forget about it."

"You're not holding onto leverage? What has happened to the vampire world?"

Angel replied, "The freakin' House of Sun."

Batu's phone had been blowing up with texts from Princess Khunbish and Miranda, both anxious for news. He was at the airport checking incoming flights that originated or connected with flights from Mongolia. It was his second night keeping watch at the airport. He thanked the gods that one of the people he searched for was a vampire, making it easier to spot them in the throng of mortals. He hoped Chang and the mortal had not split up to elude detection.

In his last text to Miranda, Batu assured her that protecting the offspring was his priority. Then the frustrated vampire texted the Princess that he was doing everything possible to find Chang and the escaped prisoner. He was tired of his vigil at the airport, leaned against a wall, took a sip from his flask, then replaced it in his pocket. The people coming out of arrivals were a mix of many cultures but few Mongols. It was midnight, and Chang would have had to carefully protect himself against the sunlight seeping in through cabin windows during the long flight.

Two women dressed in burkas, one tall and one short, passed quickly by him. Batu sniffed the air and smiled. He followed them through the airport, ducking behind passengers every time the shorter one looked back.

When they stopped by a line of taxis, he quickly came up behind them and grabbed both their arms. Chang and Odgerel struggled against him. He whispered, "I don't want to shed blood at the airport." When the taxi driver raised his eyebrows at the commotion, Batu asked, "Have you ever had to deal with two wives?"

The driver shook his head and turned away to take the next fare.

"Come with me, so we can figure out what is in all of our best interests."

Chang said, "Let's go with him. I must find shelter and nourishment. Let's not do anything to make our situation worse."

The petite Mongol tried to pull away from Batu. "Fine! But keep your hands off of me."

Batu let go of her arm, and they walked to the parking garage. Chang and Odgerel pulled the coverings from their faces and heads. Chang asked, "How did you know it was us?"

Batu touched his nose. "I would recognize your scent a mile away."

Odgerel anxiously wrapped her arms around her chest. "What are you going to do with us?"

"Honestly, I couldn't give a rat's ass about you, but the Princess and the Baroness are not happy you're here." He opened the door of a rental van. "I'm taking you to the Baron's guest house, and if you don't do anything stupid, you'll be safe there. But I'm betting you'll ignore what I just told you."

She insisted, "We've come to see the Magus."

Batu scowled and said, "You couldn't even wait until we left the airport. I thought you were the bright one. Don't even talk to me until we get to the house." He mumbled something in Mongolian as he slid the door shut.

Chang whispered, "He switches to your tongue when he is very angry." He leaned back in the seat, crossed his arms, and said nothing more.

She whispered, "We must find the one with power."

Batu called back. "You'll wish you stayed in Choibalsan."

Chapter 28

Vampires Without Borders

Los Angeles had not seen such an influx of the undead in ages. Hotel suites in five-star hotels were being filled by guests who demanded not to be disturbed during the day. The most loyal of the Haute Caste, Sir Raf, Dr. Kyoto, Lady Amelia, Sir Borgia, and Lady Antoinella, had been invited to stay at the Magus' estate where he could keep a close eye on them. They all gathered in the living room of the Magus' mansion.

"Did you enjoy your stay at the refuge?" The ruler of the undead inquired of Lady Antoinella.

She smiled as though it had been a mere recreational visit and leaned back on the couch. "It was delightful to be around such amazing creatures. I was impressed by how well they are cared for."

Sir Borgia moved beside her and touched her hand. "You seem refreshed."

She pulled her hands away to his dismay, stood, and went to the fireplace as though desiring warmth though the room was quite comfortable. "I might visit there again."

Lady Sarah walked in with Sir Ruben trailing behind. "Good evening. Thank you, dear Magus, for the accommodations at the Fairmont Hotel."

"You're most welcome, Lady Sarah." The Magus shifted his attention to Sir Ruben. "Tell me about the online response to our gathering tomorrow."

Ruben nervously swallowed, then plopped down on the couch right next to Sir Borgia. Borgia, obviously not pleased being so close to Ruben, unsubtly moved over. "Well, there are two camps. Those who think it's time the Mordecais should conform to our society's social norms and act like they belong in our world. Then there are those that think they should continue as they have been doing." Ruben knew the powerful ruler would not be pleased with the latter, and he waited for the backlash.

In a cold tone, the Magus inquired, "And how is our world split?"

"About evenly."

Lady Sarah interjected, "For my brother, I'm sure it's more about gambling than conviction." She found a leather chair next to Dr. Kyoto and gracefully seated herself.

Lady Antoinella did not let her amusement show as the Magus balled his hands into fists. She said, "Please excuse me. I need to make sure all my luggage has arrived and unpack. Good night."

She left as the Magus railed, "They are idiots to bet against me, against the future of our kind."

The Congolese House of Wands had made their own arrangements. Lady Kananga had leased a house on the beach in Malibu for two weeks, though she envisioned a much shorter stay. Her knights, Sam and Kabedi, made arrangements for daytime security while she sat on the back deck, looking out at the waves glimmering in the moonlight. She received a text from Lady Cassandra.

All is as planned. Sir Omar is ready for us.

She texted back.

Then we shall proceed.

Memories of her long history with the Magus skipped from the night he transformed her to their trysts over the centuries. She had always enjoyed his intellectual and physical company until recently. Darkness born of resentment had overcome his judgment as he tried to stop the Mordecai family, his own creation. His current path strayed from the code that had enabled their kind to survive and flourish. Lady Kananga blinked rapidly to stop her tears as the reality of what they had planned for the Magus pained her heart. As painful as it would be, she knew something had to be done to protect their society. She wiped her eyes, gaining composure before anyone could see her sadness. She shook her head and uttered, "He is such a magnificent vampire."

Sam stepped out onto the deck. "Did you say something?"

"No, nothing." She managed a smile.

They had been intimate for several years. He tenderly took her hands, and she rose. "Mbuyi Kananga, I know you too well. Let me help ease your burden." Their lips touched lightly at first, then his arms pulled her to him, and she allowed a deep, slow kiss.

She leaned back and stared at his handsome face and soft brown eyes. "Hopefully, we will create a power shift that will bring about a new sense of community for our kind." Lady Kananga raised her hand to his cheek. "And Sir Sam will not be an empty title as you will be given the same respect as those with HH blood."

"I appreciate the honor, but as time goes by, it becomes less important what others call me, as long as you allow me to be your knight and lover."

They embraced again, and he easily lifted and backed her up against a wall. "Now!" she cried. Lady Kananga pulled her dress up as his cock became free of his pants. He kissed her neck, letting his fangs tease the spot where her artery pulsed. She took his cock with one hand, stroking it and guiding it to her pleasure center. Sir Sam thrust into her as Lady Kananga's fangs found his neck. Her bite released the pain-to-pleasure response vampires adored.

He moaned, "My love."

With all her control, she released his throat, reeling from the hit of blood. "Harder!" she demanded as he continued to enter her. With each thrust, their breathing quickened. The exquisite tension of their building climax was almost unbearable. He rubbed her hardening nipples. She gasped, and his lips teased her neck.

His fangs penetrated Kananga's throat at the excruciating moment of climax. Her HH blood gave him an energy-packed sensuous meltdown. Sam collapsed against her, and they slid down to the deck. He pulled back, breathless, and lay beside her. Kananga rested her head on his chest. He was not the most gifted lover, but his enthusiasm made up for that. "I'm glad you take your pleasure so seriously, Sir Sam."

At a four-star hotel near the Narcissus club, Common Caste from several houses congregated in the bar. A vampiress with long purple hair and black leather garments sat alone. Sophia was the only member of Sir Borgia's house allowed to come because he considered the other Common Caste untrustworthy. There were some vampires from the House of Arrows, some chic New York

showed up for the House of Plows, and a few vampires dripping in diamonds from Africa representing the House of Wands, but there was no representation from the House of Cups or Sir Omar's House of Swords. Sophia had heard they were on the outs with the Magus, like the House of Sun.

"There she is," a man in a bowler and vest walked over, accompanied by another in a fine black suit. He doffed his hat and greeted her. "Good evening, Sophia from London town."

"Bug off." She had her eyes on a flirty female from the House of Arrows.

"Name's Billy, and this is Robert."

Robert quietly said to her, "Lady Kananga asked that we have a word with you."

"You blokes don't appear to be from her House."

Billy said, "You could call us emissaries."

Sophia saw their serious expressions. She took note of the gathering nearby and said, "Right. But not here."

They followed her to a back corner table away from the other undead. Robert sat across from her and began. "Lady Kananga believes you're an ethical vampiress. She wanted you to know that whatever might happen at the concert, it will be for the stability and progress of our kind."

"Could you be more specific?" She looked from one to the other.

After a moment of silence, Billy advised, "No matter how down and dirty things may appear, it would be best if you didn't intervene."

"I'm of the House of Pentacles." She sat up straighter.

Billy smirked. "And Sir Borgia doesn't give a shit what happens to you or the other Common Caste."

Sophia flipped her hair over her shoulder and leaned towards them. "Who are you to talk about Sir Borgia?"

"I'm Sir Billy, and he's Sir Robert. Though we do not have HH blood, we've been elevated to Haute Caste status. I don't suppose Sir Borgia ever mentioned that possibility to you."

She hung her head, looking dejected. After thinking about it for a moment, she blew out a breath and said, "Well fuck me if you're Haute Caste. After all my centuries of being a loyal toady to the Lord of Pentacles, I'm a glorified nothing."

Robert laid on the Southern charm. "Darlin', I've been around that pompous ass long enough to know he probably feels threatened by someone of your intellect and beauty. Lady Kananga will reward you for simply staying neutral." He glanced around the room and added, "We'll be going now so as not to keep you from finding a sweet distraction tonight."

After they left, Sophia sat quietly, lost in thought. Sir Borgia barely acknowledged her existence. "Bollocks!" she shoved back from the table and returned to the bar scene.

At the Narcissus Club, the Magus arrived to check on preparations for his planned glorious display of power over the vampire world. Those most loyal to the House of Sun would hear about the amazing event they were not invited to. Rumors of his ability to make the Mordecai offspring fall into line would shore up his control of their world. When the undead witnessed the unruly part-vampires allowing him to take their blood for his research, they would give the proper respect to him again.

Sitting in a chair in the main room, he pictured Dr. Kyoto drawing the offspring's blood as they stood in a line on the stage, as though doing penance. Leif would be last with instructions from the Magus to jab him harder than the others. The ruler of the night had prepared a gracious speech about showing mercy to those who had opposed him if they repented and asked forgiveness on bended knee.

Lady Jacquotte approached him with apprehension. "Magus, I got word you wanted to see me."

"Yes," he replied, then called out, "Sir Raf!"

Raf emerged from the kitchen, where he was ordering the workers about. "What do you need?"

The Magus gestured for him to come close. Raf nodded to Lady Jacquotte but gave no greeting.

"I have an enjoyable task for both of you. If you succeed, I shall forgive both of your lapses of judgment." He waited for them to respond.

They both mumbled versions of willingness to do his will. The Magus touched Sir Raf's shoulder. "Tomorrow night, I wish you to get the attention of Phoebe in a way that will anger Tomas. Keep him fuming during the performance. I wish his jealousy and lack of control to be on display."

Raf looked pleased with his assignment. "I look forward to performing that task."

Jacquotte had a bad feeling about what was coming next. The Magus addressed her with an icy glance. "You will use your blood connection and succubus charm to draw Leif to you in front of Marie."

She shrugged. "That's all you want?" Jacquotte was careful not to say what she would do. "I thought you might want me to start an orgy with the band."

"Leif will be enough." The Magus stood and walked through the exit.

When he was out of earshot, Jacquotte said, "Fucker."

Raf's eyes lit up. "Do tell."

She wanted to vent. "He set me up with the Day Fanger before, not knowing if his blood was toxic. It turned out we were compatible, but I don't want to press my luck."

"Or piss off the Baroness."

"Yeah, that too." She gave him a hard look. "You're not concerned with making enemies of the Mordecais?"

He lowered his voice as the staff was arranging chairs near them. "I fear the Magus more, and you should too. Anyway, I have unfinished business with Phoebe."

"Well, Raf, you'll regret listening to your prideful dick. I shouldn't care what happens to you, but you're one of the ancients. Try thinking like one. Good evening."

Lady Jacquotte had one stop to make before returning to her schooner at the harbor. The pirate could not shake the feeling of impending disaster. Though not one to steer clear of chaos, the Magus' blind need for revenge was making her nervous. She'd have her crew be ready to leave at a moment's notice.

Chapter 29

Meanwhile...

Hannibal complained as he carried Casandra's luggage into their weekend getaway house in Venice Beach. "Did you pack one of the baby elephants?"

She merely smiled and called out, "Hello! We're here."

A young androgenous looking, Asian vampire with short blond hair emerged from one of the bedrooms.

Hannibal took in the stranger, turned to Cassandra, and demanded, "Who is this? I thought we agreed to keep our plans to our select group."

Cassandra and the stranger burst out in laughter. The stranger told the Seer, "It worked better than I had hoped."

"So, you really don't recognize our good friend, Lady Lily?" Hannibal looked confused, and Cassandra laughed again, then explained, "The House of Cups wasn't invited to the Magus' party, and Lady Lily is out of favor with him due to her support of the House of Sun. Since she has a central role in our plans, we decided a disguise for her would be in order. Lady Anastasia used her gift to alter Lily's appearance temporarily."

Hannibal did not hide his disapproval. "I hope when this change wears off, you'll grow your hair out again."

Cassandra regarded his overalls. "Ignore him. He has the fashion sense of a turnip. You look fabulous, and hopefully, the Magus will not recognize you until it's over."

Always focused on the task, Lily asked, "Do you have it?"

188

Cassandra pulled a small wooden box out of her tapestry shoulder bag. "I'm sure it will be enough."

Lily carefully withdrew a vial from the box. "It must work. The drug cocktail I'm preparing would take down Godzilla."

Hannibal said, "Remind me never to upset either of you." He paused, trying to find a way to correct his earlier faux pas, added, "Your hair looks very modern."

Lily smiled. "Nice try."

Cassandra embraced Lily. "We would not be able to attempt this without your help. Thank you for being willing to stand with us against the Magus to save our kind and help the Mordecais. I realize this must be difficult for you."

Lily bowed her head slightly. "They are our future. It is an honor."

Hannibal frowned. "But you'll be opposing Dr. Kyoto as well. I know you were inseparable in the past."

"He would not recognize me now. And I am not only speaking of my appearance." She took Cassandra's box containing a small glass vial and headed back to her room.

A knock on the door surprised Lady Casandra. She was not expecting any more guests until the next night. She checked the peephole in the door and saw an old acquaintance.

She opened the door and gestured for the visitor to enter. "Lady Jacquotte, please come in."

She followed Jacquotte into the small living room. Hannibal warned. "Don't try your charms on me again!" He abruptly turned away and left the room.

Lady Jacquotte snickered. "Fun times on the bayou."

"Not to be inhospitable, but the sun will rise in a couple of hours. Would you care to tell me why you've come?"

"Lady Cassandra, I know you've disapproved of my behavior at times, but I hope you can put that aside. I'm worried about the Magus. To be frank, I think he's lost his mind when it comes to the Mordecais. We need him to regain control of his judgment and vision. He has kept our society safe for centuries, but his current loss of control is troubling."

"I'm listening." Lady Cassandra crossed her arms.

"My intuition tells me something is going on besides whatever the royal offspring are planning for tomorrow night." Before Cassandra could respond, Jacquotte raised a hand and said, "I am not asking for the details, but the Magus has a secret I am willing to share with you. I hope that information might help all of us." She handed a folded piece of paper to the Seer. "An old wound that needs attention."

Lady Cassandra took the note and read it. "I always had my suspicions, but being a direct descendent of the Magus' blood has blocked me from seeing his hidden world. I will consider what you've shared with me." She lightly touched Lady Jacquotte's arm. "Thank you for risking his wrath." Then her eyes lit up. "You should consider a visit to Key West soon."

"Not to worry, I have already made my plans. Goodnight, Lady Cassandra." As she left, Jacquotte wondered how she knew her next destination. "Freakin' psychic," she muttered.

At the House of Sun compound in Granite Falls, Miranda sat in the living room watching in amusement as Alejandro conned Benny out of one of Guillaume's chocolate chip cookies. Wendell happily played with his dinosaur toys ignoring his brother's antics.

"Ali, give it back to him. You already had enough." She shook her head.

"I'm hungry." He was about to jam it in his mouth when, with vampire-like quickness, she took the cookie from him, surprising Benny.

"Grandma!" Ali's lip started to curl up.

"You just ate three. Dinner will be in an hour. Go help Grigoryi in the kitchen."

"Not sorry," he mumbled.

Miranda using her "I'm disappointed in you" mom voice, said, "Alejandro!"

He pouted, looked at his feet, then said, "Okay, I'm sorry," and headed to the kitchen.

Miranda grinned and handed the cookie back to their guest. "He reminds me more of Alexander than Jacques. Sharing is a very difficult concept for him."

Benny shook his head. "Seriously."

"You don't have to be so nice to the kids. We aren't going to send you away because you tell our little tyrant no."

Benny looked a little embarrassed. "Is it that obvious? I feel like I don't deserve to be here. I'll understand if you want me to go."

"Not gonna happen." She hugged Benny, smiled, and said, "We've all sort of adopted you. There is no going back now."

He teared up a little, wiped his eyes, then asked, "You don't have to worry about me. You've got enough going on. Have you heard from anyone in L.A.?"

She pulled Wendell and his triceratops onto her lap. "It's quiet for now. They are getting ready for the show." She smiled at her grandson. "We have a lot of allies, all sworn to keep the kids safe, but there's a lot I've been kept in the dark about. It's not easy to trust Lithuanians."

Benny, looking puzzled, asked, "Lithuanians?"

With all the current stress, Miranda laughed for the first time in days and explained, "Tristan was born in Lithuania. When the kids were little, we called vampires Lithuanians until they were old enough to understand the truth. They started calling them that around outsiders to make things easier."

Miranda kissed the top of Wendell's head. "He deserves a more normal family."

Benny quietly said, "I think this family is amazing."

Wendell looked at Benny's cookie and declared, "Triceratops hungry."

Benny burst out laughing. "Is it okay?"

Miranda waved her hand and said, "Fine, but only give him half."

"Thanks, Benny." Wendell smiled and held the treat up to his dinosaur before devouring it.

Miranda said, "Now go help your brother in the kitchen."

He scampered off as she turned to Benny. "For a very long time, some of the more ancient Haute Caste have viewed the Common Caste as servant-class vamps. Now the vampire world is going through a power struggle. It began when I was born. I am half vampire but still a mortal. When I married the Baron, I was given the prestige of the ruling class. Some of the Common Caste were angry about that and that they had remained second-class citizens. At first, there was a lot of resentment towards me and the kids. Over time we've won many of them over, and their resentment turned to the Magus. I'm hoping they will stand with us when the Cringe tells off his highness."

"After everything you all have done for me, I wish there was some way I could help them."

A crash sounded in the kitchen. River could be heard yelling, "Ali, stop it!" Then Grigoryi spouted off in Italian.

Miranda said, "I think you've got enough to do here."

Tomas was coming back from the mini hockey rink when he saw a short woman peering into a kitchen window. He quietly approached her unnoticed. "What do you want?"

Startled, she jumped back and turned, ready to fight or flee. Tomas blocked her path but didn't seem threatening to her, so she explained, "Leif. I must talk to Leif."

191

He raised his hands to show he meant no harm. "You're the Mongolian woman Batu talked about. It's cool, as long as you don't want to harm any of us."

Her stance relaxed. His dark eyes and calm voice reassured her, and she took a step closer. "I don't want to hurt anyone. I don't trust Chang or Batu, but I believe Leif will tell me the truth."

"Okay. Follow me." He turned his back on her and went through the back door, hoping she would keep her word.

He led her to the kitchen, where Leif was eating a very rare roast beef sandwich. Surprised to see her in Tristan's mansion, he swallowed, trying not to choke. "Hey Odgerel, I heard you made it here. Why do you want to be around more vampires?"

The room was tense as she moved next to Leif. Tomas tried not to laugh when he noticed Tilly pick up a butcher knife. The new and improved Leif would not need any help, but it was a sweet gesture.

"Chang said you have the mark of the witch. Is that true?"

"He wasn't lying. I hate to take my shirt off for women, but just this once." He pulled off his T-shirt and displayed his dragon brand.

She gasped and raised her hand to gently touch the mark with her fingertips. "Unbelievable."

Frustrated, Leif said, "Why does everyone say that?"

"Do you two want a room?" Marie quipped from the doorway.

Leif pulled back and put his shirt on. "This is Chang's friend, Odgerel. We met once while I was staying with Princess Khunbish."

The Mongolian addressed Marie. "I mean no disrespect. I had to know if it was true. He has been honored by the witch, so I must pledge my loyalty to him. This is a sign. I wanted to meet the Magus, but no more. Now I will follow Leif."

Tomas laughed and said, "Be careful! You might end up following him off a cliff."

Leif took Marie's hand. His eyes pleaded for mercy.

Marie realized they were all waiting for her response. "Okay. We'll figure out something." She added coldly, "Odgerel, don't even think of touching him again. Got it?"

Odgerel was startled by the implied threat. "You're his woman?"

Leif said, "She is the love of my life."

Marie smiled at Leif. "Sometimes, somehow, you manage to say the right thing." To everyone's relief, that broke the tension.

Tomas gestured for Odgerel to sit down at the table, but she remained standing. He asked, "You don't want to return to Mongolia?"

"I have nothing there since Batu and Chang killed my employer. No future and little money." She looked around. "I was living in a two-room apartment with another, above a café where we worked."

Marie said, "Go back to the guest house. You can trust Sir Batu. He's one of the good guys."

Leif added, "And don't forget, whatever Batu says goes."

She bowed respectfully. "Because you say so, I will listen to Sir Batu. Thank you, Leif."

Tomas said, "I'll walk you back over there. It's almost sundown, and they should be up soon."

Marie pulled Leif into the dining room, out of Tilly's hearing. She put her hands up, cradling his face. He leaned down and kissed her gently. She let go and said, "You have to grow up, Leif. This new power is not something to play with. You've got fuckin' devotees now. I don't think she'll be the only one to follow you."

"But you'll always be the center of my world." They kissed again, and he started to move his hands lower, but she pushed him back.

"Many of the Common Caste, and now a Mongolian mortal is looking to you for guidance. You didn't want this bullshit, but it's your fate. You can't ever let anger make you act against what you know is right. Promise me that. No matter what the Magus or others do."

"I promise." He whispered, "But it's awesome, right? I mean, there's a team Leif out there."

Maire blew out a short breath in exasperation. "Awesome! And tell your new follower to keep her hands off you."

He grinned. "I'll tell her you're the only one who can touch my dragon."

"You're such an asshole."

The Magus arrived at Lady Pomp's hotel to make a last-minute request. A wave of confidence rolled off him as he swept into her suite. "Lady Pomp, so glad you were able to come. I hope these accommodations suit your needs."

She straightened her little black dress and adjusted her pearls. "Yes, dear Magus, the accommodations are fine. I will have the maid lay out my gown for the fete."

She came forward, and he kissed her cheek, avoiding her mouth. Surprised and a little perturbed, Lady Pomp asked, "Is all going well?"

"Yes. The offspring have promised to give me their blood in front of representatives of our world. Finally, they will admit my dominance." He smiled. "I have a small task for you."

"Anything, mon cher. What is it?"

"I recall that Des was attracted to you when he was younger. Would you tease his libido at the club in front of Sigourney, his girlfriend? That should cause some friction between the lovebirds."

She gave him a small nod. "Very well, but I would rather please you with my gifts. They are wasted on such an inexperienced mortal." Her history of pleasing a king made his request somewhat odious to her.

The Magus replied, "Not tonight, but perhaps another time when our society has returned to its former glory. As always, I appreciate your loyalty."

Chapter 30

Anxiety Rising

Tristan sat beside Miranda on the back deck, watching the moonlight reflected on the constantly moving river. He tenderly pulled her against him, putting his arm around his love's shoulders.

She touched his cheek. "I know it would be more comfy inside, but the sound of the rushing water is soothing.

"Miranda, everything will be alright. Our Haute Caste allies will ensure their safety."

She shivered, but it wasn't from the cold. "I think you're right, but the guilt is overwhelming. I feel like I should be there."

"Have our children asked for either of us to help them?"

"No, and that worries me even more. They are so full of themselves sometimes. Who knows how that bastard will react?" She turned towards him. "The Magus' obsession to dominate us has caused him to lose sight of everything else."

"You're not wrong. Though she has always been a close ally of his, Lady Kananga has grown concerned, and she is not alone. The eldest members of our world understand how his instability jeopardizes our entire world. They will act to save our society at the right moment. Our society has survived many threats over the centuries, and we have learned not to act rashly. Have a little faith in vampires for once," he admonished her.

"You think I should be like that Mongolian chick, who is now pledging to serve Leif? How crazy is that? Marie texted me, and she's afraid that Odgerel and some of the Common Caste wanting to follow him is going to his head."

"I am troubled by the powers given to Leif. His primal reactions and impulsiveness are troublesome. He only became more problematic after visiting Mongolia. We must take on the challenge of educating and guiding him. Loving acceptance and trying to protect Leif is not enough."

"You're looking at a woman who had kids by three different vampires. I think I'll leave the lessons in self-discipline to you and Alexander."

Tristan smiled in a rare show of emotion and said, "I would never want you to change." Tristan nuzzled her neck. "I love your scent."

"Seriously? The kids are facing down the Magus, and all you want to do is fuck?"

"Yes." He pulled her into an encompassing embrace and kissed her long and hard. When he released her, he said, "I'd appreciate it if you pledged yourself to me."

She snapped, "I'd rather be thrown in the river than say I belonged to anyone."

"As you wish." He scooped her up and started walking toward the riverbank.

Miranda, ineffectually, started pounding his chest with her fists, yelling, "Stop it! It was only a figure of speech."

He reached the riverbank and held her over the water. Hearing Miranda's yells, Grigoryi, Guillaume, and Benny came running toward them from the house.

"Put me down!"

"Certainly."

She looked down at the flowing water and felt his grip on her begin to loosen. She yelled, "On the ground! Put me on the ground!"

Tristan turned to her would-be rescuers and said, "Everything is fine. I'm just helping the Baroness relax and take her focus off the children."

Benny saw the others trying not to laugh and said, "I think it worked."

The three helpers returned to the house, and Tristan slowly lowered Miranda to the pebbled bank of the river. "Better?"

She straightened her clothes and shoved him hard, though he barely moved. "Idiot!"

Tilly had fixed an early dinner for the offspring before the big event consisting of filet mignon, stuffed baked potatoes, and Cesar salads. She even made a chocolate and strawberry cheesecake. Phoebe was now a vegetarian, saying it somehow helped her deal with hanging out with vampires. So, their "chef" also had grilled veggie burgers.

They all sat around the dining room table. They were all nervous about the upcoming confrontation. Except for Leif, no one had much of an appetite. It was unusual to see the offspring not devouring their food. Tilly, sounding concerned, asked, "Should I call the Baroness?"

Des quickly responded, "No! Thanks for all this, Tilly. We'll probably be starving when we get back after the show."

Tomas added, "It's just pre-performance jitters."

Leif burped. "Tilly, the steak is fantastic."

Marie shook her head. "Sometimes I can't believe you eat like a teenage boy."

Tilly, feeling relieved, went back into the kitchen.

Sig, all business said, "Okay, let's go over the plan one more time before we get our goth on for the undead hordes."

Des complained, "Again? We've been over this a dozen times."

Jacques said, "She's right, we've got this one chance, and we better not mess it up. Tomas, go over everyone's part in the plan."

Marie poked Leif. "Pay attention. No winging it tonight."

"Okay, whatever." He turned his attention back to his plate and started chowing down on the potatoes. "So good."

Phoebe crossed her arms. "Focus, dude!"

Despite the seriousness of the moment, they broke out in laughter. Leif said, "What?"

Loretta demanded, "Put down your eating utensils and pay attention before I get that Mongol witch to give you an ass-whooping."

Leif winced. "Sorry. I'm serious as a heart attack about tonight. I get so hungry. Like all the time."

Marie leaned over and kissed his cheek. "We know. Okay, so let's go over it again."

At his Paradise Cove mansion, the Magus regarded the contents of his walk-in closet like he was perusing paintings at a gallery. He turned to his new butler, "Nothing here is quite right for the occasion. Pierre, I desire a more contemporary look."

The older Frenchman had once worked for a clothing designer. "Of course, sir. Might I suggest leather pants and a silk shirt, untucked."

He frowned. "I don't want to emulate the Cringe."

The butler pulled up pictures of celebrities on his phone until he found one of a movie star advertising cologne. "If I might say so, this look would be appealing. A bit wild and seductive."

The Magus took the phone, studied the picture, then nodded. "Yes. Purchase three similar outfits, and I will choose between them."

The Magus excused the butler with a wave of his hand. Never had he been so concerned about appearance. A finely tailored suit that flattered his build and Italian shoes were his usual look for such an affair, but he suspected that held no appeal for Marie.

He raked a hand through his dark locks and suddenly felt foolish. The young woman had shared an intimate evening with him. She knew exactly what was hidden under his clothes. The ruler of the undead wondered why he felt so apprehensive. He sank in a tufted velvet chair beside his shoe collection. The thought she would continue to reject his advances made him wince.

"Damn, Marie."

The Magus walked out on his patio and gazed at the moonlit coast below. He wished he was spending this beautiful evening with the young baroness. The thought that she would choose Leif over him was a wound that did not heal. He recalled how Marie had expressed her appreciation of his lovemaking when she thought the Magus was unconscious. Recalling her words, the night he had tasted the offspring's blood kept his hope alive. He knew she had feelings for him despite her protestations.

The butler stepped into the garden with a crystal glass of blood on a small silver platter. "Dinner sir?"

The Magus took the glass and waited for the servant to leave. Then he raised it to the dark sky. "I drink to Jacques de Molay, whose descendants are a royal but welcome pain in my side."

Sir Ruben called from the doorway. "Magus, I can't find anything unusual about the Cringe performance this weekend. They seem to be going along with your demands."

Without regarding Sir Ruben, the Magus replied, "I doubt that very much."

Carmen was directing her crew to finish the final touches to the club. Angel came over dressed in a fine black suit and dark purple shirt. She smiled at him. "Lookin' good, homeboy."

His serious expression did not change. "Thanks." Then he whispered, "How supportive are your staff of the current regime?"

She spoke softly with a twinkle in her eyes, "Loyal until we're not loyal. You know, the king is dead. Long live the queen! Or something like that."

He held up a thumb drive loaded with and set to play one song. "One of the Cringe will signal you to play this on the P.A. system at the end of their second song. Would you do that?"

"No problem." Her brow furrowed. "What are you up to?"

"After tonight, I might be gone for a while. I've got Magus drama burnout. Your crew is going to need a strong leader. Don't fail them."

"You're starting to give me the creeps. Are you skipping town? It's either a woman or some heavy shit going down tonight. Thanks for the heads-up, but...," she gestured to the Common Caste crew, "we got this. Always have and always will. Fuck the elites."

A meeting of the Haute Caste conspirators was taking place at the house at Venice Beach. All cell phones had been left behind or disabled. They had to ensure the utmost security and prevent any chance of surveillance by the Magus. Lady Kananga, Lady Lily, Lady Antoinella, Lady Cassandra, and Sir Hannibal gathered in the living room.

After half an hour of lively debate, Lady Kananga raised a hand to silence them. "Enough! Do we have a consensus of who shall be the interim leader of the vampire world?"

Sir Hannibal cleared his throat. "Yes. I now believe that is the best choice. I must admit, I first thought I would be the better option."

Lady Antoinella concurred. "Lady Lily, your idea is brilliant. I also wanted to be considered for that honor, but now I see you have proposed the best solution."

Lady Cassandra took a deep breath. "I shall be the messenger. I'll leave as soon as we have completed our task."

Sir Hannibal's eyes narrowed. "You believe they will agree?"

Lady Cassandra asked, "You doubt my powers of persuasion?"

He quickly shook his head. "Not at all."

Lady Kananga addressed the group. "We'll rendezvous at the club. Tonight, we make history."

Sir Hannibal grumbled, "One way or another."

Chapter 31

What a Night

"Lady Amelia, you look stunning," Sir Borgia purred as he took her hand and gently kissed it in a courtly fashion.

She felt the passion behind his touch and pulled away as her gut became uneasy with his praise. "Thank you, Sir Cesare. Please excuse me." She headed to the far side of the ballroom.

Sir Borgia watched her go with a perplexed expression. Antoinella regarded the interaction from a few feet away. She was glad that Amy had the sense not to be seduced by her lover. She had once thought the moon rose on his words, but now she could barely stand his subservient attitude to the Magus. "What a waste of his power and intelligence," she thought. She knew that being the bastard son of a powerful pope motivated Cesare to want the approval of the most ancient vampire.

Amy found Angel at the back entrance. "I've never seen you so dressed up before. I'm impressed."

"Sorry if that's what impresses you." His tone was cold.

"Look, I didn't mean to be rude to you at the restaurant. I only want to do what's best for my kid." She was hoping for understanding and empathy: anything but his disdain.

"Good luck with that. I have to help set up for the performance." He leaned closer and whispered. "You might want to stay far from the stage." Then he walked out.

"What are they planning?" she muttered. Amy considered how much she'd paid for her little black leather dress and decided to follow his advice.

Amy noticed dozens of vampires in the main room that she'd never seen before. Most seemed to be Common Caste, and we're trying to get the attention of Sir Cesare, Lady Sarah, Sir Ruben, and Dr. Kyoto. She thought it was funny how Sir Ruben ignored everyone while busily texting on his phone.

Amy walked up to him. "What are the odds the Magus gets want he wants tonight?"

Ruben looked around, then whispered, "The smart money is on the Mordecais."

She shook her head. "I hope for your sake the Magus doesn't find out you are betting against him. I am sure your sister wouldn't be too happy either."

"What they don't know makes me rich."

Amy noticed Lady Kananga at the entrance. "I wasn't sure anyone from the House of Wands would show up."

Ruben said, "I'd never bet against her."

Lady Kananga entered with her knights, Sir Sam and Lady Kabedi. The attention of the assembled vampires turned to the new arrivals. A minute later, Amy spotted Lady Cassandra wearing a simple purple robe reminiscent of a priestess. As she approached the Seer, the Common Caste began to crowd around them.

"Lady Cassandra, I hope you've seen a positive outcome for this night's activities."

The famed Seer spoke coldly, "We all play the parts we must. That is all I will say."

Before Amy could respond, Cassandra turned to walk away. The throng of Common Caste parted, giving the Seer a clear passage. Amy's attention was drawn to the arrival of Sir Jorge and Sir Franco. Amy mused aloud, "Now, if Sir Batu arrives with the band, almost every house except the House of Swords will be here to witness the event, which is exactly what the Magus wants. I guess Sir Omar and Lady Anastasia didn't want to be here to see the offspring surrender to the Magus."

Everyone would notice their absence at this historic event. They had fallen out of favor with the ruler of the nocturnal world because of their allegiance to the House of Sun. There was no way to know how Amy's loyalty might be judged after tonight.

When the offspring arrived, the noise from the gathering crowd increased. Loretta's hand trembled as she handed an equipment bag to Jacques. "Hey, Lolo, it's okay. We got this." He gestured for her to have a seat behind his keyboard. "Do you need anything?"

She looked unhappy. "I need this to be over so we can get back to the kids."

"I miss them too. "Funny, I thought it would be good to have a break, but it turns out not so much."

Marie nudged Jacques. "Hey, Raf just showed up. Keep an eye on Tomas."

Jacques walked over to Tomas and Des, trying to block the sight of Raf as he approached Phoebe. Trying to sound casual, he said, "Be sure the guns are within reach."

"Yeah, bro, we know." Des plugged his guitar into the amp.

Tomas' stare went past Jacques. "What the fuck!"

Jacques put a hand on his arm. "C'mon, trust Phoebe. Let her handle him."

Des immediately grasped the situation and called out, "Hey Phoebe, Sig needs some help with the microphones."

Phoebe smiled back at them. "In a minute." She pulled on the sleeves of her favorite Castlevania hoodie and looked straight at Raf. "You are nothing but a troublemaker. You don't care for anyone but yourself. Sad."

He tried to reach out, but she avoided his grasp. "Very well. But remember that a night does not go by that I don't think of the time you came to my bed in the hotel and we…."

"Did nothing. Because you're an asshole." She turned abruptly and went to help Sig with the equipment.

Des smiled at Tomas. "Phoebe's only into you. Give her more credit."

Tomas stared down Raf, who seemed unaffected by the threat the Mordecai's eldest son's stare conveyed. Before things could escalate, Franco and Jorge walked up to the Magus' minion and put a hand on his shoulder.

"Sir Raf." Franco cleared his throat. "Perhaps you should set your attention on someone as shallow as yourself. Ah, there's Lady Pomp."

Jorge added, "And we will erase your existence if you cause harm to Phoebe. She is under our protection like the rest of the offspring." He moved right in Raf's face. "And it will be two to one. We never fight fair."

"And your headless body will never be found," Franco assured Raf. "Though it will be rumored it is somewhere in the Amazon."

Raf struggled to look smug. "You've spent so much time devising my demise. Too bad you'll never be able to carry out your plan. But I'll be sure to inform the Magus."

Franco laughed, which further shook Raf's composure. "It's not as though the Magus would lose any sleep if you suddenly disappeared."

Des stepped outside to get away from the tension in the club. He took a deep breath and expelled it slowly. A familiar perfume got his attention.

"Good evening, Desmon. It has been too long." Pomp came up beside him. She held out her hand, and he almost took it, but self-preservation made Des step back.

"Yes, it has. You look good, I guess. How's France?" He was still attracted to her smile and the way her long blonde, perfectly curled hair stopped at the top of a revealing neckline. "Same old Pomp," he thought.

"Paris is too noisy, but out in the country, it is still wonderful. You should come and visit me. Perhaps come for a weekend?" She stepped closer and touched his arm. He began feeling a sense of attraction drowning out his caution. He would've died for attention from her when he was a teenager. "I could take you on a special after-hours tour of Versailles."

"Des, you're needed inside!" Sig called from the doorway. She stood with her arms crossed, ready to take on Pomp. "Stay away from him!"

Des said loud enough so that Sig would hear, "You should find someone else to invite to the home of the guillotine."

He winked at Sig and tried to pull her inside, but she resisted.

Pomp flashed her fangs. "If only you were a vampiress, you might have a chance to keep him."

Before Sig could respond, Angel stepped out of the shadows and ordered, "Everyone inside. Now! Except you, Pomp." After the mortals went in, Angel admonished the French aristocrat. "Seducing a mortal to make the Magus happy? How far you've fallen from being the favorite of a king."

Pomp scoffed. "I have the full confidence of the Magus."

"Ah, but you failed him tonight. I wonder how much Ruben will pay me for this juicy bit of gossip."

Her eyebrows raised. "No! You would not dare."

"You have no idea what I would dare. It would be best for you not to stick around, Pomp." Angel didn't wait for her to respond, turned, and headed back into the club.

"Merde!" She stomped her high heels and clenched her fists. Pomp pulled her phone out of a hidden pocket in her dress. "Get the jet ready! We leave for Paris as soon as possible." She did not want to incur the Baron's wrath if she persisted in pursuing Des. Pomp decided to leave before anyone got a chance to humiliate her further.

Des went back into the club and saw Marie was adjusting her drums. He realized that he needed to focus, grabbed his guitar, and started tuning it.

Just as Marie was satisfied with her drum kit, she heard her name whispered from the stage wing. She looked over and was surprised to see Lady Jacquotte.

She checked to see where Leif was, to be sure he was safe. Then she walked over, keeping her eyes fixed on the pirate. "What do you want?"

Jacquotte raised her hands in a show of peace, then spoke softly. "I'm trying to keep my promise to yer mother and also not get in any more trouble with the Magus. He'll be here in a few minutes, and I have to put on a show for him. I am supposed to make it look like I'm having fun with your man. Give me a minute alone with Leif when the almighty vamp arrives. After that, I'll be sailing far away from you all."

She gave the pirate the "evil eye." "You got a lot of nerve. Why should I care if the Magus is pissed at you?"

"Because if you don't help me, I might have to break my word." Her eyes pleaded with the young woman.

Marie's lips got tight. "No succubus power!"

"None. I swear. It'll be just like I'm talking to you right now."

"Then you promise to leave?".

Jacquotte spoke in a serious tone, "I swear on my dead mother's grave."

"She's probably undead, but you better keep your word."

Marie went over to Leif, who was killing a bag of nacho chips. "You need to talk to the pirate when the Magus shows up. Pretend that you're into her. We don't want to suspect that his scheme is going off track. She'll leave once the Magus sees you two hanging out. She gave her word to not use her powers on you and to go far away after it's done. It'll be worth it. Can you handle that?"

He looked at her a little suspiciously and said, "Sure. But this means you can't be pissed about it later."

She kissed him. "I won't."

Commotion at the entrance signaled the Magus was about to enter. Leif walked over to Lady Jacquotte and stiffly stood a foot away. Sir Jorge began to approach them, but Marie warned him off.

Leif put his hands in his pockets as she moved closer. "Shit. I hate it, but I still want you."

The vampiress felt the same attraction due to their blood connection. His shirtless vest displayed his brawn and a bit of the dragon tattoo. She tamped down the sexual attraction, which was triggering her succubus nature. He didn't need to be any more excited by her.

Leif burped nacho fumes. That helped cool Jacquotte's ardor.

The Magus strolled in wearing a glistening dark suit and was seated near the stage in an overstuffed chair. Sir Cesare, Lady Antoinella, Dr. Kyoto, and Lady Sarah stood by him like courtiers vying for attention.

His eyes landed on Leif and Lady Jacquotte. She whispered to Leif, "We're on."

Leif grabbed Jacquotte and kissed her passionately. There was no doubt they both were into it. Then Marie ran over and pulled him off the vampiress. Lady Jacquotte ran out through the back of the club with a smile. "Damn!" she exclaimed. As soon as the door closed behind her, she stopped and bent over, catching her breath.

She heard clapping and turned around to see Angel. He said, "You'd deserve an Oscar, but I don't think you were acting."

Lady Jacquotte came up to him and put a finger to his lips. "That's something Marie doesn't need to know."

His hard expression softened. "You're getting soft. You care about the offspring as well."

"Blasphemy. I only care about myself," she said a bit unconvincingly.

A car pulled up, driven by one of her crew. Angel called out as she got in, "Liar."

Marie was relieved the drama with Jacquotte was over, at least for the time being, slugged Leif in the shoulder.

He chuckled. "I thought you wouldn't be mad. It had to look real."

She put her hands on his cheeks. "You're not that good an actor." They kissed, and she shoved him away. "The worst part is that she's ruined pirate movies for me."

Leif thought, "Not for me." But he kept it to himself.

"Fuck her. Get over here and help me with the drums."

Chapter 32

Unbelievable

The house lights dimmed in the club; then, a spotlight illuminated the Magus. In her Morticia finery, Sig rounded up all the band members and their significant others. The eyeliner, sexy goth clothes, and rebellious glares gave them a dangerous vibe that the vamps adored. They were gathered in the center of the stage, whispering.

Marie said, "He's already targeted Leif, Des, and Tomas by sending his loyalists to mess with us. Whatever happens, we can't be distracted from our main objective. Got it?"

They all nodded. Jacques put his arm around Loretta. "Stay close, baby."

"Always." She smiled back.

Leif said, "I can't wait to scare the crap out of him."

Phoebe straightened a rainbow unicorn pin on the lapel of her black jacket. "We'll be lucky to mess up his suit."

Tomas said, "Whatever happens, leave everything behind and run for the limo when it's over. I mean it, Leif. Don't fuck around."

Leif put his hands up. "No problem."

Des said, "We're doing this for Mom, Ali, River, and Wendell. It's time that royal dick learns he can't manipulate us."

Sig shouted, "Cringe!"

The others roared, "Cringe!" and then moved to their spots on the stage.

Lady Kananga and Lady Lily were off to the side near the Magus, deep in conversation. Suddenly a man ran thru the crowd to the ancient leader and threw himself at his feet. "Master, you cannot trust them!" Chang gestured to the stage. Gasps could be heard from the crowd.

The Magus rose and began laughing. "What makes you think I trust anyone? Chang, I remember when you tried to help Sir Alexander unseat me. It is not as if I need your advice." He signaled to Sophia and another Common Caste vampire standing off to the side. "Take him to the kitchen where he might be useful and keep him there." He looked towards the back of the ballroom and called out, "Lady Amelia, please join me."

She reluctantly came forward in her little black dress that flattered her in every way. He glanced at Jacques to see if he was watching, then pulled Lady Amelia into his arms. Jacques' hands became fists against the keyboard. Alexander approached Jacques from the rear of the stage and whispered, "Don't let him play you. Think of Loretta and let this go."

Whispers from the crowd filled the room as the Magus kissed Amelia. Keeping his arm around her, he called to the Cringe, "Play!"

Des stood in the center of the stage with Tomas to his left and Jacques behind his keyboard on Des' right. Marie was behind her drums on the platform to the rear of the stage. Their significant others stood off to the side. Des smiled broadly and acknowledged the audience, which was made up mainly of Common Caste vampires. "Good evening, all you nocturnal maniacs! This number is called Rage!"

The crowd applauded as the Cringe filled the club with passionate anger while the Magus watched the stage as though bored. Des gestured towards the audience as he sang, pulling them in closer. Sig, Phoebe, and Loretta stepped forward and began throwing Mardi Gras beads. Loretta purposely hit the Magus on the head with a few strands. Amy took them off him, and he pretended to ignore the incident.

The crowd caught the beads while gyrating to the loud primal beat. They layered the colorful plastic beads with their jewels over slinky evening gowns and tight suits. The crowd was into the rebellious feeling of the music.

Lady Kananga and Lady Lily inched up behind the Magus. After having been an intimate partner with Lily for many years, Dr. Kyoto quickly saw through Lady Lily's disguise and started to make his way over to her. She saw him approaching her and quickly disappeared behind the stage, and he followed, yelling, "Wait!"

Lady Lily gave him a bitter smile and ran out the back door. Dr. Kyoto followed and looked around the parking lot, but she was gone. This did not bode well for the Magus. There could only be one reason for her disguise. He should have tried to warn the Magus, but after seeing his treatment of Chang, he decided to leave the party rather than take sides in the battle. He hoped Lady Lily would realize that he had not betrayed her. Kyoto took one last look around and departed.

When Des sang the line in the song, "Fuck all the vampires!" the crowd erupted with delight, and everyone showed off their fangs. Lady Kananga was relieved when Lady Lily reappeared. Lady Cassandra made her way to Sir Henry and said, "Buckle your seatbelt. The Haute Caste conspirators are about to act."

Henry, always concerned about Leif's poor self-control, came up behind him and shouted over the music, "Be careful, Leif!"

Sir Henry moved to the side of the stage where he could have a clear view of the club. There were ruling-class vampires surrounding the Magus, and it appeared their smug leader thought he was surrounded by loyalists. Powerful confidence emanated from him. In his arrogance, he didn't sense anything amiss.

As the first song ended, the Magus stood. "Enough! I will have what was promised."

Des was not about to be intimidated. He spoke directly to the ruler of the night. "One more song, and then we'll give you the blood you deserve." He turned to Sig and winked. All the significant others drew close to their lovers on stage for the second number. Des scanned the audience. "No matter our blood type, we belong, just like all of you."

Loretta surprised the crowd when she started singing "Because the Night," and the band joined in acapella. Their strong, clear voices enthralled the audience. They added guitars, drums, and keyboard as the others began to sing with them. Soon the crowd joined in and filled the room with the power of the popular song. The servers from the kitchen came out, and Carmen patted Angel on the back.

Raf moved beside Angel and said, "I fear the momentum in the room is not going the way the Magus expected."

Angel said sarcastically, "That's too bad."

The song ended with Loretta and Jacques kissing. The room became quiet, all attention on the stage as everyone expected to witness the offspring finally submit to the Magus.

The Magus called out, "Dr. Kyoto!" When his ally did not appear, he searched the crowd and grew angry when he did not find Kyoto.

Des signaled to Carmen and yelled, "Now!"

"Ballroom Blitz" blasted on the club speakers confusing the crowd. The offspring pulled Super Soakers out of their equipment cases and began firing at the Magus. Streams of blood hit him from four different angles. The crowd screamed and ran, afraid of what the Mordecai blood might do to them. With incredible speed, the Magus leaped on stage, headed straight to Leif, and clutched his throat. Marie reached down, grabbed her stool, and hit the Magus in the back.

Before Sir Henry could intervene, Leif pushed the Magus away, raised his arms, and flames shot out, engulfing the Magus. He staggered back, on fire.

"Damn it, Leif!" Tomas cried. He dragged the Magus to the edge of the stage and pushed him into the reflecting pool. He had never felt so conflicted in his life. He yelled at his siblings, "We gotta go!" He took Phoebe's hand, and they all ran off the stage and out of the club.

Lady Sarah, covered in Super Soaker spray, got to the Magus first. She was relieved to see his face was barely touched by the fire. Lady Kananga, Lady Lily, and Sir Borgia came next, helping the Magus climb out of the pool. He looked like a wet charred rat. The ground began to tremble. Lady Antoinella got between Sir Borgia and his ruler, while Lady Lily and Lady Kananga swiftly injected the charred vampire with a combination of Marie's blood and a powerful animal tranquilizer.

Lady Sarah cried out, "What are you doing?"

The Magus glared at them. "Traitors!" He struggled for a moment then his strength and ability to speak were gone. The trembling ground quieted. Lady Kananga's knights got to him before he collapsed.

Sir Borgia pushed Lady Antoinella aside, grabbed Lady Lily shaking her, and shouted, "How dare you?"

Lady Sarah came to his side and said, "Get control of yourself. Others are watching." She tried to appear serene despite the fact she was covered in blood.

Sir Borgia noticed the kitchen staff crowding around them. He released Lily and asked, "What is the meaning of this?"

Lady Kananga signaled to her aides to carry the Magus away, then said to Sir Borgia. "We are saving the vampire world by keeping our founder from self-destructing."

Some of the kitchen staff cheered as the Magus was carried out. Sir Borgia gave them a hateful glare, and they disappeared before Borgia could take any action against them.

Lady Antoinella said, "Cesare, this is for the best. You will see. The Magus will be well cared for while he regains his sanity and judgment. No harm will come to him."

Raf ran over to the exit as the Magus was being taken out. He pulled out a silver knife and advanced toward Lady Kabedi and Sir Sam. "Let him go!"

A fireball hit him from behind! He shrieked and tore off his jacket before the flames burned him. Sir Henry grinned. "You have no idea how long I've waited to do that. Just a little payback from me for the snake attack."

Raf snarled and said, "One night, Henry, I will see you squirm."

A shuriken Japanese throwing star pierced his thigh. "Fuck!" He reached down and pulled it out as blood ran down his leg.

With cold anger in her voice, Lady Teri said, "Never, ever threaten my love."

Raf stopped himself from responding, then limped across the club to exit through the kitchen. Sir Henry and Lady Teri followed the House of Wands' aides and assisted them as they strapped the Magus to a gurney in a van for transportation to the airport.

Lady Lily and Lady Kananga promptly got in the vehicle to oversee his transport. They would ensure he stayed sedated until the Magus was secured in Lady Kananga's private jet.

Lady Lily scrunched her nose. "We'll wash him soon and get him out of those ruined clothes. What is wrong with the blood splattered on him? It has a disgusting odor."

Sir Henry replied, "The offspring mixed a little of their plasma with Hollywood movie blood. They kept their word, but I don't think he'll appreciate that when he realizes what happened." He bowed to Lady Lily and Lady Kananga, "You're doing a great service for our kind. I wish you well."

"I was never totally convinced this would work," Lady Lily said as Henry closed the van doors.

The offspring's Limo sped away several minutes before the van left with the Magus. Everyone was leaving the venue, eager to give eyewitness reports to their houses. Sir Ruben approached Lady Teri and Sir Henry in the parking lot. "That was wild! Where are they taking him?"

Sir Henry said, "To a place where he can heal. He has invisible wounds that need tending. If you start placing bets, I will wager that he will return a wiser, more restrained leader in time."

Vampires heading away from the club slowed down to look at the trio. Ruben ignored them and said, "No one can believe the Magus was taken down before he could demolish the building. When I felt it start to shake, I thought it was all over. That was epic! The Mordecais pulled it off. Even I wouldn't have bet that they would have been able to take down the Magus." He fingered his Mardi Gras beads. "Let the good times roll."

Lady Teri asked, "Will you and your sister return to Toronto now?"

He shrugged. "Yeah, well, it seems Lady Antoinella is off to visit Sir Hann at the elephant sanctuary. Sir Borgia's world is shaken, and he needs my sister to comfort his bruised ego. I think I'll stick around here for a little while and help redecorate the club. But I have to say, that was the best rock concert ever! It ended in total chaos and social upheaval." He pointed to the red stains on his Ramones T-shirt. "I'll probably never wash this. So where is the Cringe playing next?"

Sir Henry raised his brows. "With the Magus, at least temporarily not in command, shouldn't you be worried about who will rule our world in the interim?"

Ruben smiled and said, "Nah, rulers come and go, but rock and vampires never die."

In the Narcissus Club kitchen, Carmen was yelling at the clean-up crew. "Everyone, help yourself to blood and raw sirloin. After everything that happened tonight you all deserve it!"

She smiled at Angel. "Did you know how this was going to go down ahead of time?"

He shook his head and leaned against a counter. "I knew something was planned. but I had no idea what the details were. I'm not sure anyone expected a shitshow of this magnitude. It was historic. Tonight, will be talked about for years, no centuries to come. The offspring have earned the respect of the vampire world. I mean, how many of us haven't wanted to ruin the Magus' custom-tailored suit and set him on fire at one time or other?"

Carmen conceded. "It was something to see. But I'm sure his highness will be back sooner or later. So, where are you going?"

He finished off a cup of blood. "I'm thinking maybe Key West. The ratio of tourists to undead is appealing."

Carmen replied, "You are incorrigible."

Angel's attention was caught by Lady Amelia standing in the kitchen doorway. Carmen saw the look in Angel's eyes and headed out to the club to help with the clean-up.

"I just wanted to say goodbye," Amy said softly.

He moved closer and touched her cheek. "What's your plan?"

"I have to try to find the Magus. After what went down here, I need to show some loyalty to him so I can keep Alejandro safe. After tonight he'll probably be hell-bent on taking down the House of Sun. I wish things could be different," she said wistfully.

He backed away from a kiss as his emotions closed down. "You don't need to worry. The Mordecais and Sir Alexander will keep Alejandro safe. You should've figured that out by now. You're blinded by the Magus. You could do better than that ungrateful waste of vampire flesh." He paused and added, "I know I can do better."

Before she could respond, he was gone.

Chapter 33

Who Knew?

It was quiet at first as the limo got on the road, and their adrenaline rush began to fade. The offspring embraced their significant others, feeling the rush of having won a battle. Leif, being Leif, couldn't help himself. He held up his hands, showing them his palms and grinning. "I fried that bastard."

"That wasn't exactly according to the plan we agreed on, but, somehow it worked out okay anyway. Good job!" Marie kissed his cheek. "Your vest is singed." Her phone pinged, and she checked the incoming message. "Mom texted that she heard what happened at the club. Alexander filled her in on all the gory details. Said she's proud of us, but we should get our asses home."

Sig asked the question that was on all of their minds. "What the fuck happened with the Magus? We were ready to get out before he brought down the building, and then Lady Kananga and Lady Lily jumped on him. I didn't see what happened after that."

Leif stammered, "It was me! I think they were saving him from me."

"No love," Marie countered him. "I was sworn to secrecy and had to wait until it was over. Some of the Haute Caste abducted the Magus. They weakened him by injecting him with a little of my blood and tranqs. He's going away to be rehabilitated by some ancient bloodsuckers."

Tomas was upset with Marie. "Damn it, Marie. You should've let us know. I thought we were in this together."

Marie trying to calm Tomas down, explained, "I had to keep my word. When you make a promise to Lady Cassandra, you keep it."

Loretta chimed in, "I wouldn't want to piss off a Seer. We should be grateful they're all on our side."

Des asked, "Who else was in on it?"

Marie smiled. "I know Lady Antoinella, Lady Lily, Lady Kananga, and Sir Hannibal. But I think Lady Anastasia and our Grandpa are involved in it too. There were probably others."

Des rubbed his chin. "That makes sense. They'd have to take him somewhere far away from the loyal House of Pentacles. Somewhere secure and remote. I think Princess Khunbish needs to try to seem at least neutral. Sir Jorge and Sir Franco are all about taking care of their foster son, so that leaves the House of Wands and The House of Swords."

Jacques said, "I hope they lock him up for a hundred years."

Loretta hugged her husband. "I felt goosebumps when we sang "Because the Night." It was so dope when you opened fire on the Magus. You all rocked and shocked those vampires! They ran off like their hair was on fire, afraid of your blood. Can't we stay in the moment and celebrate our win!"

"Ruben was taking a video of us with his phone," Jacques told them. "I can't wait to see that. It will go viral on undead social media."

Leif said, "Hey! The Cringe made them cringe."

Groans and pleas for him to shut up only made Leif smile. He put his hand over his dragon mark. "That witch gave me the power to overcome the Magus. Call me the Dragon King."

"No! Marie, make him stop." Des drained his soda can and threw it at Leif.

Tomas shook his head. "The witch must have been off her game that day; it happens to the best of us. She probably confused you with Batu."

Leif huffed. "Jealousy is not a good look Tomas."

Loretta changed the subject before they started fighting. "Hey, what happened to Batu and Chang?"

Des said, "Batu was going to deal with him. We gave Chang shelter then that dick turned on us. Maybe we should give Chang a job cleaning at the Narcissus."

Sig said, "At least his little friend is all about following Leif. She'll stay loyal."

Marie frowned. "And we can't leave her here in L.A. Mom is going to love another guest."

Leif said, "No problem. I can teach her to help with the goats."

Phoebe was frank. "Goats? She's a human being. Find out what her hopes and dreams are. Help her become a legal immigrant with a work visa. Throwing flames is cool, but it doesn't make you a hero, like actually helping her would."

Loretta looked at Jacques. "This freakin' family. No sooner do we take down the Magus—okay with help—and after everything tonight, we're still arguing about crap. Can't we just feel gratitude for a minute?"

Jacques pulled her close. "House of Sun rocks!" He put up a hand, and they all high-fived. But Leif slapped Tomas' palm a little too hard.

Tomas said, "Damn! Leif, King of the goats."

Leif retorted. "King of the greatest of all time? I'll take it. Leif one hundred and the Magus zero!" With a flourish, he grabbed a bag of snacks and started eating with relish. "I saved this for my victory."

Des shook his head. "Flaming Hot Cheetos?"

Sig asked Marie, "It there any of that tranq left they used on the Magus?"

Once aboard the jet, Lady Lily and Lady Kabedi cleaned up the Magus as the medication slowly wore off. His fine suit was ruined, but it had protected him from the flames. There were superficial burns to his hands that would heal soon.

Lady Lily spoke softly, "Let us hope he stays unconscious until we arrive."

Lady Kananga gently pushed his hair away from his chiseled features. "And that he realizes we wish to help him."

They settled in the comfortable cabin, sipping blood and keeping an eye on him. The weight of their actions hung heavily in the air. Lady Kananga would rely on her centuries-old relationship with him to help convince the Magus that they were acting in his and the vampire world's best interests. The head of the House of Wands quietly watched the Magus lying motionless on the bed. She was amazed at how peaceful he looked without emotional fire in his eyes, glaring at perceived enemies. She might have laid down with him if the others had not been present. A few years had passed since their last memorable tryst. She hoped he was not truly lost to his obsession with the Mordecais.

Lady Lily closed her laptop. "The address and other information from Lady Jacquotte check out. The captain has made the arrangements for our arrival in several hours."

Lady Kananga mused aloud, "I hope this has the effect of awakening his regard for humanity."

Sir Sam said, "The house we'll stay in is about a block from the address you were given and rented for the week."

Lady Kananga knew she could always rely on her aides. "Thank you both for all you've done for our kind this night. Please get some rest. We'll take turns

215

watching over the Magus. We'll stay at the airport until nightfall, then leave for our final destination when he has recovered enough to be mobile."

Lady Lily checked her phone. "Sir Omar sends his congratulations and states all is ready in Qatar. I will let him know what night we shall arrive."

"Splendid. After this brief visit to the French Quarter, we must get the Magus safely to Qatar. Our world depends upon it."

Chapter 34

Miles Away

Sir Jorge and Sir Franco stood in the living room of Miranda's home, waiting while Benny packed up his stuff. During his stay in Granite Falls, he was given a laptop, new shoes, and lots of clothes. Benny wheeled his luggage into the room with a huge smile. "Ready."

Sir Franco smiled at Benny. "I can't believe you would want to leave this verdant paradise for Seattle."

Benny glanced at Miranda. "You've been great to me. Thanks for everything! In my whole life, I've never owned a computer or had this many clothes and shoes. I do like it here, but I have always lived in the city, and the club feels more like home."

"No problem, but I want you to know you're always welcome here." She hugged him, and his eyes got teary. It was the kind of hug he used to get from his mom.

He blinked hard a few times, swallowed, smiled, and then went to the car. Sir Jorge asked, "What do you think of him?"

Miranda said, "That kid deserves everything we can do to help him reach his potential. He's bright and kind. You should've seen how patient he was with the kids."

Sir Franco laid a hand on her arm. "If he's ever in need of a mother's touch— we'll come get Grigoryi."

"I love you, but you can be such an asshole."

As Franco turned to leave, Grigoryi came rushing in with a large bag. "Where's the boy? He forgot the meals I packed for him."

They pointed to the front, and he ran to catch Benny. Miranda watched Grigoryi, then conceded, "Okay. You may have a point."

The Offspring and their partners decided to fly home that morning, hoping to return to Granite Falls before Sig's uncle and Loretta's auntie arrived. Jacques and Loretta drove their car that they had left at the airport. The rest followed in a limo. This suited Loretta as she wanted a little "quiet" time alone with Jacques. On the way from SeaTac, She snuggled up to Jacques and quietly said, "Next time we take a weekend off from the kids, it's gotta be just the two of us. Somewhere peaceful, without any family drama."

"Is that a real thing? Do places like that actually exist?"

She leaned away and hit him on the shoulder. "Yes. And those places have five-star ratings, spas, and…."

His phone lit up, and he held up a finger and said, "Hold that thought for a second." He read the message on his phone. "It's Mom. Your Auntie Gloria and Dion just arrived. About that getaway, you might want to go more rustic. Somewhere off the grid where they can't reach us."

"I hoped we would get there before them so I would have a chance to change and clean up a little after last night. How does my hair look?"

"Great, but I'm not sure Gloria is into skull beads."

"Are you kidding? She's from 'Nawlins. I'm glad Odgerel isn't arriving for a few days. We got enough to try and explain." Loretta got busy sending texts to everyone so they'd have the same story; the band was getting back from a concert in Portland after a late-night show. Miranda texted her a thumbs up; they weren't too late with the cover story. "So, babe, we beat the Magus; what's next?"

"We're going to Disneyland!"

Dion and Gloria had arrived a little earlier than expected, and Grigoryi was beside himself. He paced the kitchen and threw his hands up in the air. "I need three hours for the cake!"

Miranda noticed his thick wavy hair starting to show signs of graying. She figured the daily chaos of the House of Sun was probably to blame for his premature aging. "Old friend, I'm sure whatever you prepare will be delicious.

Take all the time you need. They are staying the night. We can order tacos from Marco's in town, so you don't have to worry about dinner. I'll keep the kids out of the kitchen, so they won't get in your way."

"Mi scusa, I shouldn't ruin this day. It is a celebration!" A little smile warmed his face. "As the kids say, "I got this', but yes, please keep the little ones busy."

The noise of the victorious Cringe crew arriving filled the house. Miranda followed the ruckus to the living room to see rounds of hugs exchanged between the young people, Dion and Gloria. Not wanting to be left out, the little ones were trying to get Jacques and Loretta's attention.

"Loretta, Wendell looks like your daddy." Her auntie said.

Dion hugged Sig, cocked his head toward Des, and asked, "Is he treating you right?"

"Most of the time," she chuckled.

Loretta grabbed her auntie's hand. "I can't believe you did it!"

Dion smiled. "We most certainly did! Elvis married us in Las Vegas. But it's legit." He leaned over and kissed Gloria.

Jacques whispered to Loretta. "Gloria and Dion getting married in Vegas by Elvis is not the weirdest thing about this family."

Loretta beamed at them, "I'm so happy for you both. But I wish you had invited us."

Gloria gave her a sly smile. "We were afraid you wouldn't approve. We haven't been dating that long."

Des said, "Welcome to the family!"

Phoebe said to Dion. "Honestly, this family is very accepting."

"I guess so. I've met Guillaume and Leif."

Phoebe left it at that. "I need some coffee." She started to head to the kitchen.

Miranda barred the doorway, ready to take on trespassers. "Grigoryi is baking, so the kitchen is off-limits. Tell me who wants coffee or tea, and I'll get it."

Loretta spoke up, "Everyone, I have an announcement. There will be a new Mordecai in about seven months."

The room was filled with surprised expressions and congratulations. Jacques' brothers made some remarks about taking the pressure off them and about his lack of self-control.

Tomas whispered to Des, "I'm not placing bets about the blood type this time."

Des said, "Yeah, me either." But they both knew that they were so competitive that neither of them would be able to resist the temptation.

Miranda hugged Loretta. "I could not be happier. You're the best! Whatever you need, you only have to ask." Then in a quieter voice, she said. "I'll try to dial back the drama around here."

Loretta shook her head. "Good luck with that."

Jacques picked up Wendell and looked at Alejandro and River. "Let's show auntie and Dion the horses."

Wendell said, "Come on, grandpa, I'll show you my horse."

As they followed the kids outside, Dion said, "Grandpa, I like that."

That evening they all feasted on barbacoa tacos with yummy side dishes and drank horchata. The Baron, Batu, and Guillaume arrived as they were finishing their meal. Miranda conveyed Alexander's congratulations to the newlyweds as he was away on business.

Grigoryi brought in a four-tiered lemon cake with coconut frosting and tiny pink flowers that formed a heart. Dion and Gloria were touched by his thoughtfulness and told him it was delicious. The offspring were amused by their father trying to appear "normal" as he managed to eat a small amount, knowing it would cause indigestion later. Guillaume and Batu refrained, saying they were trying to eat healthier and had given up sugar.

Miranda felt a sense of well-being that had eluded her for months as she looked around the living room filled with her safe, happy family. Tristan leaned over and whispered, "You look radiant."

She displayed a Cheshire grin and whispered back, "Our family is okay, and the Magus has been taken away. I couldn't be happier."

The front doorbell rang. Des said, "I'll get it."

A moment later, Lady Cassandra appeared dressed in a long purple hooded cloak. Miranda went to her and hugged the unexpected arrival as though her appearance was no big deal. The Seer led Miranda aside and spoke quietly to her.

The matriarch's countenance darkened, then she did her best to smile. She turned to the gathering. "Gloria and Dion, this is my friend and writing collaborator, Cassandra." The visitor waved a greeting to the family. "A publishing issue has come up. Tristan, would you mind meeting with Cassandra and me for a few minutes?"

"Of course." No matter what Cassandra had to say, he was glad to be given an excuse to stop pretending to eat cake around the mortals.

The kids acted like everything was fine and talked about Cassandra and her animal refuge. Gloria's serious expression showed she wasn't buying it.

Miranda quietly told Tristan and Cassandra, "Let's not put a damper on the celebration. We can talk in the fencing barn." She wanted to be sure no one would overhear them.

The three slipped out of the house and headed to the barn. Baron set three chairs close together. Lady Cassandra waited until they were seated to speak. "I'm sorry to interrupt your family time, but this can't wait. By now, you know that during the chaos at the Narcissus Club, a small group of us took advantage of the distraction and abducted the Magus. He is being transported to Sir Omar's home in Qatar for—shall we say rehabilitation and healing."

Miranda asked, "You believe you will be able to keep him there against his will?"

Lady Cassandra answered with confidence. "Yes. It is a remote compound and well-protected. We have taken measures to diminish his powers temporarily. He will be given the respect and care he needs to regain his former rational brilliance."

Miranda crossed her arms, clearly not satisfied with Cassandra's explanation. "You came all this way just to tell us that?"

The Seer replied, "No, not only that. While the Magus is incommunicado, someone must take his place as head of our world. I've come to tell you whom we have chosen."

Tristan calmly said, "I was expecting this."

Miranda blurted out, "You are the second most powerful vampire. Of course, it must be you. This will be great for us."

Lady Cassandra leaned forward and gently laid her hands on Miranda's arms. She was trying to give her comfort before the next blow. "Dear Baroness, the rest of the Parliament, save for Sir Borgia, have chosen you."

"No way is that happening!" She shook off Cassandra's hands and shot to her feet. "Are you all batshit crazy?"

Lady Cassandra frowned. "I understand this comes as a shock to you, so I'll ignore that comment."

Tristan silently mulled over the news, then said, "Yes, of course. I understand it now. Miranda, it makes perfect sense. You are the only logical choice."

Lady Cassandra calmly explained the decision. "Lady Kananga, Lady Lily, Sir Hannibal, Lady Antoinella, Sir Jorge, Lady Anastasia, Princess Khunbish, and even Lady Sarah insist you take the Magus' place temporarily."

Tristan nodded in agreement. "Miranda, because you are mortal, there is no concern that when it is time for the Magus to return, you will attempt to retain power and remain ruler for eternity."

221

"I am tired of all of you making decisions about my life without consulting me. I won't do it!" She sat back in the chair, crossed her arms, and glared at Lady Cassandra.

They sat in uncomfortable silence until there was a low, muted rumbling. Tristan put his hand to his stomach and grimaced. "Excuse me; it's the cake." Attempting to maintain his dignity, he slowly walked to the bathroom.

After the door closed behind him, Miranda cocked her head toward the faint sounds of retching. "That's how I feel." She got back to her feet and started pacing. "Sometimes I hate this whole fuckin' vampire world! I just found out a new grandbaby is on the way, and the Magus is out of the picture, at least for a while. Things are starting to look up, and now this." She stopped and stared questioningly at Lady Cassandra. "What about the others? Any one of you bloodsuckers, no offense, is more qualified than I am. Even Sir Ruben."

Cassandra suppressed a laugh. "Ruben? You can't be serious. The centuries have not diminished his immaturity. Sir Borgia would challenge any other vampire, fearing they would not relinquish power. We believe he'd start a civil war against any other Haute Caste. None of the elite would ever accept a Common Caste. The only logical solution is for you, a half-vampire mortal that can take away or diminish our powers with your blood. We were all sure you would not want to do this, making you the perfect choice. And not to mention that you are the only one who has successfully faced down the most powerful vampire in our world. You are unique and in a special category."

Miranda growled, "Being special is overrated."

Tristan returned, appearing as though he was feeling much better. "I heard your remark about Sir Borgia. You won't have to feel threatened by him. He would think it beneath him to kill you, a mortal half-vampire."

Miranda scoffed, "Great, that makes me feel much better about the whole thing."

Lady Cassandra asserted, "In any case, in my visions, I've only seen Sir Borgia as the head of the House of Pentacles."

Miranda put her hands on her hips. "Aren't your visions ever wrong?"

Tristan replied for Cassandra, "I have never known a more accurate seer."

Miranda clenched her fists. "Fuck me!" Tristan smiled. "Don't even think about it." She paced around the barn several times, then turned and asked, "What if I decline this wonderful offer?"

"No matter." Lady Cassandra smiled and added. "We already regard you as the leader of our world for now."

"So that's it? The nocturnal maniacs have put me in charge of the asylum?"

"Even at this moment, the news of your appointment is being spread."

"Let me guess, by Sir Ruben." She collapsed in her chair and dropped her head into her hands.

Tristan checked his phone. "Congratulations are already coming in." He smiled. "Sir Franco says he refuses to call you Your Highness."

She drew in a long breath, slowly exhaled, and looked up at Cassandra. "Unlike you, I never, ever saw this coming. I imagined Lady Kananga, Tristan, or the other Haute Caste stepping up. This is insane. Can you imagine what my mother would have said? She hated the Magus."

Tristan gazed fondly at his love. "I think she would say it's about time he got his comeuppance and would congratulate you."

"You're right, and I think she would."

Lady Casandra said, "You will have to meet with all the other Houses to allay any misgivings they may have about you. Especially the House of Pentacles."

Tristan's tone became serious. "Sir Borgia won't challenge you outright, but he will try to undermine and sabotage you to make you look weak. We must always be vigilant."

She mockingly said, "He's a mini-Magus. I got his number. I'm not worried about that self-absorbed elitist. Anyway, Lady Antoinella is my ally."

Lady Cassandra coughed politely. "In case you weren't aware, she's Sir Hannibal's 'friend' at the moment. Lady Sarah has gone to London with Sir Borgia. Beware Lady Sarah and the House of Plows. As head of the newest House, other than the House of Sun, they desire to increase their status by association with the House of Pentacles, the oldest House."

Miranda laughed. "Wow! Seriously. Antoinella and Hannibal." Her amusement was brief. "Damn Sarah! She has been tight with the kids and me at times. I never thought she would stab me in the back."

Tristan leaned over and kissed her cheek. "My Empress, the court intrigue has begun."

Miranda focused on Lady Cassandra. "You haven't mentioned Dr. Kyoto. He's the most loyal to the Magus and would never abandon him."

"He disappeared after the events at the Narcissus Club. I was somewhat surprised that he didn't try to interfere with our actions. Perhaps Dr. Kyoto desires to see how this plays out before committing himself to a side. Lady Pompadour and Sir Raf have also not commented on your appointment."

Miranda said, "I'm sure they're thrilled."

Tristan stood and moved in front of Miranda. He held out a hand. "There are others who will come to your aid when news of your new appointment reaches them."

Miranda took his hand, closed her eyes, and drew in a deep breath. She slowly exhaled and opened her eyes. "I can't even think about this anymore right now. We should go back to the house. We have guests. and we shouldn't ignore them." She rose to her feet and rested her head on Tristan's chest. "What the actual fuck!"

Tristan kissed the top of her head and said, "Go ahead. I'll be in shortly."

She slowly walked back to the house, trying to regain her composure.

After she left the barn, the Baron said to Cassandra, "I will stay by the Baroness' side and help guide her as much as she will allow."

Lady Cassandra smiled. "I'm pleased you agreed with the decision. In many ways, you are the most qualified to rule."

"It's time the vampire world comes to know Miranda and the offspring better. It will ensure their place in our society." He looked down thoughtfully for a moment. "After Jacques was arrested, I wanted to decapitate the Magus. If I had that kind of power, I might give in to temptation."

"You have excellent insight. For the same reason, Sir Omar was not considered. Do you think it will take long for Miranda to come to grips with her new position?"

"She has been trying to distance herself from our world. It is why she allowed the children to take on the Magus at the club without her. Miranda barely slept while they were gone. Now she's being told to stand at the heart of our society and keep order. She never wanted any of this, but she'll be a formidable leader. I have no doubt our family will encourage her to take the reins and step up."

"Very well. The Magus' jet is waiting for her at Paine Field. His property, homes, and whatever resources she needs will be available to the Baroness while he is in 'recovery.' I must be going. I fear the elephants' care might slip Hann's attention while Antoinella is visiting."

The Baron said, "That is not a match I had ever imagined."

With a tight smile, Lady Cassandra replied, "She likes powerful ancient vampires. At least she has chosen someone more ethical than Borgia."

"Goodnight, dear friend. I will keep you updated."

She nodded and disappeared into the night.

Chapter 35

Secrets

Gloria and Dion returned to the mansion on the lake in Seattle to stay with the kids and grandkids. Early the following day, Jacques wandered into the kitchen for coffee to find Loretta's aunt working the espresso machine.

"Macchiato?"

Jacques replied, "Sure." He was surprised she knew what he liked.

He watched her carefully make his favorite bean juice creation. Her braids were coiled high on her head with a touch of gray at the roots. Her expression was tight, her eyes searching as she handed Jacques a mug.

She grabbed her cappuccino and said, "Let's go out on the patio."

Though it was chilly, he didn't question her. She sat at a wrought iron table for two in a patch of morning sun. As soon as he was in the chair, her expression became cold.

She leaned forward. "I hope you don't think I am stupid or oblivious. We are supposed to be family. So, stop lying to me. What is going on with the Baron and some of the others?"

She was a bright woman that didn't miss much, and he knew that at some point, she would start asking questions. He had prepared himself for this moment a hundred times, but all his rehearsed responses failed him. He sipped the creamy brew, knowing he wouldn't get past her bullshit detector any longer.

"Okay, here it is, straight up. My dad, Guillaume, and some of the others are vampires. They would never harm you or anyone we love." He unconsciously held his breath, waiting for a response.

Her brows raised, and she said, "I suspected something like that. All the explanations of their behaviors were starting to get pretty thin.".

Astonishment showed on Jacques' face, and he stuttered out, "You knew? How? When? I mean…."

Gloria was amused at his discomfort and said, "Darlin', I am old enough to have seen things you probably can't imagine. Did you forget that I grew up in the city of voodoo and vampires? That said, I don't think Dion could handle this. He's a lovely but sensible man, rooted in reality."

"I was prepared for you to suspect something wasn't right, but not that you would believe they are vampires. To be honest, I'm a little shocked. Are you really okay with this?"

"It doesn't seem to have done you any harm, and Loretta seems happy. I may be Loretta's aunt, but I think of her as a daughter. I want to know that Wendell, the new baby, and Loretta will be okay. Can you promise me the dark side of the family won't hurt her or my grandbabies?" Her face hardened, and her eyes bored into Jacques. "Be assured that I will find a way to destroy anyone that harms any of my family—vampire or mortal."

Somewhat relieved, he leaned back and said, "I promise you that my mom, dad, sibs, and our allies won't let anyone hurt our kids or Loretta. I have been around them my whole life. I know this may sound weird, but even though they are vampires, they are like everyone else in many ways. Some are good, some not so much."

Her features softened. "With a vampire as your dad, how does it affect you? Does that mean you will become one of them?"

Jacques straightened his shoulders. "Well, it's a little complicated. No one automatically becomes a vampire. They have to be willing and become transformed by a full vampire. Dad is one hundred percent vampire, and Mom is half but still mortal. My brothers, sister and I are mortal but sort of enhanced. Brighter, stronger, and quicker than other people. In school, we had to hide our abilities to not draw attention to ourselves. We sort of joke about being hybrids."

"What about Wendell? Is he a 'hybrid' too?"

"It's a little early to tell, but we think so. By the way, we refer to 'them' as Lithuanians around outsiders or people like Dion that don't know the truth. We'll wait to tell the kids the whole story till they are teenagers like our folks did with us."

Gloria laughed. "Good luck with that." She took a sip of espresso as her thoughts raced. "So, you are mortal, but do you ever get sick?"

"Not really. We have strong immune systems, and we heal from injuries quickly." He smiled and added, "Being a hybrid has its upside. "He thought for a moment, then decided to tell her more. "My mom was the first half-mortal half-vampire. My dad wanted her to transform so he would never lose her, but she decided that she wanted to remain mortal. She's aging like anyone else but much slower than normal. Dad artificially aged himself so she would feel more comfortable, but it's temporary for him."

"I had no idea she was…."

"Don't feel bad. A lot of people have underestimated her. She is much more than most realize. You definitely don't want to get on her bad side."

"Speaking of mothers, you take good care of my girl. You don't want to get on my bad side either."

"Of course I will."

Loretta opened the sliding glass door and poked her head out. "What are you guys doing out here? It's cold! Come inside. I'm making waffles."

Gloria whispered to Jacques as they walked in, "Don't tell her I know till we leave. She can call me when she's ready."

Inside, Loretta cornered Jacques in the kitchen. "What was that about?"

He pulled her into his arms. "She wants to be sure I'll be good to Wendel and my pregnant wife."

Loretta said. "I wanted to tell you. It was weird; Franco and Jorge knew before I did."

"Of course, they did. Freakin' vampires' sense of smell. A change in hormones or something."

Gloria appeared in the kitchen doorway. "Something's burning."

"The waffles! Crap!" Loretta fussed with salvaging breakfast.

Jacques smiled at Gloria. "My bad. I distracted her."

Loreta's auntie shook her head. "Not the first time, and I am sure it won't be the last."

The Magus and his chaperones made a stop in New Orleans while he recuperated from being singed and drugged. His powers still appeared to be diminished by the small amount of Marie's blood remaining in his system. His captors hoped it would be enough to make it impossible for him to escape. By the second night, he had recovered enough to visit an old acquaintance.

The temporary change in Lily's appearance had faded, and she once again looked like her old self. The Magus silently studied her face and then said to her, "At the Club, I was fooled by your disguise. It was only because I was distracted by the antics of the offspring. I would have seen right through it if it had not been for that."

Lady Lily replied, "Honestly, I hadn't expected it to fool you for more than a brief moment. Now I think it is time to call upon your old acquaintance."

As he, Lady Lily, and Lady Kananga stepped out on the street, he said, "Lady Jacquotte, like all of you, are risking much to force me to confront my decisions and actions, of which you disapprove. Though I might not agree, I understand you think you are doing this for the good of our society."

"I apologize for our methods," Lady Kananga said, "But we only wish to help you see you are not infallible, and you have made some unwise decisions."

The trio walked toward a three-story house built during the antebellum period in the French Quarter. The Magus had insisted on walking to the grand home he had gifted someone he had cared for seventy years earlier. The ornamental streetlights and old buildings made it seem as though they had traveled back in time.

Lady Kananga glanced at him and asked, "Are you sure you wish to do this?"

He stayed focused on the house at the end of the street. "Even if not in your lovely custody, I would still feel compelled to endure the pain that awaits me now that I'm here. Lady Jacquotte used to frequent the French Quarter and knows the delight I once experienced in this place."

They stopped at a wrought iron gate that led to a small courtyard. He rang the bell, and an old man in gardening clothes appeared. He stared at the Magus as though he was seeing a ghost.

"You look like…"

"…Desmon Dontinae. Yes. I have a striking resemblance to my grandfather. May I visit Miss Camille?"

The old man's eyes fell appreciatively on Lady Kananga and Lady Lily, then returned to the Magus. "You all might be just what she needs right now. A little distraction from her maladies. Follow me, please." He led them through the courtyard filled with fragrant flowering plants, past a tall, stately oak that provided shade during the day, and into the house. He asked them to wait in a sitting room and went to tell the nurse."

"Thanks, Jesse," the Magus said.

The old man turned around, looking puzzled. "How do you know my name?"

"My grandfather told me about Camille's younger brother, how he always doted on her and cared for her. I assumed that's who you are."

"Huh. Imagine that." Then with a little smile, he added, "After all these years, you remembered me." He returned a few minutes later. "Right this way, and don't mind the nurse. She's a sourpuss."

Lady Kananga and Lady Lily had discussed letting the Magus be alone for this reunion but for fear of him escaping decided against it. They followed Jesse through the beautiful home filled with antique furnishings, plush oriental carpets, and vases of fresh flowers. They went up a narrow set of stairs to a large bedroom that might once have been a living room. One wall was taken up with large windows with a garden view. A collection of Mardi Gras masks hung above a large four-poster bed, and bright paintings of Mardi Gras floats decorated the remaining walls. A small white-haired Cajun woman was propped up on lavender and pink pillows in the center of the bed.

"Desmon?" She lifted a hand while a nurse who appeared to be almost as old as Camille fussed with a satin comforter.

The Magus moved to her side, gently nudging the nurse away. He leaned close to the frail woman on the bed and said, "Camille, my love." Then his voice seemed to fail him.

Lady Lily whispered to Lady Kananga, "Is he crying?"

The most powerful and feared of their kind gently took Camille's frail, bony hands between his and kissed them. "How I've missed you."

In a raspy voice, she said, "You were right to leave, but I have never been with another."

"I should have visited. All these years…," his voice cracked.

"You gave me this house and ensured that Jesse and I were taken care of. We turned the brothel into a respectable hotel. Not as interesting as it used to be when we first met." Her laugh turned into a fit of coughing. The nurse came around the bed and helped Camille take a drink of water. She shot the Magus a dirty look.

Lady Kananga softly told Lady Lily, "The nurse is lucky he is in a weakened state."

With profound sadness in his voice, the Magus said, "I regret every moment I have been away from you."

"I still have memories of the years we had together. I eagerly waited for the sun to go down. Those midnight rendezvous, dancing for you and helping those poor women. I have no regrets, cher." She lifted a hand to his cheek. "I'm glad you're still the handsome fool I've loved forever. I wish you could see me like I used to be."

He leaned down and kissed her gently. "I do. I always will."

Camille caressed his cheek and closed her eyes. "Desmon, I waited," she said with her last breath.

"No!" The Magus looked about frantically. "I need a knife!"

Lady Kananga and Lady Lily grabbed him as the nurse tried to throw herself over Camille's body.

"But I can save her!" the Magus cried out.

Jesse went to the bed and told the nurse, "Don't call anyone except the funeral home like she told us."

Then he turned to the Magus. "Mr. Dontinae, she stayed alive, hoping to see you one more time. You gave her her wish and set her heart free. I thank you." He picked up a small, framed picture of a beautiful young woman and handed it to the Magus. "You all should be going now."

The Magus slipped the picture into a pocket with trembling hands. He said nothing as they walked back to their rented home. Once inside the French Quarter mansion, he turned to the others with reddened eyes, "We must leave. If not, I will see that I'm buried beside her."

Lady Kananga replied, "Of course." She signaled to Sir Sam and said, "Please help Lady Kabedi gather our things. I will notify the pilot and arrange transport."

Lady Lily touched the Magus' sleeve. "I was not sure we could trust Lady Jacquotte, but it seems she was right about bringing you here."

His gaze went past Lady Lily as he spoke, "Yes. Camille's death would have been a hundred times more excruciating had I not had a chance to say goodbye. Because of her, I once felt the lightness of being." His voice became rough with emotion, "I now realize that one night, the Baron will plunge into the depths of this sea of grief. I will show him compassion."

Lady Kananga's looked surprised. "At this moment of agony, you think of another? Desmon, there is hope for you."

He said, "Perhaps it is a side effect of Marie's blood. I hope it shall wear off soon."

Chapter 36

Alone

Miranda refused to talk with Tristan or the kids after the guests left that night. She told them she needed time to think when they tried to engage her about the Parliament's decision. They had all heard about it from Ruben's texts before she or Tristan had a chance to tell them. Tristan and Miranda went to their room without further discussion.

The young folks stayed up discussing how it would affect all their lives. After a couple of hours Jacques said, "You know guys, let's not forget how much Mom hates all the drama the vampire world generates. It's going to be awfully stressful for her."

They all sat thinking about it until Tomas said, "True but she knows we all have her back. Right?"

Sig answered, "Of course she knows that, but she is going to need more from us all than that."

Des asked, "What do you mean?"

Marie jumped in. "I think what she means is that Mom is going to need us to step up and take the whole situation really seriously. We're not kids anymore. We can't be fucking around and doing stuff that will only add to her stress."

Loretta spoke up, "I don't mean to talk out of turn...."

Marie gestured for her to go on and said, "It's okay, you're family."

Loretta went on, "Marie is right. We all have to start acting like adults. She will have enough to worry about without us making things worse."

The following day, Des found his mom alone on the deck while Grigoryi was letting River "help" with the breakfast dishes. In a soft voice, he asked, "Can we talk about what you're planning to do?"

She looked at him with a mother's eyes that took in his whole life at once. "Des, I'm not ready to discuss it with anyone yet—even your father. I need to be alone right now. I have too much to think about. If you want to help, entertain River. I'll let you all know when I've figured out my next moves."

He hugged his mom, though it felt one-sided. He realized that emotional exhaustion was overwhelming her. "Sure. I'll take her over to Marie's and Leif's place. No matter what you decide, we're all behind you. You know Grandma would be proud of you."

Miranda smiled. "Thanks. Since Cassandra told me what they wanted me to do, I've been thinking a lot about her. I think she hated the Magus more than I do. Your dad said he thought she would love it."

Des returned to the house, got River, and took her to Leif's and Marie's house. Miranda wandered down to the river and watched the water flow past. The river's soothing sight, sounds, and the ever-present scent of the fir trees always helped her think. After a while, she shook herself out of her reverie and walked to the fencing barn.

Miranda took a rapier from the wall rack and gracefully moved through the exercises she had learned from Guillaume without much thought. In her mind, she was facing off against the Magus, Sir Borgia, and Dr. Kyoto. As the blade cut through the air, her confidence increased. After vanquishing her foes, Miranda was a little out of breath.

She put the rapier back in place, tilted her head back, and shouted, "Fuck them all!"

She pulled her phone out of her pocket and dialed an often-called number. She felt comfort when a familiar voice responded, "It's about time, Your Majesty."

"Alexander, you must be in Qatar by now."

"Yes, I arrived shortly before the Magus was brought here."

"If I do this, are you ready to help me rule the shit show that is the vampire world?" She sat down in a chair and focused on the call. "If you think it's a bad idea, I will bail, no matter who insists I do it."

"I was only half joking when I called you by a royal title. I am of the opinion that if not me, you're the only logical option."

"Well, I mean, there's always Tristan or Anastasia."

232

"A terrible idea! Heads would roll." Sir Alexander sat in a luxurious bedroom at Sir Omar's compound. "She is here with Sir Omar waiting to meet with our distinguished guest. I look forward to seeing him in a diminished capacity. The Magus' current state gives us a chance to help him gain some much-needed insight. After my attempted coup against him, my time in 'exile' at Sir Hannibal's sanctuary, weakened by your blood and cleaning up after the elephants, humbled me. I saw things in a totally different light. Hopefully, his time here will have a similar effect on him."

"Humbling the mighty warrior was a true miracle." She chided him. "Before I jump into this, I have a lot of planning and strategizing I have to do. I still want you for my consigliere."

"Of course." In a seductive voice, he added. "Whatever you need, you have but to ask."

"Goodnight, Alex. Thanks." She hung up and took a breath to calm herself. He would always have that effect on her. Sir Alexander was one handsome, sensual charmer, but Tristan had all that and her heart.

She still needed to confer with one more advisor.

Leif had a soft spot for kids. Des suggested 'Uncle Leif' teach River how to play guitar so he could talk with his sister. Marie and Des heard squeals of delight from River in the living room as they stepped outside. The morning air was cool and smelled of pine. They sat on an old log with a view of the river.

"Do you think she should do it?" Des asked.

Marie pushed some pine needles around with her boots. She frowned, then said, "It's Mom. It doesn't matter what we think. I know she doesn't want to deal with all the nocturnal freaks, but what choice does she have? She'll do it to protect us."

They heard a loud crash coming from the house. Leif yelled, "No drums! Just the guitar today."

Des laughed. "I think Leif might need some protection."

"Bro," Marie said in a serious tone. "We have to start looking out for the little ones. The only way we can help Mom is by keeping River, Ali, and Wendell safe."

"And the new Mordecai on the way."

Marie nodded. "This time, I hope it's a girl. There's already too much testosterone around here."

"Fuckin' Jacques and his super semen." Des yawned. "Luckily, the rest of us are happy with being aunts and uncles."

"Where's Sig?"

"She's hanging with Dion and Gloria at Jacques' place."

Marie grinned, "And playing with the kids. You better be careful, or you'll end up knee-deep in diapers and wipes."

"Same for you and Leif." He smirked. "Thor Mordecai. I can just see it."

She shoved him so hard that he fell off the log. "The world is not ready for a little Leif to be running around."

That evening Miranda went to the Funeral Pyre. The club was open, but there was no live music. She had texted Sir Henry and asked him to meet her in a back booth without Lady Teri. She slid into the curtained booth, and Andre, the flirtatious blond waiter, was immediately at her disposal.

"What is your pleasure, Baroness?" He leaned in a little too close.

"Back off, Andre. All I want from you is black coffee."

"No cream? Or maybe some sugar?" He smiled seductively.

With vampire stealth, Sir Henry appeared behind Andre and pushed him aside. "Go get the coffee and then leave us."

"Whatever." Andre left in a huff. Alexander closed the curtains and sat across from Miranda.

Miranda gave her loyal friend a weak smile. "Is Teri pissed?"

"Why would she be? Because we're meeting without her, or you wouldn't answer her texts or return her calls? Of course, she is, but she'll get over it. I explained you needed some advice and time to process this messy situation."

"I'm relieved you understand." She searched his face. "This will impact you the most. You know what I'm getting at. While I'm off running the insane asylum, I'll need you to be the head honcho of the House of Sun."

They fell silent as Andre delivered her beverage without a word and walked off quickly. Henry assured her. "I will fulfill my promise to you as long as needed."

"How can you be so calm? Taking on the House of Sun is like trying to put out a volcano with a squirt gun."

"Well, a squirt gun was effective against the Magus." He countered.

She took a sip of coffee. "You know there's a good chance I'll never want anything to do with the undead when this is all over."

He responded, "Except, of course, the Baron. How is he taking being passed up for you?"

"Better than I ever would have expected. I still don't get why I was chosen. Sir Omar, Lady Kananga, you, and so many others, I mean, real vampires have a better understanding of your world than I do."

"First of all, I think you underestimate yourself. Although you haven't been around for as long as most of us, you have a better grasp of the motivations and schemes of those in our society than almost anyone. You would never use the power for your own agenda or enrichment. If one of us had been chosen, petty resentments and jealousy would drive us to challenge every decision and try to grab power. You, like the Magus, have a unique status. Though he is currently detained, we all know he will return eventually. Your reign will be accepted as a stopgap measure and respected as such."

"I'll only do this if you agree to take over the House of Sun. My only agenda for taking the position is that it will enable me to protect my family. That is all I ever wanted." She stared into her cup of coffee, then up at Sir Henry. "Fuck it! Guess I'm the empress of the night."

Lady Teri's voice came through the curtain. "About fuckin' time!"

Chapter 37

Departures and Arrivals

Tristan arranged for his jet to fly Gloria and Dion back to L.A. from the Everett Airport. Jacques was unusually quiet after returning home, thinking about how to break the news that Gloria now knew the family secret.

Assuming he was concerned over how things went with Gloria, Loretta said, "Hey, hon, you were cool with my auntie. I know she can be judgy, but you were great with her. She is worried about Wendell and me. Thanks." She sat beside him on the couch.

Jacques rubbed his face. "You have no idea."

"What are you talking about?"

He calmly replied, "She knows that some of our relatives are Lithuanian."

"You told her?"

Wendell and Alejandro picked up on their serious tone, stopped playing, and stared at them. Jacques told the kids to go play in Alejandro's room. They grabbed their toys and headed off. Wendell wasn't happy about being left out, stuck out his bottom lip as he grudgingly obeyed.

Once the kids left the room, Loretta asked, "How did she know? Did someone say something?"

He sat beside his wife again and touched her hands. "She's pretty observant, and having lived in New Orleans with all the paranormal shit that goes on there, made her suspicious. Your Auntie Gloria came right out and said that she wasn't stupid and knew we were lying about the family and demanded the truth. I knew she wouldn't let it go, so I told her. She asked me to wait and tell you after she left and said there was no need to tell Dion. He sees only what he expects, eccentric mortals with a lot of money."

"Sheesh. I'm surprised she didn't demand Wendell and I go back to L.A. with them."

Jacques kissed her. "I told her that the family and our allies won't let any harm come to you guys. She'll support us as long as you and her grandbabies are okay. But she was clear that if she thought you or the kids weren't safe, there would be hell to pay."

Loretta rolled her eyes. "When I was in third grade, some kid made a racist remark about my hair. She went to the principal and the Board of Education. And that's not even to mention the NAACP. The school had an assembly about diversity, and the kid apologized in front of everyone."

Jacques said, "I pity any vampire that pisses her off. But if anyone does that to Wendell, I'll make sure they regret it."

She shook her head. "Babe, it's not if; it's when. Last week in Nordstrom, I was followed around by store security. It's how the world is. Well, you know, the mortal world, anyway. "We'll do everything we can to protect our kids." She touched her tummy. "And prepare them for the racist crap they'll experience."

"I only want a better world for them," Jacques said. "I'm glad he'll have a little sis or bro so that they can be there for each other. I know me and my sibs fight, but we always have each other's backs."

She snuggled into his arms. "It's weird, but I've never picked up a racist vibe from vampires."

"They're all about blood type, and Wendell has HH, which means he's upper class. It's just a different form of prejudice."

"Same old shit. Some people always need to feel that they are better than someone else."

"It's why the other blood types are usually running errands for the Haute Caste."

Loretta asked, "Like Angel?"

"Exactly! Even though he got moved up to Haute Caste, it hasn't changed the way he's treated very much. Now that I think about it, I wonder what happened to him after the concert. Hope he stays loyal to our house."

"I got a text from him that he's going away for a while."

Jacques pulled away from her, feigning shock. "He's texting you? What an asshat."

Loretta fluttered her eyelids. "What can I say? Vampires like me."

"Maybe Angel likes you too much." He pulled her into a sweet kiss. They fell to the couch as his hands cupped her breasts. Her hips rose and moved against him.

"Stop it, Ali!" Wendell came running into the room crying.

Loretta pushed Jacques away and pointed at the kids. "Your turn."

He smiled. "Later?"

"You better take advantage of me now, 'cause after this baby arrives, I will be wearing one of those chastity belts."

"We'll figure out something. You know I'm not giving up your fine...." he noticed Wendell sniffling in the doorway. "...self."

The Magus arrived at the Qatari estate of Sir Omar. Lady Anastasia, as always, greeted him with due respect, but it was clear he wasn't a guest.

The grand room had colorful rugs and comfortable low furniture with lots of pillows. They were seated around a beautifully engraved copper-top table`. A servant brought out a tray with glasses of O positive. After being served, they all sat quietly, avoiding looking at each other.

Finally, Lady Kananga put an end to the uncomfortable silence. "Dear Magus, we will withhold further injections and allow you to regain all your strength and ability if you give your word to remain here until it is agreed that you are fit to rule again."

With an odd look of amusement, he looked to each in turn until his eyes settled on Sir Alexander. He said nothing, and after a moment, his old adversary nodded without a word or sign of emotion.

Sir Omar cleared his throat. "We made this difficult decision because you seemed to have lost focus and understanding of your essential place as our leader."

"I must admit I'm struggling with what has happened to me." The Magus took a sip of blood and looked out the large windows to a lighted fountain. "My visit to New Orleans, where I witnessed the death of someone I cared for deeply, was emotionally taxing. Strange how a mortal life can impact us. She was the first mortal to win my devotion, but I abandoned her when she aged."

Seeing his sad countenance, Lady Anastasia sympathized and said, "We understand that has been painful. But are you not also angered by this abduction?"

His eyes met hers, and she saw a hint of amusement. "I resent seeming to be bested by that ill-mannered goat herder. But the almost unanimous concern by

238

the Haute Caste for my well-being has given me pause. Perhaps I should question my approach to the Mordecais, and a visit with you might assist me in that endeavor."

Lady Lily appeared confused. "Visit?"

The Magus raised one hand, and they felt a tremor shake the building. After a few seconds, he lowered his hand, and the ground settled. Sir Omar rose to his feet. A tight smile came to the Magus' lips. "Having survived Marie's blood in the past, I have developed an immunity to its ability to weaken me, and the tranquilizer wore off quickly. I allowed you to bring me here because I was curious about your intentions."

Lady Lily began, "The whole time in New Orleans, you could have...."

"Yes, I could have punished you all, but you made me face my greatest regret. For that, I'm beholden to you."

Lady Kananga smiled. "You never fail to amaze me, dear Magus."

Lady Anastasia sounded stern, "We still desire that you stay with us until you have moved past your obsession with the House of Sun. A few nights will not be enough time to heal your wounds."

His haughty, arrogant manner returned. "You put yourselves in peril to bring me here—especially Lady Kananga and Lady Lily. I do not know how long I will indulge in your hospitality. I only promise not to leave without your knowledge, though I have no need of your permission."

Lady Kananga reminded him, "When you renewed your spirit in the Congo, your brief absence only increased your desire to control the Mordecais."

Sir Alexander finally spoke, "And that singular preoccupation has brought about a surprising outcome. Due to your absence, the Parliament has appointed an interim leader who shall relinquish all power when you return."

His face became stern. "Not you or Sir Borgia. I would accept Lady Kananga or Baron Tristan to preside in my place."

Lady Lily said, "It is the Baroness Miranda. The decision was almost unanimous."

He sputtered, "And you think me mad! Has our society forgotten who we are? You dare replace me with a mortal?"

Sir Alexander retorted, "She is the only one powerful enough to rule and sensible enough to relinquish leadership when the time comes."

In a rare show of emotion, the Magus shouted, "She has beguiled you all."

A brief, mild tremor rattled the room until the Magus regained control. There was a long pause. Then Sir Omar spoke, "As long as no harm shall come to my daughter, you will be welcomed back to rule when the time is right."

The Magus leaning back against the cushions, scoffed, "You presume to make this decree? This is ridiculous. I have not given my permission for her to reign in my place."

"As a royal who lost a palace," Lady Anastasia began, "I understand your difficulty accepting your current plight. But in order to save you from my father's fate, we shall keep you here for the sake of our world until you show your sense of ethical, rational decision-making has returned."

Sir Omar reached over and touched the Magus' hand. "It might take all of us, but we will use our powers to protect you from yourself, old friend."

The Magus stared at Sir Omar as though sizing up an enemy. Then he drew in a long breath and slowly exhaled. He sat up straight and squared his shoulders. "Have I truly behaved in such a way that you, one of my oldest confidants, question my sanity?"

Several voices said, "Yes!"

He noted the concern of the Haute Caste he had transformed. "You have given me much to contemplate. Miranda is in charge? I'm at a loss to understand this decision. Let us hope that you will soon believe I have recovered my faculties. I shall retire now. The last two nights have been grueling."

A servant entered and whispered to Sir Omar, who said, "She was expected. Show her in." The servant opened the door, and Sir Omar called out, "Welcome, Lady Amelia."

The Magus turned his attention to Amelia as she entered the room. "Have you come to gloat?"

"No!" She quickly knelt at his feet, causing the others to feel a bit nauseated by her behavior. "I'm here to comfort you. To be sure you are not ill-treated."

Lady Kananga said, "You show how little you understand our society. The Magus would never be maltreated."

Sir Alexander regarded the late arrival kindly. "We assumed you would appear to ask that your child, my grandson, would not be harmed if the Magus desired to exact revenge."

The Magus leaned towards her, gesturing for Lady Amelia to rise. "No matter. I am glad for your company. But now I will retire. These unexpected events have made me weary." Despite his youthful appearance, his movements were weighed down by emotional pain.

"Of course," Lady Anastasia said and signaled a servant to show the Magus to his suite. "Lady Amelia will be taken to an adjoining room."

The most ancient vampire's presence was felt even after he had left the room. Sir Omar said, "We cannot let down our guard, but his response was less dramatic than I expected."

240

Lady Lily shook her head. "His powers are back. I thought Marie's blood would thwart his abilities, but he appears as powerful as ever. Still, he came with us when he could have overpowered Lady Kananga and me."

Lady Anastasia said, "There are cracks in his defenses. He felt that something was not right but pushed it aside. Now that that has happened, he can no longer ignore it."

"And Lady Amelia," Sir Omar mused aloud, "appears to be a devoted mother. Let us hope that is truly her motive for being here."

Sir Alexander said, "Indeed."

The servant led the Magus and Lady Amelia to a luxurious suite, opened the door, and bowed. A Siamese kitten was lounging in the center of the large, canopied bed. It raised its head, barely acknowledging the intruders, then resumed grooming itself. The Magus, taken aback, pointed to the cat and demanded, "What is that doing here?"

The servant smiled. "That is Seraphina. A gift from the Baroness Marie." He handed a note to the temporarily dethroned ruler.

> **Magus,**
> *You need to remember what it's like to care for a life if you are ever to figure out how to get along with our House. Seraphina will be taken away if you don't feed her and clean her cat box yourself. I'll know if you screw up. Get your act together.*
>
> **Marie**

A faint smile appeared as though a fond memory came to his mind. "She has offered me redemption."

He handed the note to Lady Amelia. She asked, "Shall I take the cat away?"

With a wave of his hand, the Magus dismissed the servant to wait outside.

"No, Amelia." He went over to the bed and reached out to pet the kitten. She batted at him playfully. Her blue eyes studied the stranger. "I'm to clean up after you to prove myself worthy of your company. How diabolical and delightful. Will you claw me or purr, little Seraphina?" He turned to Lady Amelia, "A kitten has pierced my darkness. Only a Mordecai could have accomplished this."

"To be specific, Marie. And you do know that she is involved with Leif."

241

"Yes, yes. I know. I gave the Baroness an elephant I rescued once, and she reciprocated." Deep in thought, he stared past Amy as if she wasn't there. After a moment, he turned back to her and said, "Amelia, It seems to me that the males of our kind, at times, feel attracted to mortals, but the vampiresses do not seem to be attracted to mortal males. Is that true?"

She shrugged. "I can't speak for others, but I find our kind much more interesting and challenging."

"But what of Jacques?"

She stepped back. "I was attracted to him at one time, and I must admit I still have a fondness for him." She carefully chose her words. "But he has a life, and a love, apart from me. We only share a child now."

"Then you know what it is like to have been touched by one of the Mordecais. Something we share. That is all. Have a good rest." He began playing with the kitten.

She left the room, and the servant showed her to an adjoining suite. She looked around the room. "No pets in here, I hope."

"I believe you shall care for the powerful beast next door. Sleep well." He bowed and left.

To no one, she said, "Ali!" and a tear fell down her cheek.

Marie's phone pinged, waking her. She sat up and reached for it. "Damn! I forgot to put it on sleep mode."

She picked it up and smiled at the text message.

You took my Komodo dragon and gave me a Siamese kitten. I never feared my dragon but this unpredictable furball is another matter. It seems my rehabilitation has begun.

Leif stirred beside her. "What's up?"

"Nothing." She put down her phone. "Remember when we took the Magus' Komodo?"

"Yeah, after it tried to eat me. Good times. The best part was how pissed off he got when we donated it to the zoo." He pulled her down into his arms.

Leif began softly snoring, but her eyes didn't close.

Chapter 38

Rise of the Empress

A week later, in Granite Falls, there was a gathering of the inner circle of the House of Sun. Grigoryi watched the little ones in the game room so that the adults could speak freely. Miranda stood in front of the fireplace biting her lip. Tristan was off to the side with Sir Batu.

Her eyes swept the room, lingering on her offspring and their partners, then on to Sir Henry and Lady Teri. "You all know I've been told to take over for the Magus while he is indisposed."

Des said, "All hail, Mom!"

Guillaume entered and shot a disapproving look at Des.

Marie elbowed him. "Shut up."

"I don't seem to have any good options other than to accept." There were hoots and cheers from Des, Tomas, and Jacques. She held up a hand to quiet them. "So, it's time to thank Sir Henry for agreeing to take over the running of the House of Sun as I move on to a weirder, more fucked-up challenge."

Henry stood and took her hands in his. "I was honored to accept your request." Then Sir Henry turned to the others. "I am relying on each of you to accept more responsibility while safeguarding our secrets and each other. There is much to be done. The Common Caste vampires in Portland have disappeared after Jeanne and Sir Bart, who have been guiding them, have gone on vacation. I want to find out what the Common Caste are up to." He looked at Des and Sig. "I will need your computer skills to help with that. Even more than usual, we must all be careful to avoid attention from the public, and especially the police. I ask that the Cringe restrict their concerts to the Funeral Pyre."

Leif, hearing that, looked a little downcast. "Damn. I was hoping to take the band to Europe."

Tristan responded. "You will have to put that on hold. None of you should go anywhere near the House of Pentacles. Sir Borgia is unhappy about the Magus' plight, and he has been known to be quite underhanded and quite adept at creating scandals. He could undermine your mother with scandalous rumors about you."

Phoebe said, "Or maybe something true." The others pointedly ignored her.

Lady Teri got back to the issue at hand. "Don't give any of those who supported your mother reason to question the wisdom of her being appointed to rule. Des, no more betting with Sir Ruben. It'll seem like you're using insider information. Trust me. I'll know if you do."

Des did his best to appear offended, causing Tomas to laugh.

Sig said, "That means you too, Tomas. I pulled up your bets over the last five years while I was researching the Magus. You have lost enough to buy a small house."

Phoebe stared at Tomas. "You did what?" She slammed down her mug. Coffee sloshed onto the table. Tomas grabbed a napkin and cleaned it up.

"I haven't gambled since Jacques got arrested. I've blocked Ruben."

Miranda sarcastically asked, "Will wonders never cease? Sir Henry, my beloved House of Sun is all yours."

Sir Batu addressed the assembled. "The tarot card, the Empress, is now her reality. The Common Caste are demanding rights and recognition that some of the Haute Caste will not receive well. Most of the ancient vampires appear friendly and supportive to the Empress, but that could change if chaos rips our society apart. Her ability to keep the peace while allowing change will garner respect and is essential to the safety of us all."

Loretta, who had been quietly listening, finally spoke. "Miranda, you will be great. Fuck Sir Borgia. You got this, and we'll back you up by behaving ourselves. I only have one question. How long will the Magus be in time-out?"

Tristan responded, "Sir Omar will update us on his progress, but Lady Cassandra believes it will take months. I received a text from Lady Kananga this evening. Lady Amelia has arrived in Qatar and will be allowed to stay as long as her presence does not hinder the Magus' progress."

Jacques swore, "Fuckin Amy, what is she doing there? Ali has been asking for her."

Phoebe said, "Believe it or not, she's looking out for your kid. I know it's hard for you to see, but she changed after Ali was born. He is all she cares about now."

Loretta shrugged. "Makes sense 'cause she could have hooked up with Angel."

Jacques looked dumbstruck. "What? When?"

"You are so oblivious. He was trying to jump her bones, but she was focused on the Magus. Angel told me she was all about status, and his blood type wasn't good enough for her." Her husband's scrutiny made her add. "He texted me a week ago."

Sir Henry shook his head. "Enough. Put aside petty issues to consider how we can protect the House of Sun and support Empress Miranda. Leif, you have been given gifts that no one could have imagined. Rumors are spreading like wildfire about how you took down the Magus. Very few know that Lady Kananga and Lady Lily weakened him before he could destroy the building. Remember, you are still fallible."

"Spreading like wildfire?" Leif grinned. "Honestly, I haven't seen a downside. We've got the Magus by the balls. Why shouldn't I flaunt what I can do to make nocturnal freaks fear me?"

Miranda fired back. "Because you'll do something stupid that will put us all in danger."

Marie took Leif's hand and said, "You're amazing, Leif, but it's not enough when you're dealing with the incredible freakin' undead. With a small gesture, the Magus could slice your throat, Lady Anastasia's touch could age you, and Sir Omar could behead you before you ever saw it coming. That's some of the dark shit we know about. We need to protect each other."

Miranda's expression softened. "Marie, maybe you should be the Empress."

Sir Henry regarded Tristan with amusement. "And the Baron could suspend you in the air and drop you off a balcony. Trust me. I know that from personal experience. But I'm not one to hold a grudge."

Leif asked the Baron, "Can you do that? I mean, would you?"

Tristan reassured Leif. "I'm sure you would never give me cause to use that power on you."

Tomas snickered. "Yeah, since he hasn't done it to Des yet, I think you're safe."

Leif's expression grew serious. "You know I'd never do anything to hurt any of you guys."

Marie crossed her arms. "Make sure you keep Odgerel at the Funeral Pyre, and we'll be fine."

Sir Henry said, "The biggest challenge will come unexpectedly and out of nowhere. With the Magus gone, some may feel free to go against the code and do something they wouldn't dream of with the Magus in charge."

Grigoryi yelled in the game room, "Ali, play nice!"

Batu remarked, "We should tell that to the vampire world."

Miranda crossed her arms. "Especially that damn pirate. I wish I knew where Lady Jacquotte is and what she is up to. Since Sybil escaped from the Magus a couple of years ago, we haven't heard anything about her either. And while I'm at it, I'm worried about the research Dr. Kyoto was doing with our blood. Who knows what happened with it and what he's working on now."

Sig asked, "Since you have the use of the Magus' property at the moment, can we sleuth around in his office?"

Des' eyes lit up. "Can you imagine what kind of shit we can find on his computer?"

Miranda smiled. "You can tear his office apart for all I care. We'll take the Magus' jet to L.A. in a couple of days. It's time I started acting like the Empress in charge. But I'm not sleeping in his house."

"Of course not." Tristan looked pleased. "My Bel Air home will be your headquarters."

Loretta looked over Miranda's outfit and said, "No offense Empress, but you've got to up your game."

Even Phoebe got the hint. "The backwoods Eddie Bauer vibe has to go."

Miranda considered her wardrobe of jeans, hoodies, and mud boots. "Point taken."

Sig grinned. "I know some amazing shops in Seattle."

"Okay but no tiaras."

River ran into the room and hugged Batu's legs. "I want cookies. Grigoryi said it's too late." The vampire's eyes shifted to his daughter's mother. "Empress?"

"Here's my first royal decree." She looked down at River. "Two cookies, that's it."

Chapter 39

It's Midnight Somewhere

A few weeks later, Angel downed a shot of tequila at the Green Parrot Bar in Key West. He liked the historical vibe of the place, and it had a nice mixture of blood types if he was hungry. His clothes were casual but a little too wrinkle-free and spotless to be mistaken for a local.

"Hey!" A drunk with a raspy voice and a pot belly leaned towards him. Beer fumes made Angel regret the lack of empty stools between them. "Bud, you got a light?" He pulled out a joint as though it was a regular cigarette.

"No."

The bartender, who might have been a heavyweight contender, said, "Get out, Jackson! I've told you before you can't smoke in here."

"All right, all right." Then he whispered to Angel, "If you want anything, let me know. I'll be outside."

The bartender said, "Sorry 'bout that. He's been banned since he sold some crap to a bunch of tourists that left them sick as dogs. They had to be taken to the hospital. Too bad they were afraid to finger him, but we all know. Steer clear of that piece of shit."

"No problem, thanks for the warning. I'm trying to find a friend. She said she was heading this way. Do you know Jacquotte?"

The bartender eyed the stranger with suspicion. "Yeah, I know her. When you see her, remind her that she still owes me for a broken window."

Angel laughed and said, "That definitely sounds like her."

The bartender moved down the bar to serve other customers.

As Angel was finishing his drink, a young woman wearing cut-offs and a bikini top took Jackson's stool. The scent of jasmine almost covered her identity.

"I know Jacquotte," she said quietly.

"Sybil!" Angel paused, letting his gaze sweep over the dark-haired beauty. "I never expected to find you here. Your recovery is phenomenal." His voice became a whisper. "The last time I saw you, the Magus had left you looking like a rotting corpse."

She stiffened and waved to the bartender. "George, I'd like a Mojito."

"Right away, Sybil." The bartender gave her a flirty smile.

Her composure returned. "Angel, I owe Alexander for my rescue and rebirth. I'm different now, aligned with the House of Sun. I'll finish my drink and disappear if you're still working for the Magus."

The bartender placed the Mojito on the bar and managed to lightly graze Sybil's hand. "On the house, babe."

She smiled and took a sip. "Perfect."

George glared at Angel and walked to the other end of the bar.

"You haven't lost your ability to charm." He turned to face her. "No worries. We're on the same team now, but I'm taking a hiatus. Maybe you haven't heard about the Magus being sequestered and Empress Miranda taking over for now."

Sybil almost spit out her drink. "Are you serious?"

He nodded and gave her a brief recap of the events at the Narcissus Club and the Parliament's decision.

She stared at him, then said, "I've been completely off the grid. This changes everything. I can come back now." She thought for a few seconds. "How long will he be gone?"

"No one knows. But most of the Haute Caste think he needs to rehabilitate his attitude towards the Mordecais before he can be in charge again."

Her eyes became dark. "I'll never forgive him."

"You and me both. So, where can I find Lady Jacquotte?"

"She told me if I saw you to, give you this." Sybil handed him a piece of paper. "When you find her, tell the pirate I've appreciated her hospitality, but I'm done hiding."

"Okay. When did she give you this?"

Sybil said, "Recently." She finished her drink, waved to the bartender then took off.

Angel unfolded the note. "Damn!" he mumbled, then pulled out his phone and googled an address in a swampy, crocodile-infested parish of Louisiana.

The bartender came over and asked, "Anything else?"

Angel put a hundred-dollar bill on the counter. "Everything. I want everything, but I won't find it here. Goodnight."

Outside, Angel looked around and saw Jackson loitering across the street. He went over to him and said, "I need a boat to take me to the mainland tonight. Can you arrange that?"

The scroungy man said, "Gonna cost ya."

"I'm good for it. Let's go."

A few hours later, Jackson was unconscious in the E.R. with a throat laceration. He had no memory of how it happened when he woke up. Angel was on his way to find the pirate who might be the answer to his unrequited passion. It was a new era for the vampire world, and he intended to enjoy it.

Des and Sig returned to their modern Seattle apartment, still feeling the buzz from Miranda's decision. She took off her jacket, threw it on the couch, and sat down.

"She's amazing. Your mom is ferocious." Sig said.

Des plopped down beside her. "I don't want to talk about her or anyone else right now."

The serious tone of his voice made her pay attention. "What is it?"

He fished a small velvet pouch out of his pocket and handed it to Sig. "I'm serious as a heart attack. Marry me."

Surprise lit up her face as she pulled the pouch open and found a sparkling dark stone in a platinum setting. "You're not fucking around."

"No, I can't imagine spending the rest of my weird life with anyone else." He gently took the ring and placed it on her finger. "It's a black diamond. It just seemed right."

Her eyes glistened as she stared at him. "Des, I don't want to be with anyone else either. It's just that I'm not sure what might happen. I mean, what if I decided that I want to become a vampire?"

"I can't stand the thought of losing you." He cupped her face with his hands. "I would hate it if you made that decision, but I would still want you. Not even that could change my feelings for you."

She kissed him gently then their passion flared as clothes became casualties of frenzied lovemaking. As they rolled onto the floor, Des hoped that meant yes.

CURIOUS WHAT IS NEXT
FOR THE HOUSE OF SUN?

HERE'S A SNEAK PEEK AT
WHAT IS COMING.

The Magus

In my extremely long existence, I rarely felt perplexed or indecisive. As the original vampire, my mission was to survive in the most artful and pleasurable way possible while ridding the earth of some of the worst of the dregs of humankind.

Though immortality has its benefits, boredom became my enemy. I continued to honor an old debt with a Knight Templar. In exchange for a wealth of Templar treasure, I would protect his descendants. A millennium later, I arranged for the birth of Miranda Ortega, the first half mortal half vampire, descended from the long-dead Templar. It offered an opportunity to expand nocturnal society and, as far as I was concerned, retired that debt. She ultimately wed Baron Tristan Mordecai and produced offspring. She and her children filled me with thoughts of grateful part-vampire mortals who would help me expand and improve my civilization. Sadly, to my dismay, I greatly misjudged them.

Therein lies the source of my current predicament and confusion. I find myself considering the plight of Napoleon, having been banished to an island. A group of Haute Caste undead, whom I once ruled, insist I stay in seclusion until I change my ways. They demand I accept the recalcitrant, disrespectful nature of the Mordecai family that I created and leave them alone.

But what fun would that be? The eldest daughter, Marie, sent a Siamese kitten to amuse me while in exile. Why did she do that? A mystery I must resolve. Yet my host, Sir Omar, contends I brought this situation upon myself by my behavior. Miranda, the matriarch of the family, has been temporarily installed by the rebellious cadre to rule our society. I could never have imagined that blasphemous possibility. Don't those who forcibly brought me here understand the potential chaos they might unleash on our world?

My obsession with the partial vampires has, indeed, removed boredom from my life, but it has added a level of pain and chaos I had long ago put behind me. I tried to come between Marie and her half-wit boyfriend, but that turned into an epic failure. En route to this exile, my captors took me to visit a past love, a precious mortal in New Orleans, only for me to witness her death of old age.

Not overseeing the empire that I created has left me time for reflection. My life, it seems, has always been greatly influenced by women. As a child in Mesopotamia, I suffered from an unknown malady that left me weak and sickly. My father rejected me and left my mother to care for me. She tried many "cures" without success until she found that raw, bloody meat restored my strength. Over time I began to understand what I was and what my potential was. I learned that I could "transform" others to be like me and I started to build my society.

For centuries, I was the undisputed ruler of the denizens of the night. Ironically, it was the woman whose birth I arranged, and her offspring, who were the first to seriously challenge my authority. Without consulting me she established the House of Sun, named no doubt, to provoke me. Her act of rebellion encouraged others to ally with her against me. It was women that should be unquestioningly loyal that planned and executed the plot to bring me here.

Like a greedy dragon, I like to keep my treasures, but now, they seem to slip out of my grasp. Like so many have foolishly done, they all underestimated me. Thought they believed they could hold me here against my will, yet I can leave whenever I wish. I have decided to humor them and take this time to reassess the future of our world, and especially the future of the House of Sun. Soon, I shall depart and make myself anew, taking time to become, once again, the most respected, powerful, and feared vampire.

Chapter 1

The Journals

Miranda stared at the six fat, leather journals on her desk. Through an open window of her bedroom, the babbling sound of the Stillaguamish River soothed raw nerves. The fact that the river had flowed past this spot before these books were created comforted her.

The cover of each book bore the name of a House of vampires. Pentacles, Swords, Wands, Cups, Plows, and Arrows. While the ruler of the vampire world was detained elsewhere, she had, over her reluctance, been put in charge of their society. "Damn, Magus!"

A familiar voice behind her said, "You must write one for the House of Sun."

Strong hands caressed her shoulders through her hoodie. Had she been a cat, Miranda would have purred. "Tristan, the lists in these books are exhausting. I can't believe the Magus has personally recorded the creation and the demise of every bloodsucker that ever existed."

"All of those that were sanctioned." He pulled his ex-wife up into his embrace. His deep blue eyes focused on the woman who held his heart. "With all that you have dealt with, bookkeeping is what defeats you?" He moved her long dark hair back while nuzzling her neck.

"That's what took down Al Capone." Miranda melted against his chest and sighed. She was used to the coolness of his touch. She looked up at his face, framed by a thick blond mane. "Are you always ready for sex? Never mind silly questions. Anyway, I don't have anyone to record. None of us have been transformed."

He merely said, "Except..."

"...Leif! That should never have happened." Sadness filled her eyes when she thought of her daughter's boyfriend. "He walks in daylight and washes pizza down with blood."

"Not just Leif. Perhaps you don't want to think about it."

"Lady Teri. That was not my idea. I can't believe how happy she is as one of you nocturnal maniacs." She paused and, with a note of apology, said, "Sorry, you know what I meant. Maybe I can pawn this record-keeping off on Sir Henry."

He shook his head. "Though he has taken over as the Head of the House of Sun while you fill in for the Magus, you need to be the one to list the vampires who have become loyal members of the House during your time, including me."

"You don't get off that easy. I'm listing you as a co-founder of our freakin' family."

He kissed her gently and whispered, "It is my honor."

He led her to the bed, and they began tearing at their clothes.

Little footsteps echoed down the hall. "Mom!"

Miranda jumped up and pulled her hoodie back down. Tristan frowned. A beautiful six-year-old with dark hair and big brown eyes, stormed in. "Ali took my dinosaur!"

"Truly a tragedy," Tristan remarked.

"Okay, River. I'll talk to him in a minute. Go back downstairs."

Tristan asked, "Can't her father help with childcare duties?"

"Batu," she thought about her old friend and protector, with whom she had a one-night stand. "He's spending the weekend with Lady Lily."

"Perhaps River will get distracted downstairs for a few minutes."

Miranda gave Tristan a sheepish look. "Raincheck?"

He sighed and played with her long curls. "Midnight, my Empress."

"Deal, Emperor. You know I'll never get used to being called by that title. That ass-wipe Magus better get his act together and take back this circus soon."

In a seductive whisper, he said, "I'd much rather kneel to you."

"Mom!" River yelled from the bottom of the stairs.

Miranda sighed. "Maybe I'll let you later."

Unknown to Miranda or the Magus, a young mortal was entering their world quite willingly. He looked around an abandoned industrial garage near the Port of San Francisco. Faint footsteps alerted him as he stared into an unlit doorway. With an Irish accent, he called out, "Show your bloody face!"

Sir Ruben stepped from the shadows; his pale features were almost colorless, but his red curls made him look less scary. "Chill!"

Felix nodded to the knight of the House of Plows. "Ruben, I feared they would send someone I didn't know. Or maybe they'd changed their mind about me."

The vampire tugged on his motorcycle jacket and smiled. "No. You're acceptable, which is not really a compliment. Do exactly what you've been told, and you'll worm your way into their favor. They pay better than Sybil. And Always watch your back."

The young man ran a shaky hand through his light brown hair. "You got my dose?"

About the Author

Susan is from Southern California and was a Peace Corps volunteer in Zaire in the late '70s. She went on to earn her master's in psychology and started in the field of Mental Health/Addictions at a street emergency shelter. She worked for several years at County Mental Health, a University Medical Center, and Cedars-Sinai Medical Center. She and her family moved to the cornfields of Illinois (like Miranda), and she became a therapist at a V.A. Medical Center. Over her career, she heard about the struggles of celebrities, bikers, walking wounded Veterans, nurses, felons, farmers, prostitutes, athletes, professors, and musicians. Being a therapist gave her insight into many diverse lives, from a housewife with insomnia to a strange ranger who walked the streets with a suitcase full of Barbie dolls. Writing became her outlet for the emotional stress of her job. In her writing, Susan created a hidden world that keeps the true nature of the inhabitants' secret.

She first considered herself a writer when her late mother-in-law, an author of English historical fiction, said she liked her stories. The manuscript of her first book was lost when lightning struck a power line and wiped out everything on her computer. Rather than take it as a sign to stop writing, she took it as a lesson to back up everything on the Cloud. It took her years to rewrite the book from her notes, but fortunately, she never gave up.

She became a widow at a young age, battled Lupus, and is a two-time breast cancer survivor. Her children, family, and friends always encouraged her to pursue her dreams. She believes there is a Miranda in each of us struggling to make sense of an insane world while sipping coffee.

Susan married a widower who accepts her obsession with shoes and helps with the technical stuff. They live north of Seattle on the banks of the Stillaguamish River with two rescued cats who rule the house. She volunteers at an animal shelter and the Unity Museum in Seattle. She loves Barbacoa tacos and consumes an inordinate amount of coffee.

Follow Susan and the continuing adventures of Miranda and her offspring at:

Susanold.com
zairesue@susanold.com
Instagram @zairesuewrites
Facebook book.com/zairesue/

Also by Susan Old

Novels
The Miranda Chronicles:
Book I: Rare Blood
Book II: Rhapsoday In Blood
Book III: Gift of Blood
Book IV: New Blood Rising
Available @ Susanold.com or Amazon

Novellas
with Susan Brown and Linda Jordan

Book I: **Witch Magic**
Book II: **Witch Fire**
Book III: **Witch Tree**
Book IV: **Witch Stone**

Available on Amazon

Short Stories
Included in Anthologies of the
Writers Cooperative of the Pacific *Northwest*

Tasting Evil
Several Deadly Sins
Best Laid Plans
The Bread Also Rises

Available on Amazon

www.ingramcontent.com/pod-product-compliance
Lightning Source LLC
Chambersburg PA
CBHW031214020726
47499CB00002B/586